GIFT OF DIAMONDS

ROBERTA SERET

WAYZGOOSE PRESS

ADVANCE PRAISE FOR GIFT OF DIAMONDS

"Seret vividly captures life under dictatorial rule in Romania and the ghastly compromises that good people are compelled to make in order to survive."

— *Kirkus Reviews*

"*Gift of Diamonds* is written in language that is flawless. I loved the well-crafted and strong themes, the well-written international setting, and the political ideas explored in the story. But what had me going from page to page is the deft treatment of the protagonist—she is real, genuine, and sophisticated."

— *Readers' Favorite*

"*Gift of Diamonds* by Roberta Seret is a spellbinding novel. It is a well-crafted, fast-paced, and a character-driven story that had me on the edge on my seat... The descriptions are gorgeous and the author leads the reader into the psyche of the protagonist with intelligence. The setting is well written, and the contrast between the horror that Mica is running from and the hope of liberty in the US is mesmerizing. *Gift of Diamonds* is cinematic, an engaging story that I would love to watch as a movie."

— *Readers' Favorite*

IN APPRECIATION

No book is written alone.

Words and thoughts come alive on the page only after they are shared with those the author respects. I have been fortunate to have family and friends who have believed in me. For without them, my literary world could not have taken shape.

My deepest appreciation goes to each one of you:

Maggie Sokolik, Senior Fiction Editor of Wayzgoose Press; Dorothy Zemach, publisher of Wayzgoose Press; Linda Langton, my literary agent; Marcia Rockwood, my editor; Mridula Agarwal, my right hand and tech Guru; Natalia Donofrio, my web designer; Greenwich Pen Women: Anita Keire, Ginger Heller, Deb Weir, and Kyle Ridley.

My friends of many years: Judith Vogel, Leslie and Norman Leben, Lydia Eviatar, Judith Auslander, Raffaella Depero, Nancy Cushing-Jones, Will Nix, Elise Strauss, Nina Saglimbeni, Candida Iodice, Andreea Mihut, Ioana and Eugen Mihut.

My sons: Greg and Cliff; my daughters-in-law: Hally and Arielle; my grandchildren: Annabel, Sam, Jack.

And my husband, Michel, who always at my side, has shared his story and our journey. Without his *joie de vivre* and optimism, these books would not have come to be.

Thank you all,
    Roberta

To Michel

One second of fate and our bikes collided. Together we embarked on paths rarely traveled. Always encouraging, you have opened me to vistas never known before. Chatting, laughing, even crying, but you, always optimistic and loving. How lucky I have been.

Your story became my story and they are now for our children and grandchildren. How grateful I am.

INTRODUCTION

Dear Reader,

I invite you to go on a voyage with me to Transylvania where my imagination has borrowed political intrigues to create a different view of Literature. Facts fuse with Fiction in *Transylvanian Trilogy.*

Gift of Diamonds, Love Odyssey, and Treasure Seekers: each book of the trilogy can be read independently or interchanged, depending on reader's choice. The main characters are Mica, Anca, Cristina, and Marina, four friends since their teenaged days in Transylvania, who appear and reappear in each book. They were known in their little town as best friends, the Four Musketeers, *Poets of their Lives.*

Gift of Diamonds is Mica's story and her escape with rare colored diamonds as Communism in Romania explodes under dictator, Ceausescu.

Marina and Cristina take center stage in *Treasure Seekers* when they are successful women living in New York City and Paris, and vacation together to exotic Turkey to fall, unexpectedly, into a web of Terrorists.

Love Odyssey is Anca's quest as she escapes alone while pregnant from those who have targeted her.

The stories flow together amidst Romania's politics. I have used the historical settings as a novelist would – to enhance the fictional storyline. Yet, I must confess, I have sometimes been tempted to make the history a little more exciting with touches of imagination. Accordingly, I've taken liberties under the guise of "poetic license" with time and place to recreate a literary fresco of Romania's second half of the 20th century. The history is the "backdrop curtain" of the novels, not center stage.

I have used Romania's dictatorial regimes to create an atmosphere of deceit that poisoned all Romanians during the Fascist and Communist years. One form of totalitarian government led to another. These were times of secret police, informers, fear, lies, double-crossing, dehumanization, shredding of documents, the destruction of the human soul. What we know today about these times is still masked with inconsistencies and ambiguities to cover up the Truth.

Yet, the world I offer you is of Fiction, and I use four female characters as dramatic voices. Each woman of the trilogy takes center stage to create her own life as she journeys through political events to survive. Each one becomes involved with history and forges forward in an existentialist need to direct her own destiny. But sometimes, the four friends find challenges that are stronger than their willpower. Those are the times when the fictional protagonists merge and interact with factual events. It is then that their courage evokes exciting narratives. Fiction that could not exist without Truth.

I hope you enjoy this colorful kaleidoscope of Fact with Fiction, Truth with Crimes, History and Art, Strife with Love. For it is from my heart that I offer you these stories from Transylvania.

Roberta Seret, Ph.D.

PROLOGUE

I ESCAPED Romania in the middle of the night, by bike, on February 2, 1965. It was the moment when the country was locked in a communist prison. I was seventeen years old then. Now, twenty-four years later, in the diplomatic and political frost of 1989, with the beginning of freedom, I'm returning. As I walk through customs at Bucharest's Otopeni airport with my American passport held tightly in my hand, I feel a strange sensation: memory is pulling me back to a lost time.

I see my seventeen-year-old self in front of me, leading me into the labyrinth of youth. She takes my hand and warns me of pitfalls while I enter a world I may have forgotten. She's cute, smiling, spunky, full of life. One would say she had been very much loved by her parents.

I follow her, admiring her short black hair cropped straight around her oval face, highlighting her high cheekbones and hazel eyes, with a small pointy chin and full lips. She's of medium height, fragile like porcelain on the outside, but more resilient than she realizes inside. She's dressed in a black turtleneck sweater and tight black leggings, wearing high black leather boots and covered with an Elizabethan-style coat that closes with a belt wrapped twice around her thin frame.

She leads me to a customs desk where I present my papers to an officer without any communication other than his indifferent stare. I understand that his silence, inherited from the communist era, still lingers. I look around me. There's only one electric bulb for the entire room and its 40 watts flicker. The wind blows through a broken windowpane, letting in a winter chill. The airport is empty except for several policemen carrying machine guns. I watch them: smooth-skinned boys, dressed up as soldiers.

At the baggage claim, waiting for my suitcase, I notice bullet holes in the cement walls and dried blood on the floor. Broken glass and bullet casings fill every corner of the room. Someone tried to clean up proof of last month's revolution, but didn't finish. There's a heavy silence permeating the air. Danger and risk still exist.

I reason to myself that I had to make this journey. And I look around, trying to find Mica, my seventeen-year-old self, my guide. I want to confess to her why I'm here, why I have come alone, despite the suffering that might befall me, now, as it did in the past. But I can't find her.

I see my suitcase coming down the conveyor belt. I pick it up and feel its heaviness. I try to grip the handle tightly and suddenly I feel a piercing pain in my right-hand little finger. I close my eyes, try not to cry. I remember...

I was eleven years old, walking home alone from school. A policeman was trailing me. He detained me, handcuffed me, forced me onto his motorcycle, and took me to the chief of the secret police.

───────

"*IN MY OFFICE, I HAVE THE POWER TO DO WHATEVER I WANT.*"

He unlocked the handcuffs, pulled my small hand into his, and removed from his pocket a pair of pliers. He flashed the tool in front of my face to taunt me and placed the metal tip under a flame. I saw it turn fiery red.

"Only you can save your father. Work for us and your father will be safe."

"Don't ask me that. Please! I can't!"

"Such a sweet little pinky you have." He took the red-hot pliers, tightened it on my fingernail and pulled hard.

"Ow!" I was on fire, burning. I fell to the floor in excruciating pain.

"Get up!" He pulled me up by my sweater. He let his pliers play with my thumbnail, burning the tender skin around it, shouting at me,. "In my office, I have the power to do whatever I want."

I'M TWENTY-FOUR YEARS OLDER AND I'M RETURNING HOME. I LIVE IN New York City and I am a goodwill ambassador to UNICEF for refugee children. This is one of the reasons for my visit. I have established an adoption agency in Transylvania for orphans, and I want to check that medicines from New York are being distributed correctly to the orphanages, and that each child has a crib or bed and food and medicines that we have sent.

I'm also returning because when I escaped, I had left something for my father in his underground bunker the night he was arrested. I need to find out if what I had hidden is still there. I'm afraid, yet excited, to learn the truth.

That's why I'm seeking my teenaged Mica to guide me to a lost past. As I search for her in these hollow halls of the airport, something unexpected is happening before my eyes: the reappearance of images from my youth. I try to hold on to the scenes as clues to help me understand how the past shaped my future. My present.

I look back to see, to feel, to relive the moments.

. . .

EVERY YEAR ON MY BIRTHDAY, MY FATHER AND I TALKED ABOUT monsters and vampires. Tata was a wonderful storyteller. I cuddled in his arms and listened to tales of what happened in the woods of Transylvania where we lived.

In Romania, when we spoke of vampires, we meant Count Dracula, Vlad the Impaler, on whom so many legends were based. In Spera, the small town where I grew up, he was remembered as a prince, a leader who protected his people from the Turks when they invaded Romania in the fifteenth century. Still, we had to accept that his heroic deeds were cloaked in bloodthirsty evil. He believed that blood preserved his youth; thousands of innocent people died at the flick of his hand so that he could fortify himself.

Mama did not approve of Tata's stories, but she never stopped him. As she cooked, she'd frown while Tata laughed with joy, telling me his tales.

As I became a teenager, what he shared became more complex. My father explained how the behavior of monsters and the character of man could intersect. Tata was an engineer, and he constructed a stage for me where his stories became lessons for survival.

By the time I was seventeen, Tata's stories had taken a different route. The characters were no longer based on legend or fairytale. I became the protagonist of the story. My father was preparing me for what I would need to know: that I was the daughter of a revolutionary.

Father was the leader of the Transylvanian anti-communists, which proved very dangerous for him as well as for Mama and me. My mother feared that Tata's secret mission would force me to grow up too fast. She realized his work would affect my entire life and she tried to counteract the dangers by preparing me for the future: I would get to America. She taught me English and read Shakespeare to me.

When Tata's clandestine activities, kept him out at night, Mama took me into the kitchen, ran the faucet strong so no one else would hear her words, and took out our shortwave radio to listen to Radio Free Europe. She'd translate the broadcaster's English words into whispers and reveal the political truths to me.

As our country turned ruthless, Tata's stories scared me. I wanted him to stop, but I stayed and listened. Now, years later, as I look back at my childhood, I understand his motive: his vampire stories were warnings. Politics had turned inhuman during that time in Eastern Europe, and his lessons became guiding principles to help me understand political realities. My father's monsters taught me that there is evil in man. Given the proper incentives, man is capable of becoming cruel and sadistic. Tata didn't want me to become a victim; yet, there was little he could do. I would be tested and I'd have to fight to survive.

But Tata's passion for life overruled the savagery that surrounded us. He was optimistic, determined to do what was right. And he had a secret treasure, which he believed could open the door to dreams. I inherited his treasures.

PART I

SPERA (TRANSYLVANIA), ROMANIA

CHAPTER 1

February 1, 1965

"NO, NO, JULIET. NOT LIKE THAT!" the white-haired director yelled. Mica stopped reciting her lines. She hated displeasing Mr. Marinescu. He had taught her so much and introduced her to the love of her life: the stage. "Your words must come from your heart," he explained. "Act as if you're a woman, not a child. Think of everything you're losing!"

Mica squeezed her eyes tightly. It was difficult to be unhappy when she was playing Juliet and Romeo was as handsome as Nicky Strancusi. But she did as directed and turned her thoughts to the secret police, who had come yesterday to their house in the middle of the night. "We'll be back," the chief had warned her father. "Until we find out what you're up to."

"That's it, Mica! I feel your fear," the director shouted. *Fear, yes, for my parents*, she thought.

"You must get this right. *Romeo and Juliet* is the first Shakespearean play the people of Spera will see."

Her eyes wandered past the chandelier with only one light

bulb, to the tattered red velvet curtains and crumbling cement walls. Modern times seemed to have forgotten her town at the Romanian-Hungarian border.

"Start from the beginning of the balcony scene one more time," Marinescu shouted. "Remember, people, tomorrow is opening night."

Mica tried to forget that the freezing room was no longer an elegant theater; that the broken chairs hadn't held an audience in years. She concentrated on being Juliet. They began and Mica moved closer to the edge of the stage. Taking a deep breath, she recited her lines:

"My bounty is as boundless as the sea,
My love as deep; the more I give to thee,
The more I have, for both are infinite.
And all my fortunes at thy foot I'll lay
And follow thee throughout the world."

Marinescu stood up and applauded. Waving his beret, he yelled, "Brava, Mica!"

She took a deep bow and smiled, imagining how everyone in Spera would applaud her tomorrow night. Emile Marinescu's production of Shakespeare in English was such a big event that even people from Bucharest were traveling to their small town to see it. And she was the leading actress.

Holding Nicky's hand, she practiced a curtsy while he bowed and then kissed her cheek. She felt her body turn warm. This was the only thing that could keep her from worrying about her parents.

Then Nicky led her into the wings, where he put his arms around her waist, pulled her near, and brushed her lips with his. It was magical, better than she'd imagined, but Mica was pulled instantly back to earth by the sound of the tram station's clock striking 5:30. "Oh, no," she whispered to Nicky. "It's almost curfew." She was afraid that she wouldn't have enough time to get her father his dinner and take it to him and then be home before seven. The police seemed to be patrolling more actively than usual.

Nicky gave Mica one last kiss. He moved her closer and held her tighter, kissing her neck. She closed her eyes to enjoy his nearness, and the thrill of his passion. Then, suddenly, upon hearing another clock chime, she moved away and put on Juliet's Shakespearean coat. She smoothed down her short, cropped black hair and whispered, "Forgive me. I must go!"

She raced through the theater's dark corridors and climbed the broken-down stairs. Still tingly from Nicky's kisses, she was struck by the freezing cold outside. Her hazel eyes teared and her face stung as if tiny knives were piercing her skin. Running through the dark, she shuddered at the thought of being alone in the empty tram station.

She moved toward the shadow of the barbed-wire fence where she had locked her bike. Someone tapped her shoulder. She stopped breathing and turned around slowly. Relieved, she saw Nicky, her Romeo, grinning down at her. When Emile Marinescu had chosen her out of the twenty-five girls who had auditioned, she had thought only of her role. But then when she saw Nicky Strancusi, a nineteen-year-old engineering student, she couldn't believe her luck. He was so handsome. Six feet tall, thin but muscular with broad shoulders. Black wavy hair that he wore long, covering his ears. He looked like a Roman god she had seen pictured in history books, with blue eyes and devilish smile. After four weeks of rehearsing together, she felt she could give herself to Nicky. Enjoy him without restraint, for the very first time.

He leaned toward her and rested his elbow on her bicycle seat. "'Delay this marriage for a month, a week. Love only me,'" he told her, reciting his lines.

Mica laughed, wanting to believe that his Shakespearean lines were what he truly felt.

Nicky took her hand into his. "Let's practice our lines together. Alone. We have an hour and a half until curfew."

She was tempted to say yes. She wanted so much to be with him, feel him close, feel his kisses, but she sighed. There wasn't time. "I can't." Reluctantly, she climbed onto her bicycle.

He unclasped her fingers and softly kissed the open palm. "Don't forget tomorrow's cast party after opening night. We're having champagne and caviar. One of the girls got them from her boyfriend." Then Nicky's face turned sad. "Only someone from the secret police can find champagne in this country when there's not even milk for a baby."

Mica nodded sympathetically. She hated the Securitate, especially after they had raided her home yesterday in the middle of the night and threatened her father. "You're on our blacklist now! We're watching you!"

She turned to Nicky and whispered, "I can't talk... 'I must be gone and love, or stay and die.'" As she got on her bike, she tried to sound more cheerful, "Till tomorrow, Romeo."

Mica biked away from the tram station, turning for a moment to wave good-bye to Nicky, who appeared as a tall black figure silhouetted in the fading daylight. Ever since Mica had joined the student Shakespeare troupe four years ago, her life had changed for the better. Every day she'd wake up excited, knowing she'd rehearse after school or perform on stage. And to help her get to the theater and home more quickly, her father had given her a bicycle. It hadn't been easy for her father to buy one. Bikes were all but impossible to find, even on the black market. No one in school, except for her history teacher, had one. Mica was lucky her father had connections.

She knew that he'd be a rich man if they were ever able to get out of Romania. But he kept saying the timing wasn't right to get past the border into Hungary without being caught by the Romanian police. He believed the moment would come when the communists would change leaders, then there'd be total disarray, and they'd have their chance to get out. He said it could happen any day.

Mica set out for her house to collect her father's dinner from her mother. She didn't ask any questions, but Mica knew that he and his followers were planning something big, and it was a secret, something not spoken about in her house. Tata was afraid that the walls could have ears or neighbors would spy, so he kept the details to himself. Mica had no choice but to continue her studies, practice her lines as Juliet, and see her friends on weekends. It was not easy for Mica to pretend her life was like everyone else's. A double life was a difficult role. For her mother and father also, who went to work as always because the police were watching them. But in the past two evenings, Mica had had to get involved with real action. It was her job to bike to the underground bunker and bring her father his dinner while he and his followers strategized every last aspect of their plan to overthrow the communist leader.

"You're late," Corina Mihailescu said as Mica stood at the front door. She had obviously been watching for her from the window, but to sound less anxious, she quickly asked, "How's Nicky?"

"He's not like anyone else." For one second, Mica closed her eyes and smiled. Then she took her father's dinner from her mother and packed it into the basket mounted on the rear of her bike. "I can't wait until tomorrow night! You and Tata will be so proud of me. I'll save you front row seats."

Her mother watched her mount the bike. "Good idea. I'm looking forward to see you on stage. Something good for once." Mica noticed her mother's round cheeks, usually flushed and full, appeared tired and pale.

"Tell Tata to eat this dinner only when he's alone," she whispered. "The message is hidden inside the cup. Then bike home as fast as you can. You know I worry about you!"

Mica pedaled away as the last rays of daylight faded. She heard the howl of a rabid dog, and she reached behind her and took out a wooden club her father had placed in the rear basket. "Just in case," he had told her. Mica hated Spera in the dark. There were no lights anywhere, no cars, no people, no life. Only the sounds of wild dogs howling and searching for scraps. They were known to nip at cyclists' legs, even maul children. People would leave their houses with a club or stick in hand because so many of the stray dogs carried rabies.

Mica veered off the main road and followed a narrow path into the woods. She had come this way so many times that she could have found her father with her eyes closed, but with the darkness closing in around her, she proceeded carefully, ducking to avoid the overhanging branches that blocked her path.

Her father and his engineering students had designed and built an underground secret labyrinthine bunker during World War II so that they could fight the fascists. After the war, they had abandoned it until a few days ago as they prepared their anti-communist rebellion. The bunker was carved inside the earth like a twisting tunnel, with a sleeping area lined with dozens of bunk beds, a large bathroom, a kitchen, an armory, and a private office for her father.

She pushed her bike slowly through brush and broken limbs using her high leather boots and a stick to clear the way. She came to a stop and hid behind a tree to see if anyone other than her father's men were near. She saw no one. She laid her bike among the fallen limbs and covered it with dead branches. She quickly went through the trapdoor next to the abandoned glass factory that marked the site of the bunker. As she made her way to her father's office, she couldn't help but notice an unusual mass of machine guns leaning against the stone walls of the armory and knew that this meant their preparations were imminent.

When she knocked on his door and saw his full head of bushy red hair shine in the light, she felt reassured. He greeted her with a red pencil in one hand and a map in the other hand. "Mica, sit with me while I eat."

"What is it, Tata?" she asked. "What are you planning? Can I be part of this?"

"No, my love," he said, kissing her forehead. "You're busy enough as Juliet. And I don't want anything to happen to you."

She put his dinner on the table, but before she could ask him more, the cement floor began to vibrate, and they both turned toward the metallic noise of wheels rolling against the bunker's stone floor.

"Stay here," he said to her as he went out to investigate.

Mica waited until she heard him talking with someone before she sneaked a look. The sound of wheels came from a slab of wood fastened to four wheels. On top of the plank was a man, his body cut off at the top of his thighs. His torso sat on top of a hollowed-out hole in the wooden plank. His hands were inside two metal cans, and he used them to balance his half body so he could stay upright. He had no legs.

The "Snake Man." That's what her father and his men called him. His head was huge, out of proportion to his narrow chest. His long, spidery but muscular arms extended to the ground as he swung them, using the cans to push himself forward. Shadows fell across his face. He had braided most of his long black hair but for a pompadour above his forehead that he had wrapped around a small stick and where a black and yellow snake now curled. The reptile was so still that Mica couldn't tell if it was dead or alive until she saw its slithery tongue snap out of its mouth.

They finished their conversation, and Anton Mihailescu patted the man on the back. The Snake Man made his way down the corridor as Mica stared, mesmerized by the way he maneuvered his half-body.

"Poor man," her father said, sitting back down at his desk and taking the tin cup that Mica had brought. "He wasn't always like that. I knew him when he was a tall, handsome student. One day the police arrested him because he was in the street after curfew. They wanted him to denounce his friends, but he refused. So they hung him from a tree upside down for several days. When they were done with him, they threw him in the mud. He had no circulation left in his legs, and he got gangrene. His legs had to be amputated."

"How awful." Mica rubbed her thighs and a shiver passed through her. She felt so sorry for him.

"That's why he's full of hate against the communists. He'll pretend to work for them and be our decoy." Her father stood up from his desk and walked over to the map he had been studying when she arrived.

"Mama said to eat this when no one is near you," Mica said. "There's a message inside."

Anton took the tin cup and with his fingernail, he pried open the false bottom which revealed a note folded in four. He read it, then burned it with a candle on his desk.

"A good way to communicate with me," he said, and winked at Mica. "Remember." The smell of beef stew and corn pudding filled the room, and her father started to eat. Then he stopped.

"*Draga mea*, my dear," he said, standing up and putting his arm around her shoulder. She felt his red mustache rub her cheek. It pricked her but she didn't move, wanting to hold on to the moment. Her father didn't move either. When she looked up at him, she noticed how tired he looked; his broad six-foot frame appeared less powerful, but he held her more strongly than ever.

"Mica, you must perform tomorrow evening as Juliet." He paused and then slowly let her go and went to his desk. He unlocked the bottom drawer and took out a map of Transylvania. It was marked with red dots.

"I keep telling myself you're a young woman now. Seventeen."

"Yes." But why was that making him so sad?

"I don't know what will happen, but if someday I don't come home, if your mother doesn't come home, you must get yourself to Hungary."

He smoothed the map out on the desk between them and drew a line from Spera to the border. "This is the route I took years ago, when I worked in the Resistance. There's a hidden trail through the forest, and when you cross the border, you have to get to the train station. You'll have to run five kilometers to get to the first station in Hungary, but you can do it."

She wanted to ask him why he was telling her this now, but she was afraid to know. He looked so sad.

"I traveled on foot. It took me six hours in the middle of the night to get to the border, but it can be done faster by bike."

He made dots along the route he had drawn and explained what each one meant: a fork in the trail, a grove of pine trees, the fence at the border, the electric wires. "I will go over this several times until you have memorized each detail."

She nodded. He opened a drawer with another key and pulled out a pile of black and white photos of the Romanian-Hungarian border area. "You're going to have to use trees and buildings as markers while sighting angles with your eyes."

He showed her photos of a dense forest, and pointed to several buildings, a twelve-foot high fence, a cable box. Then from another drawer he took out a ruler and compass.

"Where the last pine tree and barn meet, right here, create a sixty-degree angle with your eyes. Then look down to the ground." Using the ruler, he drew a diagram. "Create an isosceles triangle like this with two equal sides at that spot. The two lines will converge at a point where you will see in the distance the chimney of Dracula's castle. This is the way explorers navigate unchartered land."

She studied the photos in his hands and watched him measure the angles with his ruler and compass.

"This is the section of the fence from which you will dig a rectangle the same size as your body," he explained, circling the point with his red pencil. "The earth will be muddy and soft there because it was once a sewer. Dig two feet deep on each side, so you can pass safely through beneath the wires."

He repeated the directions again, and then cautioned her not to give in to the impulse to run toward freedom after crossing over. She needed to stay focused to keep from attracting any attention that might alert the guards on either side of the border.

After an hour of listening and then being quizzed by him on the plan's details, Mica's sweater was damp even though the room was unheated. She noticed her father's face was red and that a vein under his left eye twitched. She watched him rip the map and photos into tiny pieces and burn them with the candle.

He took her hand, put her palm against his lips. For several seconds, he stroked her fingers. *"Draga,"* he whispered. "If you can't find me or your mother, if you know in your heart that we've been taken, then you must take the diamonds from the basement. Remember how I've shown you where to dig them up. They will buy your freedom. They will protect you for the future."

"Tata, no. Don't say that."

"Whatever happens, you must be strong. Don't ever give up hope, no matter how hard things seem. Think with your mind and act with all your heart. When in doubt, go with your instincts."

She hugged him with all her strength. He wiped his eyes and looked away, sighing. Sensing his silence as a signal to leave, she kissed him good-bye on each cheek. He held on to her for several moments more. "I love you more than life," he whispered. "Never forget that. Use our love for your strength."

She wanted to answer, "I love you too," but she said nothing; her mind was filled with his map lesson and what he had told her she'd have to do. She couldn't absorb yet the reality that her life was about to change and that she'd be responsible to achieve that change. She felt almost in shock; even though she had known for years that her father's anti-communist work would have grave consequences for her. She didn't realize that it would come now. But now it had.

She felt it was best to leave him to his work, or she would break down and sob, or he would cry. She took the hidden staircase, then tiptoed through a secret corridor and climbed out into the night from a different section of the tunnel. Glancing from one side to the other, she searched for a moving shadow or noise. No one, just rats trying to move faster than the bitter wind.

On her way home, she took a detour through Gypsy[1] town. The people of Spera believed Gypsies stole children and took them far away. Whenever Gypsies marched through town, parents took their children's hands. The Pied Piper was a Gypsy who led children away from home with his magic flute. Yet, when Mica watched Gypsies dance with their colorful costumes and their arms thrown up to the sky, she was surprised to see they looked like everyone else, except they were so happy.

She passed their broken-down shacks and saw that rats were scurrying into ripped garbage bags. Cracked flower pots with garlic pushing out of the earth were all over the muddy ground. There was no food to buy in stores, so the Gypsies planted garlic, which they ate whole. Some people said they also ate dandelions from the mountains and even pink poppies. Mica wondered if that's why they acted so strangely.

A stray dog ran after her, barking and growling while reaching for her boot. Mica gripped her wooden club tightly. She didn't want to hit the dog, all she wanted was to get home quickly so she could sit by the fire with her mother. She wanted to feel safe, protected.

Spera was in sight; Mica could see the church steeple. Free from the dogs, she slowed down while passing the infirmary, a dilapidated two-room shack. Her arm ached in memory as she recalled going there to get shots for tetanus and polio when she was small. Now the facility was closed. The doctor had disappeared one night along with his wife. People said he had bought visas for France, visas that cost a fortune. Her mother had said, "Lucky man. He traded his Brancusi for freedom."

Almost home, she couldn't help feeling as though someone was watching her. Something moved against the wall of an abandoned building. She glanced from one side to the other, looked over her shoulder and moved faster. A noise from a motorcycle; it grew louder. Someone was breathing. There was the slow tapping of footsteps down the cobblestone street.

Mica's heart pounded as she accelerated, thinking of the big green armchair at home by the fireplace and her mother next to her on the couch.

"What's a schoolkid like you doing out so late?"

The man's voice made her jump. She froze, stopped her bike, her heart beating faster. She saw that the man's nose was red and swollen and streaked with blood vessels. She had once seen another man with a nose like that and her father had told her, "Too much drinking."

The policeman ordered her to get off the bike and to drop her club. She noticed he couldn't walk straight; he wobbled. He searched her, starting with her back, touching her shoulders, and moving from top to bottom, down her legs.

"Turn around."

As he touched Mica's chest, he jumped back. "My God. You're a girl!"

She pulled away before he could come near her again. She was furious at him for touching her, and furious at herself for not fighting back. But she had to keep herself in check.

"Show me your I.D."

She handed over her card, wishing she could throw it at him, and got back on her bicycle to defy him. The policeman grabbed the handlebars and pulled her toward him. She smelled his clothes, bitter with wine and sweat. "You shouldn't be out this late."

She considered just riding away, but it would be risky. He could shoot her or follow her. He asked, "Where do you live?"

Mica pointed toward her parents' house beyond the road and up the hill.

He came closer. She remembered her father's advice after the police had raided their house. "If anyone should ever start questioning you, cooperate. Don't fight. And don't be angry with yourself for giving in. Pretend you're acting."

She blinked her eyes and put on the flirtatious manner and voice she had seen in a French movie that had been shown months ago in their little theater. "Yes, you're right. I'm going straight home. Need to do my homework."

He glared at her, then pushed her hard, and laughed. "Go! *Vede-ti de treaba*," the policeman yelled, puffed up with power. "Get out of here before I put a bullet through you."

---

1. I use the term *Gypsy* with no intention of disrespect. The official term is *Roma,* but I use *Gypsy* as a colloquial word, spoken by Europeans in their daily conversations.

CHAPTER 2

As Mica biked along the last kilometer to her house, the wind lashed her cheeks. Her eyes watered and her bike swerved. Several times, she almost lost her balance. She pedaled faster.

"I'm stronger than you," she yelled at the wind. But she knew she wasn't. Not at seventeen years old.

Arriving home, Mica pushed her bicycle up the cement walkway to the bike rack and waited for her mother to answer the door. She needed to talk to her about Tata's map lesson. What did it mean? And why now?

When her mother opened the door, the smell of *mititei* greeted Mica. The meat sausage, grilled with garlic and herbs, was her favorite dish. But tonight she wasn't hungry.

"Did you give your father the *mamaliga* and stew?" her mother asked, leading Mica down the dark hall to the kitchen.

"*Da.*"

"Was he alone?"

"*Da. Da.*"

"The note was to warn him to take special care tonight."

Mica didn't say anything.

"We'll eat together while we listen to the radio," Corina suggested. Mica watched her mother's trembling fingers take the shortwave radio out of its hiding place. Then she put on the sink's water faucet strong to drown out the sound of her voice. "Radio Free Europe is on in English tonight."

"Maybe we shouldn't do this. If a neighbor hears the English, they'll report us to the police. They'll get an extra ration of sugar if they denounce us..."

Mica stopped talking. Something about her mother's manner made her reluctant to continue.

"I think I'll put on another radio with a Romanian station," her mother said.

"Then it'll be hard for us to hear Radio Free Europe."

"Maybe the neighbors want to hear something else. I want to keep them happy."

Her mother's change of mind was strange. Usually she was so precise about what she said and did.

"I'll first put on the portable radio with the Romanian station," her mother said. "See, I'll set it here by the window so the neighbors will enjoy the Romanian news. Let's go to the kitchen table where I'll put the shortwave radio on for us."

Mica went over to her mother and put her arms around her, placing her cheeks against her chest. Mica wanted to hold her, talk to her. "Mama, what's wrong?"

"Let's huddle closer to hear the English."

Mica hugged her mother again. She wished she'd say something reassuring.

"They're enforcing the curfew strictly tonight for a reason," her mother whispered, turning down the volume and the English message. "Your father told me that he might be a little late tonight. Tomorrow night might be the one we've been waiting for."

Mica tried to keep from shivering. She wanted to think good things. What if the Mihailescus could escape to America all together? They had waited so long. Their friends who had survived the war had left between 1945 and '48, when there was a window of freedom to emigrate. Then the Russians took control and the Iron Curtain came down. Her parents had lost their chance.

Mica closed her eyes so she could hear better. The broadcast was full of static, but it delivered news from England and America. The shortwave radio was the only link they had to the free world.

> *"Several years ago, during the red hot summer of 1962, Gheo-rghiu-Dej, the dictator of Romania then, thought Khrushchev had weakened because of losing in the Cuban Missile crisis. The moon took an independent stand against the sun. Now the Romanian dictator of seventeen years is dying of cancer. Intelligence indicates that a Russian radioactive doorknob was installed in his office."*

Mica looked at her mother to see her reaction. But she didn't move a muscle, so intent was she on deciphering the hidden meaning of the broadcaster's message. She explained to Mica:

"Rumors are that the Dictator Gheorghiu-Dej has been irradiated by the KGB. They weren't happy with his reducing Soviet influence in Romania and increasing his own form of nationalism. He's paying: he was poisoned. Lung cancer."

Now Mica understood why there was an eerie feeling in the streets. "Does this mean there will be a new dictator?" Selfishly, she didn't want any change to come this week because of her début as Juliet.

"Your father says there will be a struggle for power among the communist leaders. Ceausescu is the inner group's choice, which means he's the most dangerous."

Mica thought all communists were dangerous. She turned to

her mother and asked, with a feeling of horror, "Is Tata's group staging an uprising?"

"I don't know," her mother said with an eerie calm.

"Mama, let me get more involved. Not just delivering messages to Tata in his dinner. I'm not a child any more. Even Tata told me that this evening. Let me help you. Work with you. I want to be part of this like you!"

"No!" her mother shouted, striking Mica on the chest with her fist. "No! I'd rather die a thousand deaths than allow anyone to harm you. No! No!"

Mica was frightened. Her mother had never shouted like that before, or pounded her on the chest. And then, within seconds, her mother became composed. Corina walked over to the fireplace, stared at the log charred almost to ashes, and mumbled, "Tata will have to chop some more wood..."

Mica stared at her mother. She had a strange expression on her face as if she had not understood Mica's request or her own outburst. Mica didn't know what to do for her mother. Her eyes looked vacant. Obviously, she was suffering. Mica wished her father would get home soon.

Corina got up. There wasn't a ray of heat left in the entire house. She put her coat on Mica's shoulders, hugged her, and walked to the window. The coat hung over Mica as if two girls could fit inside. Corina was a head taller than Mica and broader, but their faces were similar with the same full lips, dainty noses, and short black straight hair cropped softly around their wide foreheads.

Sometimes Mica thought she looked very much like her mother, but in reality Mica resembled no one else. Her eyes were hazel but if she wore green, they changed to emeralds. If she stared at the sky too long, her eyes absorbed the same hue to blue. Her high cheekbones were as soft as a painter's brush.

Her mother walked over to her, took her in her arms and

kissed her cheeks several times and held her tight. She asked Mica, "How was rehearsal? Was Mr. Marinescu there the entire time?"

Before Mica could answer, she saw her mother's lips twitch. In a quavering voice her mother continued, "Did someone visit him? Someone he didn't know?"

Corina must have realized she was frightening Mica. She tried to change the conversation and her voice took a lighter tone, "Let's talk of something pleasant. Tell me about Romeo. I hear he's very handsome. I'm sure he likes you."

No matter how bad things got, Mica's mother always tried to think of something good and she encouraged Mica to do the same. That's why she had taught Mica English. "One day you'll need English to make your dreams come true," she had said.

"Would you like some tea?" her mother asked, returning to her chair at the table. "I got your favorite rose honey from a friend of mine. I traded a book for it."

"No." Mica felt her stomach tighten from the tensions of the afternoon and evening. "I think I'll go to bed, or should I wait with you for Tata? Maybe I should?"

"No, I fear he may be late," her mother said again in a detached way as if her words were being said by someone else. "You should go to bed. Tomorrow is your big day."

Mica bit her lip and stood up. She wanted to go to sleep and pretend she was Juliet and Nicky was wooing her like Romeo wooed his love. But the child in Mica longed to stay near her mother. She wished she could cuddle in her arms like a little girl and never leave her.

Instead, Mica sat down and took her mother's hands in hers. "Mama, I love you." She kissed her mother's fingers. Closing her eyes, Mica remained still. With her mother's hands in hers, she was afraid if she'd moved, she'd lose this closeness forever.

CHAPTER 3
FEBRUARY 2, 1965

MICA WOKE up to a layer of snow covering their yard. Pulling the blanket to her chin, she lingered lazily in bed and practiced her first lines, "'O Romeo, Romeo. Wherefore art thou, Romeo?'"

She picked up the clock on her night table: seven a.m. The glass of water next to it had iced over. She jumped out of bed, put on slippers, and went to see if her father was home. She looked for his hat at the front door. Nothing. His boots and coat weren't there either. She ran into the kitchen where her mother was preparing breakfast.

"Where's Tata?" Mica asked.

"He's gone out early," her mother answered quietly. "He said to tell you he will see you tonight at the play. He can't wait."

Mica watched her mother. Her lips were trembling, and she didn't look up when Mica went to stand next to her. "Is he okay? Is everything okay?"

"I'm sure everything is fine," Corina said, as much to herself as to Mica. She finally looked up and Mica saw tears in her mother's eyes. "He didn't come home last night," Corina confessed. "Sometimes that happens when it gets too late."

"I'll go by bike to check on him in his bunker before I go to the theater."

"No!" her mother shouted. Mica jumped, surprised. "You have the play. We'll be there tonight, and your father can tell us what happened afterwards."

"Mama, tell me the truth. Do you know what happened to Tata? What is he planning?"

Her mother leaned in close to Mica and shook her head. "I don't know," she said, but Mica got the distinct sense she was lying. Her mother set a plate of hard-boiled eggs and goat cheese cakes on the table. "You have to have a good breakfast today to keep up your strength!"

Mica choked down a few bites while her mother bustled around the kitchen. She tried several times to ask for more information, but her mother wouldn't answer and only interrupted her to remind her to bring an old jacket that one of the boys wanted for his costume. "Mica, I can't wait to see you tonight. I know how hard you've worked for this."

For a moment, Mica let herself believe that all was well, even though her instincts told her that wasn't the case. "Maybe someone from Bucharest will see me, and I can find a place in the theater program after I graduate next year."

"One thing at a time," her mother said, trying to smile. Then she turned serious again. "When you get to the theater, ask Mr. Marinescu if he wants to come to our house for your father's birthday so I can talk to him."

"But we just celebrated last week," Mica said.

Her mother crossed the room, beckoned Mica over to her, and turned on the faucet. She talked quietly as the water roared. "Ask him if he wants to go swimming with your father. He knows which sharks to avoid. Above all, you must trust him. Do whatever he says. No matter how hard."

"I always listen to him. It's through him that I discovered my passion for the theater."

"Yes, I know, my darling. But this is different."

Mica sensed something was very wrong. "Can I really trust him?" she asked.

"Yes. But make sure you speak to him in English. Only in English."

Mica couldn't get her mother to explain what was going on, despite her insistence; so, she decided to go to the theater early to get ready for the evening. When she arrived at the stage door, she was immediately drawn into the whirlwind of preparations.

Mica and the rest of the cast spent the day finishing the set and getting the theater ready for opening night. She should have been exhausted by the time they went backstage and started putting on their costumes, but she wasn't. She had never been so excited. Her friends, Marina, Cristina and Anca came backstage with a bouquet of blue mountain flowers. Marina said they picked them for her at their favorite trail. Cristina added, "To bring you good luck." And Anca laughed. "You've been so busy rehearsing that you couldn't hike with us Saturday, so we brought something from the valley to you." They chattered and laughed until the troupe's seamstress told Mica she needed to adjust her costume.

Mica, Anca, Marina, and Cristina had grown up together in Spera. What they liked to do the most together was to hike. Saturdays, in all weather, was their time together, to feel free wandering in the woods of Transylvania and the Carpathian Mountains. They'd hike through pine forests and valleys carpeted with purple heather and laugh. Their favorite game was to hold hands like a human chain. "One for all and all for one," they'd sing, walking in a line, and chant their motto, "We are the poets of our lives." Then they would bend down low, swing their arms to the sky and start again, holding hands, walking in a line, feeling so free, singing and shouting, *"We are the poets of our lives."*

Sometimes after they hiked, they'd go to the Saturday market in town. There was never much to buy there, but once, when they were thirteen years old, they saw a Gypsy, all by herself, seated in a corner, hiding, selling something that Mica, Cristina, Anca, and Mariana had never seen before: a lipstick, not completely new, but more than half full, of a hot pink color. Next to it in the Gypsy's rough hand was a little pointed glass bottle of nail polish, also half full, the same color pink. Mica ran home and got some *lei* to buy the treasures. Every Saturday until it lasted, the girls would put nail polish on their toes. They wore the lipstick on special occasions.

Everyone in class called them the Four Musketeers because they were always together. They even sat at the same table every day in the school cafeteria. Anca was the poorest of the four. She'd bring just one slice of bread for lunch, carefully packed in the same old gray scarf. Mica always brought two sandwiches, two pieces of fruit, and two slices of bread with rose petal jam. She always sat next to Anca and made sure her friend had one of each.

On Friday evenings, the four friends would go to the Youth Center and listen to records. Often the boys joined them and they'd all dance to the 45-rpm records of the Beatles that Mica's father had given her for her fifteenth, sixteenth, and seventeenth birthdays. Mica loved to dance. It was the only time she could stop thinking.

She never knew exactly how or from whom her father got "Yesterday" and "Michelle." When she asked him, he smiled and answered, "My friends want you to have a happy birthday. I told them you like the Beatles."

Birthdays were special for everyone in her class. Whenever someone had a birthday, their favorite teacher, Doamna Rosa, would make a cake and bring it to school. It wasn't easy to find butter or eggs or milk or even flour in Romania. Such delicacies were available only on the black market. But no one questioned the teacher. They were all too busy enjoying the treat.

What Mica enjoyed the most was going to a movie with Anca, Marina and Cristina. Every two months, Mr. Marinescu got a reel of a 16- millimeter film which he showed in their little theater. Usually it was in Romanian, but sometimes it was in Hungarian or Russian. Once, he showed a film from France starring Yves Montand. Mica couldn't believe how beautiful Paris was. For months afterwards, she dreamed of strolling on the grand boulevards of Paris or chatting with her friends at a café. At night, in bed she'd imagine how sweet a chocolate croissant must be. A movie was the only way she could glimpse the free world and dream to become part of it one day.

But Mica already knew what she wanted to do with her life. She wanted to continue performing no matter what. Emile Marinescu had been a wonderful teacher, but if she wanted to be a real actress, or even more importantly, a serious dancer, she would have to find a way to get to Bucharest and study at the Conservatory for Dance and Performance. On stage, she felt unbridled in a way that she never did as she went about her life from day to day.

Often, she was afraid that someone was always watching, ready to inform on her, and she had to be careful what she said, who she spent time with, and where she went. But when she danced, before an audience or even alone for herself, she felt her true nature come out. She'd lose herself in the movement of her body and feel free, as if she were floating in air. Mica realized that dance is only true if it comes from the need to give meaning to life. For that reason, she needed to study and work hard. She hadn't asked her parents yet, but her plan was to go to Bucharest in September to audition. The thought thrilled her: dance, theater, and the big city.

Mica slipped into the long Elizabethan coat she was wearing to play Juliet, and the seamstress knelt to pin it up so that it didn't drag on the ground. The coat had been used before, but Mica was shorter and thinner than the previous actresses.

There was a knock at the door of their makeshift dressing room, and Nicky stuck his head in. He smiled when he saw Mica. "The audience has started arriving," he said. "Twenty minutes until places."

Anca, Cristina, and Marina waved good-bye. Cristina, with her long, fiery red hair worn braided in a crown, led the group, as always. Marina, the tallest and strongest, was the one to help them navigate the backstage scenery. And Anca, the intellectual, reminded Mica as she kissed her good luck, "Your tragedy as Juliet will prepare you to be more courageous in whatever else you do."

Mica hugged her friends and returned to putting on her high black leather boots and arranging her coat. Nicky crossed the room, took her hand, and ruffled her short dark hair. "I love your cropped hair. It really suits you," he said. "You're so lovely. 'Delay this marriage for a month, a week. Love only me.'" And he kissed her on the cheek. "Let me adore you."

Mica beamed, and her nervousness evaporated. She felt so lucky, her friends truly cared for her, and Nicky thought she was *lovely*. He wanted to *adore her*. When she stepped on stage, she'd be confident. She'd focus on Nicky, only him, her Romeo. He kissed her again and whispered, "I know you'll be great. You're my Juliet."

Romeo and Juliet walked behind the curtain to take their places. But before they stepped on stage, he took her hand and squeezed it tight. "Good luck." Seconds later, the threadbare curtain went up.

All Mica knew in the two hours of their performance was the sound of Nicky's voice and the swelling of her heart. The audience was swept away, and with their enthusiasm, she threw herself passionately into her role as she never had before. She would make Marinescu proud. She would make the whole town of Spera proud. But most of all, she would make her parents proud. As the final lines of the play echoed through the hushed, dark theater, Mica lay on the stage, feigning death even as her heart beat quickly. The curtain fell, and she heard the roar of applause from the crowd.

She and Nicky stood up and kissed, unembarrassed, before taking their places at the front of the stage. The curtain went up, and the crowd was on its feet. The company took a bow, and then they pushed Mica to the front of the stage where she curtsied. Everyone cheered for her. It was the happiest moment of her life.

She looked to where she had reserved two seats in the first row for her parents, but they weren't there, and her heart immediately sank. Where were they? She looked around the theater, in the back, on the sides. Why weren't they there? She knew her parents would not have missed it for anything. Unless, unless…

Mica rushed backstage to grab her purse from the dressing room. Nicky saw her heading to the side door. "Where are you going? We have the party."

"I forgot something at home," she said, not meeting his eye. She knew that if she said more, the truth would come spilling out, and she had to keep herself in check.

She jumped on her bike and pedaled as fast as she could. When she got to her house and rushed inside, she saw that it had been torn apart. Lamps were broken. Chairs overturned. Even the walls had been punched through and ripped apart in some places.

In her parents' bedroom, clothes were thrown all over the floor. In the kitchen, broken plates and silverware were scattered everywhere.

Riddled with panic, she remembered her father's words. He had known that something like this might happen, and he was trying to warn her and prepare her. She went to her room and sat on the bed to think. "Take the diamonds with you," he had told her. Mica knew what she had to do.

She thought for a moment about the cast party and Nicky. He

would be wondering where she was, but there was no time for that now. All she knew was that her house had been destroyed and her parents were gone. She had to get out of Spera at once.

Though she didn't know where her parents were, she knew they would have never have missed her performance unless something beyond their control had happened. She feared they had been arrested. Or worse... Mica couldn't think about that. No! But she knew, if she stayed, the communists would certainly come for her next and use her to put pressure on her parents.

Six years ago, her father had shown her the colored diamonds for the first time. She felt then that her father was ashamed of having them, even if she didn't understand why.

"Your Uncle Simion gave them to me," he had told her. "I just wanted to help my brother, so he wouldn't be arrested when he escaped. No one should ever know."

"I won't tell," she said, rolling the colored stones over and over in her hands. She had never seen anything like them.

He rubbed his bushy mustache. "I don't know if it was my good luck or bad luck to have these.... I believe the green and red ones came from Auschwitz."

"What's that?" she had asked.

He hesitated, then sat down next to her.

"Auschwitz was the largest of all the Nazi concentration camps during World War II. Terrible things happened there. As many as nine thousand people were killed each day. More than a million human beings were murdered."

She looked down, sad and uncomprehending. "Why?"

He shrugged his shoulders. "People from all over the world worked with the Germans with one goal in mind—destroy Jews. Some believed what the Nazis were saying, and some became animals because of prejudice. But the worst creature of all was Dr. Josef Mengele. These are diamonds that he took from prisoners.

They all died horrible deaths." He closed his eyes. "I didn't go out and seek these diamonds."

Remembering his words, "Take the diamonds from the basement," she took the secret stairs and found the hand rake and shovel that her father had hidden. At the opposite corner of the room, she stood against the wall and took three giant steps forward. When her toe landed on a specific spot, she went down on her knees to dig in the muddy floor. Several minutes later, she hit something—the steel box. She took a brick off the shelf, picked up a key concealed beneath it, and opened the box. Inside was a leather pouch, and she untied the string. Twenty precious colored diamonds lit up the dark cellar.

Mica rolled the diamonds in her hands as she had done so many times before. The green, red and blue ones were so brilliant they created a rainbow in the dust. She put them back in the pouch and slipped them into her pocket, where their weight seemed to give her strength.

Back upstairs, she triple-locked the front door, closed the living room curtains, and went to the kitchen, where she turned on the faucet and both radios and went to work. Mica went to her mother's sewing box, found a needle and thread, and removed her bra. From a kitchen drawer, she took out a razor, a knife, a screwdriver and shoemaker's glue. She went to her father's closet, where she searched desperately for his black engineer's bag.

She returned to the kitchen and sat down at the table with her mother's sewing box. Remembering the many afternoons with the theater's costume designer, Mica began with her coat. She opened the hem and hid the green and red diamonds next to the seam, sewing circles around the jewels to fix them tightly. Next, she did the same with her bra, and once she had put it back on, she counted six tiny bumps from the six diamonds she had secured in place. Last came the soles of her boots. *Juliet's boots will bring me good luck*, she said to herself as she hollowed out the soles and heels of her boots with her father's tools and placed six colored diamonds in the bottom layer of each boot. She executed all these steps as if she were acting a role. She knew what she had to do and refused to allow emotion to take center stage.

Afterwards, she got dressed, put on her tight black leggings and black sweater and long coat, and sat on the floor to pray. Then she went to her father's dresser and pulled the bottom drawer out all the way. Against the back of the drawer, he had fixed an envelope with $300 US that Simion had given him along with the diamonds. Mica tore the envelope from its hiding place and tucked into her pocket two one-hundred dollar bills and an assortment of one-dollar bills, tens, and twenties. All the time, she was going over and over the secret route that her father had shown her on the map. By his calculations, it was twenty kilometers to the border between Romania and Hungary. It would take her five to six minutes per kilometer depending how thick the brush was and how strong the wind. It was ten o'clock; she hoped to be at the border by midnight. Then, she'd need time to dig her way under the fence and run to the first train station in Hungary.

Mica was confident that she knew the woods well. Not only because of her father's photos, but from the dozens of Saturdays when she and her friends went hiking.

She found it odd that their pleasure was now to become her danger.

She slipped out the back door of her house and began biking into the woods. She looked up into the night sky, hoping the wind would clear the clouds. Escape would be more difficult in the snow. Hearing gunshots, she took a path deeper into the woods. She lowered her body and leaned into the handlebars, trying to make herself invisible, but there was no escaping; there was more gunfire and then shouts of, "*Ceausescu! Traiasca Ceausescu!* Long live Ceausescu!"

As her path turned closer to the road through dead brush, she saw hundreds of men marching into town. With soot-and grime-smeared faces, they looked like a horde of subhuman monsters. Each man wore a helmet with a yellow light and carried a heavy bicycle chain, which he snapped with every other step as they all marched in lines of five toward Spera's center.

A helicopter flew so low that she was able to see a large "C" painted on it. For a second, she thought that someone from inside it might fire on the miners, but then she realized the helicopter was actually guiding the miners to Central Square. *C for Ceausescu*, she thought. The miners are working for Ceausescu. He has staged an uprising to use the miners to wipe out anyone who opposes him. Mica stared at the mob of miners who were blowing whistles, throwing stones, and hitting people with chains. Blood splattered on the road where they marched.

She watched a man run into the street, trying to cross the road. Dozens of miners surrounded him, flicking their chains and taunting him. He darted into a building, but a second later, he ran out, a fiery torch in his hand. He threw the torch into the middle of the miners and laughed as the flames filled the air. The miners retaliated by knocking him down and shattering the building's windows. Chaos exploded on the road. Gunfire. Sirens. She saw a woman run out of a bus carrying a baby. The infant's clothes were on fire! Mica tried to crouch down and hide behind her bike. She had never experienced violence before, and now she found herself in the middle of it. Surrounded by it.

Frightened, she squatted low behind a row of bushes. A voice from a loudspeaker mounted on a streetlight and warned the people to obey. "Go home! Don't fight back!" The distorted voice urged people over and over to stay inside and not resist the miners storming into town. Then Mica saw a squad of secret police marching toward Central Square. They seized the few people left on the street and beat them with wooden clubs.

Mica stared, afraid to move from her hiding place. She knew

the uprising had been intended to terrify the people and create hysteria. Then Ceausescu could appear onstage and create a semblance of order. It was a classic communist strategy, her father had told her so: treating citizens like cattle, rounding them up, bringing them to the range, and then locking them in cages. The iron curtain padlocked tightly.

Even from her hiding place behind the bushes, Mica could smell gasoline as the crowd became increasingly hysterical. Through the chaos, she could just make out the Snake Man on his wooden platform moving quickly through the mob. Dressed like one of Ceausescu's men, he had infiltrated the group of miners without being stopped. Though she couldn't tell for sure, it looked like he had a canister of some kind in his hand. Then a flame shot forth from his other hand and the ground all around the miners caught on fire as he lit the fuel and watched the flames before his eyes.

The miners looked around them to figure out who had started the fire, but the Snake Man had disappeared. Within seconds, he reappeared and shot one of the miners before rolling his slab of wood out of the way. In the confusion, who would suspect a cripple on a makeshift wooden board of having sabotaged the attack? But then, a van moved toward him. Soldiers dressed in riot gear and armed with machine guns rushed out and shoved him inside.

Her father had said it would happen like this. The communists would come, setting fire, shedding blood, and shrouding Spera in red. That's when he had planned their escape, their little family, the three of them together in the middle of the night. It would have been so easy with all the police in town and none at the border. Her parents would have protected her.

Not seeing her parents anywhere in the melee, Mica pedaled as fast as she could into the protection of the forest. She slowed down as she passed the dirt path to the abandoned glass factory and then came to a full stop. She didn't have much time, but she had to check to see if her parents were hiding in the bunker. She bit her lip and prayed, *Please Mama, Tata, be there. Then I won't have to escape alone. Or maybe even at all.*

Getting off her bike, she was careful not to entangle her long coat in the brambles. It kept opening even though she had wrapped her father's belt around twice. The coat was warm and black. She had worn it on stage all evening and now she was one with the night.

She pushed her bike slowly through the brush and broken limbs, watching for anything that might pop a tire. She couldn't have a flat tire. Not tonight. Looking around, she studied every moving leaf, every shadow, to ensure she wasn't being followed. Then, she laid her bike down and covered it with branches. This section of the forest was desolate and eerie, quiet, as if time had completely passed it by.

Walking slowly to avoid stepping in a ditch, she felt for the trapdoor and then kicked some dead leaves off it before descending the secret stairs. Her father's office door was wide open. She stood still behind a column and listened. No one. She touched her heart as if to quiet its thumping, then stepped inside the room.

Maybe her father and mother were hiding? She pressed a button she knew opened a secret door that led to a dark closet and, beyond that, to a safe room. She moved a rug from the floor and slid open a wooden panel. "Tata, it's me, Mica," she whispered, leaning down to peer into the bunker's lower floor. No one there.

She went to the lamp on his desk and felt the bulb. Cold. She moved toward the stove where he made his beloved espresso. The coals were cold too. Her parents hadn't been there at any time during the past day, and Mica realized, terrified, that it was the first time in her life that she was truly on her own.

She sat down in her father's chair, filling the indentation his body had made over time in the soft leather, moving her body into his form. Staring at the maps on the walls, she remembered his sadness of the previous night and felt the weight of his words when he had traced the route to the border and told her, "Memorize each detail."

Her foot bumped against something metal, and she bent down to look under the desk. It was the tin cup that she had used to bring her father his dinner. She pried open the false bottom, hoping to find a message—a word for her, something. But there was nothing, not even when she turned the tin upside down and shook it.

She moved to return the tin cup to the desk, but stopped as the diamonds sewn into her bra pressed hard against her breasts. The diamonds! A message! She'd leave two diamonds for her parents so they would have something to escape with if they returned to the bunker.

She slipped off her bra, undid the stitches with her teeth, took out two pink diamonds, and dropped them into the cup's hidden bottom. The jewels rattled against the metal. No good. She took a handful of cold ashes from the coals, mixed the ashes in the cup with two pink diamonds, and buried them. Satisfied, she placed the cup next to her father's espresso machine, reasoning if anyone snooped around, the tin cup would look like an ordinary cup for coffee. But her father or mother would understand. They would know there was a message inside.

Mica made her way out of the bunker as quickly as she could. Even though all the papers were gone and there was no evidence that it was her father and his men who had been hiding out there, anyone could know now about the bunker's existence, and she had to get as far away as possible. Back in the woods, she pedaled faster, all the while, crying and replaying in her mind the details of her escape. And yet, she felt a surge of hope.

CHAPTER 4

THE DIN of an engine nearby left her fearing the worst: the police. Turning around, her body rigid with terror, she looked in every direction, struggling not to lose her balance. No one was there. The main road was far behind her, and ahead of her there were only trees and brush. Yet, Mica sensed that someone was getting near her.

She was taking the secret route to the border, which her father had circled many times in red on the map. He had assured her that no one ever used the path anymore. Most people didn't even know it was there. As she pedaled, Mica said a silent prayer that whoever was out there meant her no harm.

A shadow moved near the trees on her left. She thought she heard a person's voice; then came the snap of footsteps on leaves and sticks. The shadow moved again, as the breaking of branches grew louder. Suddenly, the footsteps stopped. Mica's heart pounded. *Faster!* she told her legs.

She'd be at the border soon if she kept up her pace, if no policeman or thief caught her first. She called upon every bit of her strength to pedal faster. The shadow loomed nearer; the branches and brush broke loudly. But it was dark, and she couldn't see anyone.

"Stop. Wait." A man's voice shouted. He was pedaling his motorbike to minimize its noise. "Mica, it's me, Marinescu. I came to help you."

He was wearing a long heavy coat and a woolen cap pulled tightly over his white hair. "When you ran off after the play, I went to check on what was happening. Your parents didn't come to the performance. I knew that meant trouble and that you'd try to escape. Your father and I took this hidden path years ago."

For a moment she wondered if he had brought someone with him. Two men to ambush one girl. He suspected she'd escape. Did he know also that she had diamonds? She looked behind him and listened for noise. Mistrust had always been a part of her life.

"I came to warn you that at the fork, the Securitate are looking for anti-communists and Resistance fighters," he said. "I'll ride with you to where the path divides and then leave you to go on your own when it's safe."

She just stared at him. Could he be trusted?

"Please believe me," he said, as if reading her thoughts. But she didn't answer. She thought of her mother, who had insisted that Mica could trust Mr. Marinescu. That she should do whatever he told her.

Mama, I hope you're right, she thought.

Pedaling on, they came to the monastery's gate.

"The fork in the path is after the gate," Marinescu said, taking the lead. "Walk your bike and bend down as low as you can, like me. There's a terrible woman who guards the gate. She works with the secret police and would denounce us. I'll go ahead, then follow behind me."

He moved first. She waited, unsure whether to listen to him or to run away, and then she spotted the hunchbacked old woman stumbling through the snow. Her clothes were tattered, and she wore no overcoat, no hat, no shoes. Her feet were bare. Even from a distance, they appeared blue and swollen. The woman grumbled and cursed as she limped along. Then she spat at a tree. Mica, frightened, felt certain the woman had seen her.

Ahead, Marinescu signaled for Mica to join him. They bent lower and went on, leaving the old woman behind.

"Who is she?" whispered Mica.

"She's the devil," Marinescu replied curtly. "I remember her from the war. She was the mistress of the leader of the Iron Guard for all of Transylvania. That was Codreanu the nationalist. He had all his followers write an oath in their own blood, vowing to commit murder whenever they saw a Jew."

Mica swerved to avoid a boulder. Her hands were shaking but not just from her near accident. She had always thought her father was exaggerating with his tales, and now Marinescu was telling her the same story in the dramatic voice she knew so well.

They stopped to rest for a few minutes, then walked slowly ahead.

"Was this witch part of that group?"

"Yes! She said that she wanted to be Romania's female Hitler."

Mica felt a chill flow through her. Whenever she heard Hitler's name, her entire body tightened. She shifted on her bicycle and felt the diamonds in her bra, press hard into her skin. Why did people harbor so much hatred against the Jews? She remembered Shylock in Shakespeare's play. "Hath not a Jew eyes? Hath not a Jew hands, organs, senses, affections, passions?"

Marinescu continued. "She helped lead a group of Jews from the neighboring town to this forest, then had them strip naked in the snow, where they were shot dead. She ordered the Romanian soldiers to take the bodies to the town slaughterhouse where her father worked. They decapitated each one, and had the heads hung from butcher hooks with a sign underneath saying: KOSHER."

Mica closed her eyes and wiped the tears from her cheeks.

"Let me tell you why I want so much to help you," he said. "I must do something good for you because years ago I was powerless to help another girl."

"What do you mean?"

"This witch that we just saw had a husband who worked in a textile factory. They had a little girl; he adored that girl. He would take her to school before going to work, then walk several kilometers to the factory, and at the end of the day he'd walk back to pick her up. I used to see them together, hand in hand, laughing and singing. She was about nine years old. Blonde pigtails, freckled face.

"But the mother didn't like the child, and she hated the father. He was Jewish; she didn't know that when they got married. Realizing she'd have a baby with Jewish blood, she wanted to punish him and his child."

Mica remained distraught and took a deep breath, dreading what was coming.

"One day, I saw the witch in the forest. She was wobbling as she walked, drunk, carrying a bottle of wine. She saw her husband and daughter walking home and went over to them.

"Drink," she said, forcing the bottle to pry open the girl's mouth. The father grabbed the bottle. They struggled. Not wanting to see her parents fight, the child took a sip. The mother laughed."

Marinescu stopped walking. He was trembling.

"I was there. I ran over to the woman, tried to grab the bottle away from the child. But the mother was too strong. She threw me down. The girl was vomiting and the father was yelling, 'No more!'

"As her parents fought, the girl was knocked to the ground. She hit her head on a rock. The mother opened her daughter's mouth and poured wine down her small throat. Before long, the little body stopped breathing. She'd choked."

"Did she die?"

"Yes. That's why her father threw himself in the river and drowned. I tried to get the mother prosecuted, but the Iron Guard protected her. And then after the war, she became a communist, switching sides from right to left, like so many other fascists did. Now she's the one who's telling the secret police that rebel fighters are hiding in the monastery."

Mica took a deep breath, wishing she could ask him to stop talking, wishing she could stop such hatred.

He resumed his pace. "I keep telling myself the past is the past and I must go on. But I don't want to lose my humanity." He paused, as if trying to find his composure. "If we don't do good for others, God will turn his back on us." He looked down and made the sign of the cross on his chest.

They moved in silence for several minutes until Marinescu spoke again. "Remember, at the fork in the road, turn left."

He pointed the way and gave her his final cue: "You'll continue from here alone. If I find out any news about your parents, I'll try to get word to them that you've escaped."

Mica pulled her bike to the side, looking around to see if anyone was following them. Mr. Marinescu gave her a kiss on both cheeks and took her in his arms.

"Be strong, Mica. Do whatever you must to survive. *Whatever! No matter how hard!*"

He turned his face, wanting to hide his tears, and then left her to travel alone. Mica continued on, holding tightly to her wooden club.

CHAPTER 5

WHEN SHE ARRIVED at the border area between Romania and Hungary, the forest thinned, and Mica realized she would have to cross open fields, making it easier for the secret police to spot her. She worried about this, and she worried that the diamonds on her were blood diamonds. She had once overheard her father whisper to her mother, "I hope they're not cursed."

But she refused to think about that. Now, more than ever, she had to think positively and stay cerebral, stay in control, focus on what she had to do. She abandoned her bike at the edge of the forest and crept up to the border on all fours. As she crawled through the snow toward the guard station, she watched as three men patrolled the road with their three dogs. Every once in a while, one of the dogs barked sharply and Mica held her breath, worried that even at a distance her scent had been carried on by the cold, snowy wind. She studied a small box attached to the gate and counted as it ticked every second. She felt as if its electricity flowed through her body—every second stung her like needles.

Her father's photos and his map of the border area had been perfect. Now, once she had observed the guards and their routines, and the way was clear, she moved slowly to a nearby barn he had said had once been used by the fascists as an arsenal. Her father had told her how he and his group had defused land mines on the surrounding grounds.

She tiptoed, all the while looking down to detect any old mines that might still be in place. Quietly, she cracked the door open just enough to slip inside, where she took off her heavy coat and collapsed on the hard ground. Even though the barn was freezing, it was a relief to be protected from the elements after biking two hours through the snow and wind.

She took a flask of water and two small tins from the pockets of her coat. After a few sips of water, she carefully took off her sweater as her skin tingled in the freezing air. She rubbed her upper body with olive oil from the first tin and then mixed dirt with it to make mud, creating a paste that covered her neck, her arms, and her torso. She did the same with her lower body.

She had once seen a Gypsy from her acting company cover her own body with olive oil and dirt before going home. When Mica had asked her why, the girl had replied, "Rabid dogs are roaming near my house. Only olive oil and dirt are stronger than human scent. If they don't smell me, they won't bother me."

Before Mica went back out into the cold, she counted the diamonds sewn into her clothes, to reassure herself. She had left two pink diamonds for her parents, but she still had eighteen. She touched her bra's padded cups, counting the bumps that hid four diamonds. She felt the hem of her coat where she had sewn the green and red jewels. There was also the blue diamond, her favorite for its unusual purplish hue and shine, which was in her right boot's carved-out heel. Eleven others—yellow, pink, brown, green, and red—were in both boots' soles and left heel.

She bent down and picked up the second tin can, which held paprika. Sprinkling the red spice on top of her black sweater and pants, she pretended, for a moment, that it was fairy dust. She rubbed the red powder into the olive oil and mud on her face and neck until she was a reddish-brown color with no human smell at all.

The long black coat, which had seemed such a good idea when she was choosing what clothes to wear, all of a sudden seemed bulky. But she was cold, and she put it on anyway as she sat down on the ground and removed her high, black leather boots. She banged the boots together several times to make sure the soles and heels were tightly glued. Reassured, she kissed her boots and raised her face to the sky. *God, please protect me. I'm all alone.*

Then she turned her attention to her coat pockets. In one, she found the rubber gloves and hand rake her father had told her to take from the basement. In the other, she fingered the metal cutter from her father's drawer. With her tools intact, she readied herself for the next part of the plan.

By the light of the moon and stars, she studied the pine trees in the distance and marked the angle between the barn and the last tree, just as her father had shown her on a photo. Then she raised her face to the wind and repositioned her body accordingly. *I can stay warmer from this angle,* she said to herself, remembering how Anca had always assessed the wind when they hiked, and suggested they should finish their hike with the wind behind them. "We're tired enough at the end." Mica followed her friend's advice.

She got on her knees and searched the ground with her fingers until she found the exact spot to dig, remembering how her father had circled the location several times on his map. She put on the rubber gloves making sure to stay clear of the electrified fence.

Looking up at the chimney of Dracula's castle once more to calculate the angle, she recalled as a child how she enjoyed dressing up as Dracula. Her mother had fashioned a black cape from one of her father's old shirts, and Mica had spent hours pretending to fly around her house. It had been so much fun.

She tried hard to focus on digging, but the work was hard

and it was windy, and despite concentrating on her task, her mind wandered. Playing Dracula as a child had kept her busy for hours, but in school, she had learned some of the real history of Vlad the Impaler. Her history teacher had told the class that Dracula had stopped the Turks from invading Romania. The teacher had moved to the front of the class, flicked his stick in the air, and with its tip, tapped a boy on the head. "How did he do it?"

When the boy shrugged his shoulders, the teacher hit him hard on the head. "With sheer terror! You all know that Dracul in Romanian means *devil*. And he was thirsty for human blood. Some people say he carried a flask made from human bone, which he hollowed out and filled with blood, just in case he got thirsty."

Some students laughed, like Mica did; others moved uncomfortably in their chairs.

"Yes, Vlad the Impaler was bloodthirsty," the teacher continued. "His greatest pleasure was to wake up in the morning and watch a line of people being impaled by his soldiers with a long, pointed stake that was thrust up the victim's rectum, coming out through the stomach.

"Count Dracul would smile and breakfast on toast rubbed with garlic and drink bloody tea. All the time enjoying his garden view."

Mica stopped digging to calculate if she had done enough. She had estimated that her body needed an opening two meters by one meter. She could then slip under the fence to the other side.

The sky had grown cloudy again, blocking the stars and light. She took out the small flashlight she had taken from her father's drawer and flicked it on quickly to check her progress. She imagined Hungary, just wires away, where the guards would be sleeping —she hoped. Her father had told her they'd likely be drunk from the evening's festival of St. Stephen. There was an American embassy in Budapest, a network for political refugees—and a visa, a new passport, a telephone call to her uncle in America. Certainly he'd help. They were family. She'd tell him she escaped with the diamonds!

All would be well as long as Mica kept digging, but her pinky ached. Putting her finger in her mouth, she started to cry as a dreadful memory came flashing back. Six years ago, when she was eleven years old. Aside from today, it had been the cruelest day of her life.

She dug and remembered...

She had been walking home, alone, from school, when she saw that a Securitate policeman on a motorcycle was following her.

"Halt! Stop!" He rode up in front of her, blocking her from walking farther.

"Get on!" He pointed with his gun to the sidecar of his vehicle. When she was seated inside, he locked her wrists in handcuffs and took her to Headquarters, where the chief was waiting for her. She had heard about his evil tactics. Staring at the man, she realized why everyone was so afraid of him. He had a glass eye that was fixed, staring, in one direction. His other eye had a tick. When he spoke, she saw that his three front teeth were made of steel and his other teeth were stained with brown spots of nicotine.

"Stand at attention!" he yelled, taking a whip from his desk and snapping it at her shoes.

She felt the tip lash her ankle. She jumped away. "What did I do wrong?"

"Your father likes radios," he began.

She didn't answer.

"He speaks English?"

She shrugged her shoulders, but even at eleven, she knew that to speak or read English, the language of Capitalists, was considered a crime. The only people she knew who spoke English were several students from her acting group, and her parents and Mr. Marinescu, who had learned it while working for the Resistance.

"I know he's an engineer," the chief said, unlocking her handcuffs, putting her small hand in his, and removing from his pocket a pair of pliers. He flashed the tool in front of her face, and placed the metal tip under a flame. She watched as it turned fiery red.

"In my office," he said louder, showing her the hot tip of the pliers, "I have the power to do whatever I want. *Anything!*"

She pulled her hand away.

"Only you can save your father. Work for us, and your father and mother will be safe."

"Don't ask me that. I can't!"

He laughed. "Don't you like me?" He pulled her pinky to his hand. "Such a sweet little nail you have." His sadistic grin showed his steel teeth reflecting red.

He took the red-hot pliers, tightened it on her fingernail, and pulled.

"Ow-w-w!" she screamed. "I'm burning! I'm on fire!" she cried, hysterically. "Please stop! Please! No!"

He pulled again, harder, until her nail dropped to the floor; she fell down crying, the pain beyond description.

"Get up!" He pulled her up by her sweater. "Get to attention! Stop that crying!"

He put the pliers under the flame again, grabbed her by the arm, and put the red hot steel on top of her thumb.

"Your father listens to Radio Free Europe on a shortwave radio. The neighbor told us so. That's a crime! What is he planning with that radio?"

His red-hot pliers played with her thumb nail, burning the tender skin around it.

"Stop!" she yelled. "Stop! Please, no more!"

"We know you speak English too. Your history teacher told us."

She tried to pull her hand away, but his grip was too tight. Her pinky was gushing blood. She couldn't stop sobbing.

"We need someone like you to work for us. A youngster who

speaks Romanian, Hungarian, and English. Would you like to be that youngster?"

"No! No! No!"

He grabbed her again, this time by her hair, and threw her into a chair. He put his pliers to her ring finger. She felt the tip burn her skin and she bit her lip to stop herself from crying.

"Do you want more? *More?*"

"Would my father or mother get in trouble?"

He smiled, pleased. "As long as you work for us, they're safe."

Mica understood. She had to save her father and mother. She couldn't refuse the secret police.

"You won't tell my parents what I'm doing?"

"You can trust me," he replied, grinning. "You'll work for us in the afternoon instead of going to school. Your history teacher will bring you here."

She looked down, crying, ashamed, and angry at herself. She put her bleeding finger into her mouth and tried to comfort herself.

And so, Mica was recruited as a child spy for the communists. Since she lived in Transylvania, the area of land that had been shuffled back and forth between Romania and Hungary for centuries, she spoke Romanian and Hungarian without an accent. English, she had learned from her mother and her Shakespeare books.

They dressed her up as a newspaper boy and put her to work on a Romanian train. Her job: to make sure that the train's bugging devices were working. The main circuit box was in the first-class bathroom, hidden behind the toilet. Only a small child's hands could fit into the narrow opening. She also taped conversations using a tape recorder buried in a large sack full of German and French newspapers, which she carried in a backpack.

On her first day of work, she overheard several men speaking in English about the Vatican's involvement in overthrowing communism in Eastern Europe. Religion, they claimed, was being destroyed. They were priests traveling incognito to organize secret meetings designed to counteract communist regimes.

Mica had been so happy to hear about their plans that she lingered next to them as they chatted. To do her share for the cause, she destroyed the tape of the priests' conversation, and for the entire afternoon, she felt redeemed—she had subverted her bosses.

On the second afternoon of work, she learned just how dangerous being a spy was. She was selling her newspapers on the train when she noticed two men, both Romanian, who were arguing. They wore green shirts that Mica recognized as being the uniform of the Romania's fascist party, and the older one was pointing a gun at the younger one.

"You'll never get this information for such a pitiful price!" the younger Romanian protested, unafraid of the weapon pointed between his eyes. He held up a piece of paper, and as he opened his mouth to swallow the paper, Mica saw he had gold teeth.

The older Romanian tried to grab the paper, but the other man ran away. He climbed out the window and made his way to the top of the train. Mica opened the window next to where she had been sitting and looked out and up to find the man. He was running on top of the train and appeared to be ready to jump off when the train passed under a power line. But his hands got snagged in the electrical wires and in a split second, his ten fingers turned to flames before her stunned eyes. With his hands burning, he jumped off the train and ran into the forest.

To calm herself down, Mica walked in and out of the first-class cabins to sell her newspapers. As she entered the last one, she saw that it was empty. On a seat lay a large book, thicker and shinier than any her mother had ever brought home. She stared at it, not daring to touch it. On the cover was a building with a tip pointed so high that it scraped the sky. The steel was surrounded by a setting sun sparkling like red diamonds.

Unable to fight temptation, she picked up the book, looked around to make sure she was alone, and stuffed the book into her newspapers. Then she rushed out of the cabin to the bathroom.

As if in a dream, she fingered the title words: *New York*. She opened the book, stroked the paper, and studied each page. There was a photo of a park covered by fine snow, a layer so pure that only God could have sprinkled the earth that white. Turning the page, she stared at a wide avenue, its dazzling bulbs lighting up theaters and billboards. Hungry for more, she whisked through the pages, greedily, until on the very last one she saw fireworks showering colored gems over New York's sky. She wondered if the photos could possibly be real. They looked as though the camera's flash had sprayed the city with fairy dust and diamonds.

She didn't know what to do with the book. But she knew she needed to own it, to touch the colored pages, to believe they were real. She couldn't help but keep it. She wanted so much to make that world her own.

Each night for the next six years, before she went to bed, she fantasized about being in New York: strolling on the avenues, exploring the hidden corners, feeling the lights lift her body. Before closing her eyes, she'd think of the photo where fog surrounded the city and closed it off from the rest of the world. She imagined the fog reaching to heaven, making New York an island for the brave. She'd caress the pages of her magic book, praying that one day she'd be free in New York.

Mica hadn't taken the book with her as she escaped. But as she dug, she thought of it and hoped that one day the photos would become real. She knew that first, she'd have to be brave.

CHAPTER 6

MICA CONCENTRATED on what she had to do. To keep herself focused, she thought of the good things ahead of her, and her diamonds and how they were certain to bring good luck. She dared not think about where they had come from and whether she had the right to own them, or if having them would bring her bad luck. She needed them to change her family's future, to secure her parents' freedom; that was her responsibility, her duty despite the danger and risk. The dilemma of right or wrong couldn't come into her mind.

As Marinescu had told her, "Do whatever you must to survive." Yet, she was afraid. And now, she was exhausted from biking and digging. She had to keep telling herself to go on, not give up, to fight—more!

She yearned for sleep. The muscles of her neck and back ached from digging. She looked around. No one was there, but she couldn't ignore the feeling that she wasn't alone. She hated the secret police with all her being. Every time she thought of them, she saw the sadistic chief standing in front of her, his pliers threatening to burn another finger, a smug grin on his face. Her mangled pinky stung as she forced herself to keep digging.

She remembered how, after finding the book on her second day of work, she went to the chief and said she was sick and couldn't work anymore. She begged him to let her go, pleaded for him to leave her father in peace. She cried hysterically and made a scene as if she were going mad, like Ophelia.

He stared at her with his one glass eye fixed in the same corner, as if it had been pinned there to frighten and bully her to work for him. Maybe he didn't need her any longer, or perhaps he couldn't trust her. Whatever the reason, she felt like screaming with relief when he insulted her, threw her out of his office, and warned her never to show her face again. "Good riddance," he spat at her. Not long after, he was bitten by one of the feral dogs roaming the town. The dog was rabid; the chief suffered before he died.

Good riddance to you, Mica responded to him every day in her private thoughts.

Mica dug for another hour until the space under the fence was large enough for her to slip through without touching any wires or setting off the alarm. Once she was sure that she had excavated enough earth on both sides, she slipped under the fence, holding her breath. She realized that her father's instructions had taken her near the guards' hut, so she crouched down to the ground, hiding her small frame behind several boughs of dead trees.

She panicked that she was so near to their hut and was even able to see that three guards were on duty. She heard a telephone ring and their conversation: "*Da, da,*" a man's voice said. "Ceausescu? Spera. *Da. Imediat.* We'll be there at once." Mica moved behind a tree, and watched all three guards leave and mount their motorcycles.

Even though her father had told her not to, Mica ran as fast as she could across the Hungarian countryside, wanting to reach safer ground. When she heard a bomb explode, she hid behind a tree, thinking her good luck was over. But as the sky turned blood red, she remembered the anti-communist uprising on the other side of the border in Romania.

Exhausted, but determined not to stop fighting, she dug her nails into the earth and threw a fist of dirt toward the sky. Feeling the flow of adrenaline fill her body, she stood up straight and stretched her arms, yelling, so all the gods would know, "I did it! I'm free!"

Turning to the West, she kicked the ground beneath her with her diamond boots and screamed, "I'm free to be free!"

For one second, she was elated. But then she realized she wasn't completely free, not yet. Mica still had to get through another fence, twelve feet high, on the Hungarian side of the border that was charged with a high-voltage control box. The thought petrified her. Despite the cold and wind, her entire chest felt moist.

Carrying her hand rake, she pressed a button on the handle to check that it worked and watched the wire cutter spring out. Her father had explained to her exactly where and how to cut the wires in the back of a specific control box to disengage the electricity.

When she reached the designated spot, she put on the special rubber gloves and without thinking further, cut the wires of the control box. It fell into a puddle of mud; she was still alive. Breathing hard, she placed the hand rake back in her coat pocket and told herself, "Go!"

On the Hungarian side, she ran toward the railway station by following the train tracks, just as her father had shown her with a photo. She stopped every few minutes to catch her breath and look around to see if she was being followed. It was still dark, a little after 5:00 a.m. The animals were still sleeping in the barns, the farmers at home. She only had an hour before daybreak. According to her calculations, she was five kilometers away from the train station. If she could keep running, she'd be on time for the 6:00 train to Budapest.

Agile and light from years of biking, hiking, and dancing, Mica ran swiftly, moving to the rhythm of the Beatles record, *"Michelle, ma belle, sont les mots qui vont très bien ensemble. Très bien ensemble."*

The more she ran, the lighter she felt. At the end of an hour, she was no longer running but floating.

Mica walked to the end of the platform where there was a bucket of water for animals. She bent down and lapped up the liquid in rasping, thirsty gulps. It was only when she tasted a clump of dirt and some bits of hay that she spit out the water and growled in disgust; yet, still thirsty, she gulped more.

The train had been sitting in the station when she arrived, but now that it was two minutes before six, she had to board. She looked around her and saw no one, so she climbed into the last train car. It was full of cattle. As she moved through the hay, two cows mooed. She feared they'd give her away.

"Shh… shh," she whispered and patted them as if they were friends. She gave them some straw and hay from the floor, which the cows placidly accepted as a bribe. Perhaps they didn't realize she was a person at all: she smelled no different from the other animals in the stall.

She burrowed her small body into the straw, closing her eyes and savoring the warmth. She had been outside for hours, and only now, surrounded by the animals, did she let herself relax just a little. In the wooden wall of the car, there was a small round hole for air, the same size as her eye. As the train started to move, she leaned against the opening to watch the hills and mountains of Transylvania pass by.

She was leaving her country, her home, probably never to return. She'd never go again to her little theater or feel Nicky's kisses. They could have fallen in love. Her life would have been so different than what it would be now. She wiped the warm tears off her cheeks. Will Romeo find another Juliet?

She'd never see again her friends—Anca, Marina, and Cristina. She thought about all the Saturday afternoons they had spent together, climbing the Carpathians, hiking through valleys carpeted with wild flowers, and singing, "We are the poets of our lives."

They once followed a trail through a pine forest where they were surprised to see hundreds of yellow needles sparkling a path. No one before them had taken that trail and not one pine needle had been crushed. Mica thought of the Gypsy proverb: "May your feet touch the earth more than the sky." She wondered if her feet would ever again touch such soft natural beauty.

Mica bent her knees to her chest and breathed deeply to stop herself from crying. Would Marina or Cristina bring lunch for Anca? And what would they do when she, Mica, didn't show up at school? She hoped the secret police wouldn't arrest them to try to find out where she had gone. But they didn't know anything about her plans.

Would her parents learn she had escaped? Would they be tortured because of it? She thought of her father's map lesson, his cold espresso. People didn't just disappear, unless… She dared not think she'd never see them again. She needed to wipe that fear out of her mind or she'd never have the courage to continue her journey.

Mica sobbed. She thought about how her life was going to change—the future loomed out in front of her unknown. What would it be like? She only had $300. How long would that last? Where would she sleep? It was winter and as cold in Hungary as in Romania. Where would she find shelter?

She tried to stop thinking negative thoughts. *Something good will happen*, she told herself. *Something to help me get to America, to sell the diamonds, help my parents.*

She counted to ten to calm herself down and leaned against the train's wall. She thought of her mother and how she enjoyed reading Shakespeare to Mica. When she was a little girl, Mica liked to cuddle in her mother's arms while she listened. Her mother used to tell her that her shoulder blades were like angel wings.

As Mica looked around the compartment, she spied another circular air hole. Putting her eye to it, she looked out, imagining it was a kaleidoscope and she was watching the colors of her country pass by. The red sun began to rise. Mica saw a group of farmers in a field, clustered together by a fire, eating breakfast. Seated on the soil, they shared their bread and cheese.

As the train traveled through the crimson path and sun greeted the new day, Mica saw wagons of all sizes, pulled by horses and oxen, driven by farmers and women. The day's farm tools were strapped above the wheels. They were chatting and laughing the same way their grandparents had done years before. The music from their fiddles was also the same. But Mica knew she'd never be the same tomorrow as she was today.

She stared at the sun as it rose and colored the snow on the mountains red. It looked as if the sky was splintering into a thousand fires. No painter could have brushed red so passionately on white and blue.

She burrowed herself into the hay and the train became her shield, protecting her as she rode toward her future, a future of risk and hope. With each kilometer the train traveled, her life in Romania moved farther and farther away. She looked through her small opening again. Colors appeared muted now, as if she were viewing them through tinted lenses: green pine trees in between mountain cliffs, blue rivers and rushing brooks, a white and blue waterfall. She put her ear to the opening to hear the silence of the hills. The sounds were softer than she had ever remembered. Only the timbre of cow bells echoed through the fields.

It was the soft mist of morning that Mica knew she would miss most of all. She'd run from her room so cold and enter the kitchen so warm. Her mother would be preparing toast with rose petal jam and tea with honey. The logs in the fireplace crackled and Mica watched from the window to see how smoke, colored pink by the rising sun, rose in straight columns. In winter, the grass was covered in a morning blanket of pink and white frost. She'd start her day happy.

It all seemed unreal. Within twenty-four hours, her entire life had changed. Before, it had been so normal. She lived a happy life: cooking with her mother, doing her homework, laughing with her friends, listening to her father's stories. She loved performing Shakespeare, being Juliet next to handsome Nicky, worrying if Romeo would die for her. But today? Her parents' disappearance, a communist uprising, a fascist witch, escape, being all alone.

These were the events of a lifetime. Perhaps it was a nightmare and she'd wake up and Mama would take her in her arms and say, "It was just a bad dream. You're here with us. You're safe."

She remembered the words of the past day from those who had taught her so much. Marinescu had insisted she act as a woman, not a child. And just before she went on stage, Anca kissed her good luck. "Your tragedy as Juliet will prepare you to be more courageous in whatever else you do."

Mica knew she had to have confidence in herself. She needed to find strength within herself to concentrate on surviving and creating a new life. Her father's words echoed in her ears: "Whenever life seems the lowest, that's when you must rise. Use your willpower to survive."

PART II

BUDAPEST

CHAPTER 7

THE TRAIN STOPPED at Keleti Station, the end of the line in Budapest. Mica quickly sneaked out of the wagon. She ran and ran, all the time feeling as if she were a movie character who had passed through a black-and-white screen into a Technicolor world. Awed by the color and light around her, she touched some flowers to make sure they were real. She looked through a clean window and wriggled her nose at her own image. Smiling, she didn't care that her clothes were soiled and her hair was sticky with olive oil. All she could think of was that she was safe and alive in Budapest! Relieved and excited, she laughed and laughed while swaying before her image in the window. She didn't even notice that a person or two were staring at her.

She walked from the railway station to the oldest part of town, just as her father had shown her on his map. Climbing up to Castle Hill, she looked down at the Gothic spires and church domes. Mesmerized by the colorful panorama of roofs, she marveled at the reality of sites that only yesterday were red circles on a map. Turning her eyes upward to a blue sky, she saw the turrets of Fisherman's Bastion and the colored, tiled roof of Matthias Church. Below her was the Danube River, winding like a snake, dividing the city into a left and right bank—the old section of "Buda" and the new "Pest." Its serpentine waters called to her, and she, tempted and willing, was being pulled toward its flow.

Running down a dozen steps two at a time, she waved to the Danube like a friend and skipped across the Chain Bridge. Touching the metal cables to make sure they were real, she convinced herself, for a moment, that the Chain Bridge existed so that she could run across it. And she did—back and forth, over and over again, only to stop to admire the river sparkling like diamonds in the sun.

At the foot of the bridge, she spied a rose bush and approached it. Putting her nose next to the red flowers, she smelled their sweetness. She looked around to ensure no one was watching her, then picked the brightest rose. She rubbed its velvet layers on her cheek and, closing her eyes, wished for good luck. Then she threw the flower into the sparkling water and watched the red rose float away.

Coming upon a water fountain, she put her mouth to the running spout. Gulping down the water, she felt invigorated. Then she cleaned her face and rubbed some of the olive oil out of her hair.

She saw a square laid out like an open market, a marvel the like of which she'd never seen before. In Spera, she and her friends would scan the paltry Saturday market in search of hidden treasures, but there was never anything to buy because there was never anything to sell. But here, despite the communist government, Budapest had goods. And the people could sell and buy without being afraid.

The displays of green vegetables, fresh fruit, cheeses, and breads was a wondrous sight. The women moved freely among the stalls, greeting friends, laughing and joking, so full of life. They seemed to like each other, even trust each other. Vendors yelled, "Come and get it." Gypsies joined in with their violins, plucking *pizzicatos* to the murmur of the crowd. Several children danced and laughed as the Gypsies played their songs.

Mica had never seen such animation in her life. It reminded her of a circus or a fair. In Romania, getting food was a misery. One had to wait in line for hours for a ration of rotting fruit or old goods. Here, the market was dotted with little worlds of round tables, laden with all kinds of fresh food. In addition to the fruits and vegetables, there were all kinds of fish with silver and gold skin sparkling in the sun. Meats, smoked and grilled, filled the air with perfume. The scent made her salivate almost beyond control. Starving and light headed, she remembered her last meal with her mother. She hadn't even finished it. She ached for Mama to tell her one more time, "*Draga,* dear, eat. I made the cheese cakes just for you."

Suddenly, her stomach twisted. She felt it knot and ache, and she bent over in pain: she hadn't eaten for twenty-four hours and she was starving. Once her stomach settled, she took two American dollar bills from her pocket and walked through the marketplace, trying to decide what to buy. She had no idea how far two dollars would go for fruit or smoked fish or grilled meat. She studied a peasant woman, short and bulky in an old coat. Her fists were wrapped in frayed socks. Red-cheeked and friendly looking, she was selling fruit. Mica tried to see if anyone else was paying with foreign money.

But she was so hungry that she couldn't think anymore. With her head spinning, she leaned against a tree, telling herself to be strong. She looked around to see if there were any police strolling through the market, like in Romania, but there was no way to know. She'd have to take a risk.

"*Jonapot kivanok.* Good afternoon," the peasant woman,

surrounded by red apples, purple plums, and green pears, greeted her in Hungarian.

"*Szia*—Hi," Mica responded. "Your fruit looks beautiful." She smiled sweetly.

"*Igen*," the peasant nodded in agreement—yes—twitching her nose and lowering her head slightly to avoid Mica's smelly clothes. "*Igen*. Are you from the countryside?" The woman frankly eyed Mica's strange coat and high leather boots.

"How did you know?"

"You're not from Budapest. I can tell from your clothes and your accent. I'm from the country too." Mica thought the woman was trying to be nice, that she wanted her as a customer. But Mica realized that she hadn't addressed her as *he* or *she* when speaking Hungarian. Perhaps she didn't know if Mica was a girl or a boy because of her short, oily hair and bulky overcoat.

"Would you like to buy some fruit?" the woman asked.

"Can you sell me a pear?"

"Sure."

"I only have American dollars."

The peasant eyed her coolly. "Let me see. I won't take them if they're counterfeit."

Mica turned her back, then like a magician pulled a dollar bill out of her pocket. "Here. What I have is real."

"Anything can be phony," the woman commented, still skeptical. "Even jewels that sparkle may not be real."

"Mine are real!" Mica insisted.

The old woman took the bill, held it to the light, touched the paper, studied the colors. She measured the portrait with her finger, as if to see if George Washington was dead center.

"I guess it's a good one," she said, handing Mica a brown paper bag. "There aren't any red dots on the left corner like the black market bills."

"How many can I have?"

"Take eight pears. That's an equal exchange."

Elated, Mica filled the bag. Then, clutching her pears, she skipped away, smiling. overwhelmed by happiness. She was free and safe and in Budapest, such an exciting city! For the moment, that was all that mattered.

CHAPTER 8

As Mica strolled on the Corso promenade that was parallel to the Danube, she began eating the pears. Here and there, she stopped to touch a tree to make sure it wasn't all a dream.

She followed the cobblestones until she saw the pointy reddish-brown towers of Parliament House. Her father had told her that the American Embassy was directly behind it and opposite the Basilica.

When she arrived outside the main gate, she saw that it was as he had described. The embassy was housed in a medieval stone building protected with Gothic fortifications and set among a series of gardens. It faced the Danube, but around the building ran a stone wall far taller than Mica, which was lined with chips of broken glass cemented into the top section of the barrier. Mounted on the wall were swinging cameras as well as lights and siren horns.

Approaching two American soldiers at a security post, she pointed to herself and then to the sign: "VISAS. REFUGEES. 13:00 to 18:00." She looked above their head at the clock; it was 17:30 by the twenty-four-hour clock.

They searched her from top to bottom, then asked her to take off her coat and boots, and pointed she should put them on the security, conveyor belt. She panicked! Her diamonds would be detected! What to do? She first placed on the belt, the brown bag of pears, and then her coat and boots. She asked them if they wanted a pear. "They're so delicious," she said, smiling with the temptation. They answered "yes," and stopped the conveyor belt, so she could take the bag and hand them the fruit. As they were eating, they restarted the conveyor belt and Mica put back the bag of fruit as well as her garments. She quickly moved her coat to an angle where the diamond hem dangled off the table and the soles of her boots off the edge. She held her breath while watching her garments pass through security. The soldiers, still eating the pears, pointed to an area at the side of the main building and waved her through inside the embassy complex to a long line with other people.

Mica stood with the others, finishing her fruit, and thinking that she had used her instincts at the last second to pass through the checkpoint without incident or problems.

Studying the line of people waiting, she wondered if the twenty-two people before her and the dozen behind her, were also trying to become political refugees. She tried to guess where they came from by their clothes and facial features. Ukraine? Bulgaria? Yugoslavia? She studied their shoes worn away from walking. Some were taped up to reinforce the frail soles; others were wrapped in rags.

She noticed a young man gardening. He was dressed in overalls, a heavy sweater, and had a large hat covering his face. *Strange,* she thought—*he's wearing Sunday shoes, not work boots.* She watched him putter in a plot of land where there were no bushes or flowers, only winter brush that was dead from the cold. She looked at the man's hand rake, and thought of her own, wondering what was he doing there.

At that moment, the gardener pulled something from his pocket the same size, color, and shape as the hand rake. Only when he pressed a button and whispered something into the device did she realize it was a walkie-talkie. A large American car was entering the main gate. As the guard opened the wooden barrier, suddenly, from the side, sneaked in an old VW Beetle, zooming at high speed toward the Ford to enter, also.

Mica saw the gardener run away to hide behind a bush. He was talking excitedly on his walkie-talkie. She heard him whisper in Hungarian, *"Igen! Igen!"* She was able to understand: "Yes! Enter with him! Go faster! Disengage the bomb and run!"

Instinctively, she leapt from her place in line and ran toward an American guard at the gate who was now shooting at the tires of the German car. The Volkswagen stopped. Mica picked up a rock and threw it at the German car, smashing the front window and yelling in Hungarian, *"Alj! Alj!* Stop!"

From the American car, the passenger bolted out and dodged into the embassy. Mica ran over to a shed in the garden and wrapped herself in her big coat for protection. She knew from the gardener's message that an explosion would immediately follow.

The Volkswagen blew up. Pieces of debris flew through the flaming air as bystanders took off running. The American guard had run away in time to be safe. The driver of the VW had jumped out of the car and ran away. Then suddenly, the same driver of the American car, rushed to Mica with a brick raised threateningly over his head and was about to strike her when she yelled in English, "No! I tried to help! I'm your friend."

Surprised, he lowered the brick and yelled, "Who are you? Where did you come from?"

Mica stood up and calmly answered, "I've journeyed from afar. I have borne myself beyond the promise of my age, doing in the figure of a lamb, the feats of a lion. Pray thee, what is thy name, friend?"

"*Freund?*" he yelled furiously. "*Nein Freund!*"

"Friend! That's why I wanted to save you."

With his gloved hands, he picked up some pieces of broken glass and pointed them at her face, ready to slash her mouth.

"Stop!" she pleaded. "Why, what's the matter that you have such a February face, so full of frost, of storm, and cloudiness?" she said, again, using her Shakespearean English.

"What language is that?" he asked.

"English. Shakespeare's. What I know best."

"I don't understand a word you're saying." In anger, he threw a handful of broken glass at her coat. She moved away.

"I wanted to help you and your passenger. Please, sir, let me explain." She knew she was dirty and smelly, but unafraid, she pressed on. "I want to be a political refugee."

"I don't believe you." His expression grew menacing. "You work with these suicide bombers!"

"No! I was waiting for the embassy to open and I saw someone in the garden with a walkie-talkie. He pretended to be a gardener. I understood his Hungarian. Then I saw the Volkswagen chase the American car. I knew it belonged to an American because I saw the red, white, and blue flag on the radio antenna."

"Take off your coat. Your boots."

"I have nothing," she said, doing as ordered.

He frisked her, picked up her boots, looked inside, then threw them back to her. He took her arm and dragged her to a guard at the gate. "Kneel!" the guard ordered, jabbing the butt of his rifle into her back.

"Play back the surveillance tape of the car bombing!" the driver said.

The guard reached up to a black box protruding from the gate. Mica twisted her head to see what he was doing, but the tip of his rifle dug hard into her neck.

"Radu, she's right," the guard confirmed, after playing back the tape. "It was the gardener. He got away. The driver of the VW got away also in the panic."

"You better not be mixed up with this!" Radu spat at her feet.

Mica wiped the dirt off her coat, put it on, then her boots, and coolly answered. "I saved your life. Now will you help me?"

"We're not finished with you," he sneered and led her through a courtyard to the largest white house she had ever seen. It looked like a castle. She saw he had gold teeth in his mouth and tried to remember where she had seen that before.

"I'm going to take you to the man you saved. You can tell him your story."

CHAPTER 9

THE DRIVER, Radu, and Mica entered the house without being stopped by the guards. "Willy, this way," he said to her.

Mica was still puzzled by his English, which didn't sound like the Beatles or the broadcaster on Radio Free Europe. She didn't understand him well and why was he calling her Willy? Was it because she had quoted Shakespeare? His accent reminded her of Mr. Marinescu's when he gave stage directions in English.

Mica stopped short when he led her into the most sumptuous room she had ever seen. Her boots sank into the room's thick red carpet. Her eyes watered at the sight of the chandelier, sparkling like diamonds in the setting sun. Every lightbulb of the fixture was lit. She felt so small, surrounded by hundreds of books lining the walls. It was a grander room than any she could have imagined. She was afraid to enter, worried that the man whose room this was must be very important and had the power to send her back to Romania.

"He's over here." Radu walked past the secretary into another room where a man was seated at a large desk. Mica stood in the doorway, ashamed to be so dirty in the presence of such an elegant person.

"Excuse·me sir," Radu said with a shyness that belied his earlier aggression toward Mica. "You said you wanted to meet the young man who tried to save your life."

Mica thought she heard him use a masculine word to describe her, but because of his accent, she wasn't sure. He called her Willy. Feeling threatened and insecure, she hesitated to correct him.

The driver waved to Mica to enter the room. "This is Neal Bridge, the American ambassador of the U.S. Embassy."

Mica nervously approached the desk as the man behind it stood up and came around the desk. Too timid to look directly at him, she lowered her eyes and stared at the trousers of his gray suit. The fabric looked softer than anything she had ever seen. His shoes were black and shiny. When he didn't say anything right away, she glanced up. He was very tall with short blond hair and reading glasses on his nose. He looked dignified, like he could be the president of the United States of America.

"Leave us alone," Bridge said to Radu, then pointed Mica to a chair. "You're very brave. Do you perform such acts often?"

"Oh no. Not unless I have to, my lord."

"Did you *have to* this morning?"

"Yes, sir. I felt there was someone important in the American car."

"Did anyone tell you that?"

"Nay. I'm a stranger in this land. This is the first time I've journeyed so far from home."

"And why, exactly, are you here?"

"I want to be a political refugee," Mica said with passion. "I want to go to America. I have an uncle in New York."

"You speak with a British accent. How is that?"

"My lord, I've been listening a lot to the Beatles, and my mother used to read me Shakespeare. Was't not to this end that I began to tell my story?" She lowered her eyes, thinking of her mother, and bit her lip so as not to get emotional and lose control.

The ambassador took off his glasses. He looked concerned. "Young man..."

"I'm not a man," Mica said, suddenly angry. "I'm a woman. My name is Mica Mihailescu." Now even more aware of her appearance with this disclosure, Mica blushed deeply. But after a moment's awkward silence, and having sensed Mica's embarrassment, Bridge continued.

"In the past few weeks, we've had several terrorist attacks." He looked at Mica with thinly veiled distrust. "Are you part of this anti-American movement?"

"N-no," she answered. "I-I don't know what you're talking about."

He walked closer to her. "How did you get to Budapest?" he asked, raising his voice. "What are you doing here?"

"I want to be free," she answered to his last question.

The ambassador walked around the room. Mica was frightened by his loud voice again.

"How do I know what you're telling me is true?"

"Search me. I have no bomb on me. No gun. I have nothing but good intentions." She stood up and indicated she had nothing to hide. "Maybe when the gardener ran away, he dropped his tool cutter?"

He switched on a small screen at his desk and studied the surveillance tape. After several minutes, he stood up and walked over to her. Mica could sense that he was conflicted what to do with her.

"Well, Mica," he said, "outside this office is a special wing for refugees. We have a medical office staffed by a doctor and a nurse, who are responsible for examining each person who applies for political asylum. There's a line out there. They've all escaped, risked their lives to get here because they know that Budapest is the only city in the East where they can get asylum in an American Embassy."

Listening to him, she felt calmer; he seemed like a good person. The timbre of his voice was far better than the broadcaster on Radio Free Europe.

"I'm innocent. I have asked myself whether tis nobler in mind to suffer the slings and arrows of outrageous fortune, or to take arms against a sea of troubles? But I did not take arms!"

"Where are you from?" he asked.

"Spera, a town in Transylvania, in Romania. I escaped."

"How is that possible?"

"I dug my way out in the middle of the night. On the Romanian side, the guards had left their posts to protect Ceausescu."

"How do you know that? It just happened hours ago! Who gave you this information?" he yelled, trying to frighten her into confessing something. "Did someone plant you here to spy on us?"

"No! No!" she said forcefully.

"How old are you?" he asked.

"Seventeen."

"What about your parents?"

"I don't know where they are. They weren't at home. I searched for them. They disappeared."

He didn't ask when or how. Instead, he moved closer to her, and his voice continued its mistrustful tone. "You escaped alone? Got here to Budapest?"

She stared at the man before her, watching his expression of suspicion change to one of pity. Feeling there was something sensitive about him, she let her heart speak. "Sir, please, you must believe me. I did escape all alone. You have no idea what it's like to live under communism. I want to build a good life for myself. I'm willing to sacrifice everything for freedom."

He didn't say a word.

Sensing she had his sympathy, she continued. "Do you know what it's like never to trust anyone? Most people in Romania would denounce their neighbor in a second."

The ambassador sat down at his desk.

Mica watched him and she kept speaking. "I'm not asking anyone to give me anything. I'll work hard. I want to live with good people. I want to be good."

After several moments of silence, he said, "I can't promise. It will take time. But first, I'll arrange for you to see our doctor; you'll be examined by him and interrogated by another person at the embassy. Then you'll be permitted to apply for a visa with our legal counselor."

He picked up the telephone on his desk and spoke English so rapidly that she couldn't understand it. He put down his phone, stared at her, and said, "As ambassador, I run the embassy here. I don't get involved with incoming refugees. But you did show bravery and tried to help..." He stopped talking when his secretary appeared at the door and motioned for Mica to go with her to the medical wing. They passed a long line of refugees waiting and entered an unmarked door where a nurse was.

"Undress and take a shower," the Hungarian nurse said in accented English. She handed Mica a changing gown. "You smell like mud and cows."

"Yes, I'm muddy," Mica answered, suddenly angry and hurt. "And yes, I smell bad! I've just escaped a communist country. Alone." She felt the need to stand up for herself.

"I'm sorry," the nurse said softly. "I shouldn't have said that. I respect and admire what you've done. As soon as you finish the exam, you'll be able to rest. But first, we need a chest X-ray, urine sample, blood tests..."

The nurse had a way of smiling and talking that reminded Mica of her mother, even though the nurse was much younger.

Perhaps it was the similar accent when they spoke English. Or maybe it was the same round cheeks, so red with warmth. Mica removed her outer clothes, leaving on her bra, underpants and boots, and then reached for the gown.

"Your boots, too," the nurse reminded her.

Mica shook her head no.

"Listen to me," the nurse said. "I'm your friend." She glanced down at Mica's boots. Mica realized that if she continued to protest, it might seem suspicious.

"Okay… I'll keep my boots next to me in the shower."

"No one is going to walk out with them."

"They better not."

The nurse looked at Mica in her bra and underwear. "You'll need to remove your bra as well. Do as I say. Please."

After he'd given Mica a cursory introduction, Dr. Michael Ingel opened the chart in front of him. He was a middle-aged, gray-haired man, with tight, skinny lips. He had a little head for a big body, and thick black eyeglasses shielded his small face. He raised his parrot-like nose from time to time to ask Mica, who was seated on the examining table, a question.

"They tell me your name is Mica. What's your last name?"

"Mihailescu."

"Well, Miss Mihailescu, we have a problem with you. We have laws here, regulations that prohibit a female minor from entering the country without a parent."

Mica jumped off the examining table. "But I have to go to America! I can't go back."

Dr. Ingel spoke calmly—the perfect bureaucrat, controlling his true feelings. "Get dressed. I'll have to call the ambassador about this matter."

He walked back to his desk. As Mica changed, she listened intently. "Neal, this is Michael Ingel. Please come to the medical clinic. Now!"

Mica's hands faltered as she put on her bra and pulled up her diamond boots. She eyed the doctor, afraid, as she watched him slam the phone down in anger.

CHAPTER 10

"WE HAVE no way to protect girls here. We'll have to send you back to Romania," the ambassador said.

Mica broke down and cried. "I'll be arrested. They'll think I'm a spy and kill me."

"What do you know about spies?" the doctor asked. He leaned forward as if to examine her more closely.

"You can't stay," Mr. Bridge repeated. "We'll arrange somehow to get you back. You must have family who will take you in."

"I have no one. I told you. Everyone was killed during the war." She was afraid to say more.

"I don't believe anything you're telling us!" the doctor said, losing his patience.

Mica started to sweat. She felt dizzy as if the floor were moving. She wanted to ask for a glass of water but was too scared.

"I'm going to ask you again. How did you escape? Are you a secret agent?"

All of a sudden, Mica lost her balance. As she fell, her right shoulder hit the steel edge of the doctor's desk.

"I can't breathe," she cried.

The doctor bent down, felt her head, her pulse, her stomach. "Your abdomen is rigid. What did you eat and drink in the past twenty-four hours?"

"I drank water at the train station. I was so thirsty, I forgot to think it was dirty."

The doctor and ambassador helped her up, and slowly put her into a chair. "The water probably contained an amoeba," the doctor explained. "I've seen several cases recently of dysentery."

"I-I ate pears, also," Mica told them. "I hadn't eaten since yesterday morning, and I was so hungry."

The doctor didn't say anything. He picked up his phone and within seconds, the nurse appeared at the door of the examining room.

"Miss Bartha," the doctor said. "Put the girl in one of the cots in the infirmary. We'll watch her. Pulse is weak; abdomen is distended. Prepare to take a stool sample for dysentery."

The nurse helped Mica stand up. "Hold on to me."

The nurse walked Mica down a corridor and into a room where she put her to bed. If her stomach hadn't hurt so much, Mica could have easily fallen asleep—she had been awake for more than twenty-four hours—but the pain, and the thought that she might not make it to the United States kept her tossing and turning. She feared what would happen to her if she was forced to return to Romania. The Romanian police at the border would be suspicious of her returning to Romania once she had been in Hungary. More than suspicious: they would likely kill her.

Nurse Bartha periodically appeared to take her temperature and to check on her. She gently tried to remove Mica's coat and boots, but Mica refused and pulled her knees to her chest.

Mica felt hot with fever, and it was making her head feel faint and her body weak. Breathing deeply, she tried to calm herself by remembering something good: when she was on stage as Juliet. Romeo was holding her hand as they bowed. The audience was cheering. But gradually the applause drifted off; Nicky was nowhere in sight. The theater turned dark, and Mica fell asleep.

TEN HOURS LATER, MICA WOKE IN A SWEAT. HER HAIR WAS WET, and the pillow and sheets were drenched. The spasms in her stomach were still there. Gasping for breath, she tried to raise herself to a sitting position, but she couldn't move her right arm. It was sore and rigid from her fall. Mr. Bridge and the doctor had been yelling at her. She felt danger for herself. She was all alone. If only her mother or father could protect her.

Nurse Bartha entered the infirmary carrying a bowl of soup. As she came closer, Mica smelled her sweetness, like honey. The nurse reminded her of the women in the Romanian countryside, who made cologne from bee pollen.

Mica studied her: medium height, not thin, not heavy, short, brown curly hair, with strands of blonde at the temples. Probably not more than thirty or thirty-five years old. Her full, round face was cheerful. She looked so healthy in her white coat.

"This is for you," the nurse said. "It'll soothe your stomach."

Mica took the bowl with her left hand, and despite the throbbing in her right shoulder, smiled at the nurse. "Thank you." Then she hesitated. "I had a terrible nightmare. Can I tell you about it?" Mica was already feeling calmer now that she wasn't alone. "I used to do that with my mother, and when I finished, she would say, 'Abracadabra,' and the nightmare disappeared."

"Of course." Nurse Bartha, seeing Mica's difficulty, took the bowl of soup from her and started spoon-feeding her as if she were a child.

"I dreamt I was in a tunnel and I couldn't escape. It changed to a village and I saw my house. Then the house fell down. I was looking for my parents, but I couldn't find them." Mica started to cry.

Magda Bartha took Mica in her arms, rocking her softly. "You're not alone. I'm here with you."

The quiet of the infirmary was interrupted by a bang.

"Damn it, Neal!"

The nurse turned her head to the adjacent wall. "That's Dr. Ingel's office. He has quite a temper."

Mica stared at the nurse and then moved her head closer to overhear the yelling. She thought she heard the doctor bang his fist several times on the desk, even though it was on the other side of the wall. She listened.

"Who is this girl? How did she get here? This will have to be investigated further."

"Yes," she heard Mr. Bridge say. "But how? We can't get any information from Romania. That country is locked tight."

"Not so tight if she got out," the doctor countered. "I know someone there. He's a Romanian doctor; works for the C.I.A. It'll take some time to get the information."

"Start an investigation. We can wait," the ambassador said.

"Who knows? Maybe she's a terrorist or spy."

"At her age?"

"Of course! She's a weathered adult," the doctor warned. "You can't compare her to an American teenager. Children from this part of the world have to grow up fast. They learn how to survive or die. They have a sixth sense, like alley cats."

"You're probably right, but I did give my word to help her. I have to honor that. And now she's sick."

"Forget about being a gentleman! We're dealing with terrorists!" the doctor said, his tone disgusted. "And yet, it's true, it wouldn't be ethical to throw her out. Sick. Perhaps our little actress will get herself in trouble and we'll learn more about her. I suspect she's very savvy if she got out of a communist country on her own. We can watch her, maybe learn something. I'm not adverse if she works for us until she's well. She can replace Radu as a translator. I'd like to get rid of him. He gives me the creeps."

"It's true. He's weird," the ambassador said. "But we have to be careful. I sense Radu could be dangerous."

For one week, Mica lay in bed in a semiconscious state. Most of the time she slept, waking up only to pain in her stomach and shoulder and the need to fight the demons that kept tormenting her. Fragmented images passed through her mind, blurred scenes without order or connection, people's faces fusing into others. She saw her father with his red bushy hair and red mustache, but his face was Marinescu's, cut and battered, and his skin was covered with dried blood.

"Tata," she moaned. "Are you safe? Mama, did you return home?"

When she opened her eyes, her pillow was wet from her tears. Magda Bartha must have heard her sobbing, for several times Mica found herself crying in the nurse's arms, being rocked and soothed until she felt her head return to the pillow, which was like a soft cloud that took her to the sky where she floated hand in hand with her mother. Then she awoke, recognizing a voice; but it wasn't her mother's. It was the nurse's, bringing Mica back to earth.

AFTER ANOTHER WEEK, MICA'S FEVER AND HER STOMACH SPASMS lessened. Her right shoulder didn't hurt as much, and she started to spend more time during the day awake. The nurse brought Mica books from the embassy library and Mica looked forward to discussing them with her new friend. The books bonded them and reminded Mica of evenings with her mother, who was a librarian in Spera's Central Library. When her father was not at home in the evenings, Mica and her mother would find comfort in front of the fireplace, reading aloud from Shakespeare, Tolstoy, Dostoyevsky, Chekhov, and so many others.

One day, Magda brought Mica a transistor radio. "I brought it from home. Do you like music?"

"I love the Beatles," Mica smiled. "Do you think this radio can get music from a capitalist country?"

"Of course, on Radio Free Europe! Besides, inside the American Embassy, you can listen to whatever station you want. The BBC plays the Beatles."

Mica took the radio from the nurse as eagerly as she was now taking food. She lay back in her bed, cuddling the transistor.

"Now that you're getting stronger and I see you enjoy the songs," Magda said, "I can teach you to play music, if you wish."

"Here?"

"Yes, it will give you something to do while you get better. I would enjoy teaching you. I miss not having a sister. My two brothers have a *naï*. It looks like several flutes put together. You play by blowing air into the different holes. Shepherds play it when they watch their sheep."

Mica knew the instrument. Romanian Gypsies played it, too.

"Brahms used the naï in his *Hungarian Dances*, and Bartòk for his czardas," she explained.

"So did the Beatles!" Mica said. She was thrilled about the idea of learning to play the instrument better. She had played it once on stage in a Shakespearean play and loved its sound, but it belonged to Mr. Marinescu. "Can we start soon?"

"Of course! I'll bring it tomorrow!" Magda said, happy to see Mica getting better.

One evening before Magda went home, she went to check on Mica and bring her dinner. Mica was still not completely well enough to join the embassy staff in the dining room and was in bed, sketching with colored pencils that the nurse had given her, and listening to the Beatles on the radio. Mica was trying to concentrate on her drawing and the music, so she wouldn't think about what would happen to her once she'd fully recovered. She feared the doctor wouldn't let her stay in the embassy, and then, where would she go? What would she do? But when she saw the nurse, Mica felt calmer and showed her a picture of the Chain Bridge she had just drawn.

While the nurse was admiring Mica's work, there was a knock on the door. Two young men were being escorted inside by an embassy security guard. When they saw Magda, they ran into the room with a burst of energy. She yelled, "Ben! Tibi! What a surprise! Mica, meet my brothers."

Mica looked at the two handsome men, one a head taller than the other. The shorter and thinner one, Ben, was older, appearing to be in his early thirties, while the taller, younger brother, Tibi, was probably in his late twenties. Ben, the obvious leader of the two, had a reddish-auburn mustache and long sideburns. His hair was also reddish, full, and wavy, and reminded Mica of her father's. Tibi, the less serious of the two, was blond with a fair complexion.

"We were passing the embassy and decided to surprise our big sister and walk her home," Ben explained to Mica as he introduced himself.

"Actually, we were curious to see our competition," the younger brother joked. "Magda talks all the time about you and I'm jealous. She says you've just started to play the naï and you have more talent than I do."

Magda laughed. "This is the only time he's telling the truth."

Mica saw how the nurse's face glowed when she stood between her brothers. They were like her children, even though she was just a few years older than Ben.

Mica shook hands with both young men. "Your sister is on a mission to fatten me up. Every day when she takes my temperature, she asks me to stick out my finger and she says, 'Too bony. You must eat more.'"

They all laughed. Mica was delighted to be at center stage. She put down her sketchbook and arranged her hair with her fingers.

"Look at the bridge Mica drew," the nurse said proudly, as if Mica were one of her children.

Ben took the drawing pad and admired the picture. "I love how you drew the river—just the right blue and green shining in the sun like diamonds."

"How did you know I tried to make diamonds?" Mica's hazel eyes sparkled the same greenish hue as the Danube.

"He sees diamonds everywhere," Tibi teased, patting his older brother on the back. "He's obsessed."

"My brothers are diamond cutters," Nurse Bartha said. "So was our father."

"Have you ever seen a colored diamond?" Mica asked, trying to sound casual. She eyed her boots next to her bed and thought that perhaps the brothers would know the value of her diamonds. She knew she'd have to be cautious, and she wondered if she could trust them the way she trusted Magda, who was so kind to her.

"I haven't seen a colored diamond close up," Ben answered. "Seen many in books and studied them."

"He's being modest," Tibi said. "My brother is a real expert. He knows more about diamonds than anyone in Budapest."

Ben looked down, uncomfortable with the compliment.

Magda glanced at Mica, worried that she was getting tired. "My dear cherubs," she said to her brothers. "It's time to leave Mica to rest and have her dinner."

"Of course," Tibi responded.

Ben approached Mica's bed and shook her hand again. "I hope you'll be able to visit us at home. I can show you some books of colored diamonds I have."

"I'd love that." But then her face darkened and the feeling of frustration returned. Mr. Bridge had told her she couldn't leave the embassy grounds. Still Mica smiled and waved good-bye as they closed her door. She wished she could get up and run home with them. Instead, she'd have to be content just thinking how pleasant it was to have made some friends.

CHAPTER 11

AFTER THREE WEEKS OF REST, medication, and care from Nurse
Bartha, Mica was fully recovered from dysentery. Her shoulder
also healed, allowing her full mobility of her neck and shoulder
without pain. Color had come back into her cheeks and her short
black hair had grown in so that her soft curls framed her white
complexion. She had managed to put on a few pounds and the fullness heightened the curve of her high cheekbones. Magda Bartha,
now her dear friend, had told her that the enforced rest had
brought out her natural beauty, and Mica was now full of energy.

Her first thoughts were of her parents. She tried to phone them
from the clinic, but the Romanian operator told her that the telephone had been disconnected. She considered calling Mr. Marinescu, but the old theater had no phone, and Mica was concerned
that his phone at home was tapped. And if she called the post
office, where there was a public phone, there would be a record of
the incoming and outgoing connections. Whether her parents
were in jail or not, her phoning would cause problems for them.

She reasoned that if her parents had been released from interrogation, which she hoped was true, they'd have been placed under house arrest. Then Mr. Marinescu would have been able to get word to them that Mica had escaped to Hungary. Her father would have checked the basement and realized she had left with the diamonds.

All she could do was to send each week, a blank postcard to her home in Spera with a Hungarian stamp. One of them at least was bound to get through, and, if her parents were home, they would understand the implied message. Magda agreed to help Mica find the postcards, without photos to give the authorities a hint about the city or sender, and mail them.

Now that Mica felt stronger, she made herself useful in the clinic by translating for the nurse. She enjoyed being busy and felt comforted in Magda's company. Mica also wanted to show Dr. Ingel and Mr. Bridge that she was grateful for their allowing her to work and stay in the embassy. Whenever Romanian refugees didn't know Hungarian or English, Mica transcribed their medical history and application forms from Romanian. And if the refugee was Hungarian and the nurse was busy, Mica felt equally comfortable serving as liaison.

She ingratiated herself, albeit reluctantly, with the doctor by preparing each patient for examination, thereby reducing the time each one had to wait in line. She asked his permission to give the refugees bread and honey after their blood tests. When she had free time, she gathered nuts from the trees in the embassy garden and put them into each person's pocket as they finished having their chests X-rayed. She even collected old shoes and sweaters from the embassy staff and distributed them to the refugees at the end of their visits. As each one waited for their medical reports, Mica offered a word of hope that they'd be able to fill out forms for an American visa.

One afternoon, Magda advised Mica about diplomatic protocol, suggesting she should visit the ambassador in his office to thank him for helping her stay and work in the embassy, and to apply for a visa.

"Can I really just go and speak to him?" Mica asked. "He's the ambassador of the U.S. Embassy."

Magda smiled. "Of course. Neal Bridge is very approachable. Our embassy reflects its location—Budapest—friendly. We try to be a family here."

Pleased to oblige, Mica waited for lunchtime, when she knew the ambassador would be alone in the library.

"Excuse me, sir, Mr. Bridge," she said, entering the opulent room. "I'm sorry to bother you...," She hesitated, always tongue-tied in his presence. "M-may I please have a minute of your time?"

"Of course," the ambassador said, putting down his papers and giving her his attention. "How are you feeling?"

"I'm well now, thank you. But then, it was like the breaking down of my entire body. I hope I'll never have that feeling again."

"Hope not. For sure." He looked down, seeming not to know what else to say. "Now, is it true you have an uncle in New York and that he's willing to sponsor you?"

"Yes! All I have to do is call him when I know I'm coming to America. I know his number by heart. I found it on a card in my father's drawer. Do you think we could call him? Now?" Mica was fizzing with excitement. *America!*

He nodded.

"What are you going to ask him?" she said.

For a moment, she felt scared. Had she been too eager to ask him to call her uncle? What would happen if her uncle refused to take her in? Over the years, her father had lost contact with his brother, and she didn't even know him. Her father knew that an exchange of letters to and from America could be used as a reason for his own arrest. In addition, she had always wondered why the brothers' relationship was fractured. She knew that if she had had a sibling—and she'd longed to have a sister or brother when she was younger—he or she would be a treasure.

"I'll ask him if he'll take you in and take responsibility for your welfare until you can support yourself," Bridge said. "He'll have to sign an affidavit in New York in the presence of a witness and send it to me."

Mica panicked again. What would happen to her if her uncle declined to sign an affidavit? She didn't know what an affidavit was, but it sounded coldly official.

Bridge held out a pen and paper for her to write down the telephone number. Then without further ado, the ambassador went to his office to use his private telephone, and Mica followed, staying in the open door as he spoke on the phone.

"Mica," he said, turning from the phone, "your uncle wants to know if this will cost him? I told him just your room and board."

Mica, bewildered by the speed at which all this was happening, was nonetheless surprised that her uncle's first thoughts were of money.

Bridge spoke to her uncle a bit more, then Mica heard him say, "Until she's eighteen." Then he turned to her. "He says he has never met you and is reluctant to sign anything that will be notarized without knowing you first."

Mica's heart leapt into her throat. "Can I speak to him? Maybe a few words from me would help?" She breathed deeply and tried to control her panic.

"All right, but I'm going to listen to what you say, so be careful."

She smiled at the ambassador and pretending to be nonchalant, took the phone. "Hello, my dear uncle. The last time I saw my father, he told me to tell you, '*Am diamantele. Nu s'a vandut niciunul. Nu stie nimenea inafara de mine.*' I have the diamonds. None of mine was sold."

She glanced quickly at the ambassador, who had obviously

heard her switch to Romanian. Under his glacial stare, she immediately changed back to English. "My dear father wanted me to give you a gift when I see you in New York. I hope you'll invite me and accept my gift."

"Diamantele? You have the diamonds?" her uncle said in a raised voice. "How did a kid like you escape Romania all alone? What are you now—seventeen?" Then he changed his tone, became softer. "The diamonds...well... the diamonds... my brother's daughter. I believe in family loyalty. Okay, I'll accept you as my bloodline, but only if there are no shenanigans!"

"Yes, thank you, dear uncle." She had no idea what *shenanigans* were, but how could he refuse knowing she was bringing a *gift of diamonds?*

Mica handed the ambassador the phone and smiled. "Sir, my uncle wants to speak to you. He said he loves his brother and he's happy to have me in his home."

Bridge grabbed the phone, still looking furious. His thick, blond eyebrows, which usually formed a unibrow, now furrowed up and down. Two small muscular hemispheres on his forehead tightened, and his entire body seemed to tense up as he struggled to master his temper. For the first time, Mica saw real emotion on his face.

Bridge spoke to her uncle for several minutes; all the while, he kept his eyes on Mica. After hanging up, he continued staring. She carefully kept her expression neutral and calm. She had to get to America, no matter what the cost.

"Mica," he said, "You tricked me by speaking Romanian. You should have spoken English all the time! How can I trust you after that?"

"I didn't realize I was using Romanian until I saw your face. My uncle spoke to me first in Romanian. I responded without thinking. I wanted to be polite."

Bridge stood up. "How do I know what you said in Romanian?"

She wanted to say something to charm him, but the furious look on his face kept her from speaking. They stood facing each other, he clearly angry and she thinking that this was not the first time that she had been in a situation where feminine guile had helped her parry with authorities. Here, at this moment, Bridge was the authority she needed to charm. Mica couldn't allow anyone but herself to determine her fate.

Neither Mica nor Neal Bridge said a word for several seconds, but neither did either of them look away.

Mica looked into the ambassador's eyes and smiled up at him. She found this took no effort, no play-acting. She was being entirely genuine. "Mr. Bridge," she said softly, "please..."

At that moment, the door opened, and a short, elegant man, carrying a folder of papers, entered the room. Mica stopped thinking of her problems and stared at him. He had visited her several times when she was sick to give her magazines.

As if on cue, she blurted out, "Hello! I love your dance magazines. Thank you so much. I read them every night before I go to bed and dream of dancing with Nureyev."

He moved toward her, shook her hand, and introduced himself. "My name is George Szabo."

She curtseyed and while lowering her eyes said, "Kind sir, it's an honor."

Bridge was initially annoyed at the interruption. But Mica's and George's short exchange had somehow given him a few seconds to take control of the situation.

He said calmly, "This is one of our men working in immigration. He'll help you do the paperwork for your visa application."

Szabo smiled. "I have more magazines if you wish. I get them from my sister in New York."

"New York?" she asked, incredulously.

"George," the ambassador interrupted, "did you want to tell me something?"

"Yes, sorry, sir. I asked your wife if she wants to audition the violinists from Café Gerbeaud for the Embassy's Easter party."

"Fine, fine." Bridge nodded his head and moved his shoulders as if to dismiss the man, but George turned to Mica. "I have some books also about ballet..."

"Good. Fine." Bridge waved Szabo out of the office, then began to pace the room. "This is what I propose," he said as he walked to the map of the United States on the wall. "I'll give you the benefit of the doubt, and a choice. It'll take up to six months until your visa application can be cleared. You can go to a refugee camp in Austria for this period. But, considering that you're alone, and in the camps, well, things happen there...."

"No," he said, seemingly more to himself than to his charge. "You'll be safer here. I feel responsible for you." He stared at her and then continued. "You can stay at the embassy and work for us."

"I'd love to stay here! I'll do anything." Mica felt like jumping up with joy, but took a deep breath instead to appear calm.

"There's one stipulation: you cannot leave the embassy; you have no papers. You're not here legally. As I told you before, if you get into trouble, I get into trouble."

"I'll behave. I promise."

"We need a translator full-time in the clinic, and you've already proven yourself. Usually Radu helps out. He speaks Romanian, Hungarian, and German, but his English isn't good."

"I'm so grateful..." Mica lowered her head to hide her tears of joy.

He raised his hand as if to stop her from talking further. "Remember, if Radu gets angry at you for replacing him, don't react. Tell me, and I'll handle him."

Mica understood. Radu had tried to slash her face with broken glass. Ever since she had been well and moving around the embassy, she had avoided him. He gave her the creeps with his gold teeth and leather gloves that he always wore. She had made it this far, and had no intention of having anyone ruin her chances for getting a visa.

CHAPTER 12

WINTER IN BUDAPEST was cold and dark. Gray clouds from dawn to dusk shrouded the sky with a heaviness that Mica had never known before. Not allowed out of the embassy, she felt as if she were in prison. At the end of the day, when everyone went home to families and friends, she'd linger alone in the garden. Sometimes she'd stand on the stone bench against the cement wall, gazing at the rooftops spread out before her. She'd think about New York, wondering if the city had rooftops like in Budapest, or only skyscrapers? And how would she get her parents to New York? How would she begin? Would her uncle help her? Their beginning on the phone had been ominous.

Often, she'd stare at the high school next door to the embassy garden and remember the good things about Romania while she watched the teenagers play. She longed to go back to school, to be with her friends, to laugh with Nicky, feel his hand in hers. It seemed so long since she felt truly happy. She wanted to feel like a teenager again, but now she felt much older than her seventeen years. No longer protected by her parents, she had to depend on herself.

In the two months of living at the embassy, Mica's life had changed in ways she had never expected. She had only laughed once on the day she met Magda's brothers. Otherwise her routine was regimented and uneventful. She was the only female refugee working in the embassy. There were several men, in their twenties, but she only saw them in the dining room. They were reserved and quiet, busy thinking about their own plans for freedom.

Her only pleasure came late at night when she practiced the *naï* that Magda had lent her. Mica was making progress, teaching herself, and could play the same Romanian folk songs that she and her friends used to sing. But Anca wasn't with her, nor was Marina or Cristina, who loved to dance with her. Mica missed dancing so much. It always made her feel alive.

Yet, despite the challenges surrounding Mica about her present and future, she refused to allow herself to be despondent. If her situation was difficult, that is when she would have to fight and overcome obstacles. Her father had told her, "Whenever life seems the lowest, that's when you must rise. Use your willpower."

She looked at the school yard from the embassy garden, and stared at a group of girls and boys playing soccer together. What fun it would be if she could join them. But how? She thought and thought. Then an idea came to her: She had Magda's radio that played American rock 'n' roll on the BBC station, for twenty-four consecutive hours. Maybe she and Magda could use the radio and organize a dancing party for the Hungarian teenagers next door?

The thought gave her so much pleasure that she didn't sleep that entire night, dreaming of dancing to the Beatles, the Rolling Stones, the Everly Brothers, the Diamonds, and so much more.

As soon as Magda entered the clinic in the morning, Mica ran to her, taking her hand. "I have an idea. Please, let me know what you think."

Magda stared at her. Mica looked like she was jumping out of a box.

"Can we organize, somehow, somewhere, a dance for the teenagers in the high school next door to the embassy?"

"You mean a party?"

"I don't know what to call it. A party or dance."

"Well, that's quite a challenge. The school is run by the communist government. You'd need someone to go around the rules."

"How about having the event, here, in the embassy, in the auditorium where the ambassador hosts gatherings?"

"Not a bad idea. Let's speak to Mr. Bridge during lunch time."

Mica had a difficult time concentrating on her morning chores of translating patients' records. She kept looking at the clinic's clock, waiting eagerly for noon. When she saw the number 12:00 on the white and black clock, she ran to Magda and almost pulling her, led her to the library, hoping they'd be able to see Bridge there.

The door was opened, but they knocked to be polite. Neal Bridge looked up.

"Sir," Mica began, "excuse us for interrupting your lunch. But we have an idea we'd like to discuss with you, if we may?"

He nodded his head.

"Wouldn't it be a good gesture to make friends with the community—with the Hungarian youth?" She continued explaining, before he could even answer. "Invite them to a dance? Nurse Bartha has a radio that can get American rock n' roll. And the high school is in our community. Right next door."

He stared at her. "Well, that would mean getting permission from the school director. I know Laszlo Fabry. He's not a communist at heart. He's actually an intellectual. Loves American history and literature. We've had some exciting discussions."

"We could host the event here, during the day," Magda said, "when we have all our security guards on duty."

"Not a bad idea," Bridge said. "I do want to open up to the community. Encourage friendlier relations. Perhaps an Easter celebration for students." Then he turned to Magda. "My wife and I are busy planning the embassy's annual Easter party. Could you manage the details of the dance to coincide with that and still not neglect your clinic responsibilities?"

"Of course. And Mica will help me. We can also serve tea and cheese."

"Oh yes!" Mica said. "Imagine dancing! A tea and dance!"

The next morning, Bridge entered the clinic, signaled to Magda and Mica to follow him to an empty room. He told them that he spoke to Laszlo Fabry, who thought it was a grand idea, and Fabry would escort, himself, twenty sixteen-year olds, who have Fridays free for sports, from 1:00-4:00. They could all come this Friday."

"Yes!" Mica shouted. "What fun!" She was in heaven.

———————

FRIDAY AFTERNOON CAME. AT 1:00, TEN TEENAGED BOYS AND TEN teenaged girls lined up at the guards' station. They were very excited, and listened carefully to the guards' instructions on how to pass through security. Mica and Magda greeted them, shaking each teenager's hand and introducing themselves. Mica felt so grown up, although she was just one year older than the group, and most of them were taller than her. The teenagers were dressed in white shirts and black pants or black skirts. Their shoes appeared freshly polished and their hair was perfectly brushed and coiffed. Their faces were all smiles.

Mica led them into the auditorium which Magda had decorated, as a surprise, with blue and white balloons. When Mica asked, "Where did you find them?" Magda smiled and answered, "My friend sells them in the park and gave us a dozen as a gift."

Mica placed the radio on the podium, and raised the volume of BBC to its loudest sound. For three hours, the teenagers did not stop dancing, not even for cookies that Magda had baked. And when the nurse finally rang a bell, to indicate the end of the party and they should pass to the dining room, they all mumbled, "Please, one more dance." After several more dances, reluctantly, they formed a single file and passed to the dining room, while dancing in a *conga line* and singing, *"Ole! Ole!"*

———————

THE NEXT MORNING, BRIDGE ENTERED THE CLINIC ALL SMILES. "What a successful event," he told Magda and Mica. "Laszlo has asked me if they can return. Perhaps with other students for another holiday event? What should I tell him?"

"Yes!" Mica said.

"I'll speak to him. Good for diplomatic relations," Bridge commented, and smiled at Mica. "Congratulations," he told her softly, and let his eyes linger a while on hers.

Mica was happy, not only because she had organized the dance, but because, she had created something different in the embassy and everyone was pleased. She had also created an afternoon for herself and others, where they could dance to American music like any other American teenager. Mica had refused to let herself get down and did something to make herself happy.

But the high school dance was a conscious endeavor that Mica planned during the day. It was at night, when the unconscious can usurp the conscious that she had less control and success. Nightmares plagued her as she'd think about her diamonds and that they came from Auschwitz. She'd twist and turn, remembering when she had asked her father, "If by some miracle, someone in a concentration camp survived, was he marked forever? How much pain could a human being endure?"

"Mengele considered the Jews to be inhuman, and so to him, they didn't have feelings nor could they suffer," her father had said. "He treated them as if they were experimental objects. Mengele was more inhuman than people can imagine. He said he was experimenting for science. Twins were his primary guinea pigs. He wanted to observe if one reacted medically different than the other."

"What do you mean?" Mica had asked.

"Mengele started by trying to change brown eyes to blue. He'd strap down his victims on slabs of marble, like carving boards, and then inject different colored dyes directly into their eyeballs. All this he did without anesthesia. Then, he'd take out their eyeballs and pin the eyes on a large board made of cork, and line the colored balls into columns as if they were butterflies. He sent the display to his mentor, Professor von Verschuer, the Director of the Kaiser Wilhelm Institute for Anthropology in Berlin, to communicate how well his experiments were going. Mengele had a Ph.D. in anthropology from the institute. When he didn't need his blind guinea pigs anymore, he sent them to be gassed."

Mica hid her face in her hands. Her father took her in his arms.

"Everyone knew misery at Auschwitz," he had said. "Even those who survived, had died. That's why I worry about these diamonds. Blood diamonds."

Night after night, Mica had difficulty sleeping, knowing that the diamonds had been taken from their original owners, and they had died.

Magda noticed how deep in thought Mica had become. Even when they ate lunch together, Mica would often remain quiet. "Tell me, dear, is there anything I can do to help?"

"No," Mica said, turning to look out the window.

"You'll get your visa," the nurse assured her. "This is all temporary. Soon you will have friends and your life will change. America is a land where dreams come true."

"You remind me of my mother," Mica said. "She always sees the bright side of things too."

"I'm glad."

"I'm afraid." Mica hesitated. She stood up, paced the room, and sat down again, clearly agitated. "Can I tell you a secret?"

"Of course."

"Promise not to tell?"

"Promise," Magda said, and she crossed her heart.

"I'm worried about diamonds." Mica waited to see if Magda understood what she was getting at.

"*Diamonds? Why?* How could something so beautiful be cause for worry? But what do you mean?"

Mica stood up agitated. "Diamonds *are* beautiful, but they have many facets. They can also be dangerous."

"I understand," Magda reflected, watching her young friend closely. "My brothers are diamond cutters for the State Institute of Gemology. So was my father before them. It's true. The cutting machines they use could take off a finger or even a hand." She paused, and when Mica did not respond, she said, "Now that you've met my brothers, perhaps you should speak to them about diamonds. Talking about something worrisome does help the soul."

Mica moved closer to her friend. "I escaped Romania with colored diamonds," she whispered. "I don't know if they're valuable. I have them hidden. Maybe... maybe, I could somehow show them to your brothers."

Magda didn't respond, but her eyes went wide. Then she smiled. "I have an idea. Sunday is Saints' Day in Hungary. It's a festive holiday. How about if I ask Mr. Bridge if you can come home with me and help us celebrate?"

"Do you really think he would let me leave the embassy grounds? He said several times that I can't."

"Let me try to convince him. I'll say it's your reward for arranging such a fun dancing party." Then Magda added, "My brothers have a lab in our basement with special machines."

CHAPTER 13

THE NEXT DAY, Magda asked Neal Bridge to give Mica "time off" for the holiday. She could spend the afternoon with her in her apartment nearby. He deliberated, but finally gave permission for Mica to leave the embassy complex under the responsibility of the nurse.

That Sunday, Mica walked with Magda Bartha to the apartment that she shared with her brothers near the Corso promenade. Mica was thrilled to leave the Embassy even if it was only for an afternoon. As soon as she entered the nurse's apartment, she was overcome with pleasure and gratitude.

It was an apartment full of light, and Mica could feel the goodness in the home: the fragrance of flowers, sweet and inviting; the smell of meat sizzling with herbs; the tang of fresh orange; freshly baked cake; and all kinds of cheeses. Books were everywhere—on shelves, on small tables, even piled high on the floor.

Multiple shades of green lit up the living room. The mint curtains were made of lace so light that the sun beamed through them. The couch had a turquoise paisley print and the chairs were emerald velvet. Even the pillows were dotted a happy green with red embroidered flowers. The inviting home lightened her spirits and the nurse's brothers greeted her with equal warmth.

"Now that you know where we live, I hope you'll be able to come often," Ben said.

After they were seated with a glass of tokay, with Magda busy in the kitchen, he explained that they had all lived together since Magda lost her fiancé during the Hungarian Revolution. "She never married anyone else; never moved from this apartment. Instead, Tibi and I moved in with her. She says she loves to mother us."

Magda had prepared all kinds of foods, and she served Mica as they all sat in the living room, settling in front of the fireplace, listening to Brahms' *Hungarian Dances.* Mica stared at the red flames burning the logs and remembered how her father enjoyed piling up their logs like a small mountain.

"Please have one. *Palachinta,* with cheese or apricot," she offered Mica.

"It's a crêpe we usually have for dessert," Tibi explained. "It takes time to make. You must be very dear to Magda if she made it just for you." He smiled with obvious affection at his sister. Mica sensed he was the lightest in character of the three siblings.

"I prefer the apricot," she said, after trying both and licking her fingers clean. "Can I have another one?"

"Of course." Ben brought the platter to her. "Afterwards, do you want to see my workshop? The door is always locked, and it's in a separate wing of the basement. No one but us will know what goes on inside."

Even though Ben and Tibi knew she had the diamonds, Mica still deliberated about what to do. She told herself this was an opportunity, and she should trust them. Who would know better than Ben and Tibi if she could trade diamonds for dollars and freedom for her parents?

Still feeling hesitant, Mica followed them downstairs and

through a long corridor to a room paneled with polished rose-wood. The only furniture was a large wooden table of the same fine wood, reminding Mica of the refectory table in Mr. Bridge's library. But on this table, there was a special microscope, a box of instruments, a loupe eyepiece, a scale and an unusually shaped lamp.

Mica began tentatively. "My father had diamonds he wanted to sell and escape with. But he couldn't get out. I did."

Ben's face brightened. "Yes?" he asked, encouraging her to tell him more.

"It's not a happy story," she said, hesitating. "He hid the diamonds for twenty years. He hoped one day, he'd be able to use them to get out of Romania, but he kept waiting, waiting for the right moment." She stopped talking, looked down and said, "My father was also afraid that the diamonds were cursed."

Ben and Tibi leaned against the table and Magda stepped forward to take Mica's hand.

"The moment came for my father early in the war, when General Antonescu, who ruled Romania, had quickly aligned himself with Hitler and realized he could make money from the Bucharest Jews. Antonescu didn't send them to concentration camps like he did with the Jews from Moldova and other parts, even though Eichmann tried to insist. Antonescu was negotiating a deal without either Hitler or Eichmann ever knowing—to sell the Bucharest Jews and send them to Palestine. But the British, who controlled Palestine at that time, didn't want to upset the Arabs. Even though Ben-Gurion, the leader of Israel, wanted the Bucharest Jews to build up the new country, the British told Antonescu no. They called it a slave trade, unethical to sell people.

"The British and Antonescu were at an impasse, so the Committee for Romanian Jews placed an ad in the *New York Times* saying that General Antonescu would give Jews away practically for nothing. That thousands of Romanian refugees were waiting to be bought for a small amount to go to another country."

"Bought? By whom?" Ben asked.

"America, Canada, and Europe, but no country wanted them; so, Arthur Sulzberger, the publisher of the *Times*, wrote an editorial, saying that twenty thousand Romanian leis, or fifty dollars, could save the life of a Jewish refugee from Bucharest. Henry Morgenthau, the U.S. Secretary of the Treasury, took the editorial to President Roosevelt, who hesitated and stalled. It was an election year and not a popular idea. The plan fell through. The Bucharest Jews couldn't leave the country. And yet, Antonescu kept trying.

"Even though my father wasn't Jewish, he knew this was the moment to plan on how to get out of Romania. Jews couldn't be saved or sold or bought. It was an evil time. But before my parents could escape, one night, Hungarian fascists stormed into our town and ordered all Jews to be at the train station within an hour. Thousands from Cluj, Dej, Satu Mare, and northern Transylvania lined up. Those who were in front were shot dead.

"The fascists were ranting and raving, 'KILL ALL THE JEWS!'

"When the soldiers went to sleep, my uncle Simion, my mother, and my father, who had been hiding some Jewish neighbors in the church's cellar, came out and they all snuck away together from Spera. My mother never wanted to talk about it, but my father told me they walked by night and slept by day in the forest for weeks until they got to Bucharest. They all joined the Resistance."

"And the diamonds?" Tibi asked.

"It was 1944, my father and his brother were working out of an underground cellar in Bucharest. On Christmas day, my uncle Simion was there alone. He made all the false passports and documents—he was their expert. A man dressed in a fur coat knocked on the door and said, '*Pax-tibi.*' That was the password. Peace to you. My uncle opened the door."

"'I need two passports immediately,' the man told my uncle. 'For myself and my wife.'

"Simion said nothing, but he let the man in and then locked the door. 'My wife is pregnant. I don't want her to give birth in this country.'

"The man pleaded with Simion. 'Raoul Wallenberg in Budapest is arranging protective passes for Hungarian Jews. Documents that say the holder is a Swedish citizen. I speak Hungarian. You must help me get to him!'

"Before Simion could answer, the man took off his coat and opened a small, leather sack that was hidden in the fur lining.

"'I'm a jeweler. I have a fabulous treasure.'

"Diamonds rolled on Simion's desk. They were red, green, yellow, white, and blue.

"'You can have *all* these diamonds,' he said. 'No one will ever know. I'll also give you five thousand American dollars to arrange our departure.'

"In one week, Simion, now the owner of the diamonds, prepared documents and visas to Sweden, two for the jeweler and one for himself. Because of his contacts with the Resistance in Bucharest and Budapest, and the jeweler's American dollars, Simion was able to arrange plane tickets for three passengers to Stockholm and then on to New York."

Mica stopped talking and looked down as if she were thinking. "He couldn't get more visas for his brother and sister-in-law. Maybe that's why my father was angry with him."

"He had no problem entering New York?" Ben asked.

"The hardest part was *leaving Romania*. Simion hollowed out the heels and soles of his oldest shoes and hid twenty white diamonds there. He hid the colored diamonds in an oversized pocket watch and its leather strap. The largest diamonds, the green, red, and blue, he secreted inside the handle of a walking stick. He was so nervous he'd be caught that he gave my father the pocket watch with its strap and the walking stick. At the airport they searched Simion from top to bottom, but didn't inspect his shoes. They never found his white diamonds." Mica smiled. "Sometimes there's good luck."

"That doesn't sound like the diamonds were cursed."

"They were! My uncle told my father that all the diamonds belonged to Jews who couldn't leave Romania, who had been taken to a concentration camp, Auschwitz, and didn't survive. He called them blood diamonds. But my father had the colored diamonds and he wanted to use them, like his brother did, to get out of Romania. Even if the diamonds had belonged to someone else, who? And how to return them? Most likely they had died."

Mica took several deep breaths and then continued, in a lower voice, "When my parents disappeared, I escaped and took the colored diamonds, hiding them in my boots just like my uncle Simion did, and now, I'm not even sure if they're genuine." Mica stopped talking. She leaned against the wall for support and closed her eyes.

It was quiet in the laboratory for several moments. Ben, Tibi, and Magda stared at Mica with their mouths slightly open. "That's really a sad story," Tibi said. Magda made the sign of the cross over her chest.

"If you want, we can look at the diamonds and assess their quality," Ben said. "I have an ultraviolet lamp and high-powered microscope."

Mica had by now decided she'd show them the diamonds in her boots, but would keep the largest and most important ones—the red and green gems—in her bra. They would remain her secret. "Okay, I'll show you."

She bent down low, took off one boot, and turned the heel to the side. She took out a small green diamond and put it on the cloth that Tibi had laid on the table. He cleaned the stone and then placed it on a black velvet cushion.

"Oh my God!" exclaimed the nurse. "What a bright color!"

"And an unusual shape," commented Ben, picking it up with tweezers and studying it with his loupe eyepiece. "A pear shape with eight cuts on each side. At least nine carats."

Mica's heart skipped a beat. She had several green and red diamonds. This one was much smaller than the ones in her bra.

"Do you think it was hand-cut?" Tibi asked his older brother, picking it up.

"Yes, a long time ago. The original stone must have been larger and hand-cut into smaller ones. Look at the edges. Not one face is cut the same as the next. That's why the green color is so deep, like an emerald." Ben took a thin metal tool and touched several facets. Each one had a different length.

"The Greeks believed that if someone swallowed the powder from a flawless diamond, they'd be guaranteed a long life," Ben said, still examining the green stone. "They believed that the powder of a flawed diamond, though, could kill."

"How did they know if it was flawed or not?" Mica asked. Then she put her hands to her stomach and pretended to keel over.

"If they died, it was flawed," Tibi said, joking. "Catherine de Medici is said to have died of food poisoning. They found powdered diamonds in her meat."

Ben put the green diamond under his ultraviolet light. Suddenly, he breathed deeply and whispered, "Your father was right. It came from a concentration camp."

"How do you know?" she asked.

He brought her closer to the light. "Look at these two fine lines and dot. You can only see it with this type of machine. That's the code of the S.S."

"You mean the green diamond belonged to Hitler?" Mica gasped.

"Not Hitler personally. But probably it belonged to a Jew, like your father said, who was in a concentration camp. That's why it's branded."

Mica held her breath: branded like the Jews in concentration camps. "Is it illegal for me to have it?" she asked Ben. "Will I get into trouble?"

"I'm not a lawyer. There's no letter or proof of who owned this before. Unlike a painting stolen in war and then sold afterward, we don't know who the diamond's original owner was. It may be a moral question more than a legal one."

Ben placed the green jewel under his infrared microscope. "This will show us what flaws and inclusions the diamond has."

"*Inclusions?* What's it including?"

He smiled. "It'll show us if the gem has a spot or crack. We can't see the impurities with the human eye. For each diamond, we hope to have a high level of clarity as well as color, cut, and carat. The four C's. All these characteristics determine the monetary value of a diamond."

Ben took the ultraviolet lamp and placed it next to the microscope. Studying the diamond, he started to count: *Egy, ketto, három, nègy, öt.* Oh no!"

"What's the matter?" Mica asked, becoming tense.

"I'm counting dark spots. I even see a short, fine crack."

"Ooh," Mica groaned, fearing the stones were worthless.

"Let's not panic just yet. Let's see what else you have in your magic boots."

Mica bent down, took off her other boot, turned the heel, and removed a heart-shaped yellow diamond. Ben took the stone and studied it with his loupe. "How unusual."

No one said a word. Mica held her breath as she watched Ben put the stone under his special microscope. "Is there something wrong with this one, too?" she asked.

"I'm not sure," he said. "It's clearly German. Has the same

branded mark as the green diamond. But there's something about this shine I don't like."

Mica went over to the microscope to look. She moved her eye from left to right, hoping to capture a different angle and detect a spark of fire. Instead, she saw a mustard-colored rock.

Even she could detect the yellow diamond wasn't good—probably a fake. What if her other diamonds were also fakes? She was filled with dread as she remembered reading about fake paintings in an article, saying that even the Louvre and the Metropolitan Museum had bought fake Old Masters. A forger had later bragged that he had tricked the curators by baking his new canvas in an oven to harden the paint and give it an old look. If the curators couldn't recognize a fake painting, how could her father recognize a fake diamond? Maybe the jeweler had tricked uncle Simion to get visas.

"Do you want something to drink?" Magda asked her.

She shook her head no.

"The facets are too perfect," Ben said. He kept turning the stone under the microscope.

"Maybe it's a canary diamond from Australia or a nitrogen Cape stone from South Africa," Tibi commented, trying to keep the mood hopeful.

"No. And it's not a chameleon from America or a cubic zirconia from Russia. I'm sure it wouldn't change color with heat."

Mica stared at Ben. His bushy mustache bristled and his face looked jaundiced as it reflected the diamond's mustard-yellow hue.

After several minutes, he turned to Mica and said, "It's artificial, made in a lab—a synthetic that the Germans made."

"A fake," Tibi agreed, after studying it. "The S.S. used Jewish prisoners in concentration camps to make fake diamonds and counterfeit British pound notes."

Ben said, "The Jewish counterfeiters, of course, had no choice.

They had to do what they were told. For them to survive one more day was the only moral code."

"*Moral code?*" Tibi repeated sarcastically. "I read how after the war, Red Cross ambulances transported the counterfeit money from Germany to the Vatican Bank in Rome. Four hundred fifty million in fake British pounds then went on to Argentina for the German Nazis living there. And they lived well!"

"Dirty history," Ben agreed. He was angry also. Then he showed them the fake stone in the light. "It seems that counterfeiting diamonds was even more difficult than counterfeiting money."

Magda sensed Mica's growing turmoil. "Do you have other diamonds, dear? Maybe we'll have better luck."

Mica took another diamond out of her boot. "I do have a blue diamond, the only blue in the lot."

Ben stared at the jewel and his blue eyes lit up. "Amazing." He put the diamond under his microscope and counted in Hungarian, "*Egy, ketto, három, nègy, öt*. Unbelievable! I can't believe it! This diamond seems to have sixty-two facets. Most diamonds have fifty-eight.

"There was a French explorer-jeweler, Jean-Baptiste Tavernier, in the seventeenth century, who hand-cut his diamonds into sixty-two facets so maximum light would enter in and out. Your blue has the same number of facets and cuttings as Tavernier's *Grand Blue*."

Mica remembered her father had spoken of Tavernier, the first European jeweler to travel the world, who didn't listen to warnings not to cut his original, 112-carat blue diamond into smaller ones. Tavernier was told that man should not interfere with nature. If he did, he'd be punished—all the smaller diamonds he'd cut from the large one, would be cursed.

Ben held Mica's diamond up to the light. The basement took a bluish hue. He stared at the diamond in amazement. "Tavernier took the diamonds he discovered in the mines and caves of India and traveled throughout Europe and Asia to sell them. In the three hundred years after his death, the diamonds continued to travel throughout the world. Some were bought by kings and princes, some were stolen by bandits, and some became the spoils of war. A few of them found their way to Russia. There was the huge, blue-green Orlov diamond, 189 carats, given by Prince Orlov to his mistress, Catherine the Great. It's now in the Kremlin Diamond Fund Museum."

"Is it cursed?" Mica asked.

"It may be. It was associated with many tragedies. Like Tavernier's pale-blue-white Regent Diamond of 141 carats. It's in the Louvre, now, also out of trouble."

Mica remembered her father saying that the Regent Diamond had belonged to Marie Antoinette and then to Napoleon. Tragedies for both.

"I dare say," Ben concluded, "your blue diamond reminds me of these famous treasures, and there were four other blue diamonds, all cut from the original 112-carat Grand Tavernier Blue. Two of them are in museums—the Hope Diamond, which is heart-shaped, and the Bonaparte Diamond, square. But the other two, the Grisha and the St. Petersburg disappeared during the war. Not found since."

For a moment, Mica imagined herself going to the Chain Bridge and throwing not just the blue diamond but all of her diamonds into the river.

"What happened to the Hope diamond?" Magda asked.

"It brought nothing but sorrow to the people who owned it. Tavernier sold it to Louis XIV in 1668. The Sun King died in Versailles from gangrene. The diamond went down the family line to Louis XVI, who gave it to Marie Antoinette to wear around her neck. Legends say it caused the beginning of the French Revolution. Who knows? But history does state that Marie Antoinette finished her life with the guillotine around her neck.

"Then it disappeared for two hundred years and reappeared mysteriously in London in 1830, where it was bought at an auction by Henry Philip Hope, a wealthy banker. Since then, it kept going into different hands, each time causing havoc.

"A Ziegfeld Follies star received the diamond as a present and was afterwards murdered by her lover. Then a Greek bought it and subsequently fell off a cliff with his wife and children. In 1908, it went into the hands of a Turkish collector who soon died in a shipwreck. Next, the diamond went into the hands of the Sultan of Turkey, Selim Habib, but he had to sell it when he found himself in the middle of a revolution and a sword pointed between his eyes.

"Pierre Cartier purchased the gem from the Sultan and sold it to Mr. and Mrs. McClean in 1911, the owners of the *Washington Post*. But still the blue diamond didn't carry much hope. In 1912, their son was killed by a car. Years later their daughter died of an overdose of sleeping pills. The husband finished his life insane and with cirrhosis of the liver while Mrs. McClean committed suicide after losing her entire fortune.

"In 1949, the Hope Diamond was sold to the jeweler Harry Winston, but no one wanted to buy it from him. They were afraid. People claimed it was cursed. In 1958, he ended up donating it to the Smithsonian Institution in Washington, D.C. It's there now."

"Do you believe these stories?" Mica asked Ben. "Did all of this really happen?"

"Before I started learning about the history of the diamonds, I would have said no; they're stories, legends," he answered. "But history is history, and diamonds have strange powers that I never understood until my father starting teaching Tibi and me how to cut them and understand their stories. And now, I see their stories as real, part of history."

Mica held on to the table. She thought she'd faint. "I have to sell the diamonds as soon as possible," she stammered.

"You can't sell them in Hungary," Tibi said. "They'll arrest you and confiscate the diamonds. If you can just get to New York, you'll be free to do what you want. There's practically no one here who could afford them anyway, and those who could, would kill you for even having them."

Ben was holding the blue diamond up to the light again. "Let me tell you about the second of Tavernier's diamond cut from the original, 112-carat-blue. After the Hope Diamond was the blue Bonaparte Diamond, square and forty-three carats. Tavernier sold it first to the Sultan of India in 1669 who in turn, sold it to a Japanese samurai who hid it in his sailboat on the way to Egypt. One of Napoleon's generals found it in a Pharaoh's pyramid when he and his army were there in 1798. Napoleon Bonaparte took the diamond back with him to France and embedded the jewel in his sword for his inauguration. Defying tradition, Napoleon raised his diamond sword and crowned himself emperor by taking the crown from the Pope's hands into his own. That's when Napoleon's good luck turned bad."

"Do you think that was because of the diamond?" Mica asked, horrified.

"Who knows?" Ben said, "but even after he died, the curse didn't end. The Bonaparte Diamond went to his second wife, Marie-Louise, and continued to cause misery."

"Yes?" Mica said, eager to hear that diamond's history.

"Marie-Louise was the daughter of Franz Joseph, emperor of the Austro-Hungarian Empire. Within a year Marie-Louise gave Napoleon a son, Le Roi de Rome-L'Aiglon.

"At this time, Napoleon's success was over. He started losing on the battlefield. After Waterloo, he was exiled to the island of Elba and then after that, he was exiled again to St. Helena, where he died alone and miserable.

"Marie-Louise returned to Vienna with the diamond, prying it from Napoleon's sword. She was a greedy woman.

"Misery followed the blue diamond. Her son, called the Duke of

Reichstadt by the Austrians, died in his early twenties. Some say he was poisoned by Metternich, the emperor's ambitious Foreign Minister.

"The Bonaparte Diamond stayed in Vienna with Marie-Louise until her father, the emperor, was afraid of the diamond's curse and insisted she send it back to France. But it was too late. She had already possessed the diamond. In fact, the story goes that Marie-Louise was quite possessed- she was a nymphomaniac.

"In 1821 she married General de Neipperg, an Austrian count. It seems he died from *over extension,* trying to satisfy her desires. Widowed, Marie-Louise continued to indulge in her favorite plea-sure—sex.

"One day, she was with her entourage strolling in the Viennese Woods. Admiring a young lumberjack, she approached him. 'Come with me,' she said.

"He, thinking she was a witch, crossed himself several times and ran away. Arriving at his cabin, he met his father and his five brothers. They all saw Marie-Louise running after the lumberjack. It was said that she had not only him but his entire family.

"Metternich was not happy with Marie-Louise; he exiled her to Palma. But in the sun, her activities were not curtailed. He sent an envoy, the Count de Bombelles, to survey her. She did what was good for her, seduced him and married the Count. Continuing her escapades, in 1834 she was exiled again. The Count sent her to Bad Ischl to drink the bromide waters hoping to calm her down. He posted guards to watch her. After seducing many guards, she returned home to her husband slightly calmer. One night she went to the opera. It was with a handsome tenor that she enjoyed her last song."

"Aha!" laughed Mica. "Here is a woman who started with an emperor and ended with a tenor."

Everyone laughed. Always the actress, she took the attention and pretended she was an opera singer. "Do re me fa so la ti do."

Ben smiled and turned to Mica. "I think this is maybe where your diamond comes into the story. Tavernier's other two diamonds from his original Grand Blue arrived in Moscow with Tavernier on his last voyage, just before he died in Russia. He sold them to the new czar, Peter the Great, and they went down the line of the Romanovs.

"The first one, the blue Grisha is round and weighs forty-one carats. Prince Orlov bought it as a gift for his mistress, Catherine the Great. But bored with Orlov, she ousted him from her bed, kept the gem, and found pleasure elsewhere.

"Apparently, Prince Orlov then wrote Catherine a letter informing her that the diamond had a mate—another round shaped blue diamond from Tavernier's original one. He called it the St. Petersburg Diamond, weighing thirty-nine carats. If she'd agree to take him back, he'd give her the mate. Catherine refused. She preferred her freedom to the diamond. Somehow, she got the St. Petersburg as well, anyway, and it, too, passed down to the Romanovs.

"It was Rasputin, the mystical holy man, who took center stage with the blue, St. Petersburg. Rasputin charmed his way into the Romanov's inner circle. He had his way with women, including Czarina Alexandra. Her only son, the beloved heir to the Romanov dynasty, Prince Alexis, suffered from hemophilia. The czarina blamed herself, for some reason, for having hemophilia in her family. She confessed this to Rasputin and he kept her secret."

"I can imagine how important Rasputin became," Magda commented.

Ben agreed. "What people don't know is that Rasputin had a friend, a Jewish jeweler by the name of Aaron Simanovich, who controlled him.

"They met every day in St. Isaac's Cathedral in St. Petersburg so Simanovich could coach Rasputin on how to act with the czar and czarina. Simanovich was very clever. In return for his advice,

Rasputin agreed to introduce Simanovich to the czarina and her court of friends so he could sell his jewels. The czarina had a passion for diamonds. But she was stingy and hated paying. Simanovich gave her credit and diamonds.

"Rasputin needed money to continue his debaucheries. Orgies are expensive. So he and Simanovich plotted to steal the Imperial diamonds and substitute them with imitations."

"*Imitations?* Are my diamonds fake?" Mica asked.

"Certainly not this blue on," he said, holding it up to the light to admire its brilliance.

"When the Romanovs were assassinated in Siberia, it was said that the night before, the czarina had sewn dozens of diamonds into her undergarments. When the Bolsheviks started to shoot her, their bullets ricocheted because of the diamonds. The only way to destroy the last Romanov was to shoot her in the head."

"These diamonds have really traveled," Magda commented.

"Mica," Ben said, excitedly, "it's possible that your blue diamond may be the St. Petersburg! People have been searching for it for decades!"

Mica's head was spinning. "For as long as I can remember, my father had the diamonds buried in our basement. He got them all from my uncle who got them from a jeweler. How the jeweler got them, I don't know."

Mica turned to Magda and asked, "What should I do?"

Ben answered for his sister. "I could appraise the green and blue diamonds in my lab at the institute, where I have more powerful instruments. I believe the nine-carat green one is an original Tavernier, though slightly flawed."

"And the blue diamond?" Mica asked, hardly breathing.

"It's possible it's also a Tavernier. The St. Petersburg! But I can't be certain. I need stronger instruments. Yet I'm afraid to take these diamonds to the institute or even try to get a second opinion. What if someone at the State Institute sees me with them?"

She understood. "No. I don't want you to get into trouble because of me."

"But you have to keep the diamonds for New York," Ben agreed. "Sell them there. We'll give you the names of trustworthy jewelers we know who have immigrated to New York. You must sell them as quickly as you can, so you can end the bad luck. Use the money to do good! The good will stop the bad. Remember that."

Magda put her arm around Mica. "I'll help you too, until your visa comes through."

"We'll take you to the airport," Tibi added.

"My bodyguards," Mica said, trying to sound pleased. She buried her father's small leather pouch of diamonds in her bra, near her heart. "Let me take all the diamonds with me and think about what to do."

"Be careful where you hide them," Ben warned. "They're very valuable!"

"Yes," Tibi agreed. "Remember history—people have been killed because of diamonds."

CHAPTER 14

DURING MICA'S third month at the embassy, Neal Bridge approached her with an idea: "How would you like to join a class to improve your English and learn about America?"

Her huge smile said it all. Her words, too, were tinged with joy: "Oh yes, please! I'd love to."

"We'll meet three times a week during lunch in the embassy library with three other students who have also applied for visas and who help us out in the consular division. Redzep comes from Serbia, Attie from Bulgaria, and Milos is Czech. I'll teach you about American culture and history as well as practical hints about business, lawyers, and things you'll need to know to adapt to a new world. You don't mind homework, do you?" he asked.

She laughed. "Not at all. I love to learn about everything!" She could only imagine being able to speak English as elegantly as Mr. Bridge. And with his American accent.

That Tuesday at noon, she went eagerly to the library. She had been waiting all morning. Mr. Bridge had arranged for them to have sandwiches during class-time, and the five of them sat on chairs opposite each other at the large refectory table that looked so much like the table in the Bartha brothers' laboratory. Mr. Bridge had taken off his glasses, and Mica noticed he looked younger without them—and more handsome.

"You speak with a British accent," he said to Mica. "Let me see if I can help you soften your accent so you won't stand out. You also roll your *r's*." He picked up some papers and handed them to his students. "We'll start each session with a pronunciation drill and work on phonetics. Repeat after me: *running.*"

"*R-Running ...*"

"No, Mica, you're still rolling your *r's*. Again, until it's perfect...."

Mr. Bridge was a strict master. After each lesson, he gave the students an assignment, which Mica eagerly worked on at night, tucked into her little room next to the infirmary. She felt energized, with a sense of purpose to absorb everything Mr. Bridge taught them.

One day, he asked the group to write about a person they disliked or who had frightened them. By the next session, Mica was prepared with several paragraphs, and her teacher suggested that she read it aloud. "The most difficult thing when speaking English is to know where to put the stress on the word. To get the rhythm of a phrase. Language is like music," he explained.

She began reading: "The chief of the *securitate*..." She stopped, put her paper down. *I don't know if I should read this aloud,* she thought. She worried he might realize she had cooperated with the secret police.

But he motioned for her to continue.

"My friend told me this story and while she was telling me, the chief frightened me. It happened to my friend years ago. The chief of the secret Police took a pair of pliers, attached it to her pinky..." Mica stopped reading and rubbed her finger.

Bridge stood up. "That's enough. Good intonation, Mica."

Looking uncomfortable, he went to his espresso machine to

make himself a cup of coffee. "Let's go on to the next. Redzep, please read us yours."

Redzep stood. As he read, Mica studied Bridge's face, and she couldn't help but notice the dramatic contrast between the two men. Redzep's face was all wrinkled, and he was only in his twenties. Mr. Bridge didn't have a line on his face. She wondered how old he was. Thirty-five?

Bridge looked at Mica with an odd expression on his face, and she glanced down at her work before looking up and meeting his eye again. His eyes stopped at her thighs before he walked away. She looked down to see if her skirt had slid up.

"Sir," Milos said, "my paragraph is about an art dealer who frightened me. I'm a sculptor. He told me strange things, like artists in America have to be businessmen to sell their art. Is that true?"

"I'm sorry to say there's a lot of truth in that."

Milos continued. "Sir, can you tell us how someone can make money from art in America? I wish to learn how I'd be able to sell my sculptures."

"A good start is an exhibit or at being taken by a gallery. The best, once you're well known, is at auction."

"What's an auction?"

"An entrepreneurial way of selling precious art or antique furniture or a rare item. It's a little like the theater."

The mere mention of the theater made Mica smile.

"In a large room of an auction house," Bridge explained, "there's the auctioneer, who directs the show. He has a valuable sculpture or painting or expensive piece of jewelry for sale…."

"Like a diamond?" Mica interrupted.

"Yes," Bridge smiled, as if pleased by her vivid imagination. "The auctioneer starts with a value for, say, a diamond, and then people in the audience bid against each other for the gem until everyone has offered their final price. The one who gives the highest bid becomes the buyer."

Mica listened intently, holding on to his every word, storing them for the moment she'd sell her diamonds in New York and use the money to get her parents to America.

"Are there a lot of auctions in the States?" Milos asked.

"I don't know about every city. New York City has two main auction houses, Sotheby's and Christie's."

Mica made a mental note of the two names.

"Can anyone auction a piece of art?" Milos asked.

"Yes, if it's accepted by the auction house. Then everything proceeds legally."

Mica listened intently, but she couldn't help noticing that Mr. Bridge looked so much younger when he smiled. He was so good looking, tall and elegant, with his wavy, blond hair and blue eyes. She thought that when he was relaxed, he was really charming. She felt a tingling sensation flutter through her body and her face blushed and heated up.

Mica turned to Mr. Bridge, as if he and she were the only two people in the room. "I once had a book about New York...." She lowered her eyes. "I used to caress the pages and pretend I could touch the entire island of Manhattan with my hands. It's that book that gave me the courage to escape."

She stopped talking, realizing she had said something too personal and that it wasn't related to an auction house. All four men were staring at her.

Bridge put on his glasses, stood up, and walked a few paces away. After an awkward silence, he turned to the blackboard and wrote two words on the board in chalk:

AUCTION. BOOK.

"Your next homework assignment is to take these two words

that Mica just referred to, and write a paragraph about what the words mean to you."

"Can you give us an example?" Redzep asked.

"I just read something in the morning newspapers," Bridge said. "It was something like this. Valuable books can also be sold at auctions. Recently, a book of photos never seen before about Auschwitz has been found and will go on auction in Berlin. Some of the photos were taken by S.S. soldiers to show how their leaders, Rudolf Hess and Dr. Josef Mengele, lived in the concentration camp. End of paragraph."

Mica raised her hand, trying to compose herself as she asked her question. "If we wrote a paragraph like that, should we give a little background information, like, say who Dr. Mengele is?"

Mr. Bridge shrugged. "If you wish."

Attie raised his hand. "My mother was a nurse during the war. She was taken from her pediatric hospital in Sofia because she spoke German. Mengele needed a nurse and translator for Bulgarian children he was experimenting on." Attie paused, and then he shouted, "Mengele was a monster! Once he ordered three hundred children to be killed by throwing them into a bonfire. When one child crawled out of the pit, he took his riding stick and pushed the child back into the flames. All the children were less than five years old. This is true! This is true, I know, I know!" Attie said, looking down as he spoke.

After a few seconds, Attie calmed down, and Bridge addressed the group. "The newspaper article I read said that the American government has been searching for Dr. Mengele. I hope he will be found and punished."

No one in the class said a word. Mr. Bridge walked over to the window, stared outside, ashamed, and Mica closed her eyes. She felt nauseous. Her diamonds. From Auschwitz. She wished she didn't need them. She wished she'd never had them.

CHAPTER 15

WINTER TURNED to spring as Mica worked in the clinic, serving as translator and liaison for the hopeful political refugees. One afternoon, she was assisting a middle-aged Romanian man who wore a black eye patch over his left eye and had a limp. Mica asked, "Did you hurt your leg and eye while escaping?"

"No," he answered, rubbing his right calf muscle. "Happened to me during the war."

Mica immediately felt uncomfortable. Most Romanians who had fought during the war had fought alongside the Germans.

"Oh," she mumbled, walking toward the door, but before she could open it, he moved closer to her and inquired, "You're Romanian?"

"*Da, da,* yes, *sunt Romanca.* I'm Romanian," she answered.

"From your accent, I'd say you're from Transylvania."

She didn't reply, not wanting to give him any more information, but he wanted to talk. "I escaped several days ago from Bucharest," he told her. "It's hell there. Ceausescu has already let loose his secret police. They're arresting everyone whose loyalty to him is doubtful."

This man was a fascist, Mica thought, which meant the communists were after him.

"I hate Ceausescu," the Romanian said. "But I agree with him on one point—our country's in a mess because of the Jews!"

Mica eyed a nearby lamp in the waiting room and considered hitting him over the head with it.

"Now Ceausescu wants to *sell* them!" He laughed. "Well, that's one way of getting rid of them. Not the first time! They were sold before—after the war."

"*Sell* them?" Now she was interested.

"Yes, for tractors. He wants to dry up the Danube marshes and plant wheat there. One Jew for one tractor. Who needs Jews anyway?"

"How do you know this?" She was angry that Jews had been persecuted for centuries; and yet, she was curious to learn more. Perhaps, she'd be able to exchange her parents for tractors?

"I was a professor at the University of Bucharest when I was younger. I was the fascist supervisor for students," he said and laughed again—like a devil. When he opened his mouth, she noticed he was missing three of his front teeth.

"You're just saying these things to make yourself sound important."

"I had a lot of power twenty-five years ago," he bragged. "I organized Romanian students to attack Jewish students. One day, we followed the dirty kikes home as they ran away, like scared rats. We forced ourselves into the house of one student, who had a beautiful sister." The man rubbed his leg, then pointed to his eye patch. "Dirty kike put a knife in my eye and leg when I grabbed his sister, but my lieutenant shot them both."

I wish I had a knife to poke out your other eye, Mica thought.

"Wait!" he said to her as she opened the door to leave. "Can I have another slice of bread?"

"No!" She slammed the door as hard as she could.

Mica thought about reporting the man to Mr. Bridge. The rules were clear: if someone was a member of the fascist party, they weren't allowed to enter the United States. But terrified of starting a scandal or investigation, she vacillated. She didn't want to be called as a witness. It could take time. She had to get to America.

She returned to the X-ray room, where several other patients were waiting. As she prepared their charts, she overheard the same one-eyed devil talking to another refugee, a man younger than him, a Bulgarian, who looked like an intellectual with thin wire-framed eyeglasses.

"Now that Ceausescu is the big leader," the Romanian said to his new friend, "he's committing more crimes. Going to get Romania in trouble with the entire world."

"What d' ya mean?" the Bulgarian asked, taking off his glasses and rubbing his bald head.

"Ceausescu has a new ally: Arafat. And to make him happy, Ceausescu has set up a training camp in the Carpathian Mountains to train Palestinian terrorists. He teaches them military tactics, even how to be suicide bombers. Human bombs—never done before. All in our own backyard!" he yelled.

"Shh, not so loud," the younger refugee whispered. "Sounds like secrets."

Mica walked over to them. She had a choice: tell them to leave the clinic; or stop talking and bothering the other patients; or—she —to become part of their conversation. Curious to learn more about what they were saying, for the information could help her strategize her parents' release, she rationalized that she'd join them.

Mica approached the two men and asked the Romanian, "Why would Ceausescu and Arafat become friends?"

He stared at her, surprised at her presence and interest, and also, flattered by her attention. He lowered his voice and explained, "Ceausescu started working with Arafat by offering him planes to train his PLOs, which Ceausescu bought for him from France. Puma helicopters that fly at night and Alouette copters that fly at high altitudes."

"I guess so he could use them secretly in the Carpathian Mountains," the Bulgarian added.

"Yes," the Romanian professor said. "France's President, Giscard d'Estaing, didn't care who bought them. He was only interested in getting the money so he could improve the French economy and win the election. When the PLOs needed instructors to teach their men how to fly the planes, Ceausescu supplied that, too. He set up a language school in the mountains with translators who speak Romanian and Arabic."

The Romanian professor realized Mica was attentive, so he went on. "Ceausescu has other tricks. He invites thousands of Iranian students to study in Romania." He moved closer to Mica. "They study engineering and learn how to build nuclear sites. They study biology and become experts in chemical warfare. In return, Iran allows Ceausescu to hide his gold in their vaults. He trusts their secrecy more than Swiss banks."

"And who pays for Ceausescu's dirty business?" Mica asked. "Iran?"

"No—Libya! Colonel Muammar Gaddafi! Libya has the largest oil reserves in Africa. Gaddafi turns oil into gold. He has to spend his billions somehow. He likes Ceausescu. Calls him *my brother*."

"I wish it weren't true," Mica said, looking down.

"But it is! Ceausescu works with terrorists like Gaddafi and Arafat."

"My God!" the Bulgarian shouted. "What will the world say?"

"They'll never know. And there's more." The Romanian was pleased with his captivated audience. He moved closer to Mica who was now actively involved in the conversation and explained: "Ceausescu had one of his agents steal blueprints from the Germans so he could build nuclear centrifuges. Then he built an institute of Atomic Physics in Magurele, ten miles from Bucharest, and put his son, an engineer, in charge. Also, he set up a nuclear power plant in Cernavoda."

The Romanian laughed, clearly enjoying the fact that he had shocked Mica. "Ceausescu does business also with Iraq's Saddam Hussein," he continued. "Sells him special bullets filled with chemicals that are produced in three of Romania's weapon factories. Ceausescu tells everyone that the factories build bikes and tools." He laughed. "Saddam is getting ready to use the chemicals. He hates the Kurds."

Mica was transfixed by these stories, even if they were horrifying.

A patient tapped her on the shoulder to ask a question. She jumped, surprised, and for a second, she was brought back to her duty in the clinic. "I'll be with you in a moment," she told the new patient, and moved away from the Romanian professor.

Now she had a dilemma: what should she do with the information she had heard?

Not only was the Romanian professor a fascist, but he apparently knew a lot about Ceausescu—information the American government would like to have. *Do I dare tell Mr. Bridge what I've heard?* she thought. *Would he believe me? Maybe the stories aren't true. After all, the Romanian hates the communists. Maybe he's just making it all up for attention.* But, in her heart, Mica believed every word he had just told her. She knew Ceausescu would do anything to get more and more money, even if it meant inventing a new type of war: terrorism.

MICA LOOKED FORWARD TO HER ENGLISH AND CITIZENSHIP CLASSES. She enjoyed the camaraderie of the other refugees, but most of all, she loved learning from Neal Bridge. In awe of the range and seemingly endless scope of his knowledge, she asked him one question after another and waited eagerly for his response.

She loved listening to him, watching him move to the blackboard, using his entire body to write sentences on it. But too often, even outside of class, she found herself daydreaming about him. She kept reminding herself that Mr. Bridge's role was to protect her, nothing more. Yet, her being attracted to him made her realize that there were two sides of her character: one of the mind and one of the heart. She knew they struggled against each other. Yet, the articles they read in class and their discussions united her to him, bringing them closer. Each lesson became a soldier in Mica's private war to conquer the West. Each topic of study was a battle, and she was determined to learn as much as she could. Mr. Bridge was her lieutenant, albeit unwittingly, advising her on strategy, warning her of rocky terrain.

Mica couldn't help but profit from her lieutenant, as generals often do. She was allowing him to guide her, but she had to keep herself in check. Intuitively, she understood that liking Mr. Bridge, even romanticizing him, was acceptable. That was her secret, one she couldn't reveal. Above all, she didn't want to get him angry, which was why she decided not to tell him what she'd heard about Ceausescu and his partners, Gaddafi and Arafat. She rationalized to herself that she had no proof that the Romanian refugee's words were even true.

After the Romanian had passed his medical exam, he stayed in the embassy for several days to complete his visa application and have them reviewed. Mica avoided him as best she could because she didn't like him, but he and the Bulgarian often spent time talking to other refugees waiting in the clinic.

One afternoon, she heard the Romanian refugee speaking of more horrible things to his friend about Ceausescu. She listened, frightened. She had decided not to stop them from such talk, and not ask them to leave. Instead, she moved closer to them and joined their conversation, again. She rationalized that she was working in the clinic and was responsible to know what people were saying there. In reality, she was curious, and wondered how far the Romanian professor would go with sharing his information.

"Several days ago," the Bulgarian began, "you started to say something about stolen blueprints to build nuclear centrifuges. I'm an engineer. I know a little about the subject."

The one-eyed Romanian blinked with his good eye. "With the help of my brother-in-law, Hamad, who speaks Arabic and German, and is a translator for the Romanian government, I've learned secrets few will ever see."

He pointed to his good eye and moved closer to Mica to show off his knowledge and impress her. "My brother-in-law translated some documents. He told me that Ceausescu began the scheme by infiltrating one of his secret agents, an engineer, to work in Germany for URENCO, a multinational nuclear fuel company known for its ultra-fast Degussa centrifuges. That man stole the blueprints of those centrifuges for Ceausescu."

The Bulgarian shook his head. "I heard a scientist from Pakistan, Dr. Khan, did something similar. Bought blueprints for centrifuges from someone senior at URENCO's office in the Netherlands when he was working there, and then returned to Pakistan with a Dutch wife and the blueprints. Became the father of Pakistan's nuclear bomb."

"How frightening are these stories about spies and secrets," Mica commented.

The Romanian eyed her. "They're not stories. It's true that high-speed centrifuges are needed to enrich uranium to atomic levels. Ceausescu manufactures them in a nuclear facility near the Danube River-Black Sea canal."

"Are you sure about all this?" she asked.

"Yes. I told you: my brother-in-law has access. He had to translate this information from Ceausescu's group to Arafat's. From Romanian to Arabic."

The engineer moved closer to them. "I hear Romania has natural uranium from Moldova, near the Russian border."

"You're right. Natural uranium is needed for high-speed centrifuges to make nuclear material." The cyclops was proud of showing off his knowledge.

"Not only natural uranium, but heavy water is also needed to create nuclear weapons. It's a rare fluid, serves as a coolant, and is not easy to produce." He nodded his head. "My brother-in-law was involved with another document. Could be major news one day—Norway has a plant that produces heavy water. The Norwegians wanted to sell some to India, but that's illegal. So Ceausescu, for a hefty fee, diverted fourteen tons that originated in Norway to Romania. Said it's Romanian and shipped it to India."

"It's true, India has nuclear facilities," the Bulgarian said, breathing deeply. "Imagine if the Western world learned about Ceausescu's business deals. He has created a global bazaar and black market for nuclear technology. And not only for India. Arafat supplies a long list of clients and Gaddafi is the banker. I once heard Ceausescu say on TV, 'I want to be the first in everything.' Too bad for Romania, he'll be the first to market terrorism."

"Yes," the professor agreed. "Nuclear business takes years to build up in any country. Terrorism will grow and the world will never know that Ceausescu was the one who started it all."

"He's evil, and his banker-partner, Gaddafi, is the devil as well."

"You're right," the Romanian agreed. "Yet Gaddafi fascinates me."

"True, he's an enigma. Some people say he's crazy. That he masquerades himself with white pancake make-up, black sunglasses, large emerald rings on his fingers, and surrounds himself with several beautiful women. Says they're his bodyguards."

"My brother-in-law said he's not crazy at all. Claims his memos are very astute. He's a military man. He even created with Ceausescu a new kind of warfare, using chemical and bacteriological weapons. The code name of the operation is Brutus—from the disease, brucellosis, which the chemicals produce. He told me this venture earned Ceausescu $350 million in cash, paid by his banker, Colonel el-Gaddafi, the richest man in Africa."

Mica stared at both men and then shooed them away.

CHAPTER 16

"Are you going to the Easter party tonight?" Mica asked Magda.

"Of course! Ben and Tibi are also invited. There's going to be music and dancing. Gypsy musicians too. I hope you're planning to come along."

"I don't know... I'm not sure," Mica said, feeling embarrassed. "I have nothing to wear."

"Don't you worry about that, dear. I have a perfect skirt for you, Gypsy-style, and some bracelets made of bells. I even have a Gypsy coin belt. I'm getting a little old for them myself. You should take them."

"Really?" Mica asked, pleased. "You know those white cotton scarves in the supply room you sometimes use with the gauze bandages?"

"Of course."

"Do you think I can have a few for tonight? They'll make me look more like a Gypsy."

"Sure. Take as many as you like."

The nurse returned to her paperwork, too busy to ask Mica why she wanted the sheer, fabric-y bandages.

"Can I play the naï tonight?" Mica asked her. "I've been practicing a lot. In sweet music is such art, killing care and grief of heart."

"Do you have another reason?" She gave Mica a warning look.

"Well… I'd like to play it while I dance. You know I love dancing."

"Yes… *and?*"

"I've always fantasized I could be a great dancer one day. George Szabo even told me that dancing is not only about your legs, but also your heart and mind."

"Yes, yes, and so?"

"Sometimes I feel all bottled up. Dancing sets me free. That's why I was so happy dancing with the high school students."

"Yes." The nurse heard a ring on the phone and left Mica to answer it. When she returned, still distracted, she told Mica, "After I finish with these test results, I want to do your hair. It's grown in beautifully. With your thick black curls and high cheekbones against your fair complexion, everyone will think you're exotic."

"Do you think Mr. Bridge will be okay with that?"

Magda stared at Mica. "Why do you ask?"

"What I mean to ask is, do you think he'll like it?"

"Mica!" she yelled. "What are you getting at?"

"It's just that he's been so good to me, teaching me, and allowing the students to have the dancing party. I want to please him." Mica didn't dare admit that whenever she was with Mr. Bridge, she felt a tingling sensation throughout her body.

"Don't please him too much! He's a respectable married man." The nurse picked up a chart and waved it at Mica, as if in warning.

"What's his wife like?" Mica asked, curious. "I've seen her a few times, but I was too shy to talk to her."

"She intimidated me too, in the beginning."

"Do they have children?" Everything about Neal Bridge fascinated Mica.

"No."

"Does she work?"

"She's a psychoanalyst. She doesn't have a formal practice, what with living in one country after another, but whenever there's an American who contacts the embassy with a serious emotional problem, she helps."

"What's a psychoanalyst exactly?" But before the nurse could answer, Mica continued, "I don't understand Americans. Is it true, they're obsessed with feeling good?"

"Well, I don't know about that. Not all Americans are alike. I only know those who work here. You can't generalize."

"If a Romanian wants to feel good, there's always a glass of wine and some romance."

"Mica, don't talk like that," Magda said, losing her patience.

Mica thought her mother would have reacted the same way.

"You're barely eighteen. Enough of this silly chatter, mademoiselle. Let me show you how I want to arrange your hair, and then I'll go home to get the clothes for you." She gave Mica a hand mirror so she could admire her new hairstyle.

"*Love-ly,*" Mica sang, and danced a two-step. Then she became more thoughtful. "Can you do me another favor?" She had an idea about how she could use the evening's event to her benefit. She felt she needed to win over Mr. Bridge completely to ensure her visa, for Dr. Ingel could learn anytime about her past as a child spy, even if she had only spied for two days. She wasn't happy about scheming, but she feared there might be some records in Romania about her past activities. Someone could find it, if they were asked to search.

"Depends." The nurse eyed her with blatant suspicion.

"I want to perform. Play the flute, your naï, maybe dance. Please, I want to prepare the stage in a special way."

"I hope you're not going to fill the auditorium with flowers and wine."

"No, Mrs. Bridge would think I'm crazy." Mica laughed. "Would you make an announcement before dinner, that there'll be a show?"

"What kind of show?" The nurse was concerned. "I'm not sure you should do this."

"No, please; it'll be exciting. Remember, in Romania I was an actress. And, you know, an actress loves to play many roles."

"I'm sure it will be entertaining. Just what's needed to add something different, but don't say I gave you carte blanche."

Mica smiled triumphantly; she didn't know what carte blanche meant, but she liked how it sounded—dramatic.

George Szabo approached, interrupting their chatter. "*Szia. Jonavot kivanok.* Hello. Good morning, ladies. I have some more magazines for you, Mica."

"Oh, thank you." She eagerly took the small bundle from his hands.

"From my sister," he said. "She's a ballet teacher at the Juilliard School in New York City. That's the best school for music and dance."

"Really? Your sister?" Mica's face beamed. "I've seen pictures of dance recitals from Juilliard in several of your magazines."

Szabo smiled.

"I'll tell you a secret," Mica whispered, moving closer to him. "Tonight, I'm going to play the flute and dance at the Easter show. Something I've been thinking about for a while."

"Good. A self-choreography," he said. "I just received a gift from my sister—a movie camera. She sent it to me with her friend who's dancing here in Budapest with a special exchange program. How about I take a movie of you dancing to show my sister how happy I am with her gift? I can give it to her friend before she leaves."

"Oh, thanks so much," and then Mica turned to Magda. "Please don't tell anyone yet that I'm going to dance."

"Why not?" Then the nurse gave her one of her maternal looks of warning. "I think there are more facets to you than I realized."

Mica smiled brightly.

As soon as the nurse and Mr. Szabo left the clinic, Mica gathered what she needed for her performance. She removed a dozen scarves from the supply closet, then she went to the embassy's air raid shelter and took an armful of candles fixed upright in short glass jars. Then she went to her room to get her most important prop: the naï.

That evening at the reception, Mica watched as the American ambassador raised a glass to his guests and welcomed them to the embassy.

"Ladies and gentlemen, tonight is our annual Easter party," Bridge announced. "We're going to mix American and Hungarian customs in celebration of the friendship between our countries. In addition to our traditional American Easter egg hunt, we'll have Hungarian Gypsy music and dancing."

Then Magda fulfilled her promise, although her words came out hesitantly. "Attention. Attention!" Ringing a bell from the top of the stairs, she said to the crowd, "We have a surprise. Something different. If you pass to the auditorium, you're going to see a show!"

Bridge eyed the nurse, but she avoided his questioning stare. Buzzing and clearly curious, everyone moved into the auditorium, where Mica was waiting. She had dimmed the chandelier and lined the three sides of the stage with jars of flaming candles, which gave the stage an appearance of being suspended in the middle of fire.

She went to the back door of the auditorium and reentered, walking down the center aisle and playing the flute. People turned to see her and then looked all around the room as if to find the notes of music that sounded like birds in flight.

Mica climbed the steps to the stage. The candles' flames shone against her bare legs and sparkled the colored sequins of her short Gypsy skirt. Her chest was draped with white sheer scarves and revealed a shadow of her chiseled breasts, which pointed firm in the flaming light. In her hair, were several strands of thin veils, that floated in the air when she moved.

She danced on stage like a thin layer of white that glided freely. The audience gasped, fearful that her mist of fabric was coming too close to the flaming candles. Szabo was filming.

Mica was barefoot, with a string of bells on each ankle. Around her hips, the belt of golden coins chimed as she swayed. She moved to the corner of the stage, picked up her flute, and blew into the reed.

Vibrating from the walls came the sounds of running horses, faster and louder. Once again, not really animals, but only Mica's flute. She played on, her musical notes creating more and more images, her music chiming her story of flight and fear.

A group of Gypsy musicians walked on stage to join her. The clarinetist echoed the sound of her flute; the accordionist played trembling chords; several violinists plucked staccato beats. Sounds of birds flapping their wings became stronger. Horses seemed to gallop from the walls in a passionate trot. Mica could sense the aura of mystery had captivated the room. The buzz, the passion.

The musicians surrounded Mica in a circle as she danced, faster and faster, to their rhythm. She put down her flute and freed her hands. When she raised her arms, the scarves spread apart, like wings, showing bare skin.

The violinists moved closer and played to her feverish pace. The candles glowed brighter. Mica untied a scarf from her hair, picked up a candle, put the flame to the veil, and danced while holding the flames. Fire spread to her fingers and she puffed the red flame away.

She danced around a candle and tore a scarf from her waist. She held the fabric to the flame and paused as fire ignited the thin veil, creating a blazing torch. She pulled off another scarf from her chest, and held it while flames burned the air. Possessed by fire and losing control, she ripped off another scarf and then another. Flames soared and Mica danced faster as the music roared amidst the red blaze.

Overcome by the surge of her own emotions, she didn't realize her breasts were fully bare. The audience, entranced by the beauty of her body, stood up and clapped to the beat of her dancing. The Gypsy musicians played louder. The walls vibrated with their song. Music filled the room. Passion filled the air.

Several young people moved to the aisle and danced to the music's rhythm. Raising their arms, swaying their hips and jumping with excitement, they danced as if the music was inside them. A young man took off his shirt and swung the white fabric in the air near the flaming candles.

For one second, Mica's eyes focused on her surroundings; she saw that Neal Bridge was standing up and clapping along with the crowd. Encouraged by his interest, and unable to control herself, she danced on and on as three Hungarians in the audience jumped on stage to join her. Each one took a candle and raised their flame toward her bare breasts.

The musicians played on in a wild frenzy. Dancers clapped their hands and cheered madly. The melody evoked desire until passion took Mica beyond her limits and she felt her soul emanating fire. She raised both arms above her head and danced, abandoning all restraint, not realizing anymore where she was or what was happening. Music and fire blended as one, and Mica, possessed, danced to the beat of her heart.

Two musicians took a chair from the stage and placed her there, then, raising her high, they swayed her in the air. The candles blazing below, she above, and tension everywhere.

"Stop!" Mr. Bridge yelled, almost panting. "Stop!"

Mica slipped off the chair and fell into the arms of the men.

The violinists stopped playing. The ambassador mounted the stage —and stared at Mica's bare breasts. He told the musicians to cover her with one of their jackets.

"Bravo!" yelled the crowd. They were still dancing and Mica shyly nodded her head in appreciation. But she saw that Bridge was not happy with her. His cold stare awakened her to what she had done. She had embarrassed him and herself.

Michael Ingel walked over to Bridge and patted him on the back. The doctor took the ambassador's arm, and eyeing Mica, led his friend away. She saw Michael Ingel whisper something to Bridge, and the ambassador appeared surprised. She wondered what the doctor had said.

Mica was also worried about something else. She had hidden her boots with their diamond heels and soles, but had forgotten to hide her bra. Not wanting to wear it while she danced, she left it in her closet. And now, she was furious with herself for letting her guard down. She had been too preoccupied planning her dance performance and should have hidden her bra better!

She wanted to run to get it, but first she had to put on her clothes. As she finished getting dressed behind the stage, Magda and her brothers greeted her. Then came smiling Redzep, Milos and Attie, and even a group of her Hungarian teenaged dancing partners. They were all congratulating her.

"Brava! You have music and dancing in your blood," Ben said kissing her flaming cheeks.

George Szabo joined them. "Mica, that was beautiful! What passion! What talent you have! A free interpretation of modern dance. I filmed it all. I can't wait to get it to my sister!"

Mica smiled and thanked him, and thanked the others who were surrounding her with praise.

Then Sybil Bridge, the ambassador's wife, walked over to the group. She glared at Mica. Yet, forcing herself to be diplomatic, she introduced herself. "I'm Sybil Bridge. Your dance reminded me of Salomé's dance of the seven veils."

Mica smiled.

"Strauss would have loved to have seen your interpretation. When you get to the States, you should pursue a dancing career. You have great talent."

"Thank you, Madame," Mica said, and curtsied. "That's my dream. I pray I'll have good luck and find the right teacher."

Mrs. Bridge turned her back on Mica and addressed her husband, who was approaching the group. "Neal, don't you think this girl has the making of a dancer?"

"Absolutely," he answered, adjusting his bow tie and rubbing his neck. "Mica has not only talent but an intuitive timing. She'll succeed in whatever she chooses with her willpower."

"Oh, Neal," his wife laughed, but it sounded like a grunt. "Always the philosopher."

He seemed to force a smile and appear nonchalant. Then he turned to ask Mica, "Did you train formally in dance?"

"Oh, no. I acted in the theater. Sometimes there was a dance in the play; that's when I felt I was coming alive."

"Yes, right." He avoided her eyes. "You've told me you enjoy Shakespeare."

"Shakespeare?" interjected Sybil. She raised her arms and in a stilted theatrical fashion, recited, "All the world's a stage and one man in his lifetime, plays many parts."

Mica applauded.

Encouraged, Sybil continued her monologue. "We are such stuff as dreams are made on.

"One day we should discuss Shakespeare," Sybil said. "Neal, don't you have a book in the library about Shakespearean actors?"

"Yes, but I don"t think Mica is quite up to Shakespeare right now." He turned to Mica, "Why don't you excuse yourself and help me bring some appetizers to our guests?"

His voice had a forced, civil tone. Mica followed him to the buffet table.

"Mica," he said, as he placed some food on his plate. "You could have set fire to the embassy."

"I'm so sorry," she answered, reacting to his rigid body language and cold voice. She wished she could make him understand her passionate nature. "I just wanted to celebrate escaping Romania. Sometimes I have a fury inside me and I must control it. I feel that I have two parts that live inside me."

He didn't let her finish. "It's okay, it's okay," he said. "If you're interested in seeing the book my wife was talking about after dinner, I can show it to you in the library."

"Yes," Mica whispered, excited at the prospect of spending a few minutes alone with him.

CHAPTER 17

MICA WAS ABOUT to go to her room when she was stopped by Radu, the chauffeur. During her three months living in the embassy, she had been so busy working that she had rarely seen him. When he approached her now, she wished he'd continue to stay away from her.

"*Buna seara.* Good evening," he said in Romanian before switching to German, *"Guten Abend, Fräulein, wie geht's?"* He clicked his heels together as if to appear gallant.

Mica was in a rush; she had to change into her bra and boots. She had already left them alone too long while dancing and chatting. "Why do you speak German?" she asked, trying to leave the dining room.

"I admire Deutschland!" he shot back. "I learned a lot from the Germans."

She noticed he was sweating and out of breath. "What have you been doing?"

"What have *you* been doing? Look at yourself."

"I'[m sweating because I was dancing hard."

"I was doing hard work too—*something secret.*" He winked with sly malice. "Why don't we have a drink of vodka and toast to what we both do? *Hard work and secret.*"

Raising his gloved hand, he signaled to the waiter.

"I'm in a rush, and sorry, I don't like vodka."

"It's not friendly of you to refuse to drink with me." His eyes had a chilling look. She moved back to keep a distance.

The waiter came over to them. Radu took a glass. After he gulped his drink down, she asked him, "Don't you ever take off your gloves?"

"I had an accident six years ago and my hands got burned."

Suddenly, through the haze of smoke in the room, Mica saw the Romanian train from when she was an eleven-year-old-"newsboy." She remembered the chase. One of the Romanians had jumped off the train, having touched some wires, and his hands were in flames. Someone on the train had told Mica the man had important information he was guarding, and that he was trying to run away. She heard the man yelling in German, *"Geld! Diamant!"*

Another person on the train said the man who burned his hands was working for both the German Nazis and Romanian fascists. Now she realized why Radu looked familiar. He was the man on the train! How could she have forgotten where she'd seen before those gold teeth and burned hands?

"Mica," Radu said, interrupting her thoughts, "you're my friend. *Meine freundin.* You saved my life when the terrorists tried to blow up my car. Maybe you like me a little?" He winked at her again and when he smiled, light reflected on his gold teeth. "I don't think your diplomat friend appreciates you like I do," he said.

"He's not my friend! He's the American ambassador for the United States."

"Sure, sure, whatever you say. I know he can help you."

Mica looked into his leering face and wondered: was it possible Radu knew she had diamonds?

"I can help you, too."

"I don't need your help."

"Well, maybe you do. We had a visitor earlier. I was alone here, so I let him in. He asked for Dr. Ingel, who I fetched. I saw the man give the doctor a letter. It's on the ambassador's desk, now."

"Radu," she said, trying hard to control her fear about the letter. "I've seen a lot in my short life. I can appreciate a man like you."

He laughed, sensing he was getting the upper hand.

"Has Mr. Bridge read the letter yet?"

"It's still on his desk. I guess the evening's show distracted him." Radu looked straight into her eyes. "It's just a matter of time until he reads it."

Trying not to show her mounting anger, Mica smiled at him. "So, did you see my dance?"

"Not all of it. I was doing some extra work—to help my future. But I did sneak in for a second. How about giving me a private show?"

"*Private?*" She was annoyed at his question.

Insulted, he raised his gloved hand. "I can be as much use to you as Mr. Bridge!"

"Excuse me," she said disdainfully, waving her hand in the air as she dismissed him. "I have to go."

"Don't think you're smarter than me!" As Mica walked away, Radu raised his voice. "I'll get even with you! But first, I'm going to drink tonight with my buddies to celebrate my good fortune." He laughed as she ran away.

Mica wanted to return to her room, but she reasoned she should first see if Mr. Bridge had read the letter. If Mr. Bridge read the letter, maybe it was about her being a spy.

She went to his office and hid behind the door, while checking to see if he or anyone else was there. Then, she tiptoed inside. The room was dark, but accustomed to getting by with little light from life in Romania, she didn't need to put on a lamp. She quickly spotted the white envelope on the black desk. It was unopened.

She took from her purse her small flashlight that she had used to escape Romania. The light was bright enough to read some of the writing inside through the white envelope. Taking the letter, she tried to make out the dark-printed words. She stopped when she read, *"Be careful. The girl worked a brief time for the communists as a spy at the age of eleven. This report is preliminary and has to be followed up. I don't have enough information yet for a decision. Until then, the status of her visa should be reexamined until we can determine what her activities were."*

She returned the envelope to its place on the desk. Suddenly, she felt a tap on her shoulder.

Laughing like the devil was Radu. "It's because of you I was thrown out of the clinic to become a porter!"

Mica dropped her flashlight, picked it up, and ran away.

Passing the library, she stopped to see if Mr. Bridge was there, as he had promised. From behind the door, she secretly watched as he studied a row of records on the shelf. He took one out from its cover and placed it on the record player's turntable. Then he walked to the bookshelf to look for Shakespeare's plays. Unaware he was being watched, he picked up a book and read Romeo's lines aloud, "Alas, that love, so gentle in its view, should be so tyrannous and rough in proof."

As he was turning the page, Mica quietly appeared behind him and recited, "Love that has a tyrannous beginning has a tyrannous end."

Flustered, he closed the book.

Mica, unsure of what to say, instead, moved closer to him. His cologne smelled of cedar. She hoped he would say something nice, but he moved away.

"You put me in an awkward situation," he reprimanded her. His criticism hurt her, and yet she felt a tingling sensation throughout her body. Like chills. She didn't want to be attracted to him, but still, she felt her body get warm.

"I didn't plan to set fire to the scarves," she said.

"Let's forget about it." His face softened. "Everyone enjoyed your performance."

"I wish I could do more for you," she said.

"You've done a lot for all of us in the clinic. Dr. Ingel says your translating has made it possible for him to see twice as many patients."

"No, I want to do something for you."

He stared at her, as if not sure what she meant.

Uncomfortable, she moved away from him, and then stood straight, leaning her elbow on a shelf of books. Passion filled her body. She didn't know what to do with all her feelings. She breathed deeply. Bridge approached her and took her hand as if to shake it good-bye and leave, but instead, he held it for several seconds, then raised it to his lips, kissing her open palm. She moved closer to him as if drawn irresistibly to a flame.

He whispered, "No," and then dropped her hand.

"I don't understand what I feel for you," she said, feeling herself tremble all over. It was as if every nerve under her skin were on fire. The strength of her emotions frightened her.

He moved toward her and closed his eyes, but then, he stopped and moved back, his arms dropping to his side. "No, I can't." He shook his head several times. "It wouldn't be fair to you. I'm a married man, more than twice your age. Let's keep our friendship as it should be, professor and student." He smiled and handed her the book.

"Please, don't be angry with me," Mica whispered. She turned and left the library and raced toward her room. And yet, she couldn't stop feeling his lips on her palm and his eyes pleading, denying, wanting, all at the same time.

Rushing down the long corridor back to her room, Mica realized what a dangerous situation she had put herself in with both Radu and Mr. Bridge. Since she had arrived at the embassy, she had been in a precarious position, needing to navigate through a narrow gate of unfamiliar rules. But now, her situation was worse. Radu, she couldn't trust. He reminded her of the devil, and he knew about the letter. And even though Mr. Bridge was wonderful, she was concerned about him too. After he'd read the letter about her spying, she'd never get to America.

She closed her eyes and thought of her parents—oh, how she missed them! She felt so sad and powerless without them. She wished she were a little girl again and her parents could protect her, guide her. Trying to get by without them, was just too much. The only thing she could do to assuage her frustration was to keep sending them postcards. Still, there was no way to know if they were receiving them, and they couldn't respond.

As Mica entered her room next to the infirmary, she rushed to check out her belongings. She had kept the smaller gems in the heels of her boots, but she had moved the green, red, and blue diamonds into her tube of toothpaste. The two yellow heart-shaped diamonds she had left in her bra.

She reached first for the toothpaste; the diamonds were intact. Next, her boots. All of the diamonds were still there. But the bra had disappeared. She ransacked her bed, she looked under the bed, she searched everywhere. No bra—and no yellow diamonds. Suddenly she remembered Radu at dinner:

"I was doing something secret. Some extra work to help my future... I'm going to celebrate my good fortune."

She ran toward the rear section of the infirmary, which was isolated from other rooms, and where Radu slept. She threw open his door, and without checking to see if he was out with his buddies drinking, she went to his armoire and opened the hatch-door to search it. The bright light from the hallway fell on two large photos in the back of the armoire. One was of Radu with Josef Mengele. The other was a picture of diamonds and two sketched maps of Hungary and Brazil. Someone had drawn on the maps, in black crayon, an arrow from Budapest to São Paulo. Mica recognized Radu's handwriting from the clinic.

Angry, she searched through his clothes, opening one drawer after another. No bra or diamonds. She went to the second bureau in the room and quickly searched each drawer. In the bottom one, hidden behind Radu's dirty clothes, she found her bra. It was torn in several places, and her two yellow diamonds were missing. Enraged, she stuffed the bra into her pocket.

Just then, from the corner alcove, Mica heard Radu move in his bed. He coughed. She ran out of his room. As she raced down the corridor, she bumped into a medicine cabinet. She spied two hypodermic syringes inside the glass door. Opening it, she took the needles and returned to his room, waiting outside to see if he'd come looking for her. She didn't have to wait long. Radu got out of bed and saw Mica at his door and moved toward her. She brandished a syringe in each hand and warned him, "If you dare come near me, I'll stab you. MORPHINE! A triple dose. It'll stop your heart!"

He moved back.

She pointed the needles at his face. "Let me have my diamonds!"

"No, they're mine now! I suspected you didn't escape Romania empty-handed."

Without warning, he grabbed her shoulders and threw her backward. She staggered but didn't fall. Then she jabbed his arm with one of the syringes. He pulled the needle out and screamed in pain. She stabbed him in the back with the other needle. He fell on the floor, trying to dislodge it. She wrestled him and bit his neck in a fury. He tried to pull away, but her teeth dug into his flesh, ripping his skin until blood gushed out. He pulled the needle out of his back and slammed his fist into her chest. She fell to the floor. He moved toward her, but she kicked him hard in the leg, and he went down. He raised his hand and slapped her in the mouth.

Blood poured from her split lip and she fell back. Her blouse opened.

Staring at her bare breasts, he stood up and straddled her, using his weight to hold her down. He unzipped his pants, shut her mouth with his hand, and ripped off her skirt. Mica struggled to lift his body off her, but he was too heavy. She fought swiveling her hips and kicking him with her legs. In a desperate surge of strength, she bit his hand and kicked him in the groin. He folded up and collapsed, groaning in pain.

She ran to the medicine cabinet and took out a pair of scissors. Before he could grab her, she plunged the points deep into his thigh. He pulled them out, and with her skirt that was on the floor, he wiped the blood oozing from his wound.

Throwing the bloody skirt back to Mica, he said, "Don't think you won! The two yellow hearts are now mine, and they should be enough for me to join my friends who live with Mengele on a farm outside São Paulo in Brazil. Mengele agreed to help me just as I helped him when he escaped Auschwitz." He smirked, pleased with his bragging.

"You deserve each other!" Mica yelled. "Two devils."

Radu zipped up his pants. "I'm the winner now!"

THE NEXT MORNING, MICA WANTED TO TELL MAGDA WHAT HAD happened with Radu, but she knew the nurse would want to report him, and there was no way for Mica to allow this without revealing that he had stolen two of her diamonds. When the nurse asked how she had cut her lip, Mica replied, "I tripped in the middle of the night going to the bathroom." When she told Mr. Bridge the same story the next day in the library, he stared at her with clear skepticism. He questioned his staff about Radu's mysterious departure, but Mica remained silent.

On the following Sunday when Mica visited Magda at home, Ben examined her swollen lip, and Tibi gave her a special cream to prevent scarring. Withdrawn that entire day, she was aloof. Even their picnic lunch on Margaret Island couldn't change her mood.

Mica's despair lasted for several weeks. During the days, she tried to block out the memory of Radu by working harder in the clinic. She volunteered to update the patient folders, classify the X-rays, and transcribe all blood tests into hundreds of patients' charts. She wanted to avoid having a free minute to think.

Forgetting Radu proved quite difficult at night when she couldn't sleep. She kept seeing his loathsome figure on top of her, unzipping his pants. If she hadn't kicked him in the groin and stabbed him with the scissors, he would have raped her.

The thought obsessed her and kept her awake at night. She twisted and turned, agitated by her drive to wipe Radu's existence from her mind. She kept seeing herself plunging the scissors into his thigh.

Several weeks passed. Mica's lip healed, as well as her mood. In hindsight, and with a degree of distance and time, Mica realized that she had not really lost anything, as Ben had said the yellow diamonds were fake. This awareness ameliorated her low mood. She was also able to be objective and feel a certain degree of pride that her actions of self-defense against Radu's violence, had helped her save herself. She was satisfied to believe that she was able to overcome her challenging experiences in the embassy.

Mr. Bridge and Mica never spoke about what had happened in the library, but Mica was so shaken up by Radu that she was relieved to be left alone with her work. The two events were so intimately linked in her memory that she was happy to suppress both. Bridge seemed relieved not to have to think further about it. Yet, despite their reserve toward each other, there was the memory of closeness between them that gave Mica a great deal of happiness.

CHAPTER 18

ALTHOUGH MR. BRIDGE had told her it would be six months for a visa application to be finished, the processing of the paperwork was moving slowly and this made her even more impatient. It had been five months since she submitted her papers, and she should have heard some word about her visa. Unless the letter about her past was holding up the process.

In the quiet of her room, she'd talk to her parents in her mind, asking them for advice. She remembered how her mother used to encourage her in everything. Whatever it was, her mother would tell her, "You can do it! Your will is strong. You can create your own life."

Every night before bed, she prayed that her parents hadn't been cursed by the diamonds. Ben believed that diamonds had strange powers; when she turned out the light in her room, the history of cursed diamonds haunted her. She began to dream not only of arriving in New York but also of freeing herself from the diamonds. Some days she was tempted to give them to Ben and Tibi and to be done with them, but she needed them to get her parents to America. She remembered how Tibi had advised her to sell the diamonds quickly and use the money to do good and stop the bad luck. Until then, there was nothing she could do but wait for her visa and then confer with her uncle.

She wondered about him, and if she'd be able to trust him. He was four years younger than her father, and as she had heard, not nearly as smart. When he was a teenager, he didn't like to study, preferring to sketch nude models at the art institute, according to her father. When the war came, the Germans had killed her grandparents, and her father and Simion had escaped Transylvania. When they got to Bucharest, Simion's artistic talents helped him become the number one forger of passports for the Romanian underground while her father, the engineer, helped locate enemy sites and bunkers.

Uncle Simion was married to an American woman, but didn't have any children. Mica had always wished for a younger brother or sister, and hoped that she might have a secret cousin waiting for her. Without her friends, she was desperately lonely in the embassy even though Magda and her brothers were good to her and Mica was grateful to them. But they weren't her age. The high school Easter dance had been a lot of fun, but Neal Bridge decided not to host it again, for fear of compromising his friend, Fabry, with Hungarian officials. Now Mica missed, more than ever, laughing with friends.

To distract herself, Mica listened to the shortwave radio. One evening, Radio Free Europe was broadcasting in Romanian:

"We are mourning our colleague, Alex Petrescu, who died yesterday in Munich from lung cancer. It's the opinion of our editorial board that Mr. Petrescu's office was exposed to radioactive material by members of Ceausescu's secret police, with the intent to poison and silence him. Mr. Petrescu was preparing an article for the *Wall Street Journal* on Ceausescu's friendship with Muammar Gaddafi.

Petrescu's investigation threatened to expose the relationship between the Russians and the Libyans. Sources confirmed that the Russians have supported the Libyan military regime by training Libyan soldiers and selling the country arms and weapons. Petrescu had recently spoken with secret sources inside the Russian government who said that the relationship with Libya was part of a broader strategy, begun by Ceausescu, Gaddafi's partner, to extend communist influence throughout the Arab world."

The broadcaster's voice stopped. Mica heard him draw deep breath. "The details will be published next month in the *Wall Street Journal*. Alex Petrescu has been silenced by chemical substances, but his words will live on."

A wave of astonishment swept over Mica. Even though she had never told anyone what she had heard in the clinic with the two refugees, she felt vindicated that this journalist had confirmed what they had discussed about the relationship of Gaddafi and Ceausescu regarding terrorism and chemical weapons.

Mica turned off the radio. She was reluctant to go to Neal Bridge to report what she knew. She doubted he would have believed her, and she didn't want to delay her visa process. But now, the *Journal* had proof of what she had heard, and the whole world would know.

Although the thought consoled her, time was moving too slowly for her visa. Mr. Bridge had never mentioned anything to her about receiving a letter from Bucharest, either.

Then one day, Mr. Bridge sought her out in the clinic. He had a thick manila folder in his hand. "Mica," he said in a whisper as he watched her help a refugee fill out his medical history, "please come with me to my office."

Once she was inside, he closed the door and motioned her to

sit in the chair next to his desk. "I find myself in a difficult situation," he said.

He leaned forward and looked her in the eye. "I have just received a cable from the U.S. Department of State. The man who sent it to me is my old roommate from Princeton. He said he trusts me to solve this matter. The cable is in English, but I need to have it translated into Romanian, so I can share it with some Romanian officials."

"Oh." She was relieved he didn't want to talk about the letter.

"Florin, our embassy's translator, had a motorcycle accident and is in the hospital. I tried to do this translation myself, but there are a number of technical terms." He showed her his dictionary as if to demonstrate his labors.

"I can do it," she said.

"It has to be ready by tomorrow when I go to Bucharest. My Romanian contact will need to read it in Romanian to discuss the matter with his group. I'm in a difficult spot. There's no one else here who can help me."

"I'm happy to do it."

"I'll pay you what the embassy pays Florin."

She shook her head no. "No payment. The embassy allows me to live here and eat here. I'm happy to help. I'll go and finish my work in the clinic quickly, and then spend the rest of the day translating."

He took a piece of blank stationery from his top desk-drawer and began writing. "If you swear never to tell anyone about the contents of the cable, this translating will work in your favor for obtaining your visa."

"I swear," she said, raising her hand and feeling elated.

"I'll need more than that." He handed her the piece of paper. "Will you sign this letter of confidentiality?"

Mica touched the raised print of the U.S. Embassy's gold seal and in her most serious tone, answered, "Yes."

"First read the words below. If you agree, sign and date where it says signature."

She read: ROMANIA. GADDAFI. SOVIET UNION. CEAUS-ESCU. TOP SECRET.

She signed and dated where Mr. Bridge pointed.

When she finished her work in the clinic, Mica returned to Mr. Bridge's office. She arranged her desk in the adjoining room, placing a pile of blank paper next to the dictionary. She had also brought three apples and a paper bag containing cheese and bread. She planned to stay in the room until she was finished.

The cable read:

CLASSIFIED BY: Michael Richardson, CDA, Embassy Tripoli, U.S. Dept. of State.
REASON: 1.4 (b), (d)
GADDAFI AS KGB-BACKED TERRORIST SPONSORED PROXY OF THE SOVIET UNION AND SUPPORTED BY ROMANIA'S CEAUSESCU:

- Gaddafi has invested a percentage of his state's oil revenues into neo-fascist pro-Palestinian groups.
- Gaddafi's affiliation with fascism is a result of his relentless, rabid anti-Semitism.
- Gaddafi is a neo-fascist as well as a Marxist supporter.
- As a supporter of the Left, he serves as a conduit for the Soviet-backed guerilla insurrections through the third world. Soviet tanks, arms, planes, helicopters and Gaddafi's money are transported via Libya to Marxist regimes, terrorist groups, PLO's, Cuba, Algeria, and African rebels.
- Libya is the site of installations and special training for terrorist camps, organized by the Soviet KGB, to train Libyan and international terrorists and assassins. Ten

camps have been identified within Libya. The list will
follow in another cable.

- Castro's and Ceausescu's security guards assist in the
overseeing and training at these camps. Gaddafi invests
hundreds of millions of dollars in cash. All of this remains
consistent with the policy, authorized in the Soviet Union,
to increase support to terrorism by 1000 percent.

- Dept. of State recommends you go from Budapest to
Bucharest to impede these connections and offer economic
incentives to those involved. To be discussed when we meet
in Bucharest. RICHARDSON

When Mica completed her translation, she gave it to Bridge to
review.

He scanned her work and then put it back in the original
manila envelope. "This cable proves that terrorism grew out of
communism," he told her. "Russia will always be a fierce
competitor with the U.S. and because of that, the Cold War will
continue long after both countries agree it's over. I wouldn't be
surprised if Romania, somehow, will emerge at the center of these
politics. You can go now, Mica. Thank you."

She stood in front of his desk for a moment, wondering if this
was the moment to talk to him about what she had heard the
refugees say about Ceausescu's nuclear facilities, his deals with
uranium, centrifuges, heavy water, and chemical warfare.

But then again she hesitated, and the moment passed.

As promised, she tried to forget what she had just spent hours
translating. Yet she was conflicted and very upset. She feared she
was witnessing the beginning of a new form of terrorism and she
wasn't doing anything about it.

CHAPTER 19

ONE MONTH LATER, during Mr. Bridge's English class, Mica and her friends were having lunch in the library when someone knocked on the door. "Mr. Bridge, are you there?"

"Y-yes," he answered, brusquely, annoyed by the disturbance.

The door opened and Magda Bartha came in. "The telephone switchboard is out of service, and your wife, who's in a meeting, asked me to give you a message. She said it's important that I find you."

She handed him a note and then Bridge excused himself, walked toward the window, and read his wife's letter.

Every day, Mica was hopeful that there would be some news about her visa. She had asked Mr. Bridge once, but after that, she had not asked again. Now, she struggled to listen to what he was mumbling as he read the note, but she couldn't hear what he was saying. Bridge ripped up the sheet of paper and told the class he had to prepare a meeting and that they could finish their lesson the next day. As Mica left the library, she noticed he was angrily pacing the room.

Had his wife advised him not to approve her visa request? Mica couldn't help but wonder if there was something more personal going on with Sybil Bridge, if she had somehow found out about the night in the library. Even if she had, would she really want to ruin Mica's life and stop her from going to America?

Mica also wondered about Mr. Bridge, whose behavior in the past weeks demonstrated to her once and for all that he was truly conflicted about her and what he should do about it—if anything. Sometimes he was cold and angry; then, he would apologize for being rude. Mica understood his struggle, and was more than aware of their attraction to each other. Fighting her own feelings, she tried to avoid being alone with him for too long. Her rational side didn't want a repeat performance of a romantic scene.

Still, by the next class, Mica decided it was time to take fate into her own hands. When the other students were leaving at the end of the lesson, she walked over to his desk and handed him a book.

"What's this?" he asked.

"Anne Frank's diary. I've been reading it in the library." Mica closed her eyes and recited the teenager's words: 'Night after night, green and gray military vehicles cruise the streets... They often go around with lists, knocking only on those doors where they know there's a big haul to be made.' Please Mr. Bridge," Mica begged. "Neal, don't denounce me."

He stood up and moved away from the desk.

"I know you received a letter about me," she whispered. "I thought you would talk with me about it. I was afraid to go to you first."

"Yes," he said. "I wanted to get more information before discussing the matter with you, which took more time than I expected."

Mica looked down; she stayed silent.

"I'm conflicted about what to do," he admitted. "Dr. Ingel knows about the letter. Legally, I'm required to submit it to the embassy's legal department with your updated forms and a political affidavit."

"What's that?"

"Information related to the applicant's recent employment situation and past political activities." Mr. Bridge moved closer to her. "Was the candidate ever involved in espionage?"

She stared at him.

"We're not allowed to accept fascists, communists, or spies to enter the United States," he said, in a professional tone. Then he looked down, embarrassed by his using bureaucrateese.

"It was two days! I was a child then, only eleven years old. They threatened to put my father in jail, to kill him, my mother too, if I didn't do what they said. I was tortured to co-operate. Look at my finger as proof!" She grabbed his hand and showed him her pinky. "I only did it for two days. I hate the communists! I even destroyed a tape from priests who were discussing how the Pope planned to bring down communism. I was on God's side."

Mica started to tremble; her face flushed. She was in a panic. "I want to get to America! I need to!"

"Calm down, calm down. Ingel must have told my wife about the letter. He probably thinks you were more involved, or that I should act more prudently so I don't get into trouble."

"You're ranked above him. Why would you listen to him?"

"I can't hide this information from security. Even if it's a question of you spying for two days. I'd get into trouble because I'm responsible for you." Then he paused, "But I can get Dr. Ingel transferred to another embassy in another country where he's needed more, and then you can reapply in a year."

"A year? I can't stay one day longer than I have to in this prison. I kept up my end of the bargain. I did the translation for you. I kept it a secret. I've worked six months in the clinic and never accepted any payment."

Bridge walked over to the windows and closed them. "Tell me," he said, quietly. "Did anyone from Romania's secret police ever contact you again?"

"No! I told the chief I didn't want to do that kind of work. I threatened to harm myself. Perhaps he was afraid he'd get into trouble because of that, so he said I could stop."

"Okay, good," Bridge mumbled. "We know from our CIA informer that the chief of police didn't have time to write a complete report about your espionage work. He died soon after. That's why there was an incomplete dossier with the information we received from Bucharest."

"I don't understand."

"He didn't write a complete report. That's our good luck."

He grinned and then he started to laugh. Mica had never seen him look so happy. He turned and wrote several sentences on a paper, and then read them aloud:

"Incomplete and inconclusive evidence. This report speaks of allegations, but the dossier was not completed, signed, or stamped by the chief of Police. Nor have I been apprised in writing from any other source about the details of Miss Mihailescu's recriminatory activities."

Mica listened, thrilled, despite not understanding many of the words he spoke.

"You were coerced," he stated.

"What does that mean?"

"Forced."

"Yes, I was coerced!"

"This is what I propose," he said, clearly pleased with himself. "I will write a report accompanying the letter I received from Bucharest and include a transcript of this conversation—a copy in legal language saying there is inconclusive evidence of your espionage activities that originated in coercion and torture. Child abuse, in other words. I will recommend that you're to be absolved of any allegations."

He was speaking too quickly for her to understand, but she followed his tone eagerly.

"I know the important people in our legal and visa sections. I promise to personally discuss your case with them." He smiled at her. "I dare say, your visa will not be rejected."

These were the words Mica had been praying for. She fell to the floor as tears poured, and covered her face. "I want so much to be free," she sobbed.

PART III

NEW YORK CITY

CHAPTER 20

SEPTEMBER 1965

John F. Kennedy Airport

MICA WATCHED the travelers in front of her stepping onto a black rubber strip between rails that moved—a moving floor. Some held the railing; most of them put their bags down on the rubber strip. There was no other way for her but to go forward. Frightened and not knowing what was coming, Mica took a deep breath and stepped on.

Trying to enjoy the ride, she looked around at the posters on the walls and started to feel calmer. She wondered about the other people; did she look different from them? Could they tell she wasn't American? When they started to jump off the moving floor, Mica followed, picking up her bag and leaping forward. Then she saw a sign overhead:

Welcome to New York

Following the crowd and reading the ads, Mica's eyes moved more quickly than her legs. She looked up at the lights hidden in the ceiling; they reminded her of round spotlights she had seen on stage. These lights, though, were brighter, and they emitted a color that was soft and pinkish.

Her thoughts turned to Romania and the secret police. Were these lights hiding cameras? Was pink the color of infrared rays piercing her body to detect the hidden diamonds?

This is America, she reminded herself. *There's no secret police.*

The crowd split up at the sign that read Customs and Immigration. The group of obviously more confident travelers lined up in front of the words: U.S. PASSPORTS. The other travelers, some outwardly nervous and carrying cardboard boxes and paper shopping bags, moved to the longer line that was marked: VISITORS.

Mica put her bag down carefully in between her feet, making sure to guard it with her boots. She studied the faces of all the people in the room. Those on the "U.S." line looked like they were returning from summer vacation, dressed in shorts and jeans. The women wore straw hats, the men baseball caps. Some of them had dark glasses on. In Romania, those were the type of glasses blind people wore.

These Americans were taller and broader than the people she was accustomed to seeing in Hungary and Romania. She imagined them as maxi-figures, fortified by milk and red meat, as if they were blown-up floats in a parade. Their skin was pink and appeared soft to the touch. Their faces were full. Yet there was something childish, or innocent in their expressions. In Romania, even the children looked old. Here, everyone looked young, with their cheerful clothing in vivid colors and their funny hats. Even the furniture looked bigger and stronger so as to be able to support these sturdier citizens.

Mica waited in the Visitors line for what seemed like forever. Increasingly nervous, she dug her toes into her boots, trying to relax. She was relieved to notice that the customs officials weren't checking shoes. She tried to seem as carefree as the people on the

American line. Imitating them, she leaned on one leg, yawned, read her forms, looked up at the ceiling. Then, pretending she was looking for something, she opened up her carry-on-bag. Once she saw her visa, she forgot her fears. She touched the words—Political Refugee—and felt protected. A rush of sweet triumph passed through her. She wanted to celebrate, to scream aloud to the entire room, "I'm here! I'm free! My dream has come true!"

Also visible in her open bag was the tip of the red and white tube of toothpaste. She was satisfied with its appearance: It looked like an ordinary tube of toothpaste, squeezed and dented. Her precious green, red, and blue diamonds were sleeping quietly in their creamy paste. The remainder of her treasure, thirteen other colored diamonds, was resting in her million-dollar boots and padded bra.

She wondered if the authorities would examine her old suitcase the way they had the day before in Budapest. She was tense at the airport, afraid they'd also search her body, ask her to undress, take off her boots and bra, then find the diamonds and stop her from leaving. But the Hungarian customs official had changed his attitude when he saw her visa from the American Embassy with its gold seal.

"Good luck," he had said, closing her suitcase and waving her through. "You're one of the fortunate few."

"*Koszonom*, thank you."

She had been very emotional when she said good-bye to Magda, Ben, and Tibi at the airport. Magda was crying, and so was Mica. Ben slipped twenty American dollars into Mica's pocket, and Tibi gave her the addresses of several Hungarian diamond dealers in New York. "Just in case an auction house won't accept the diamonds," he said. Mica couldn't stop hugging and thanking them. She wondered if she'd ever see them again.

"You're next!" the American customs officer shouted while

turning the pages of a big, black notebook. "Do you speak English?"

"Yes," Mica said.

"Ever been to the United States before?" the custom's officer shouted, as if she were deaf or dumb.

"No."

"How old are you?"

"Seventeen, almost eighteen."

"Traveling alone?"

"Yes."

"Is someone here responsible for you? Anyone picking you up?"

"Yes, my uncle."

"His name." A command, not a question.

"Simion Mihailescu."

He wrote something on her declaration card, stamped it, verified her visa, and without ever looking at her, nodded her through.

She wanted to say, "Thank you. I'm so grateful to be here. God bless America." But his gruffness and the swiftness of the transaction diminished her euphoria. He didn't look as if he wanted to make small talk. She picked up her bag and moved on to the next room, marked Public Health-Immigration.

When it was her turn, Mica handed the officer the medical report that Mr. Bridge had arranged for Dr. Ingel to write.

"I hope you find happiness in America," Ingel had told her.

She was touched, thinking he appreciated her work in the clinic.

"Where are you coming from?" the immigration officer asked while reading the doctor's report.

"Budapest."

"Been anywhere else in the past six months?"

"No, just Hungary."

"Ever have tuberculosis?"

"No."

He moved closer to her and tightened his thin lips. "Do you have anything to tell me?"

Alarmed, she asked, "What do you mean?"

"Are these papers correct?"

"Of course."

"Have anything to declare? Bringing in anything you shouldn't?" He stared hard at her, clearly trying to unnerve her.

"N-no," she stuttered. She glanced up at the ceiling. Was she being watched?

"Bringing in any plants or food?" he recited. "Any art objects from your country?" He pointed to the small suitcase Magda had given her, filled with magazines and books. She wondered if diamonds were art objects. No, they were stones. She remembered the salami in her bag.

"Food?" she said. "Why should I bring food here? You'd hate what I ate there."

"All right." He chalked her bag. "Go down the steps for your luggage."

"Thank you, thank you."

He nodded and waved her on. "Next."

Mica watched the suitcases go around and around on the carousel. The tall, blond man next to her picked up his valise and walked away. He reminded her of Neal Bridge—elegantly dressed, a gentleman.

When she had said good-bye to him, she told him she'd never forget him. He took her hand and whispered, "You will be happier in New York, but you'll be missed here."

Mica was so overwhelmed by his tenderness that she couldn't say another word. She held back her tears and said good-bye again without telling him how much she had worshipped him.

Picking up her suitcase and carrying her overcoat, she turned to the attendant and asked, "Which way is the lobby?"

"Through the glass doors," he answered, without even glancing at her.

I guess this is it, she said to herself as she pushed her way through the crowd in search of her uncle.

Hearing the jingling of bells, Mica turned to see a circle of people, holding hands and singing, "Hare Krishna. Hare Krishna." They were turning around and around. All were dressed in loose-fitting, orange robes. Their skin looked flaky white, as if they had covered themselves with flour. They wore sandals and had shaved heads that were also floured white. She couldn't tell which were girls and which were boys.

Mica stopped to listen to their chanting. Charmed, she started laughing. *This is surely America,* she thought. *In Romania, these kids would be thrown in a psychiatric ward.*

She noticed another group of girls her own age wearing flowers in their hair, each one holding a straw basket. One of them, a girl, with golden curls, approached Mica and gave her a white rose. "For you," she said smiling. "Love for all our brothers and sisters."

Mica took the rose, smiled in return and wondered how many brothers and sisters the girl had. "Thank you for welcoming me to America. I'm so glad to be in New York. I…"

But the girl had already floated away, and Mica heard her say to someone else, "For you, a flower for peace."

Mica moved through the crowd, wondering how she would find her uncle. She had some money, the $300 she'd taken from home and the $20 Ben had given her, but it wouldn't go far in New York, and she had refused to take any of the money from Mr. Bridge that he had offered when she went to pick up her visa.

She walked in circles, looking for a man who resembled her father. Maybe Uncle Simion is fatter, she thought, staring at each man who passed by—all those American hamburgers and French fries. Maybe he's taller—milk and vegetables. Maybe he's bald—not enough garlic or onions.

She walked toward the main building. Seeing a sign for taxis, she went that way to find her uncle. When they had made their final plans, he had told her that he'd meet her at the "main door." But now, seeing all the doors, she wondered which one was the main door? Just then, she saw a large sign in black letters: MICA MIHAILESCU.

As if in a dream, she walked toward her name, staring at the man holding the sign. He was wearing a wide-brimmed white hat, white trousers, a white shirt, and a navy-blue blazer with gold buttons. Tall, thin, and elegantly dressed, he looked exactly the way a Romanian actor did when he dressed to play the role of an American playboy. He was of medium build, thin, not muscular, cleanly shaven and rather plain looking. She tried to find something in him that reminded her of her father.

She felt a little uncomfortable dressed in her black leather boots, black leggings and old Elizabethan coat. She walked past him, observing him for a moment and wanting to compose herself before she finally met him.

Her uncle was pacing back and forth, chanting, "Mee-high-les-ku! mi-ha-les-ku!" The way he was saying her last name harmonized with the orange people singing, "Ha-re krish-na! Ha-re krish-na!"

Her uncle's forehead was furrowed, and the curly brown hairs of his bushy eyebrows sprung out in different directions, giving him a look of distraction. This man looked nothing like her father. When he glanced at his watch and lowered the sign, she noticed he looked annoyed, emotional.

Still, he was the only family she had in America. Whatever kind of person he was, he was her link to her parents' freedom. She waved her hand and shouted, "Uncle Simion!"

They walked toward each other, and when they were finally

face to face, she said timidly in Romanian. *"Buna dimineata.* Hello, Uncle, it's me, Mica. We're finally together."

He kissed her on both cheeks, at first a little shyly. Then he put his arms around her and held her for several seconds without speaking. They stood looking at one another, both overcome by emotion.

"I'm so thrilled to be here," Mica said, trying not to cry. "It's been a long journey."

"Draga Mica. My dear! I'm happy to see you. Let me look at you. Who do you look like? My mother. Yes. The same strong chin and oval face, the same high cheekbones, full lips, and slanted eyes, hazel, golden, like hers. What a joy to see her in you! *Mi-ghty* pretty," he chuckled. *"Mi-ghty* pretty."

He took her suitcase and, still chuckling, said, "Let me take your bags."

Mica smiled as she saw a ring on his finger sparkle bright in the sun. She looked up at the sky and whispered under her breath, "Thank you God. Thank you for helping me get here."

"Come, come! My car is parked away from the terminal. It's a bit of a walk. Saved me a few bucks. We'll have time to talk," he said. "I hope you're not too tired?"

"No, I slept on the plane. And how can I be tired? I'm here!" Again, she wanted to yell and jump with joy, but something in her uncle's demeanor cut her euphoria.

"I feel guilty about your father," he confessed, looking down as they walked. "I'm in America. He's there. Not free. I never forgave myself that I couldn't get two more visas for your parents. When I got to the States, I tried to help them. Sent letters, even money. But I couldn't help more, and I didn't send more money because I didn't want to get him in trouble. I feel terrible. Whatever you'll think about me, I do believe in family loyalty and that's why I'm glad you're here."

Mica didn't know what to say. She wiped a tear from her

cheek. Her uncle had been right to be circumspect; yet it had been hard for her father.

"My wife and I don't have children. We tried, but they never came. I hope you'll let us treat you as our own."

"Oh, yes," she heard herself say.

When Simion opened the glass doors of the airport terminal, she covered her eyes and gasped, "Oh, my God!"

"What's the matter?" he asked, concerned.

"The sun. I've never seen such bright light in my life."

"Yes, it's a clear day, no pollution."

"I've never seen a sun like that. In Romania and Hungary, there's so much pollution that the sun's rays are filtered from morning to night. Communism has even stolen sunlight from us. Here the sun is surreal."

"Take my hat. Then you'll be able to see as much as you want."

"I want to see *everything*. That's why I escaped from *there* to come *here*."

When he put his wide-brimmed hat on top of her head, she saw that he was bald. *Aha, not enough garlic or onions.* He took off his sunglasses and gave then to her also. "If the sun's in your eyes, you won't see a thing."

As they walked toward the parking lot, her uncle asked her, "What kind of accent do you have? Sounds like a Limey's."

"What's that?"

"British. How's that possible?"

"Oh, I had a very good teacher. Willy Shakespeare."

He laughed. "You're a treasure, Mica. A gem." He stopped talking. And stopped walking.

"Tell me," he said as he slowly picked up his pace again. They were walking through a huge parking lot. Mica had never seen so many cars in her life.

"How many diamonds do you have?" he whispered, as if he were afraid spies were listening.

"Sixteen."

"Sixteen?" He raised his voice. "I gave your father *twenty colored diamonds!"*

"I had to leave our house immediately, and I found sixteen. I took all I could. Can we talk about this tomorrow? It's too painful for me now." She didn't want her uncle to know about the two yellow heart diamonds that Radu had stolen, or the two pink ones she had left for her father in the bunker. She was afraid he'd reprimand her for making decisions on her own. She didn't want to begin their relationship with a scene.

"Strange." He stared at her, obviously thinking and looking unhappy. Then he asked, "They're all different colors? What colors?"

"One blue, four yellows, three greens, three reds, three pinks, two browns, no whites, all different sizes and shapes."

"I've been waiting all these years to *share* those rainbow jewels and get our pot of gold."

"Share?" Her father had never mentioned sharing. She thought the white diamonds were her uncle's and the colored ones were her father's.

"Of course! I gave them to your father so he could join me in the States and be my partner. You came instead, so you're my partner now. Fifty-fifty. That's the deal. We share. *Right, partner?"* He looked at her with an obvious challenge.

Mica was surprised and discomforted by her uncle's aggression. "Fine, we'll share them, but before we share anything," she said, "we have to agree on one thing. To use our earnings first to get my parents free."

"You mean out of Romania?"

"That's exactly what I mean. Agreed?"

He stared at her. "Not agreed! Fifty-fifty! Equal partners. That's the deal. And you pay for the lawyers with your share. If you need more money, I'll pony in."

Pony? What could this mean? But not wanting to confront him, she thought it best to turn the conversation. "What did you do with your diamonds?" she asked.

He seemed to relax a little. "I cashed them in. Went to one of those religious guys in the diamond district. Asked him what they were worth and drove a hard bargain. Bought myself a house in Long Island, in Hewlett Bay Park. Also bought myself a business."

Mica perked up when she heard the word *business*. "What kind?"

"Construction. Always liked the combo of action and design. I buy land in Long Island and get the bank to be my partner. Things went well when the housing market was bullish. I did the architectural plans myself, got a crew to build, sold one house a year. But then the market fell through the roof."

"Roof? The house lost its roof?"

"No, the bubble broke. The market."

"Bubble? Like soap bubbles?"

He laughed. "I guess you can say it popped! Burst!"

"Is that what you call real estate?" she asked, remembering Mr. Bridge's lessons. He had spent a good deal of time during his weekly classes talking about American business and law and how to adapt to American ways.

"How do you know about real estate? There's no real estate in a communist country." He smiled at her. "Come to think of it, you seem to know an awful lot. Are you some kind of genius? Your father was the smarter brother. Very brainy, must have taught you a lot. And your mom, lovely. Such a good match, those two."

He narrowed his eyes. "So, tell me how did you get out of Romania?" He smiled at her in a strange way.

"It's a long story. I'll tell you later when I meet your wife so I won't have to tell the same story twice." She knew she would have to tell him the whole story, but she wasn't ready yet. "Did you get a good price for your diamonds?" She wanted to change the conversation.

"Yes, but I would have liked more."

"I want to sell *my* diamonds at an auction," she announced.

"*Our diamonds*," he said. "Remember, *partner?*" He had stopped smiling. "Auction? How do you know about auctions?"

"I studied a lot of things at the American Embassy."

"I didn't hear you say how you got there in the first place, to Budapest from Transylvania, and how you got the diamonds out all the way to New York." Then he added, "I hope you didn't do anything illegal."

"Don't worry, Uncle Simion," she said in a theatrical voice. "I didn't do anything you wouldn't have done if you were in my shoes." She laughed, looking down at his cowboy boots and then at her own.

"Are you telling me everything about the colored diamonds?"

"Yes…" She was alarmed that he sounded like the custom's official in the airport.

"We'll make a lot of money with our rainbow," he said.

"How much do you think they're worth?" she asked. After all this time, she was eager to assess what could be their value. "I'd like to know, for my own education."

"You're mi-ghty educated." He laughed.

Mica didn't respond. He was family, but there was something in his attitude she didn't trust. For one thing, his mood seemed very changeable. She also worried that he was greedy. She was willing to give him half, that was fair. But how could she make sure he wouldn't trick her and take a larger percentage? She remembered Mr. Bridge had said that lawyers were expensive in America. And she'd probably need more than one lawyer to get her parents to America. She'd need her fifty percent.

"Here we are." He wiggled his car keys. "She's over there."

"Which one?"

"The black one." When Mica didn't say anything, he said, "Guess it's a little ratty."

"Ratty?" She imagined rats in his car.

"I had a red Cadillac before, but the bank took it back."

"What do you mean?" These new concepts were confusing to her.

"Well… unexpected things happen." He looked down, fumbled with his keys. "In fact, I-I might have to file bankruptcy."

"What's that? Something with the bank?" Another word she didn't know.

"I lost a lot of money in my real estate ventures. Bought high, sold low, and then the market tanked. We have our house though."

Mica was amazed. How could he be poor if he had a *house*? His shoes were so shiny. He had a pinky ring, a blazer with gold buttons. "I bet you have more here than my father has there."

He laughed. "Could be. Guess you can say, I came a long way. The American dream. But now things will *really* change!" He gave her a big smile and slap on the back. He put her bags in the trunk and opened the passenger door. Bowing dramatically, he whispered, "Milady, welcome to America. I'm delighted you and our diamonds are here."

Mica curtsied just as theatrically. "We're all happy to be here."

Before getting into the car, she looked up again at the sun to make sure it was real. The round bright circle looked like a kaleidoscope filled with a rainbow of hope.

"I'm here!" she wanted to shout at the sun. "I'm free! And I swear I will bring my mother and father here!" And then she started to laugh.

"What's so funny?" he asked.

"You're so different from my father."

CHAPTER 21

MICA TWISTED and turned in bed, but not unhappily. She had never had the pleasure of sleeping in such a spacious bed. She felt as if she were floating in the sky on a huge white cloud. The sheets were soft, the pillow fluffy, the room huge, the air so pure. Then she heard a noise and opened her eyes, wondering, for a moment, where she was. *Am I in heaven?*

She looked up. Across the room, her uncle was picking up her suitcase. Instantly, she recalled Radu. She touched her bra, felt the diamonds next to her heart, and tightened her body in protest.

She looked to see if her boots were still standing guard next to the carry-on bag. Her uncle was walking over to them. She jumped out of bed as he turned toward her, holding a boot in his hand. When he saw her nearing him, he said, "50% is too much for you. The jeweler gave the diamonds to me! I foolishly took the white ones. Your father got all the colored diamonds although he didn't do a thing to earn them."

She was tempted to remind her uncle that he agreed yesterday that they were partners—fifty-fifty. He gave his word. He couldn't take the diamonds for himself. But something told her she'd better keep herself in check, for the moment.

Simion pointed his finger at Mica in warning. "Remember, you're not eighteen yet, and I'm responsible for you." Then he changed his tone as if he was thinking. "I'm a gentleman and I won't go back on my word. Family loyalty. Fifty-fifty. We'll have to trust each other." He left the room.

Mica was dismayed. She hadn't done anything to anger him. She had hoped that her uncle might be a second father to her, but in the one day she had been with him, he kept changing his behavior. One minute he was warm and charming, and the next minute he closed down and became cold. He was so unlike her father, who was sensitive and kind, always in control. She would have to get used to her uncle's change of moods and hope, he would act according to family loyalty. She hoped that she'd be able to win him over.

"MICA, DO YOU WANT BREAKFAST?" AUNT DIANE'S TONE WAS cheerful and warm. Unlike her uncle, her aunt had been nothing but consistently kind and welcoming, and as far as Mica could tell, she had no ulterior motives. Mica sensed that her being with them was more important to Diane than the diamonds.

"Yes, please. I'm coming." Mica followed the voices, and skipped into the kitchen. She gave her aunt a kiss on the cheek, walked over to her uncle, and gave him an exaggerated slap on the back.

Aunt Diane chuckled, amused. Her double chin and full buxom chest moved up and down with seeming pleasure.

Mica looked around the sunny kitchen. Diane's beautifully framed needlepoints graced the wall. She was particularly enthralled with the one reproducing Marc Chagall's "Green Violinist."

The day before, when Mica had first met her aunt, she was overwhelmed by the luxuries of their home, which did not appear to her at all as poor. Her own house in Romania was much smaller and more modestly furnished. Mica especially loved Diane's own oil paintings and needlepoints. "You're so talented," she told her aunt. "Works of art, inspired by works of art!" Mica kissed her and Diane hugged her. From the start, they liked each other.

"I'm hungry," Mica said. "And I don't think I ever slept so well in my life."

"Mica, dear, you're finally safe," Diane said, waving a slice of buttered toast. "You can finally sleep well. We're here to protect you like you're our own daughter."

"Is that really true?" Mica asked, hungry for reassurance and signs of affection.

"Of course it is!" Diane kissed her niece on the cheek and gestured for her to sit by her side at the table.

"Not only are you free," Simion said, "but our diamonds will free us forever."

"That's right." But Mica's mood fell—he seemed to be more interested in the diamonds than anything else.

Diane noticed her serious expression. "Mica, what can I get you for breakfast? You have to eat so you'll get stronger."

"She seems pretty strong to me," Simion cut in.

Mica laughed and then settled into her chair. "After breakfast, can you teach me how to do needlepoint?"

"I'd love to!" Diane answered. "I can show you how to knit as well, and paint using oils, if you like." Diane seemed touched but embarrassed; she ran her fingers through her long, blonde hair, with a happy look on her face. She stood up and kissed Mica on the cheek.

As Mica was relishing a glass of fresh orange juice that Diane had just squeezed for her, she was thinking that in Romania, it was all but impossible to find materials for needlepoint. Even having a TV was a luxury that they did not have. Mica and her mother enjoyed reading books together and discussing them. There was the secret short-wave radio, cooking together, and her mother also helped her practice her lines as Juliet. But most important, they had been together, even if they were silent, doing nothing, watching the flames in the fireplace and feeling warm.

But here, even though her uncle wasn't rich, everything seemed abundant. They had a car, a house with a garden, a TV, telephone, radio, and so many more things. Even Diane's plump body exemplified the fullness of life, and she was far more attractive than thin, nervous Simion. Mica thought of Shakespeare's words: "Yon Cassius, he has a lean and hungry look."

Diane said, "Okay, my dear. Breakfast time. You can have whatever you want. We consider food a priority even if we have to save money somewhere else. We have eggs, fruit, cereal, pancakes, muffins, milk..."

"Milk? In Romania," Mica replied, "there's a law that no one can have milk after they're seven years old." She recalled looking into her aunt's refrigerator the previous night and being amazed at the wealth of food, enough to feed two families in Romania for a week.

"Mica, my dear," Diane was saying, "You must promise me not to lose your accent. I love how you speak English. It becomes you." She smiled and turned to Simion. "Isn't Mica's accent charming?"

"Yes, sure," he answered. "But let's get down to serious business. I'm all yours today," he said to Mica. "Would you like to tour the city or start on our diamonds?"

"The diamonds," Mica quickly answered. "Can we make some phone calls and see if we can get the diamonds appraised this week?"

"I've already made an appointment for tomorrow at Christie's."

"Bine! Bine!" she said, feeling excited. She couldn't contain her excitement. She jumped in the air, doing a pirouette and whirling her body like a Turkish Dervish dancer.

Aunt Diane smiled. "I hope these diamonds bring you good luck."

Simion looked at her as if he had never seen a creature like her before. "Let's get back to business," he said. "Before I reconfirm, would you like me to read you a letter the jeweler wrote me?"

"Yes. I want to know everything about our diamonds."

Mica went on a survey of the kitchen, opening cabinets and drawers. So much abundance. She touched every box, can, bag, and in between, yelled, "Wow!" She wanted to sell her diamonds as quickly as possible so her parents would never be hungry again.

When Simion returned, he asked Diane and Mica to join him in the living room. He was holding several sheets of yellowed paper in his hand. "When I first met the jeweler in Bucharest in 1944, he told me he had been working in Poland. But I suspect he wasn't there as a jeweler. This is what he wrote."

December 25, 1944

Dear Mihailescu:

This letter is to be used as proof that the twenty colored diamonds and twenty white diamonds I have transferred to you in good faith and trust, once belonged to me and now are rightfully yours. I have been satisfied by how you have compensated me.

Let me give you some background about the diamonds:

In the summer of 1941, the Germans entered Leningrad. The

Russians knew they were coming and hid their art treasures in St. Isaac's Church before sending them on to warehouses in Siberia. However, the Russians could save only 18,000 items out of 54,000. The Germans got the rest. They also got the entire Amber Room, including the Romanov collection of Fabergé Easter eggs. Inside the eggs, Czarina Alexandra had hidden the Romanov collection of rare white diamonds. The Germans got those, too.

The person in charge of the Nazi Treasury in Berlin was Colonel von Nesse. He had a mistress who was born Jewish and had been deported to Auschwitz. He wanted her out. But in order for him to get her out, he had to negotiate with the head commander in charge of the concentration camp. Diamonds were the only way to talk to Commander Schlüssel.

Von Nesse sent a crate of fruit to Schlüssel as a gift. Inside the fruit, he had hidden twenty colored diamonds that he had received from Mengele. All sizes, all shapes. One of Mengele's responsibilities was to document and collect the gold and precious jewels that were stripped from the prisoners. After Mengele catalogued the treasures, he sent the colored diamonds to von Nesse in Berlin for Germany's official War Treasury. Also inside the gift of fruit were white diamonds from the Amber Room's Fabergé eggs that the Germans had stolen.

Commander Schlüssel freed von Nesse's mistress, but he was worried about being discovered with the diamonds, so he took the colored and white stones that von Nesse had given him and hid them in a muddy creek near the men's barracks.

But what Commander Schlüssel didn't know was that Jewish prisoners also hid their gold and diamonds in the same creek. Not much escaped the Nazis, but every once in a while, chance was with a prisoner and he got away without having his valuables detected. Because I had been a jeweler in Warsaw, some of the prisoners came to me to help them. The creek was a perfect hiding place for their diamonds, and a few of mine as well. Guards were afraid to go there because venomous snakes lived among the rocks.

I was in Auschwitz for two months when I was able to escape with some good luck on my side. For sure, you needed a lot of luck to survive Auschwitz. But I am ashamed to write how I escaped. If one day we should ever meet, I will tell you.

All I can say is that it would have been him or me.

Mihailescu, you are now a lucky person, the owner of the gift of diamonds. Use them so you, too, can survive.

Signed: Jacob Hersh,
Date: December 25, 1944

"I imagine," Simion said folding up the letter and putting it in his pocket, "the jeweler left Auschwitz in an unorthodox way. Probably before escaping, he dug for his own diamonds in the muddy creek. Unexpectedly, he found Schlüssel's diamonds that von Nesse had sent him, the white ones from the Amber Room along with the colored diamonds that Mengele had taken from prisoners and had sent to Berlin. That's how the white Russian and the colored German diamonds got mixed up with the jeweler's and the prisoners'."

"So," Mica said, "there were four kinds of diamonds hidden in the same creek: the white Russian diamonds from the Fabergé eggs; the colored diamonds from Mengele; the jeweler's gems; and the diamonds from other prisoners."

"That's right," Simion agreed.

"The Amber Room contained the Russian diamonds, the white ones?"

"Yes."

"What was the Amber Room?" she asked her uncle.

"Aha! It was once called the *Eighth Wonder of the World*. It was in Catherine the Great's summer palace, about an hour from St. Petersburg. It was a large room paneled with walls made of the finest amber and gold leaf. Originally, it had been given to Peter the Great in 1716 as a gift from the king of Prussia. The Germans believed it was still theirs. When they stormed through Russia during the war, they dismantled the room's twelve amber walls which were decorated with rare jewels. They also took the collection of Fabergé Easter eggs that contained white diamonds and transported everything to Germany. Some people claim the Germans buried most of the looted treasures in a secret tunnel." Simion took a deep breath. "All we know today is that the Amber Room has never been found."

Mica put her head in her hands. Simion had meant for the letter and story to document and reassure her that the diamonds were theirs, but all the letter did was to cement her suspicions that the diamonds had definitely come from Auschwitz. Blood diamonds. The horror of war. People losing their lives, their families, their treasures, everything and everyone dear to them. Experiencing horrors. Suffering. She knew she shouldn't have the diamonds. None of them should have them. It was wrong. Yet, what could she do now? She needed the diamonds to buy her parents' freedom.

The guilt and moral wrong of having the colored diamonds weighed heavily on her. Somehow, someday, she would make the situation right. She promised herself that—she would do what was right.

CHAPTER 22

MICA SPENT the next day's morning getting to know her aunt. Diane was warm and giving, and eager to love Mica like a daughter. She told Mica that she was looking forward to introducing her to the teenagers in the neighborhood and would like to invite them and their families to meet her. Then she showed her dozens of photos that she had taken of Hewlett High School, not far from their house, where she'd register Mica for school, which would resume in a week—after summer vacation. She even gave Mica a preview of the school with snapshots of the classrooms, the tennis courts, playing fields, and groups of students laughing and having fun.

Excited about things that she had never dreamed were possible, Mica spoke of her love for dancing and asked if there was a dance school nearby where she could take lessons. Like magic, Diane, showed her several photos of their town with the dance school and studio not far from the high school.

But then Diane became sad. She said, "Dance lessons are not free, like school is. They're very expensive. Maybe you can think of taking lessons after you sell the diamonds. Then you can pay for them on your own."

Mica was disappointed, but she understood. "Is it possible for me to work and make some money? Then I could start now."

"That's good of you," Diane said. "But working is a little complicated. I have to register you for a Social Security card and that can take some time." Then she hesitated before saying, "Janet Linden, our neighbor, told me she wants to go back to school. She was accepted at the law school which begins in two weeks. She needs someone to take care of Jack, who's seven months old."

"I never did that before."

"Janet will show you everything. She said she needs a sitter on Mondays, Wednesdays, and Fridays from four to eight."

"It would be like I have a baby brother."

"In a way. And you can take dance lessons three times a week."

"Sounds ideal."

"The downside is that you'll have less time for friends. And..."

"And?"

"The baby is still colicky."

"What's that?"

"A kind of stomach upset. It's not really understood. But it means the baby cries a lot."

"Oh. What can I do to stop him?"

"He stops eventually." Diane tried to smile.

Mica thought a few seconds and then answered, "Can you tell Janet I'm interested?"

"I will. I'll give you my bike so you can get around the neighborhood faster. It's old, but functional."

Mica remembered her bike in Romania. How hard it had been for her father to get it. She had left it near the border. *What lucky person found it?* she wondered.

"I'm glad to work." Mica kissed her aunt on the cheek. "I want to be as independent as possible. I don't want to be a burden to you."

"You're a good sport. I'm so happy you're here," Diane said, hugging her. "You're my real gift. Now tell me about life in Romania," and she took Mica's hand into hers.

She told Diane about her parents, her friends the Musketeers, and her love for the theater. She also told her about the bad side of her life in communist Romania, about informers being everywhere, but not knowing who they are. "They could be teachers, neighbors, friends' parents, even the priest. They'd inform on anyone who wasn't a communist or someone who'd talk nicely about America. 'A pound of sugar for a pound of flesh' was a phrase that everyone feared, but it became a way of life."

"My poor child."

"That's why it's so hard for me to trust anyone other than my parents. When I do trust someone, I have to think hard about it. That makes me very sad. The worst part is that under communism, you have no free will. I want to create my life, and choose to learn what I love to do so I can achieve something special and help others."

Diane put her arms around Mica, and Mica cried the tears that she had not cried for months. Diane held her for a long time until Mica's sobs lessened, and Diane promised she'd never let Mica feel alone again.

To lighten Mica's mood, Diane asked how she wanted to begin her day, and Mica said, "Can I take a bath?"

Aunt Diane chuckled. "Of course. Would you like bubbles with that?"

Afterwards, feeling like a different person, clean and warm and relaxed, Mica and Aunt Diane watched TV together, while Mica learned to do needlepoint and tasted chocolate chip cookies for the first time. She was fascinated at watching students demonstrate against the war in Vietnam and fight for civil rights, things that would never be possible in a communist country.

After lunch, Mica and Simion drove into Manhattan. She strained to understand the fast-paced talk on 1010 WINS radio. She wanted to absorb all she could about New York City. At the same time, she studied the people through her open window and was amazed to see how they all looked different from one another. Communism had drained Romania of all its colors, and there was a sameness to the way people dressed in shabby, colorless, baggy clothes. They even had the same ashen, worried look on their faces.

Simion parked the car, and they walked a few blocks to Christie's, which was located in an elegant building. The people working there looked as if they had stepped out of a fashion magazine. Mica felt a little ashamed of her modest, flowered dress that Magda had given her along with an old pair of sandals.

They were immediately escorted to a private room, which Mica found was even grander than Neal Bridge's office in the American Embassy.

"Miss Mihailescu, Mr. Mihailescu, let me introduce you to Michael Walters, Christie's diamond expert. He has written several books about the history of colored diamonds. I am Stanford Ericson, Christie's auctioneer and executive vice-president.

"Michael, please close the door. Miss Mihailescu, you can put your diamonds on this table. We have a special light that will enhance the diamond's purities."

Mica took out the first gem, the blue diamond, and rubbed it with a silk cloth from the table. She immediately thought of Ben and Tibi and wished they could have been there for this moment. The reflection from the diamond lit up the entire room. In Hungary and Romania, the jewel had never sparkled its glow.

Walters picked up the diamond and studied it with his loupe. Suddenly he shouted, beyond control, "This is fantastic! Fantastic!"

He put the blue diamond in a 3-D imaging machine and looked through the eyepiece while he counted out loud each tick. "Sixty-two facets! Look at the machine! Look!"

"What does that mean?" Uncle Simion asked. Mica leaned back, breathless.

"Diamonds are usually cut into fifty-eight facets."

Just what Ben said, Mica thought.

Walters continued, very excited. "But a French jeweler in the seventeenth century, Tavernier, cut his diamonds differently than anyone before, into sixty-two facets so that more light would pass through."

"Oh no," Mica moaned. Ben had been right.

"Tavernier had been warned that his original blue diamond of 112 carats was cursed, and even if he cut it into smaller diamonds, they'd be cursed also. But he didn't listen."

"Oh no!" said Simion. He was hearing this for the first time.

"This diamond that you have has been missing for decades. I read about it in Tavernier's diary in the French National Library in Paris when I was a student." His horn-rimmed glasses fell off his nose. His hands were trembling. "Where did you get it?"

"M-my father gave it to me," Mica said, hesitating. She didn't want to implicate or embarrass her uncle—tell the entire story of war and Resistance and the jeweler.

"Let me see if I can find some documentation." Ericson excused himself and left the room. Walters continued to examine the blue diamond, placing it under a halogen light. He kept turning the facets under the rays, and Mica saw the jewel make shadows on the wall. She was startled to see multiple pointy swords of light reflected on the wall. She counted sixty-two.

Walters took another instrument from a wall cabinet. Mica remembered Ben had used the same one. "Look at the spectrometer's reading. Only the diamonds that Tavernier cut himself can phosphoresce red under ultraviolet light!" His face reflected the same fiery color. Mica thought even the white of his eyes looked red.

When Ericson returned carrying several books, Mica and Simion sat down at the table with him and studied the photos of famous diamonds. Walters took out a recorder and narrated the day's findings.

Mica felt as if she were in a race and was coming close to the finish line. *Just a little more*, she said to herself. *Don't be afraid. Your diamonds aren't cursed. You will sell them, be free of them, and your bad luck will be over.*

Turning to Mr. Walters, she nervously twirled her short black hair in her fingers.

"I'm thinking about ownership papers," she began. "We have a letter from a jeweler saying the diamonds were his and that he gives them to us. Is this legal enough? If not, can you arrange some other type of documentation for us?" She remembered Ben had warned her that not having ownership certificates might be a stumbling block in selling the diamonds at an auction house.

"I can only answer your questions, Miss Mihailescu, after we see the rest of the diamonds and then we'll discuss your quandary with our legal department. Please, let's continue."

Two hours later, Mica was drenched in sweat. She didn't know if it was due to the bright lights, or the question of who owned the diamonds before the jeweler, which neither she nor Simion knew, or the two piles of diamonds on the table. Three diamonds were in the "good" pile, the large red and green and blue. Thirteen were in the "bad" pile.

"We have a lab on the premises, of course," Walters informed her. "I can't say for sure the value of the good diamonds. Our expert can do a complete analysis and appraisal tomorrow."

"Can you take a Polaroid of each diamond?" Simion asked.

"Of course. And you don't have to pay for anything as long as you both sign papers agreeing to sell with us. We do hope there will be at least one extremely valuable diamond. I think it will be the blue one." Walters smiled, pleased at the coup for Christie's. "In addition, on a business note, our legal department will have to do a search to verify there are no lawsuits related to ownership, and they will want to see what proof you have of provenance—the history of who owned the diamonds before you."

Uncle Simion reached into his pocket and took out the yellowed paper and handed it to Ericson, who, after reading it, made a face.

"That's the documentation I have," Simion stated.

Ericson's expression didn't soften. "It's not notarized."

"Notarized?" Uncle Simion said. "During the war? Most lawyers and notaries were in concentration camps!"

Walters waved his hand. He appeared to think the problem of documentation was minimal. All he wanted was to sell the blue diamond. He kept taking it from one machine to another and muttering, "Unbelievable! Incredible!"

Mr. Ericson turned to them and said, "Please understand that our House—Christie's—takes a ten percent commission on all sales."

"I see." Simion made a strange grimace. He wasn't happy with such a high amount. And Ericson wasn't happy with Simion's sole source of ownership papers.

"Can we get a second opinion?" Mica ventured.

"S-sure," Walters said, almost gasping with the thought. "The diamonds are yours, but if you decide to do that, we'll have to charge you for the appraisal."

"Can I speak privately to my niece?" Simion said, still not happy that he couldn't bargain down the commission.

"Mr. Ericson and I will get a cup of coffee. Can we bring you something?"

Both Mica and her uncle shook their heads no. The mood of jubilation had evaporated. Once they were alone, Mica fingered the diamonds that were spread out on the table. "In addition, these aren't ours to sell. There's something in me that keeps saying it's wrong. Mr. Ericson seemed to agree when you showed him the jeweler's letter."

"Mica, don't be ridiculous. Even if we wanted to return the diamonds to their original owners, we couldn't. Do you really think we should give them back to the Nazis? Or to Hitler? Or Mengele? Who is the original owner of these diamonds? Tavernier? Don't be naïve. The diamonds have passed through a dozen hands, each time changing by cutting and polishing them into another shape. Diamonds don't fit into the same law as stolen paintings or war booty. These are ours."

"True, the original owner was somewhere in India before Tavernier," Mica said, trying to rationalize the situation. "Not even the prisoners in Auschwitz were the original owners. But that doesn't make this right. It's all stolen. It's wrong, Uncle Simion. Wrong! The diamonds belonged to people who were killed in the Holocaust. I'm so conflicted what to do."

"Mica, Mica." He put his arms around her. "You're such a good person. I'm so proud you're my niece. But just think that it's your good luck to have them. Not bad luck."

Mica started to cry. "What are we going to do? Maybe they'll decide for us and not take the diamonds. Their legal department might put a stop to an auction. We don't have professional certificates of ownership," she said.

"We have the letter from the jeweler. It's legally binding. He wrote that he gave me the white and colored diamonds in good faith and he was compensated fairly. He signed and dated it. We had a business exchange. I gave him passports. Life! That's enough proof for a just exchange."

"Maybe it will be enough for the auction house, but not enough for us. We know the truth. I feel these diamonds are not ours to sell." She wiped the tears from her cheeks. "Oh, Uncle Simion, what should we do?"

He moved closer to her and took her hand. In a minute of true warmth, he was moved by her suffering. "Mica, if we give up the diamonds, no one wins. If we sell them, we can use the money to do good. We'll bring your parents here. Besides, Christie's won't let us do anything *terribly* illegal. The scandal would destroy their reputation."

"I-I don't know," she hesitated, also, worrying that she and her uncle didn't know anything about the legal aspect of selling a diamond. "Maybe we should speak to a lawyer? Or go to another auction house? Get a second opinion?"

"I don't know about a second opinion," Simion responded, shaking his head. "I don't want to bring more attention to owner-ship papers. Could erupt into a scandal even before an auction takes place. Walters, here, wants the sale. He'll calm the waters. I don't know who to trust for another opinion."

Mica remembered that Mr. Bridge had said there were two famous auction houses in New York City. Maybe the second one was worth a try.

CHAPTER 23

MICA WOKE up early in the morning before her uncle or aunt. She took out her suitcase and rummaged through the pile of clothes. Finding a package containing peppered salami that was wrapped in newspaper, she put it in her pocket and tiptoed down the stairs. In the kitchen, she cut tomato and cucumber, grated cheese, and mixed it with the spicy salami that she had brought with her from Hungary. Diane walked into the kitchen as Mica was arranging the food.

"I'm going to make you a Transylvanian breakfast," Mica announced while putting the salami under the broiler. "I know from my father that Simion used to love Hungarian salami slightly roasted. I brought some with me from Budapest as a gift. I wanted to give it to you yesterday, but I was so excited that I forgot."

"Smells good," Diane said. When it was ready, she put a warm slice in her mouth.

Simion walked in carrying a telephone directory and singing, "Good morning, sunshine. It's a great day to celebrate. Today we learn from Christie's how our jewels will rate."

"Soon, we'll celebrate," Mica sang in tune. "And to feed your hungry soul, I have a special breakfast for you."

He surveyed the feast and put a slice of warm salami from the broiler into his mouth. "Um-mm, a taste from my youth." Then he put the heavy phone book on the counter and explained that he was taking Sotheby's address just in case they decided to get a second opinion.

"Who wants coffee?" Mica asked. "I can read your future from the coffee. I made friends with a Gypsy woman who acted in our troupe. She taught me how to dance, Gypsy-style, and to see the future in the coffee grounds."

"As long as our future includes a pot of gold from our diamonds," Simion said, "that's fine by me."

"She also taught me how to use herbs to create magic."

"*Magic?*" Diane repeated.

"Yes. Herbs have special powers. I remember that Rasputin used herbs to try to help Alexis, the son of Czar Nicholas."

"I always wanted to meet a Gypsy," Diane commented. "What are they like, Mica? Do they really have supernatural powers?"

"Of course. They know everything about magic and spells. Potions are no laughing matter in Romania. Isn't that true, Uncle?"

"Umph," he answered, not interested.

Mica continued, enjoying Diane's enthusiasm and being on center stage. "When Gypsies get angry, they concoct a potion of cat stools and dead dogs and cast a spell on their opponent. I once saw a witch throw a mandrake into the Danube River, so evil would befall her enemy."

"A *mandrake?*" Diane asked. "Don't tell me that's a type of *man?*"

"It's a plant. Poisonous. With long roots and a purple flower. Looks like a poppy. Has narcotic powers."

"Oooh." Diane winced.

"I saw a Gypsy use it to put a spell on a field of wheat. She was angry with a farmer and wanted to destroy his harvest. She took a jar of river water and put pieces of mandrake inside. She held a flaming candle to the jar and in a cackling voice chanted, 'My curses always work.' Then she spilled the water on the farmer's earth."

"That's enough nonsense," Uncle Simion said.

"It's true," Mica insisted. "Even Ceausescu and his wife believe in curses. They have their own Gypsy advisor who tells them when to dress in purple to ward off evil spirits. On parade days, Ceausescu wears a purple tie."

"How about if I tie your mouth?" Uncle Simion joked. He pretended he was tying a knot with his hands. But then he put his hand to his stomach and bent over in pain.

"The salami had too much spice. Not good for my ulcers."

"Ulcers?" Mica asked, concerned.

"You can't tolerate pepper or paprika," Diane reminded him. "You shouldn't have eaten the salami."

"The meat wasn't fresh!" Simion complained.

"Of course not. It's smoked." Mica took a slice. "Look, I'm eating it and so did Diane, and we're fine."

"I hope this isn't a Gypsy curse you've put on me," Simion yelled. "We have important business today."

"I'm so sorry," Mica said, sincerely. "I didn't know you have ulcers. Let me do something to help you. I'll go to Christie's myself and bring you their written report."

He eyed her suspiciously. "With a few days of rest and medicine, I'll feel better. We'll go then. Together."

"I can't wait," she said, suddenly afraid that something might go wrong with their plans. Simion was sick now, and it was her fault. It seemed like the diamonds were bringing her bad luck. She wanted everything in place, positively, so she could get rid of the diamonds as soon as possible. She wanted to sell them fast. "You arranged for a driver. He can take me."

"Let her go," Diane coaxed him. "The driver will help her. She'll start the process, and you'll save time."

"Please, Uncle Simion. Let me go. I didn't know salami irritates your stomach. I wanted to plan a surprise for you after all you've done for me. Please believe me."

"Okay, okay," he said. Then bending over in pain, he warned her, "Make sure they take a Polaroid photo of each diamond so they can't switch them on us. I'll make you a copy of the letter from the jeweler to prove ownership. It's addressed to Mihailescu. That's you also. Remember to show them that the jeweler signed and dated it. Tell them that he gave me the diamonds in good faith and trust in exchange for passports that gave him life!" Then quickly, he ran to the bathroom.

Mica felt bad. The last thing she wanted was for him to get sick. She didn't want to wait to get another appointment. It would take time—too much time taken away from getting her parents free. She felt as if a clock was ticking for their safety.

CHAPTER 24

MICA RODE into the city alone, chatting with the driver, Hassan, a Lebanese immigrant and friend of her uncle's. He told her about his country and about Beirut, where he was born. "But, there's no place like New York," he said. "Stimuli coming from all types of people. Keeps you alive."

Arriving on Park Avenue, Hassan said he'd be waiting in the car on the side street. She walked toward Christie's and gave Hassan a wave and smile.

"Good morning, Miss Mihailescu," Mr. Ericson greeted her as she came in, shaking her hand warmly. "Are you alone today?"

"Yes, my uncle got sick."

"I hope it's nothing serious."

"Oh no, just an irritable stomach." She glanced at the clock in his office. "Sir, have you begun the analysis yet?"

"No. Our appraiser comes in at ten, and it's only nine forty-five."

Mica made a snap decision. "My uncle wanted me to tell you that we're going to come back together in a few days to watch the procedure, if we may?"

"Yes, of course."

"In the meantime, I'd like to take the diamonds, if I may?"

"They're yours, but be careful with them. New York can be a dangerous town. How will you get home?"

"My uncle arranged that his friend will drive me."

She now had an opportunity to take fate into her hands. She'd have to seize the moment. Her father had told her, "Go with your instincts."

"We wouldn't want anyone to steal your diamonds," Mr. Ericson commented.

She waited while he retrieved the diamonds. Now she'd be able to get a second opinion. She rationalized that it was fate that her uncle had become sick, and that she'd have the chance to get advice from another expert who might even offer a better commission. Her uncle would like that.

Carrying the diamonds, she crossed the street and opened the car door to get in. "I want to make another stop." She took out the paper with Sotheby's address. "Madison Avenue and 77th Street," she told Hassan.

Her uncle had been kind to her, taken her into his home, and he was showing family loyalty, but on some level, she didn't trust him completely. He was obsessed with the fact that the diamonds had once been his. All Mica wanted now was to get a second opinion, and to see if they could learn more about the legality of selling the diamonds. But no matter which auction house took the jewels, she would keep her word to her uncle—equal partners, fifty-fifty. Then she'd have enough money to save her parents. That's all she wanted. Her uncle could keep his share of the money. He'd be happy then, and rich.

"Miss Mihailescu, I'm Willy Reinhardt. My secretary told me you don't have an appointment and yet, you asked to see the diamond expert at Sotheby's... *Ya?*"

"Please," she said, "just give me a few minutes of your time. I don't think you'll be sorry. I have some unusual gems to show you."

Reinhardt looked at the leather pouch she held in her hand. "You're lucky. I had a cancellation this morning. I have a few moments free. *Ya,* this *vay.*"

She noticed his accent and smiled, thinking, New York City, lots of people with accents. Mica studied him: tall, blond, steel-rimmed glasses, middle-aged, something heavy about him despite his thin body. As he led her to a small room, she eyed the security equipment along the way, convincing herself that there was nothing risky about her plan. She just wanted a second opinion, to learn a little more about the diamonds, and maybe get a better commission deal.

When Reinhardt closed the door behind her, and they were seated, she slowly poured the diamonds onto the table. The entire room sparkled with all colors of the rainbow. Reinhardt's face appeared green, blue, pink and then red.

"*Mein Gott!*" he gasped.

"I was wondering if they could be sold in an auction?"

Speechless for a moment, he slowly picked up a green stone with tweezers and studied it with his loupe. In an excited tone, he kept saying, "*Wunderbar! Wunderbar!*"

"Why wonderful?" Mica asked.

"The stone is a very high quality: GH range, VS clarity, FG color." Then his expression changed from pleasure to concern. "Where did you get these diamonds?"

"From Romania."

He took the green diamond to a special ultraviolet light and then staring at her, he asked sternly, "Are you sure they're not German?"

"No, and I've never been to Germany."

"Did you get these on the black market in Bangkok?"

"How could I have gotten to Bangkok from Romania? I couldn't go anywhere."

"Once, when I was in Chiang Mai," he said, "a sleazy dealer tried to con me into buying a stone like this diamond. It wasn't even a genuine emerald." He picked up his eyepiece and studied the square, green stone. "Are you sure you're not working for someone?"

She was getting nervous and didn't answer. She stood up and opened her coat; feeling warm, she took it off. She was afraid that she had made a wrong decision to seek his advice.

He stared at her and moved closer. "Do you have legal provenance to sell? Proof of ownership?"

"I inherited these diamonds from my family."

He sat down, picked up the green diamond and then the large red diamond and put each one under another machine. Suddenly his tone became very dark. "Take a seat, Miss Mihailescu. Do you realize these two diamonds come from a concentration camp? They have specific markings."

She surely regretted seeking his advice. He would call the police and she'd be arrested. She remembered that at Christie's they hadn't said anything about the German markings. And yet, Ben had spoken about it.

"Let me show you." He placed the red diamond in a cup and took a thin pointer. "These are two lines and a dot, very finely hand carved. It's the mark of the S.S., a code. Today, most diamonds that have passed through concentration camps have these marks polished out. Then it's hard to trace their origin. But not yours. The mark is still there.

"Even though I'm German, I don't look very kindly on Nazi

war criminals. Did someone ask you to sell these diamonds for him? Someone who is afraid of being denounced as a Nazi war criminal?"

Mica got angry. "I got them from my father! He's not a criminal. He's still in Romania."

Reinhardt sat down next to her. "Why should I believe you?"

Mica stared at him. What should she do? Stay? Leave? Go back to Christie's? She was cornered. She could be in trouble in both places. She pulled out the letter from the jeweler and pushed it across the desk to him. He read it—and then put his head in his hands.

After a few moments, he stood up and starting pacing the room. "My brother Hans was in the Schutzstaffe—the SS. He worked in the jewelry room next to one of the crematoriums at Auschwitz. He was twelve years older than me. I was a child then. His job was to examine the living and dead bodies, for precious jewels and diamonds. What he found, he turned over to Dr. Mengele, who sent them to Berlin. Before I came to the United States, he told me about colored diamonds like these.

"After the war, he was worried about being prosecuted in war tribunals." Mr. Reinhardt took a cigarette from a pack in his pocket and lit it. "To hide, he lived in South America. He saw Mengele again in Brazil, in Rio. They used to frequent the same Clube Germanico in the southern district of Gavea. Then again, in Argentina, in Buenos Aires and again, back in Brazil in São Paulo. But my brother didn't tell anyone that Mengele was alive or where he was hiding. My brother feared for his own safety. I told him to call the Brazilian and then the Argentine police to give himself up and also tell them about Mengele." Reinhardt shook his head and his shoulders slumped.

Mica, shocked to hear all this, wondered what to do. Should she just pick up her diamonds and walk out? Should she go back to

Christie's? Say she decided to wait until her uncle was better so they could continue together? But his brother was the SS soldier, not him.

"Listen, Mr. Reinhardt," Mica said, "I just want to know if these diamonds can be sold in an auction."

She watched him as he loosened his tie and wished she could choke him, along with his brother and all their friends. She wondered if Reinhardt's brother or Mengele had handled her diamonds. If they had, they were definitely cursed. She stood up, ready to leave.

"Stay," Reinhardt ordered. He picked up the red, green and blue diamonds, the most valuable ones. "Hans told me that one of the camp commanders he was working with stole two colored diamonds, smaller ones than yours. Hans never told anyone because the commander was Mengele's childhood friend. No one ever reported the theft, and no one ever found the diamonds.

"When my brother saw Mengele for the last time, Mengele said he wished he had some of the jewelry and diamonds that SS soldiers had stolen. Theft was a big problem in the camps. You know, exile is expensive, and Mengele had to pay lots of people along the way to help him move from one place to another and safely. He learned a lot about the survival of the richest."

Mica didn't say anything; just shrugged. She didn't want to be reminded about Mengele being associated with her diamonds or his own escape.

Reinhardt continued. "After Brazil, Mengele lived in Argentina for several years without being found out. But the International Jewish community, the Mossad, the German prosecutor, Fritz Bauer, and Simon Wiesenthal—all of them knew that Nazi criminals were hiding in Buenos Aires and they wanted them. So when Adolf Eichmann was kidnapped, just a few streets from Mengele's apartment, Mengele had to get away the next day. He lived in Paraguay for a year, but then had to move on. He went to Brazil where he hid with a fascist Hungarian couple, Geza and Gitta Stammer, on their farm outside São Paulo."

"Hungarians?" Mica asked. "Did your brother ever talk about anyone else who lived there? Someone from Transylvania who wore black leather gloves? His name is Radu."

"No, never heard that name, but my brother did tell me there were other men on the farm whom he had known during the war. Mengele was almost always together with a man who spoke German with a Hungarian-Romanian accent. Mengele called him Eduardo. Why? Do you know him?"

"It must be Radu. He almost stole something from me more precious than diamonds."

"When my brother was on the farm," Reinhardt commented, "there was a scandal. This Eduardo, or Radu, raped the daughter of a farmhand. The father cut off his hand with a machete, and then Eduardo gave two yellow, heart-shaped diamonds to pay the farmer's daughter."

"They were fake!" Mica shouted. "He stole them from me! They were mine!"

Reinhardt looked at her incredulously.

"Mr. Reinhardt," she said. "Why didn't your brother go to the police to report the whereabouts of Mengele? Why didn't you?"

"I didn't want to be punished."

"Mengele should be punished! Your brother should have been punished for not reporting him. You were all accomplices."

Mica felt like throwing up, but she realized that she and Reinhardt shared something in common. Even though she had asked him why he had not informed the police about Mengele, she knew perfectly well that it was the same reason why she had not told Mr. Bridge about what she had heard between the two refugees in the clinic. She had not wanted any suspicion to fall *on her.* She had been afraid her plans would be derailed from saving her parents. It was the same behavior of conflict and fear, wanting to act but not acting, fearing the consequences were too great. She wanted to speak up, do what was right, but the risk was too high—like now: conflicted about what to do, not being strong enough to do what's right. Reinhardt, for his own reasons, had not wanted anyone to think he was like his brother. He feared he'd lose his job at Sotheby's.

Mr. Reinhardt nodded his head. "Yes, my brother was guilty of war crimes. He should have gone to the police. The last time my brother saw Mengele it was in São Paulo. *Herr Doktor* was getting more and more paranoid. He always wore a straw hat with a big brim and pulled it down to cover his forehead. He never smiled, even kept his hand over his mouth and grew a stubby mustache so no one would see the wide space between his two front teeth and recognize him. He rarely spoke, for he didn't want anyone to hear his German-accented Portuguese or Spanish. My brother said he was getting crazy."

Mica shrugged her shoulders. "At least that."

"While in São Paulo, Mengele had been hospitalized for an obstructed small intestine. The diagnosis was *trichobezoar*. He had small balls of hair imbedded in his intestine due to his nervous habit of biting and chewing bits of hair from his mustache. Doctors say they see such cases with cats and psychotics."

Mica grimaced.

"My brother died this year."

She mumbled a few words of condolence and then said, "My father gave me the diamonds. And his brother gave them to him. And the jeweler gave them to my uncle in a trade. The jeweler was in Auschwitz. He suffered. Six million innocent people and children died in the Holocaust. Millions more were never the same."

Her heart beat fast. She was furious with herself for listening, for staying. She was also trying to comprehend the complexity of the evil being revealed. "If you want to sell my diamonds, we can discuss that. If not, I'm going. I wish I had never come here."

He nodded, then rubbed his brow. "What should we do?" he asked her.

"I don't know." She put her face in her hands and slumped down in her chair.

"I can *either* contact the police about these diamonds—war booty." He gave her a threatening stare. "But I don't want to chance an investigation on me or my brother."

She bit her lip waiting for him to come up with another idea.

"*Or...* if we don't represent you, someone else will." He gave her a shrewd smile. "We can make a lot of money with these diamonds."

She shrugged again. "Can you give me a better price than ten percent for commission?" she asked him. "And can you write up a paper saying that I'm entrusting you with these diamonds until the day of the auction, and that you will insure them? Can you take a Polaroid photo of each diamond?" She tried to concentrate on the business aspects and suppress her instinct of mistrusting him.

"Yes to all your questions. I can insure the diamonds and I can get you a nine percent commission for our contract. That will still give Sotheby's a sizeable profit, for I believe the diamonds will sell high. Also, we'll have to make a copy of the letter from the jeweler for our legal department and insurance company. I'll use my influence, so there's no problem."

"How long will the appraisal take?" she asked, wanting to be reassured he was on her side.

"By the end of the day, we'll know what we're talking about, and then we can arrange the auction for a quick sale—for Christmas."

"We have a deal," and she shook his hand. "But there's one more thing..." She hesitated. "Can you advance me some money? I had all my money and suitcase stolen at the airport in Romania."

"Better that than the diamonds," he said, laughing.

She felt a twinge of guilt for lying to him. "I just arrived this morning, and I'll need to stay in a hotel until the auction."

"Sotheby's cannot give you money up front, but I can lend you $100 max from my own pocket."

"How will I live on that until the auction?"

"You could work. Like everyone else."

"Do you know a cheap hotel?"

"There's the Y on 92nd Street and Lexington Avenue. They have a few rooms. Try there. It's not far."

She thanked him, nodded her head, and left.

He yelled after her, "Come back at the end of the day when we'll have the analysis finished. I'll get the legal department to write up a contract."

Mica went back to the car. "Can you please give my uncle this message?" she said to Hassan. "Tell him I went to Sotheby's. I'll have them send him a copy of the contract later today. Everything is being done legally. They'll accept our letter from the jeweler as proof of ownership and give us a better commission. We'll be part-ners—fifty-fifty. But I'm going to stay in the city."

"I promised to drive you back home. My job isn't done."

"I apologize. Tell my aunt that I'll do what's correct. I promise her that, and I will contact her. Tell her I love her and I appreciate all she and my uncle have done for me. I must fight to the end to save my parents."

With a heavy heart, because she knew she was not doing the right thing and she was hurting her aunt and uncle, she walked into the streets of New York, all alone and very sad.

Eyeing a tall mailbox on Madison Avenue, she moved toward it and leaned against it. She was feeling nauseous, thinking of what Mr. Reinhardt had told her about Mengele. Her knees were shaking. She hoped she could trust Reinhardt—that he wouldn't go to the police. She dug her fingers into the cold steel and breathed deeply, feeling wobbly, counting, *"Unu, doi, trei, patru, cinci."*

What should I do? Should I go to the police and confess everything? Tell them about Mengele? That he was last seen in São Paulo and could still be there? Who would believe me? What would happen if the authorities accuse me of having secret information because of spying and send me back to Romania? If I don't sell the diamonds, I won't have money to save my parents. If they die, I'll never be able to live with myself.

She thought of her aunt, that she'd be so hurt that Mica didn't return with Hassan. But, then Mica thought of her uncle. She had to take control of the diamonds. She trusted herself more than she trusted him.

Mica breathed deeply, counting in English, "One. Two. Three. One. Two. Three."

She remembered the promise that she had made to herself when she was still in Budapest, that if an opportunity came to do the right thing, she would do it. She would tell someone that Mengele was still alive and last seen in São Paulo, Brazil. For now, all she could do was to make that promise to herself. She would make right her wrongs, after the sale, after she had enough funds to start the process to get her parents free.

CHAPTER 25

Mica crossed from Madison Avenue to Fifth, taking the sunny side of the street parallel to Central Park. Feeling the warmth of the late September Indian summer, she decided to change her dark thoughts and take a walk before going to the Y for a room. Autumn leaves in New York City were just beginning to turn, and she was eager to see the change of colors for the very first time. She hoped it would cheer her up.

At 89th Street, opposite the circular building, the Guggenheim Museum, she entered the park, eyed the reservoir and considered following its circular path toward the West Side. But then she looked northward and climbed up a hill that led to a dirt path marked for cyclists. Thrilled to be in the big city, and wanting to think of only that, she followed the midday sun playing hide-and-seek behind the trees and marveled as the light brightened green leaves that were turning orange.

The trail was all hers, leading to an unknown world. Every minute of being in New York evoked the adrenaline-fueled excitement of dancing on stage. She told herself not to look at her watch and instead, to delight in the pleasure of discovering New York.

As she hiked, she approached an opening at Fifth Avenue and 105th Street and, curious, walked toward a gate that was cast in the style of Old Europe. *How odd*, she thought, the wrought-iron door looks out of place in Central Park. She opened the gate, read the sign, Conservatory Garden, and entered a large rectangular area brightened by an emerald lawn. Opening up before her like an oasis of colors, the path was lined with roses as if it were a rainbow.

On the right was a hidden trail that led to another circular garden with a fountain in the center that was highlighted by a metal sculpture of three dancing maidens. Water sprayed from their smiles in a vibrant rush.

She sat down to marvel at the garden's array of flowers. Yellow pansies, blue-green hydrangea, black-eyed Susans, and hundreds of white chrysanthemums created a palette more vibrant than anything from an artist's brush. She leaned back on her bench, took deep breaths and watched the flow of people pass by. She smiled, enchanted by the city's mosaic of people speaking different languages with a variety of different faces. It appeared magical to her and her future looked bright. She would soon be free of her diamonds and have enough money to save her parents. No more would she be haunted by memories from the past.

As she was taking in the diverse colors of the scene, her eyes focused on the fountain where she saw a little boy about three years old. He was running in and out of the spray with his sister, who looked about four or five. The children were wearing bathing suits and sandals. Each one was holding a bucket, which they filled with water from the fountain, and then poured it on the head of the other.

They laughed and shrieked as the cold water dripped down their hair. The boy was blond and his sister had long auburn braids with red ribbons at the end. Over and over, they bent down together to fill their buckets and pour water on each other while the sun brightened their shoulders, making them look like angels.

Mica was mesmerized watching them play.

"Let's race over there to the flowers," the sister said, and laughing ran to the rose patch. Her little brother followed and raced toward her.

"Let's do it again," she told him, holding his hand. "You see the tree over there? You run toward it, and I'll count how long it takes you."

He smiled and ran before she even started to count.

"One, two, three, four!" she shouted.

"I won!" he yelled and touched the tree.

"Wait there," she told him. "Watch me do it in three."

She raced toward him, screamed *three*, and kissed her baby brother. "Let's go back and play with the water!" Then she ran away. He followed, but fell, and started to cry. His sister ran back to him and hugged him. Then a tall woman with braids like her daughter and blond hair like her son, went over to her children and wiped the boy's knee clean.

"Come sit with me," the woman said gently, and took him in her arms and kissed his teared cheek. The big sister followed skipping at her mother's side.

Mica watched as their mother dried them with a large towel and put a fresh t-shirt on each one. Taking out two cans of juice, she put a straw in each drink and gave them to the children. Then she took out two slices of bread and a plastic container of honey and squeezed the thick honey onto the bread. The children ate quietly at their mother's side and cuddled into her arms. Then they started to sing, "Row, row, row your boat, gently down the stream…"

Mica's eyes watered. She moved to the edge of her bench to block the sun from her face and wiped a tear away. She wondered what would it be like to have children, to be a mother. Yes, she thought, one day, she could see herself taking care of her children, protecting them. She felt that she had so much love to give.

It was at that moment, in an epiphany, that Mica realized she was a woman. All the experiences she had so painfully passed through during the year had made her understand a woman's joy in loving and wanting to give more.

She tried to hold on to this hope.

MICA WALKED TO 92ND STREET AND LEXINGTON AVENUE AS MR. Reinhardt had directed her. There was a large building that extended the entire block. Being there was no sign indicating its name, she approached a woman on the steps and asked, "Is this the 92nd Street Y?"

"Go to the next building for the entrance," the woman said, pointing.

Mica entered the building. The only furniture was a desk with a girl seated behind it, reading a book.

"Can I help you?"

"Good afternoon," Mica said. "Do you have a hotel here?"

"Hotel?" the girl laughed. "We have dormitories."

"What's that?"

"Four girls in a room. Bathroom down the hall."

"Is it possible for me to have something?"

"Let me see if I have a bed free."

"It's free? No money?"

The girl laughed again. "Free, meaning available. It'll cost $20 a night, which includes a small breakfast." She opened a big black book, turned some pages. "Yup, one is empty. We reserve for three nights at a time. Pay me up front: $60."

Mica calculated. $100 that Mr. Reinhardt had just lent her. The $300 from her father's drawer minus $2 for the pears in Budapest, and the $20 that Ben had given her, were all hidden in her room at her uncle's house. She certainly couldn't get that now. How would she manage for three months on Mr. Reinhardt's $100?

Trying to stay cheerful, she searched in her pocket, and gave the girl three of her five $20 dollar bills."

"Want a receipt?"

"Is the receipt free?"

The girl laughed again. "If you have luggage, you have to carry it. Elevator is down the hall. Second floor, number three." She handed Mica a key and returned her attention to her book.

Mica just realized that she hadn't brought her suitcase. She hadn't planned to stay in the city alone. Her decision had been impulsive—to take advantage of the situation. Now she had nothing with her: no pajamas, no toothbrush, no change of clothes or underwear. Whatever she'd need, she'd have to buy.

"Excuse me, please, Miss, do you know how I can find work?" she asked the girl.

"There's a bulletin board behind me," the girl replied, pointing without letting her eyes leave the page. "Maybe you'll get lucky."

"I need good luck. One more thing, please—is there a phone here?"

"On the right. Not free. Takes a dime. I can give you change for a dollar, if you need it."

"I only have $20 dollar bills."

"Nope, no change for that big a bill."

Mica looked down.

The girl sighed. "No problem. Here. Take this and give it back to me another time." She gave Mica a dime from her purse.

Mica wanted to phone her aunt and uncle. She became very unhappy thinking of them, and tried to rationalize and convince herself that she had to do what she had to do—she needed to be sure that her uncle wouldn't take control of the diamonds. By going to the second auction house, she became the contact person and would make sure that Sotheby's lawyers send a copy of the contract to her uncle, assuring him that he and Mica were equal partners.

She phoned her uncle and confessed what she had done.

"I took the diamonds from Christie's to Sotheby's, a nine percent instead of ten percent commission." She hoped this detail would soften his anger. She told him about her meeting with Willy Reinhardt. But when he reprimanded her for negotiating on her own, she took the phone receiver away from her ear, waited for silence and then continued.

"I'm living in the 92nd Street Y near Sotheby's, so I can oversee their preparations for the auction." She realized her reason was weak—surely Sotheby's would not require her help, would they? But she needed to give him a concrete reason for staying in Manhattan. "Everything has been done legally," she assured him. "Their lawyers are appraising all the diamonds and they're preparing a contract. They have not asked for documents of original ownership. The jeweler's letter was enough."

Simion was silent.

"I think Mr. Reinhardt was eager to have the auction."

"When will I get the contract?" His voice was angry, but she sensed he was also hurt.

"This afternoon, when they finish the paper work, take photos of all sixteen diamonds, and write up legal documents. Sotheby's will insure the diamonds and keep them in their vault until the auction. One week after the auction, they'll divide our earnings in half, minus their nine percent commission. The lawyer will send you a summary that documents the process with dates and figures."

Then he whispered, "Mica, my dear, *draga*, it's not just the diamonds. We've been worried about you. If anything would have happened to you..."

She felt like crying, touched by his soft tone and his caring, but she needed to stay resolute despite her conflicts. "I'm safe. I'm trying to bring my parents here and our family can be all together. Please try to understand and forgive me for what I've done."

"But you need money to live on."

"I will work."

"Ask her what she'll do," she heard her aunt Diane say.

"I don't know yet. I'll find something."

"Can we see you?"

She started to sob and hung up.

MICA WENT TO THE Y BULLETIN BOARD TO STUDY THE JOB opportunities. She couldn't help but feel grown up and independent; and yet, she prayed her venture of being alone in New York City wouldn't bring her bad luck as punishment.

She read what jobs were available:

- Wanted: person needed to clean apartment, cook, iron, care for 3 children, walk dog
- Escort Services: Handsome young men looking for beautiful young women
- Massage Parlor: assistant needed for body building and exercising
- Ice Cream store: part-time, six afternoons, Lexington Avenue and 99th Street; bonus: free ice cream

The last one sounded promising. She made a mental note of the address and asked the girl at the desk to direct her to 99th Street. As she walked north, she realized it was her second day in New York and apart from her hike in Central Park, it was a new experience of walking in the city's streets.

Not wanting to miss anything, she was busy looking everywhere. But as she neared 96th Street, she noticed the buildings and stores change. There were no tall buildings, but three-and-four-story buildings, with graffiti and funny designs painted on the walls. Stores didn't have fancy, large front windows, but steel bars bolted across the doors. Bags of garbage lined the sidewalks and smelled awful on this sunny day. Water hydrants were leaking while children in their underwear played in the spray.

She heard people around her greet each other, with *"Hola, qué tal?"* and she wondered what language are they speaking. Men eyed her as she passed by and she felt their stare. She was uncomfortable and looked down, eyeing her best floral dress she was wearing for her morning appointments and thinking that now, it looked out of place.

At 99th Street, she came to a store with a big ice cream cone painted on the door. Inside, a dozen people were waiting in line for ice cream. There was one girl behind the counter trying to satisfy all the people, many of whom were shouting at her in the same language Mica had heard in the streets. *"Chiquita. Ahora, no mañana. Tengo hambre. Más rápido."*

A heavyset man with a big stomach and tight t-shirt came out of the kitchen and approached Mica. *"Qué quieres aquí?"*

Mica didn't understand him, but she smiled and said, "There was a sign at the 92nd Street Y for a job."

He eyed her from head to toe, stopping at her breasts for several seconds and then grinned, obviously pleased. "You're interested?" he asked her.

"Yes."

"It's every afternoon except Sunday. One o'clock to six o'clock, five dollars an hour. You can eat one ice cream a day, but all the tips in the can go to me. I need to cover my expenses, plus a little more. Agree?"

She calculated: five hours at $5 an hour. She'd be able to pay her room and food and maybe, have a little left over. "Sounds good to me."

"Great. You can start tomorrow at 1:00." He called the girl behind the counter, Estancia, and introduced them while business continued. Mica didn't find him pleasant or polite, but she said nothing, determined to make the first job in her life a success.

She left the ice cream store and walked south to Sotheby's to get her copy of the contract and tell Mr. Reinhardt that she needed another copy sent to her uncle. When she arrived, Reinhardt was all smiles. Obviously, the appraisal had gone well and he was confident. He assured her that the diamonds would bring in a big price.

Taking advantage of his good disposition toward her, she asked him if she could assist with preparing the sale. He said he couldn't pay her, but he'd allow her to work a few hours each morning with his staff on press releases and publicity. He told her she'd be able to create a buzz for the sale by talking directly with journalists and sharing her story of how a seventeen-year-old girl escaped Romania all alone with rare colored diamonds.

He had chosen the three best diamonds, the green, red and blue. "Perfect cut, color, clarity, and they're huge! The others are flawed." He advised Mica not to sell the thirteen other diamonds in the first sale, but at another time.

Mica couldn't believe that the auction was going to take place and that she was going to sell her diamonds in New York City. It was a dream more real than anything she could have ever imagined.

CHAPTER 26

THE NEXT DAY, Mica woke up at 6:00 when the Y breakfast room started serving tea, juice, and toast. She had several hours before going to assist at Sotheby's, and didn't have to go to her job at the ice cream store until 12:00.

She just couldn't wait to explore the city. She decided to take Fifth Avenue because she remembered how beautiful it looked when she had hiked yesterday in Central Park.

She took the eastern side of the avenue from 92nd Street and walked south, admiring the luxurious apartment buildings, so regal and finely sculpted. Every few seconds she looked on the other side of Fifth Avenue to admire the soft velvety green of the park. She never felt so excited or so happy. From time to time, she'd touch a bush and caress its leaves and put her nose to the flowers and smell their sweetness. She looked into a store window and saw her reflection. In a second window, her lips turned into a smile. So thrilled, Mica jumped to the sky and kicked her heels with her lucky boots and performed a soft shoe dance.

On her return, she strolled on the western side, starting at the Plaza Hotel. She greeted each horse from its carriage with a rub on the nose. She spoke to the birds and pretended to fly with them and when they flew away, she kissed them good-bye with her arms stretched high. She thought of her colored diamonds and prayed they would bring her parents to her as a treasure dearer than any jewel in the world.

ARRIVING AT SOTHEBY'S, SHE SET HERSELF TO LEARN FROM MR. Reinhardt and his staff. She enjoyed chatting with journalists and sharing her story of how she escaped a communist country. She always finished by telling them, "Please write about the auction, not me. It's a sale of rare colored diamonds that will make history."

At 12:00, she left Sotheby's and walked north to her job at the ice cream parlor. As she approached 96th Street, she noticed two boys, about twelve or thirteen years old, following her. When she turned around to shoo them away, they ran inside a store and she heard them yell at her, *Puta! Puta!* and laugh. Frightened, she started to run. She didn't understand the word, but she understood their menacing laugh.

She ran into the ice cream store, put on a white coat and confessed to Estancia, her co-worker, what had just happened. "Not a nice word," her co-worker told her sympathetically. "You should take the bus."

Mica felt at ease with Estrancia. She was sure she would help her navigate this new part of the city. She asked her for a brief training of what she'd need to know for the job: how to put a scoop on a cone without breaking the cone, where to rinse the scooper before reusing it., and a tour of the flavors and cups.

After the five-minute session, Mica began filling orders from customers as they asked for a single scoop, *una bola de helado,* a cone, *un cono,* a cup of ice cream, *una copa,* a milk shake, *un batido* and a malted, *malteada.* But Mica wasn't sure which Spanish words meant what and what the English words meant as well. She never realized there were so many different ways of ordering ice cream and numerous choices of flavors. Luckily Estancia was there, calm and steady, and ready to help with explanations. But both languages kept mixing together and Mica felt more and more confused. This this was what travelling from one culture to another felt like. She had known the feeling before. And was grateful to have a friend and interpreter. Yet, the tension grew.

Mr. Cruz, the owner, was clearly impatient with her learning curve. She needed to work faster he told her each time he passed by. Mica kept trying.

But there was a question of pricing. It took her several minutes to calculate and collect the unfamiliar currency. She had never seen American coins before. This was what it was like to be newly arrived in a different culture. Exciting yet frightening as well. As her mistakes compounded, Mica became overwhelmed. She was not used to failing and it was not so simple to fit in. She had miscalculated her decision to work there. Instinctively, without analyzing what she should do, she fled.

Mica ran all the way to 92nd Street. Sitting on the steps in front of the Y, she put her face in her hands and sobbed. *What should I do? Where should I go? I'm making so many mistakes*, she thought. Shaken up by the incident, she tried to reassure herself to be more patient with learning new ways. Maybe she'd need to be more circumspect in her decisions, act more slowly, think of others.

Mica remembered how she acted with her aunt and uncle. So unkind of her. Such a mistake. *They treated you as if you were their own. You were wrong to walk away.*

As she sat sobbing and shaking, she looked up and saw her aunt standing next to her. Mica was speechless, but then she heard her speak. "Mica, dearest, we've been worried sick about you. Please, let us take care of you. Let us love you."

Mica leaned into her aunt's arms and stayed there for several minutes, hoping the moment wouldn't leave her. Then she saw her uncle standing nearby. He came over to her and put his arms around her without saying a word and kissed her on the cheek. After a few moments, Simion asked her, "Why did you go to live on your own without discussing it first with us? Young ones never realize how much there is to learn." He paused and then hugged her. "The most important thing is that we've found you."

Diane said, "Come home. School begins next week. I've registered you. I also spoke to my neighbor, Janet, about you helping with her baby. You'll have a chance to learn about your new home at a pace you can manage. There is much to learn and to look forward to. I went to the dance studio to get their schedule."

Mica wiped tears from her face. She was happy in her aunt's arms.

CHAPTER 27

THE FIRST FEW days as an American teenager living in the suburbs was like theater for Mica. She couldn't believe it was her life and not a role. But she acted accordingly, and day by day she surrendered her defensive façade of mistrust and allowed her inner person to be confident.

The first thing Diane did was to take her into town to a Levi's store and buy Mica two pairs of jeans in the latest bellbottom style, along with several matching shirts—plaid, stripe, and solid green to bring out her hazel eyes—and white sneakers and tennis socks. Then she took Mica to her beauty parlor where she had her hair cut and shaped to a shoulder length. Everyone came over to Mica to admire her new style, flowing freely with natural waves. "You look beautiful," several women told her, and she thanked them, shyly. When she looked in the mirror to assess the image, she saw an American teenager—and then realized it was her.

Next, her aunt took her to Hewlett High, where she was given the choice to begin as a junior, which would mean she'd be a year older than her classmates, or as a senior, which would mean she'd have to study very hard to catch up. Without hesitation, Mica chose the more difficult path.

Diane proved to be a tireless and faithful tutor: reviewing with Mica each assignment, explaining new concepts and editing all her English assignments. For math, Mica was on her own. The Romanian curriculum was at least two years ahead of the American program, and this allowed Mica the chance to make friends: she knew the material many of them struggled with and she was always available to help her classmates understand trigonometry and calculus. She had a knack for explaining what was complicated so it appeared easy.

Simion and Diane threw a party and invited the teenagers in the neighborhood and her classmates to meet Mica. They even set up a record player in the yard and arranged a dancing area on their lawn. That's when Mica came alive. She couldn't stop dancing, wanting to celebrate her new life. Her new friends wanted to learn each one of her dance steps. The pleasure reminded her of how she and Magda had arranged the dancing party in Budapest. She had felt then, as now, the joy of being a teenager.

BABYSITTING WAS A NEW ADVENTURE AND A CHALLENGE. MICA HAD never taken care of children—she had no siblings or cousins. At first, she was hesitant, taking care of a baby was a big responsibility. Jack was only seven months old, not crawling yet and was quite heavy to carry at twenty-one pounds. He still had colic and was teething, and cried a lot. Mica didn't know what to do when he 'd trade his smile to tears and cry. The only thing that would settle him down was to carry him in her arms and dance with him. She soon realized how much pleasure she had in doing that, and little by little, he didn't cry anymore.

She taught him how to laugh and chuckle, make noises with his mouth, and even clap his hands. But what he liked the most was when Mica would take him in her arms and sing to him. She'd sing to him in Romanian because there was no other way she could express her joy of holding him. Even when he fell asleep, she continued to sing softly and rock him in her arms. Every few minutes, she'd kiss his soft cheek and remember the songs her mother used to sing to her.

Mica's schedule of babysitting meant she had time to do her homework before going to bed, or all day on Sunday. Tuesdays, Thursdays and Saturdays were her days to dance. Using Diane's bike, she was able to get from school to town in five minutes. She couldn't wait to get to the ballet barre and warm up. Dancing was the best part of her week. She felt it was a reward for her escape from a communist country.

She loved dancing, every movement of her body was a liberation, a reminder that she was unbound. She loved to challenge each muscle to move faster, to absorb the music and let it flow through her blood. Dancing for her was not only physical but spiritual. It was her inner world. Her moment to be free. It was during this time, that Mica knew for certain, she wanted to be a dancer.

September and October flew by quickly. Mica studied hard at school, babysat, and danced. All this she did with passion and gratitude as she waited nervously to sell the diamonds and prayed that after the auction, she'd find a way to get her parents free.

CHAPTER 28

DECEMBER: CHRISTMAS AUCTION AT SOTHEBY'S

THE NOISE from taxis and curious seekers overtook Sotheby's from 77th Street to 86th on Madison Avenue. Uncle Simion dropped Mica off in front of Sotheby's while he and Diane parked the car. Mica pushed her way through the crowd toward a side entrance for staff only. She was dressed in her boots and Shakespearean coat for good luck.

The *New York Times* Metro section loved a Cinderella story, and one journalist, Rudy Beyer, a Metropolitan reporter, was particularly fascinated by Mica and the diamonds. Sotheby's had cooperated with the press, providing photos of the diamonds and arranging for Mica to give interviews. They hoped the buzz would garner deep-pocketed bidders. And it had, also provoking interest in the rare colored diamonds and their owner, the Romanian teenager—her escape, her wiliness, her skills as a negotiator with Sotheby's.

Beyer interviewed Mica and wanted to know more about her. "How did you escape all alone from a communist country?" was his first question. Readers were intrigued. They enjoyed his story about Mica, which he titled, "A Diamond in the Rough." She was living the American dream, rags to riches, now at eighteen.

Slipping through the door, Mica walked toward the auction room. A sign on the door read:

By Invitation Only
Register at Desk Inside This Room

She entered and saw a platform furnished with a desk that held three telephones, each a different color. A skinny man with spectacles perching on his long nose sat there alone. In front of him were a Rolodex and a large black book similar to an accountant's ledger.

Not knowing who Mica was, he started his speech. "Print your name to register. Write your bank account's information. Commission for the house is added to the bill. Here's your paddle, number 237."

"I'm not bidding. I'm Mica Mihailescu." She moved into the large auction hall and stopped where rows of chairs began. Several people stared at her and whispered. She smiled back as if she were Juliet on stage.

She surveyed the packed room. There were very few seats available. Simion and Diane were just entering. Mica waved to them to sit next to her with some of the staff from the auction house. But security guards were placed strategically at each corner, and blocked their movement. Diane threw Mica a kiss and mouthed, "Good luck." Uncle Simion waved his wide-brimmed white hat.

Off to the side of the room were two armchairs, each occupied by a beautiful woman wearing a pink Chanel suit. Their role was to take down the bidders' names and paddle numbers. At the head of the room was a platform with a podium for the auctioneer.

Mica watched as the crowd slowly filled the room. An old man, hunched over and leaning on a cane, was trying to find an empty chair. Not being able to walk well, he bumped into a few chairs, made a lot of noise, and tripped over several peoples' feet. A few people stood up to help him, as did Mica. Then she heard the sound of the auctioneer's gavel. She turned to look at Simion and Diane, and they exchanged nervous glances.

"Everyone please be seated!" the auctioneer yelled. His voice vibrated throughout the room. He was now in charge, director as well as star of the show. The stage was all his.

"My esteemed clients, today we will make history. Years from now you will read about this day, these diamonds, and you will say, 'I was there.' Three, rare, colored diamonds, green, red, and blue, each one larger than 30 carats, will be auctioned today.

"All kinds of famous people have owned them: King Louis XIV of France, Marie Antoinette, Napoleon Bonaparte, Peter the Great of Russia, Catherine the Great, Czarina Alexandra, the last Romanov, and now three of you!

"Is everyone ready? Let's begin.

"First exhibition, the green diamond, size: 32.175 carats, 82 millimeters, square shaped. Observe its image on the overhead screen. Remember, one colored diamond exists for every 100,000 white diamonds."

The auctioneer banged his gavel on the podium. "Ladies and gentlemen, do I have one million dollars for this square green jewel? Yes. Do I hear one million one? Yes. One million two? Yes. Do I hear one million three? One million four? No? Going... going... *gone* for one million three to the lady in the green-feathered hat." And then he nodded to her, "Please raise your paddle."

"Bravo!" the crowd yelled.

"Let's go on to our next diamond. We have a red one. It's 34.224 carats, 85 millimeters. Red is the rarest of all colored diamonds. Do I hear a bid of one million one?"

"Yes," came the bid from a woman in a red dress.

"One million three?"

"Yes," said a man in the corner wearing a white suit, black shirt, white tie and white Borsalino hat.

"One million four?"

"Yes!" shouted the woman as she waved her numbered paddle and red alligator purse.

"One million five?"

"Yes!" countered the man who stood, holding his paddle up and waving it with his black sunglasses.

"One million six?"

"Yes!" bellowed the woman, her voice getting louder.

"One million seven?" the auctioneer asked, turning to the man with the Italian hat.

"*No, basta, prego.* Boss said no more than one million five." The man with the hat sighed and sat down.

The woman bidding against him yelled, "It's mine!"

"Bravo!" shouted the people in the room for the lady with the alligator purse.

"Let's continue," resumed the auctioneer. "The blue St. Petersburg diamond. Here it is on the screen. Owned by Russian aristocrats, their prized jewel. This is what dreams are made of: power, wealth, and fame. May the luckiest person here win this prize. May the most famous or *infamous* among you get what he or she has always dreamed of."

On the overhead screen, a film clip from a movie appeared. Marilyn Monroe, dressed in furs and jewels, was singing, "A kiss on the hand might be quite Continental, but diamonds are a girl's best friend."

The men in the room whistled, the women applauded. "Yay!" they all cheered.

"Ladies and gentlemen, silence. The bidding will now start for this 39-carat, round-shaped, blue diamond. Remember, when you are bidding, take into consideration its rarity, its history. It's the only blue diamond in the world that's available for sale.

"Do I have two million? Two million one? Do I hear two million two? Yes! Do I hear two million three? Yes! Two million four? Yes! Two million five? Again, two million five? No? Two million four it is! The winner is the man sitting in the corner. Sir, stand up so we can all see you."

"I am standing."

Laughter followed his words.

"So you are. Do you realize that you're the winner of the most fabulous blue diamond living outside a museum? How do you feel?"

"Alive. Like I can fly. Tomorrow is my mother's eightieth birthday. I think she'll have a great deal of pleasure when I give it to her."

"Does she have an occasion to wear such a treasure?"

"Of course. A woman is never too old to enjoy beauty, even if she thinks she has lost her own. For me, my mother is as beautiful as she's ever been and I'm proud to give her this gift."

"Folks, I leave you today with that parting thought: may we all have gifts and loved ones around us. Bless you all and that's the end of our show."

As Mica prepared to leave, she was busy calculating her earnings: one million three for the green diamond, one million six for the red, two million four for the blue. Five million four from all, minus nine percent, and fifty percent of that. *"Oh my God!"* she shouted: two million four for me! She was going to be extremely rich.

While she was holding on to a chair to steady herself, the old man she had seen earlier, approached her. "Mihailescu," he said. "I have something important to tell you."

Mica walked toward him. "Yes?"

"Let me introduce myself." He spoke slowly and pointed to a corner of the room where they could talk alone. "My name is Jacob Hersh."

She remembered his name.

"I'm the jeweler, the original owner of the colored diamonds."

"Y-yes," she whispered. "What can I do for you?" She put her hand in her pocket where she had placed the copy of his letter in case she'd need it at the auction. And now he was here. She hoped he wouldn't say he was the rightful owner- the letter was clear on the point of ownership. He had been satisfied when justly compensated.

"I thought you would like to know how I got the diamonds."

"Of course."

"I'm not very proud of the story, but in a concentration camp, the only thing that mattered was to survive."

She pulled out an empty chair and helped him sit down.

"I was deported to Auschwitz in the summer of 1944," he began. "Because I was young and strong, the Germans used me to work. I carried heavy crates of food from the trucks to the kitchen. One evening, the German driver of the meat truck came into the kitchen alone. Usually, there were two German soldiers for each truck.

"*'Wo ist Ihr Freund?'* Where's your friend?' I asked.

"'He has gout. Can't walk.'

"I wanted to spit at him, thinking of all the prisoners in the camp who were starving, but I didn't say a word. If I had, he'd have shot me on the spot. Instead, I decided on a plan.

"I had amassed money—gold and diamonds that I received from other inmates because I had access to food from the kitchen. People were starving; they paid whatever I asked. I hid my valuables in a box deep in a muddy creek. That night while everyone was sleeping, I retrieved my treasures from the earth. But as I was digging, I heard a clink. I didn't know what I'd hit. I thought someone else must have hidden something in the same creek. Then I saw two steel boxes. I opened them and couldn't believe my eyes. The most unbelievable diamonds! All colors, all sizes.

"One box had a German flag in the corner. The other box had a tag with Russian words. I couldn't read the Russian, but I certainly recognized a treasure. The diamonds were now mine.

"The next evening when the driver and his meat truck arrived at the camp's kitchen, I had my own treasure hidden on me plus the German and Russian diamonds. As usual, I went to the truck to pick up the crates. The German soldier was alone, sitting in the driver's seat. He was smoking and listening to the radio with his door open.

"In one second, I sneaked behind him, and with one blow from a butcher's knife, I gave him a chop at the back of his neck. In the next second, I stabbed him in the neck, over the larynx.

"I quickly changed clothes with him, put on the Nazi cap, hid his body behind some crates in the kitchen yard, and drove off with his truck. I had to take the risk. What did I stand to lose? My life? There was no life at Auschwitz. Only death.

"The guard at the gate gave me a *Heil Hitler* salute. I nodded and saluted back, and then continued down the road. At the first sight of trees, I abandoned the truck and ran.

"The rest of the story? False passports in Budapest for white and colored diamonds, plane tickets to America, no more persecution. A life."

"You did what you had to do," Mica whispered.

"Yes, but I'm ashamed. People were dying of starvation. I took advantage." He picked up his cane, leaned on it, and adjusted his hearing aid. "Every day I thought I should be punished for what I did."

Mica looked down and closed her eyes. The price of survival. Guilt.

"I understand." And she did. The diamonds had once belonged to other people, many of whom had been murdered. To assuage her own conscience, she told Mr. Hersh, "If your story is true, and the diamonds were originally yours, you're entitled to be compensated from the auction's earnings."

He gave her a hint of a smile.

"I hope you don't mind," Mica said, "but I'd like you to prove you are who you say you are."

"What do you mean? I am me."

She took out a pen from her pocketbook and a piece of paper. "Could you sign your name?"

He did as asked. She took the paper and walked away, while reading the jeweler's letter and comparing the signatures.

She returned to the old man. "I'd like to help you..."

But before she could finish her words, Uncle Simion called Mica's name and ran toward her. "My beautiful niece, today's our day to celebrate! We made a fortune! It's a done deal!" Simion yelled and threw his hat in the air. Diane took Mica in her arms and kissed her cheeks several times. "You're a genius!"

Mica smiled and then gave her attention to the old man next to her. "Uncle, let me introduce you to your jeweler friend."

"We-ll... I'll be damned." Simion was shocked. "I do recognize you—your cleft chin, that nasty scar on your left cheek. It's been a long time." Simion bowed respectfully and took off his white hat.

"Uncle Simion," Mica said, "we did earn millions, and we can afford to do what is right. We must be good to Jacob, or God will turn his back on us."

"What are you getting at?" He eyed her suspiciously, and then took her to the side. "Let's discuss the matter first. What do you have in mind?"

"We have to share with Jacob. It's because of him that we have the diamonds. I propose that you and I pay for all his expenses, and much more, to the end of his life. He should be comfortable and be taken care of."

Simion stared at Jacob's cane and hunched back. "I guess we can all be happy with such an arrangement. We did earn a fortune." Then Simion hugged her. "Mica, my beautiful niece. You're such a good person. Now, on to our next challenge. We'll fight together to get your parents with us."

As Mica was smiling, she saw two guards moving toward the door, carrying a table. On top of the table were the three diamonds, covered with a Lucite electronic device. She walked over to the security men and asked, "May I say good-bye to my jewels?" They glanced at one another. One guard, recognizing her, answered, "Yes." He disengaged the wires and took out his gun.

Mica held up the blue diamond. As the overhead light beamed on it, she heard her father's words when he showed her the diamonds for the first time: *Look more, go deeper, don't be afraid.*

And now, in the middle of the diamond, she thought she saw a face. It was hard to say if it was a man or a woman. It was old. The eyes were squinted, surrounded by creases and lines. The face was frail, the skin weathered and wrinkled. The short, white hair was covered by a cap of gray and white stripes. The person spoke, and Mica tried to hear the words, but the striped hat disappeared, and Mica saw the face of Mengele. Then his face transformed into other faces that were distorted by tears.

Mica moved closer to the diamond, and the facets became another screen with a moving image of faces from her journey. Evil devils who tried to kill innocent people: the fascist witch, the miners, Radu. Their faces merged together, and the blue diamond appeared red in the overhead light. She thought she saw streaks of blood.

Mica returned the blue diamond to the guard. *How strange life is*, she thought. *I should be relieved. I'm free of the diamonds.* But the emotions of the auction had been too much for her and she started to sob. She was afraid she'd have to pay, somehow, for having possessed the diamonds.

Uncle Simion approached her and took her in his arms. "Mica, my brave niece, don't be sad. We have work to do."

CHAPTER 29

AFTER THE AUCTION, the first thing Uncle Simion did was buy Mica a bicycle.

Certainly as a millionaire she could buy her own, but Simion wanted to give her a token of his love and a symbol of her success. He had custom-painted red, white, and blue stripes on the 24" Schwinn. She was delighted with the gift, riding her American bike all over town, going to school with it, visiting friends, and taking dance lessons.

She loved dancing, all types—ballet, tap, modern—and was so good at all of them that Uncle Simion transformed their finished basement into a dance studio with walled mirrors and a ballet barre. He even had a special stereo system installed so she could listen to music that she loved so much while she practiced. Uncle Simion wanted to do more for her, but Diane thought it best that Mica should live like any other teenager her age. Mica agreed, and told them that she didn't want to use her wealth for herself. The money was meant to get her parents to New York, and to use it to pay lawyers to achieve this. To pay for her dance lessons, she continued babysitting for she loved Jack like a baby brother.

At Simion's advice, Mica invested half her money with a financial company and she kept the other half liquid in an account in her parents' name for their legal expenses.

Yet her life did change after the auction, for she discovered the importance of dance. The best part of her week was Saturday when Aunt Diane drove her into the city to a special high school dance program. George Szabo had sent his film of Mica dancing at the American Embassy to his sister, Anna, who then contacted Mica to apply for a special dance program for high school seniors who would be interested in attending Juilliard in the fall. She was a teacher at the school.

Every Saturday, from early morning to late afternoon, Mica was one of fifteen eighteen-year-olds who took lessons in tap, ballet, jazz, classical, and modern dance with Juilliard professors. For Mica, it was better than any dream.

She loved dancing. To lose herself in the movement of her body in harmony with the music was special for her. And best of all, she was beginning to understand that dance is only true if it comes from the need to give meaning to her life. For this reason, she gave all of herself to learn.

Her best friend at Juilliard, Annabel Grace, was smart, funny, spirited, and talented. Mica loved warming up with her. They made a game out of all their ballet pliés at the barre while their knees were busy bending. Even during modern dance and tap practice, they found time to joke and laugh.

Annabel brought out the happy side of Mica. They made an interesting pair of friends, Mica with her dark, almost black hair that she wore shoulder length, and her hazel eyes shaped like almonds above high cheek-bones, and Annabel, with long, blond hair that she wore in a ponytail, and her round cheeks sprinkled with freckles and two charming dimples.

Like dancing butterflies, they were always laughing and chatting. Annabel was fascinated by Mica's stories of Romania. "Such an exotic world. Sounds unreal. Tell me more." And Mica, a natural storyteller, was thrilled to have her friend as an audience.

But it was at night when Mica was all alone that her beautiful life turned dark as she thought of her parents in Romania. It was eleven months since she had escaped. She didn't know what had happened to them, but she refused to think they were dead. Many nights, she couldn't sleep. Horrific nightmares kept her tossing and twisting.

Immediately after the auction, Mica and Simion set out to try to discover what had happened to Anton and Corina Mihailescu. They went to two different law firms to discuss immigration procedures with communist countries. Both firms charged a considerable consultation fee, but after several weeks of multiple attempts, the lawyers' efforts were stymied because working with a communist country was too complicated. Not one lawyer wanted to continue with the case.

It was at another firm, made up of only immigration lawyers, and recommended to Mica by Janet, that the senior partner, Stefan Bernard, who was also Janet's professor, offered help. He explained that he spoke often with Romanian ministers, on behalf of another client, but the only words they seemed to understand were *wire transfer*. They used a specific Swiss bank in Lugano to receive funds for their assistance.

Mica was not surprised about the bribes, or as the Romanian ministers called it, *consultation fees*, and agreed to pay. However, she was surprised when Bernard got down to brass tacks and specified his firm's fees. "If you want to take this route, you'll need to put up $100,000 as a retainer. That will get the ball rolling," Then he added, "The retainer will also show good faith that you have enough money to continue to the end."

Though she had the funds, Mica would never have considered giving so much money up front. But Simion said, "Sounds interesting." He took Mica's hand to stop her from arguing, and addressed the lawyer. "What do you estimate the *total* price will be?"

"We can't say. This is just an initial payment to begin a dialogue. To make friends."

Uncle Simion poured himself a glass of water. He knew what lawyers cost. He had just paid his lawyer a hefty fee to stop filing papers for his bankruptcy and clear his name. Simion certainly wasn't bankrupt anymore.

Mica looked around the wood-paneled room and saw multiple photographs of foreign countries. Would her money pay for Mr. Bernard's travels all over the world?

"How long will this take?" Simion asked.

"Can't say."

"Have you ever gotten anyone else out of Romania?"

"We're working on it."

"Is this deal legal?" Mica interrupted.

"We're lawyers," the assistant answered. "The best in town."

Simion turned to Mica. "Well, my dear, the decision is yours. We start paying from *your share*. Once we see some progress, and if you're feeling tight, which I don't think you will, I'll pony up some money also."

She leaned forward and began to read through the documents. "Sure, sure," she assured everyone. "It's my responsibility."

"Did you bring your checkbook?" the junior lawyer asked her. She nodded yes. Satisfied, he made a note on his document and said, "Let's get the ball rolling. Of course, this is all confidential."

His chief continued. "There's a deal we're working on with Romania's Ministry of Agriculture. Ceausescu needs tractors and machinery to clear land and create farms. He has agreed to allow us to buy this equipment, with an added price to be negotiated for each Romanian he lets out of the country. One tractor for one Romanian."

Mica remembered hearing about this from the Romanian refugee in the clinic. She bit her lip, thinking what he had said about Ceausescu, Arafat, and Gaddafi was also true.

"You begin by reading this affidavit carefully and signing," the assistant instructed her. "We'll also need power of attorney; in case we have to do some signing as your representative."

From then on, Uncle Simion, Aunt Diane, and Mica met at the lawyers' Park Avenue office on Saturday, late in the afternoon after Mica's dance program at Juilliard. As soon as the first check of $5,000 was wired to Switzerland, her lawyers were informed that Mica's parents were alive, being kept safe and sound under house arrest so the negotiations could proceed as the minister instructed. Mica was thrilled to learn this. They were alive! Yet, the Romanian official was sure to mention that her parents were being guarded twenty-four hours a day. This detail indicated to Mica that she'd have to dance to the music of the Romanian authorities, and pay more.

Mica always began the meetings in the law office by presenting a list of requests she wanted her lawyers to make to the minister in Romania. But it seemed to her that each week there was another minister as their contact person. And each week she had to write another check with a different account number, secret name, SWIFT code, and numbers used to make an international wire transfer for another account in Lugano. The $100,000 retainer had to be increased after a few months, for her lawyers were complaining that they were working very hard. She'd have to pay more *consultation fees* for other ministers. She wasn't happy, but she didn't complain. All she wanted was results and she made her requests stronger.

"Can you arrange that my parents get a telephone in their house? Gas for heat? Food?"

The response was always the same, although the message was from a different minister: "Very complicated... too difficult. The neighborhood has to be rewired for a telephone cable. New pipelines are needed for the entire region for heat. And food? I don't even have enough!"

Just as she was about to give up hope after six months of negotiations and unending wire transfers, Stefan Bernard took a manila folder from his desk drawer. It was marked TOP SECRET.

"You once asked me if the tractor deal is legal," he began, "and it is. But I'm working on another deal..." He paused and cleared his throat. "This is for another Romanian client. Our contact man works for the CIA and Mossad."

"Sounds legal enough to me," Simion laughed. "Who is this special contact?"

"He's a friend of our tractor contact. We can work with them both at the same time. But all these deals are done in cash."

"This is going to cost," Simion whispered to Mica.

"Henry Jacober—he's Hungarian-born, lives in London, and buys Romanian Jews from the Romanian government, meaning from Ceausescu. Also buys non-Jews for a heftier donation. Some go to Canada. Some to America."

"He buys them?" Simion asked. "You say that's legal. Is it ethical?"

"Is buying a dog ethical?" the lawyer responded. "That's how Ceausescu looks at anyone who wants to leave the fatherland."

Simion loosened his tie. Mica squirmed in her chair.

"I want to know if I should include your parents in this *research?*" Bernard asked in a flat, professional tone.

"How much will that scholarly work cost?" Simion inquired.

"Don't know yet. It's a work in progress."

Simion turned to Mica. "Let's have an alternative to the tractor deal."

"Yes," the lawyer agreed. "To start the ball rolling, we have to make friends."

"Money talks," Simion replied, and Mica said, "Include my parents in your research."

THEN, UNEXPECTED GOOD NEWS CAME MICA'S WAY. NOT ABOUT HER parents, but about something else. She would be able to write a letter to Magda Bartha and communicate with her in another way, other than just sending blank, touristy postcards, which she had been doing since she arrived in New York. She knew the nurse would understand the postcard message, and that Mica was safe in New York.

Annabel had been chosen to perform in Budapest as part of an American-Hungarian Christmas exchange program and would be able to take a letter to the nurse, as well as gifts. She'd go personally to the American Embassy and speak to Magda.

Mica had not written sooner because she believed it would go through the regular Hungarian mail service. She feared any letter would be confiscated as well as reported to the police. Mica didn't want to risk having her friends be interrogated, or their jobs jeopardized.

Mica was thrilled that Annabel would be able to contact them personally. She cried while writing a letter, for so many emotions flooded her mind. She was reliving her ordeal and at the same time, feeling so much gratitude toward her friends who had helped her. She wanted them to know how appreciative she was, and sent lots of gifts with Annabel.

At the end of the letter, she wrote:

I miss you all very much. I think of our Sundays at your home next to the fireplace and our picnics on Margaret Island. I thank you for doing so much for me. Without you, I would have never been able to continue fighting. I am eternally grateful to all three of you. I pray one day soon, I will see you again and we will all laugh together.

With all my hugs and love, Mica

P.S. My Aunt Diane bought me a naï for my high school graduation last week. When I play my naï, I play for all of you. I see the three of you before me and I realize how much I miss you.

CHAPTER 30

SIX MONTHS HAD PASSED since the sale of the diamonds, and a hot July was underway. Janet didn't need Mica to babysit during the summer, and Mica decided to take dance classes near home rather than travel to Juilliard for a summer program. She was feeling tired and had recently had a great deal of pain when she tried to raise her right arm. When she rode her bike, she used her left hand and kept her right arm at her side in order to rest it. She even told her friends that she couldn't play tennis because she couldn't raise her arm to serve or volley. The pain was worse when she danced. Sharp pangs pierced her right side from shoulder to elbow.

After a week of not being able to dance or ride her bike, or even turn on her right side to sleep, she complained to her aunt. "I don't know what's wrong. I have shooting pains in my right shoulder all the way down to my elbow. I can't raise my arm. The muscles are weak. I can't even pick up Jack when I play with him."

Concerned, her aunt suggested they see a doctor. She phoned her internist, explained Mica's situation, and listened as he said they should go at once to see an orthopedist he worked with at

Mount Sinai hospital in the city. Diane asked if he'd call and make the appointment. They could be there in an hour. Mica was scared, and she sensed that Diane was also.

Dr. James Grant's office was located in an annex behind the hospital's main building. Mica and Diane followed the signs down a long series of hallways to the elevators. Arriving at the fourteenth floor, Mica stopped for several minutes to lean against a wall and gain some strength. As she and Diane walked to the doctor's office, Mica held her right elbow with her left hand so her shoulder wouldn't swing. Any movement caused her excruciating pain.

It took her almost fifteen minutes to fill out three forms while writing with her left hand. She tried hard not to let the pain show on her face, for she didn't want to frighten Diane even more. Once Mica finished, she handed the secretary her papers and studied the other patients in the waiting room to distract herself from the throbbing sensation in her arm.

In Romania, the waiting room would have been filled with families chatting and eating. There would have been children rolling on the floor, playing, and making noise. Here, no one spoke or looked at anyone else. She wondered if all American hospitals were so heavy with silence.

A nurse called Mica's name, then led her down a corridor to a small treatment room. The walls were decorated with the doctor's diplomas. Each drawer of the file cabinet was labeled. There was not a speck of dirt on the floor, no peeling paint on the walls, no chipped furniture, no foul odor—very different from a doctor's office in Romania.

This was the first time she had been in a private hospital. There were private clinics in Romania, but nothing as clean or as modern as this.

Dr. Grant walked into the room. With his crisp white coat, he seemed to blend in with his ordered surroundings. Yet there was something about his soft eyes that comforted Mica. "It seems you like dancing," he began, reading her chart.

"Yes." Despite her pain, she tried to give him a smile. Then she bowed her head. The pain was torturing her. Sighing, she wiped a tear from her eye.

Seeing her suffering, the doctor said kindly, "I see a lot of injuries with dancers. Tell me what the problem is. Can you raise your right arm?"

"No," she answered, wincing. "It hurts too much."

"Can you extend it to the side?"

"No."

"Are you right-handed?"

"Yes."

"Do you have pain when you move your body? When you walk?"

"Yes."

"Can you get on the examining table and sit towards the front?"

She did as he asked and didn't speak. She watched the expression of his face, his mouth, and the lines on his forehead as he moved her arm slowly up and down—gently. He gave her no hint of his thoughts, so impenetrable he was, encased in his white coat. She stared at his tie—red with touches of yellow and blue—so full of life, such a contrast to his work.

"Please take off your blouse and skirt and lie down. I'm going to examine you." He pressed the glands in her neck and under her armpits. He examined her breasts, her stomach, then he slowly assessed every bone and muscle of her body. She wondered what was he looking for.

"Good. Nothing." He smiled at her. "How long have you been having pain?"

"A couple of months. I tried to brush it aside as a discomfort every dancer has."

"Has the pain stopped you from doing any other activities?"

"I've stopped playing tennis." She watched him write something on her papers. "Do you think this is very serious?" she asked him.

"It's hard to tell without further tests. My technician will take some X-rays. After I read the films, we'll talk." He pointed to her clothes. "Please get dressed." He left the room.

A nurse opened the door. "Honey, let me help you. I don't want you to struggle."

She led Mica down the hall and helped her undress again for the X-ray. She reminded Mica of Magda and that first day in the Budapest clinic after she had escaped from Romania. She had told Mica to shower before being examined because she was dirty. "Dirty?" Mica remembered saying to her. "I spent the night digging in the mud under a wire fence."

"Please follow me," the nurse said. "The technician will take a few pictures. In ten minutes, we'll have a better idea of what's going on."

Mica thought about the diamonds. She began to feel tears welling up in her eyes. *What happens if I'm very sick? How will I be able to continue to work with my lawyers? How will I save my parents?*

The x-ray technician said softly, "Please stand here. Move your right arm away from your body, so I can get a clearer picture."

"I can't raise it," Mica said, trying to be calm.

"Let me help you. Hold on to this bar for support."

The technician placed a film in the machine and disappeared behind a heavily padded door to protect herself.

Several minutes later, the nurse returned and helped Mica get dressed. "Let's go to the doctor," she said.

In the office, Dr. Grant picked up the X-rays the technician had just placed on his desk. "I want to review these films with you," he said, "but first, let me give you a sling. It will immobilize the arm so you'll have less pain."

He concentrated on wrapping her arm and shoulder so as not to put pressure on them. When he was finished, he patted her good shoulder, sat down at his desk and studied her X-rays. After a couple of minutes of silence, he pointed to another chair closer to him. "Please, sit here."

He's being too nice, Mica thought. She remembered doctors from her childhood. When the news was bad, they were kind. "What's the matter?"

He didn't answer. His silence frightened her. Her shoulder was aching so much that she felt it would fall out of its socket if she moved.

Raising an X-ray to the light, Dr. Grant asked her, "How old are you?"

"Eighteen."

"Are your parents with you?"

"I left Romania alone. But my aunt is here. She's in the waiting room."

She wished her parents could have been there. Her father would have told her what to do. Her mother would have taken away her pain.

"I see. May I ask her to join us?"

"Yes." Mica felt the blood drain out of her face. She loved her aunt, but she wished very hard for her mother in that moment.

When Diane was seated, Grant walked over to the X-ray viewer. "If you look at this middle section of Mica's right arm, you can see the humerus; that's the bone from the shoulder to the elbow. You see this gray area. That's a tumor pressing on a nerve. That's why she's having so much pain."

"A tumor?" Aunt Diane's voice shook.

"We have to find out if it's malignant, which we don't want," the doctor explained, "or benign, not so bad."

"I don't understand what you're saying," Mica said. "Please tell me in words I know."

"Tumors can be a sign of cancer. We must do another test to see how serious the situation is, and whether it *is* cancer." The doctor looked directly into her eyes.

She stared at him as he spoke, but she couldn't absorb what he was saying. Yet *cancer* was a word she knew. Everyone knew it. Cancer of the bone. She closed her eyes. Afraid.

Aunt Diane put her face in her hands and wept quietly. Then, composing herself, she took several deep breaths. "Why did this happen, doctor?" she asked.

"I don't know. Probably, no one knows."

"She's very active—she's dancing and biking all the time. She just started playing tennis. Was it too much?"

"No. All normal for a teenager. Cancer is no respecter of age or even health. Let's hope the tumor is benign and that in a couple of months, she'll be back to her activities. After the biopsy, we'll know for sure."

"Biopsy," Mica whispered. Another strange word.

"What will you biopsy?" Diane asked.

"The bone where you see the gray matter," he explained, pointing again to the X-ray. "Also the muscle and tissue surrounding the gray matter to determine if it has spread."

Aunt Diane bit her lower lip. Mica thought her face looked distorted. She didn't look like Diane.

"I want to do the biopsy tomorrow," Grant stated. "First thing in the morning. No need to waste time."

Grant helped Diane up and walked with her toward the door. "Mica, could you please get dressed? I want to speak to your aunt for a moment."

Mica sat alone, stunned. *The blue diamond was cursed!* she said to herself. *Oh, Tata, why did you call the curse a superstition?*

She looked for a tissue to wipe her tears. Noticing the telephone, for the thousandth time since she had arrived in New York, she wished she could call her mother and ask her what she should do. But that was impossible. Instead, she thought she should call her lawyer to see how the case was progressing, but her right arm wouldn't move. The muscles wouldn't work. If only he could speed up her case and get her parents to America. She'd pay anything the Romanian government wanted. But afraid her parents would never be able to leave, she cuddled her arm like a baby and sobbed.

Mica left the room and walked back to the waiting room, but Diane was not there. She wandered into the hallway, looking for her aunt, and saw a door marked 'oncology.' Despite not knowing what the word meant, she hoped to find her aunt there. Mica entered, found an empty seat, and sat down, thinking she'd wait for her aunt.

Fidgeting, frightened, and unable even to concentrate on a magazine, she studied the people in the room. A frail woman next to her was wearing a turban. A young boy in the corner was bald. He wore a baseball cap. His face was bony and white; his skin looked like flour. His mother sat next to him, crying.

Everyone in the waiting room looked thin and ill. They all had the same ring of dark skin under their eyes. A young man was sitting on the floor, barefoot, holding his shoes in his hands, sobbing. "I can't walk. My feet are swollen. I just had a baby boy."

Mica stood up when she saw her aunt and nurse walking toward her. She felt as if she were a stranger to herself, not absorbing what she was seeing or hearing.

"What time tomorrow morning?" her aunt asked the nurse.

"Eight o'clock. Go to Ambulatory Care on Madison Avenue and 100th Street." The nurse put her arm around Mica's left shoulder. "Now you go home and get a good night's sleep. Dr. Grant is very good at what he does."

"Thank you," Mica said automatically, but inside she felt numb. Outside, her arm pierced her like an electric shock every time she breathed in or moved. Yet Grant didn't want to prescribe a painkiller. "I prefer no chemicals yet," he had told her.

She and Aunt Diane walked past a line of offices. Ahead, they saw the EXIT sign and walked out of the building to a rainy day.

CHAPTER 31

MICA WOKE up not knowing where she was or what time it was. Before she opened her eyes, she touched her right arm, hoping to find it healed. But it was still in the sling the doctor had made. She thought to go back to sleep, and from habit turned on her right side. But the shooting pain jolted her awake. Looking at the clock, she saw that it was only 3:00 a.m.

She got out of bed and put her weight on her left side. It helped reduce some strain on her right arm, so it would hurt less. She thought if she walked slowly and held her arm at the wrist, she'd have less of the stinging sensations that felt like pins and needles.

She roamed through her room and moved toward her bookcase. She wished she had her magic book about New York. But there was no way she could have brought it when she escaped. She remembered showing her mother the book after she'd taken it from the train. They were at the kitchen table by the fireplace. Her mother had been fascinated. Mica wished she could go back to that day, return home, speak to her mother, cuddle in her father's arms, feel the hairs of his mustache tickle her cheek. She'd laugh.

She tried to go back to sleep—she dreamt about her house at

the moment when she knew she would have to escape. The shattered dishes in the kitchen, shredded wallpaper, ripped carpet. She had thought her home was indestructible, but it wasn't. She had thought she'd have her youth protected, but the government destroyed that also. Then she dreamt she was wandering through many rooms, looking for her parents, and she roamed into a room where there was a coffin. She looked inside. She thought she saw herself. But she didn't look like her regular self. She wondered, was it because her soul had left her body and her face was no longer hers? She leaned over to the no-face, the no-voice, and she cried. *No! I'm not broken yet.*

She woke up, remembering when she did feel broken—in the embassy, when she got sick. Her entire body was in chaos. She wondered whether there was a connection between cancer and acute stress. An uncontrollable breaking down of every cell in the body that causes disease?

Mica, Diane, and Simion arrived for her appointment thirty minutes early. Mica gave the O.R. nurse her clothes and took the green hospital gown the nurse held out. "How long will the biopsy take?" she asked, wondering how to put on the gown with her arm in a sling.

"Not too long." The nurse helped Mica raise the gown over her head and her left arm and then went out. Simion and Diane stayed with her and kissed her several times. "We'll be waiting outside," Simion said, and hugged her softly.

"I love you," Mica whispered and kissed them both. It was the first time Mica had told them she loved them, and she said it with all her heart.

The nurse came in. "You'll be groggy afterwards. We'll keep you here all day."

"When will I know the results?" She didn't want to wait long to know what was wrong with her arm.

"It's hard to say. Dr. Grant needs to have the biopsy slides read by the pathologist." She saw Mica's puzzlement. "The pathologist studies tissues and cells," the nurse explained. "The doctor relies on his report before he advises the patient about the next step."

The nurse left her in a little cubicle with one small chair. Waiting all alone, Mica felt frightened. "I've gotten everything I wanted, and now I'm going to die. The diamonds that brought me here are going to kill me. I have paid for them with my life."

Another nurse came in and brought her to the operating room where there was a long table, surrounded by more lights than anything Mica had ever seen illuminating a stage. But here, there was no illusion, no make-believe. She let the nurse lead her to the long table where a doctor helped her lie down.

"I'm Dr. Roberts," he said in a friendly tone. "I'm the anesthesiologist. I'm going to give you an injection and in several seconds you're going to sleep." He took her left arm.

Dr. Grant came in. He was dressed in pale green with a mask on his face and another one covering his hair. A nurse was holding a tray of small bottles and many types of knives. The anesthesiologist continued, "I know you like dancing. How do you feel when you've finished your performance and everyone is clapping for you?"

"It's like being in heaven..."

———

WHEN MICA WOKE UP SHE FELT RESTED, AS IF SHE HAD SLEPT FOR A long time. But the table was now a bed, and the room was dim. Looking at her arm, she saw it was heavily bandaged from shoulder to elbow. Dizzy, she looked around and realized she was in a large room with other patients.

"Nurse," she called to the woman in white. "Where am I?"

"The recovery room. Your biopsy is finished."

"Do you know the results?" Mica asked.

"No, not yet," the nurse answered, wiping Mica's sweaty brow with a tissue.

Dr. Grant entered the room. "How do you feel?" he asked.

"I feel stiff. The bandages."

"Mica, I took biopsies from multiple spots in your right arm—bone, tissue, and muscle—the shoulder and rotator cuff also. But the pathologist cannot read them immediately, as I had hoped. The area of the arm, where it meets the shoulder, is complicated. He wants to look more closely at each biopsy specimen. We have to be sure of the diagnosis."

"What do you mean? Is the tumor positive or negative? Do I have cancer?"

Grant shook his head "There's no diagnosis yet. The pathologist needs a few days to be sure. We have to let him do his work."

She couldn't answer. She pushed her head deeper into her pillow, wanting to feel something soft, wishing she could burrow herself inside the feathers and be protected.

"Go home," Grant said. "Your aunt and uncle have been waiting here all day. Come back Friday and we'll discuss the pathology report together."

"I have no choice."

He took her good hand. "Mica, just a few days more."

SIMION AND DIANE MADE HER FEEL MORE COMFORTABLE AND MORE loved than she had in a long time. Diane bought Mica all her favorite cookies and chocolates. "We have to fatten you up and keep you strong." She even bought a blender to make malteds. "We can mix your favorite ice creams—chocolate and raspberry, and also make fruit drinks."

Simion bought her Beatles and the Everly Brothers records, her favorites.

Mica was very moved by their loving care. "You've been so good to me. I know I'm a burden to you. I'm so sorry."

"No! We love you, and you'll be fine," Diane insisted.

"You'll lick this thing," Simion reassured her, kissing her cheeks.

After two days of rest and attention, Mica did feel a little stronger and decided she'd like to take a walk. Diane wanted to join her, but Mica wanted time alone.

"Sure. The sunshine will make you feel better."

Mica took the path toward town, usually a ten-minute walk, but now with her heavily bandaged arm in a sling, it took longer. She usually looked at each house on her way to admire their gardens, but today she wasn't interested.

Approaching the public library, she entered through the main door and went to the librarian's desk. "Excuse me, do you have medical books?"

"Yes, a few. What are you looking for?"

"A textbook on orthopedics and another one for oncology."

Mica followed her to a corner of the reading room.

"You'll be comfortable here, next to the window. It's quiet." She smiled at Mica. "Can I do anything else for you?"

"No, I'm fine. Thank you."

Mica arranged herself at the table. She opened the thick book of orthopedics with her left hand and turned to the table of contents. Finding bone cancers, she turned to the page of malignant bone tumors. She stopped at the chart of statistics:

- 90% of patients with diagnosed malignant bone tumor die within the first year.

Treatment:

- Most Effective: Amputation of limb followed by radiation therapy.
- Experimental: Surgery to remove tumor followed by intensive chemotherapy for one year.

She turned the page. The photo on the left was of a woman with an amputated arm. The photo on the right was a man with an amputated leg. He was standing with the help of crutches.

Mica closed the book. She tried to review what she had just read, but all she could remember were the photos.

She rubbed her right arm and whispered to it: "I won't let anyone take you from me. I've just started my life. I want to be a great dancer, love a man, have a baby to hold in my arms." She put her head down on the table and cried.

Slowly she got up, walked to the window, watched a bird taking a worm to a nest where there were two baby sparrows raising their beaks. After a few minutes, she returned to the table and brought the oncology textbook close to her. Stumbling with the pages, she found the table of contents. She looked for causes of cancer. Would there be anything about acute stress and emotional crises? Nothing. She turned to the chapter titled: Treatments: Chemotherapy.

She skimmed down to the section on side effects. There was a chart and list:

- Loss of all body hair
- Inflamed, swollen and bleeding soft tissues of the mouth, throat and esophagus
- Difficulty eating solid food. Liquids needed as replacement

- Feet swollen. Difficulty in walking
- Bladder affected. Two quarts of water per day needed to stimulate urination and avoid possible kidney failure.

Mica closed the book, softly, so as not to put pressure on her right arm. She put her cheek on the hard cover and let her tears warm her face.

"Oh Mama," she whispered, as if she were near. Mica wished she were back in their kitchen in Romania. How she wished she could breathe in the sweet fragrance of logs burning in the fireplace and watch Mama cook. She could almost smell the roasting meat. Mica would read Shakespeare to her and Mama would say, "How beautiful, Mica, please read more."

"Nothing that can be, can come between me and the full prospects of my hopes."

It felt to Mica that the three days were three months. On the third day, Simion and Diane went with her to Dr. Grant's office in the city. Throughout the car ride, Mica sat in the back seat, holding her bandaged arm with her left hand as if by protecting it, she could make it stronger.

When they entered the waiting room, the secretary told her gently that she'd tell Dr. Grant she was there. She's being too nice, Mica worried.

Inside the doctor's office, Mica looked up at the X-rays on his wall viewer, and felt that each picture represented her death. Dr. Grant came in behind them.

"Good news!" he said. "The biopsies are negative."

"Thank God!" Simion yelled. "Hooray!"

"Yes!" Diane clapped her hands and kissed Mica, taking her into her arms. She was crying.

"Negative? Bad?" Mica asked. She couldn't figure out the meaning of the word.

"Negative is good," Dr. Grant explained. "Not cancer. A benign tumor. During the surgery, I removed it. The tumor was very small —the size of a pea."

"A pea?" She was trying to visualize a pea next to or near or inside her bone.

"The tumor was putting pressure on a nerve. Now you'll be free of pain. You'll be fine!"

"There's no spreading?" Diane asked.

"No. It's all clean. The pathologist is sure."

"Can I dance?" Mica asked him.

"Not yet. Come see me in three weeks, and I'll remove those bandages. You'll work with our physiotherapist for the summer." He smiled at Mica. "I hear you're starting Juilliard in September. Dancing will be your best therapy."

"Yes! Yes!" she shouted. "Thank you, doctor. Thank you for giving me back my life. What a wonderful hospital you have. What a wonderful country this is. God bless America."

"One more thing, Mica. You'll notice that you have five little circles on your arm; that is, on a line from shoulder to elbow. That's where I had to take multiple biopsies. They will scar. Don't have them removed in the future with plastic surgery."

"Why not?"

"In case we ever have to go back inside. They show where we need to go."

She didn't want to ask specifically what he meant. Not now. But she did ask, "Are they big?"

"No. But they will heal slightly puffy."

She grimaced.

The doctor took her good hand and patted it. "You've been very brave."

She remembered her father's words: "Whenever life seems the lowest, that's when you must rise. Use your willpower to survive."

She didn't want to think of the bad. Instead, she thought of everything good in her life and how much she wanted to live. Soon, she'd be a student at Juilliard with her good friend, Annabel. She thought how lucky she was to have her aunt and uncle. She felt that soon, she'd be able to get her parents to safety. "Don't lose hope," her heart told them.

CHAPTER 32

ONE YEAR LATER AND TWO YEARS AFTER ARRIVING IN
NEW YORK

MICA'S ARM was completely healed. She went once a month to the
hospital for follow-ups with Dr. Grant to be certain there was no
reoccurrence. At each appointment, Carmen, the technician, took
Mica's index finger, cut the skin lightly with a special needle, and
allowed several drops of blood to fall on a glass slide. Then she'd
insert the slide into a machine while Mica, seated at her side,
waited nervously until she'd see a green light blink and a digital
sign indicate 'normal.' Then the slide with her blood sample would
pop out.

Often, Mica would rub the dotted, puffy scars that ran from
her shoulder to elbow where Dr. Grant had taken biopsies. She'd
think about how her life had changed since she left Romania, two
and a half years ago. Persistence was a secret she kept inside her as
a treasure that she had learned from suffering and surviving. She
had been tested by life and understood that she should never give
up fighting.

Once she had fully healed, Mica set to work even harder with
Uncle Simion and their lawyers. However, the Romanian officials
they worked with had other plans. They passed her back and forth,

filling their Swiss accounts. Anton and Corina Mihailescu were at home, together, but they were still under house arrest. Mica arranged that they could leave their house once a week to buy food and do errands. But for that, they needed to be escorted by a guard from the authorities, at an extra cost to Mica. Unfortunately, no one could visit them, their phone remained disconnected, and their mail was regularly checked. Mica didn't dare write them. She was allowed no communication.

But one thing was certain, Mica remained as fixed as the Rock of Gibraltar. She'd have no peace until she found the right contact person to facilitate and ensure her parents' departure.

MICA WAS NOW TWENTY YEARS OLD AND BEGINNING HER SECOND year of college at Juilliard. She remembered how Dr. Grant had said that dancing would be her best therapy. He had been right, not only for her arm and body, but for her mind as well.

Her interest in choreography had led her to join a student-group working with Martha Graham on her ballet, *Dark Meadow*. At the beginning, Mica struggled and had a shaky start in her role as "One Who Seeks." Yet at the première, she received kudos for performing a difficult role gracefully. At night, when she was unable to sleep while thinking of her parents in Romania, she'd visualize herself dancing and remember Martha Graham's assistant praising her talents. She'd fall asleep, but then the next morning, she was brought back to the reality of a list of greedy communist officials to whom she had to write check after check.

She still had a sizable amount of money remaining that was to be used for her parents. She had $250,000 in her parents' bank account—three quarters had been spent. There was also another account of one million dollars that was in her name and remained in her investment fund. She knew if the funds would run out, she'd be able to sell the remaining thirteen diamonds. Willy Reinhardt had told her he could cut and polish out the flaws, and even if the diamonds would be reduced in size, they were valuable.

One Sunday in July, Mica felt the need to free herself from endless disappointments with her lawyers and their deals. It was a sunny day and she thought a bike ride would relax her. She took her bicycle from her dorm at Juilliard and pedaled to Central Park. The lanes inside the park were closed to cars and she was enjoying the pleasure of feeling strong with the sun on her body. As the path leveled flat, she began pedaling without holding on to the handlebars when suddenly her bicycle swerved out of control and she collided with another rider.

He almost fell off, but instead of being angry, he smiled. "I knew today was going to be a beautiful day."

He was handsome, with eyes the color of the sky and curly blond hair. She introduced herself, and he shook her hand. "I'm André Blau."

They chatted and laughed while they biked together around the park, around and around, until the sun set and they knew they'd have to part.

"Can I see you again?" André asked.

Mica didn't hesitate. She felt immediately that he was special.

They met often during the week for an evening to bike in Central Park, to listen to steel drumming, have coffee, or see a movie, or just chat and laugh. André was a doctor, a resident in internal medicine at New York Hospital.

Two months after they met, André said he'd borrowed a friend's car. He said he wanted to show her the change of autumn colors in Connecticut. He asked if she'd like to spend the day hiking in a vineyard he knew.

It was one of those warm autumn Sundays when the leaves of chestnut trees turn yellow, and everything is bright gold. They hiked for hours until the sun lingered over the horizon. They approached the vineyard's main house to rest and enjoy the festivities under way to celebrate the season's harvest. Children were playing amidst the vines while older folks chatted on the grass. Two fiddlers were playing music and several couples were dancing.

"Will you dance with me?" André asked.

Mica curved into his open arms. It was the first time they had danced together, and she hadn't known that André was so such a good dancer. Tall and broad at six foot one and athletically built, she felt him strong and tender.

They danced until they were tired, and then slowly he led her away from the crowd toward the wooden vats where the wine mellowed. Thirsty and hot, they drank the wine from the barrel. They leaned against the barn and laughed as they listened to the music and let the wine flow to their heads.

Suddenly, there was thunder. André put his arms around Mica as the lights on the dance floor blinked. She inhaled his manly scent, like sandalwood, and sweet. The fiddlers stopped playing. Instead of music there was rain.

"I know a safe place," he whispered. "Let's go."

When lightning lit the sky, she saw a path of golden pine needles and a barn. For a moment, she was transported back in time to her hikes in the Carpathians and the beautiful bed of untouched pine needles that she and her friends had discovered. But then it started to rain harder, and André opened the door and led her in to the barn. Shyly, she groped for his hand. He kissed her wet lips and brushed the leaves from her sweater, touching her breasts. She fell into the straw, and he dried her skin with his kisses. She moved into him closer, tighter, stronger. Awakened to passion, she wanted more.

He removed each layer of her clothes. He kissed her neck, her breasts. She unbuttoned his shirt, his pants and stroked his body with her hands, her lips. She moved closer, tighter. The heat of passion burned inside her. She was on fire. He took each breast in his palm and kissed the nipples hard. Then he moved into her, entering deep and strong. Passion raised her higher and higher. She floated up. She wanted to burst. Scream. Yell. Become one with him.

There was no time, no place, only now. He pressed his mouth against her skin, soft and moist with desire. Their bodies filled with longing. They forgot where they were, what they were doing, where they were going. Only wanting more and more.

Awakened to love-making, Mica felt a new passion overtake her. Every evening after her dance classes and after André finished seeing patients at the hospital, they met at his one-room studio at Payson House on York Avenue. As soon as they were inside, they'd rush to the bed to make love. The only thing that mattered was the moment of passion, of pleasure, of being close together.

Afterwards, they'd dress, she in her black leggings and leotard, André in pale green hospital pants and shirt. And with love making still inside them, they'd dance. Mica loved the way he moved. Agile, with natural rhythm, he held her strongly and moved lightly.

"I think I'll kidnap you and take you to my dance classes," she laughed. "Would you be my partner?"

"Forever."

"Were you a dancer in another life?"

"No, I was on the tennis team at college." He whirled her around. "Timing, rhythm, balance, that's the key to sports. Like dancing."

Every evening, after they made love and danced, André wanted to have more fun. "Let's go get something to eat. I'm starving." He enjoyed matching the choice of restaurant with their dancing. "A tango deserves an Argentine steak and a Malbec."

And after a samba, he'd say, "I feel like a Brazilian *feijoada* and *caipirinha.* I know a place in the Village." Whichever restaurant André chose, he always seemed to know someone there.

"How do you know so many people?" Mica would ask.

He smiled, shyly. "High school friends. College friends."

She even remarked how charming girls lingered at their table to chat and laugh with him.

"Med school friends," he said, seeming almost to apologize. She tried hard not to appear jealous.

One evening in his apartment, Mica surprised him with a Romanian Gypsy record. "I think you can dance anything, even this. You're so good."

"Not as good as you," and he bowed and kissed her hand. "Let me listen first. I'll have to study this."

He turned down the lights in the apartment and together, they sat on the sofa with Mica curled into his arms. At the end of several songs, she confessed, "I miss this music. I miss my mother and father."

As another Gypsy song began, she moved away from him and went to the window of his twentieth floor apartment. She stared out and the city lights brought her to another level of feelings. She raised her bare arms, stretched her body tall from the points of her shoes to the tips of her fingers and began to snap her fingers to the music. She moved as if on stage, a thin layer of black that glided freely with the lights behind her. The wild Gypsy sounds vibrated with desire and took her beyond control. She clicked her shoes, her hands stretched high. Possessed as if fire burned inside her, she snapped her fingers and yelled, "Ay! Ay!"

She danced as if no one was watching her, with all her soul, clicking her heels, snapping her fingers, wanting more and more. André clapped and yelled, "Brava! Brava!"

She heard him. The spell was broken. She fell down, folded her arms into her lap and cried. Tears from deep inside flowed without control and vulnerable to all that she remembered, she felt the need to tell André everything about her.

"Please don't judge me," she begged. "I want you to know who I am. Let me tell you the truth."

He sat on the floor next to her, watching her lips. She began to speak of the past- especially the bad.

"I was almost raped... in the American Embassy... by a man named Radu. I can't forget it. Sometimes I wake up in the middle of the night sweating and I see Radu. He had gold teeth and wore black leather gloves to cover his burned hands."

Mica started to sob.

André took her in his arms.

"He stole something from me. Diamonds. When I confronted him, he tried to rape me. I stabbed him with scissors until blood oozed out. He stopped."

André held her tightly. "You defended yourself. You had no choice."

"I try to tell myself that, but his evil brought out the evil in me and I have to live with that—accept how violently I acted."

"You didn't kill him," André replied. "You were strong, stronger than him."

"I had scissors. There are times when I am so angry that I have no control over my emotions. Afterwards, I feel sad and dark inside, like a cloud shrouding the sun and taking away its light."

She dropped her face into her hands and mumbled, "I have not been able to save my parents. Uncle Simion and I have been trying for one year and a half to get them out of Romania and to America, but we cannot. I think of my parents and my heart feels heavy— inside me—taking in their pain. I've tried so hard to get them free, but I've been hampered by ministers who just want more money."

He listened as if they were important clues and could make a diagnosis. He tried to take it all in.

Then she told him more about herself, things she had never

really talked about to anyone—having diamonds that had belonged to Auschwitz victims. She confessed to André, "When I took them to escape Romania, I had nothing else. I try to soften my guilt by saying I'm using them to save my parents. And I haven't even done that!"

She wiped tears from her cheeks. He remained silent and she admitted more. "I heard horrible things in the American Embassy when the refugees spoke about terrorism, and when the diamond expert, Mr. Reinhardt, said that Mengele was still alive. I was wrong to withhold important information. I didn't report what I knew and I should have. I keep doing wrong."

"Who could you tell such horrific things? Let me speak to a lawyer friend of mine who works with Simon Wiesenthal, who's been searching for Nazi war criminals in South America. He told me that Wiesenthal is obsessed to get Mengele."

"Maybe I can help?"

"My friend told me that the last time they knew about Mengele's whereabouts, he was hiding in Paraguay. Wiesenthal offered five million to President Stroessner to give him up. The Mossad offered six million more. Stroessner refused and Mengele fled."

"I know where he is!" Mica yelled.

André stared at her, amazed.

"He's in Brazil, outside São Paulo on a farm with some Hungarians."

"What? I'll speak to my friend tomorrow," André said, trying to control his surprise.

She stood up and went to the window. "I want so much to tell what I know about Mengele and also about terrorism." She stopped talking and stared at New York's lights. "There's no country in Europe like Romania that has witnessed the political turmoil of the twentieth century," she said. "In fifty years, fascism there led to communism, and communism planted the seeds for modern-day terrorism."

She slammed her fist on the wall. "I know this from my own experience, what I saw in Romania and Hungary because of the fascists, my parents' work in the Resistance, my father's plans to overthrow the communists, what I heard from the refugees in Budapest about terrorism, what I translated from Mr. Bridge's confidential source.

"One day the world will point their finger at Mengele, Ceausescu, Gaddafi, and Arafat and their terrorist evil. Why have they committed such horrors? What do they want? Mengele wanted to get rid of all the Jews of Europe. Ceausescu wants to be the richest man in Eastern Europe. Gaddafi wants to be the leader of the Arab world. And Arafat wants an Arab state centered in Jerusalem. And to achieve their goals, they create terror—terror that's hard to stop once started."

Mica took a deep breath; she was shaking with anger. Feeling that André understood her, she went to him, cuddled in his arms to share with him more. "These five scars that you know are from biopsies. Bone cancer, the doctors thought. Thank God the biopsies were negative." But she didn't tell him she feared she had been cursed.

"Do you go regularly for follow-ups?" the doctor in him wanted to know.

"Yes, once a month. Dr. Grant said I'm fine, and I should enjoy my life." She smiled. "Which I do." She poked him in the stomach and tickled him. André kissed her.

"I wish I could give back for my beautiful life in America. I would like to help somehow."

"I have an idea. My good friend, Sam Mayer, is in charge of the pediatric-oncology clinic at the hospital. He started a program to bring in artists, musicians, and singers to spend time with the children and cheer them up a little. Are you interested?"

"Of course! I can play my flute and teach them to dance. I can even do a magic show."

André laughed. "Wasn't Houdini Hungarian?"

"Yes. And I can bring in some herbs and show them how Gypsies use them. "Abracadabra," she sang, while pretending to spread herbs on his face.

He pretended to hide. "I'll arrange with Sam and let you know when you can start."

She hugged him. "Thanks."

"Aha! I have an ulterior motive. I want something back."

"What?" She laughed.

"Move in with me," André said. "Then you can talk to me all the time and use me as a sounding board. I'd love that so much. I want to help you."

Mica felt a surge of conflict. She loved André, but she felt she was too young at twenty years old to make such a commitment. A little voice inside her said, "I want my independence."

"You have my key already," he teased her. "Stay all the time with me. I hate to see you leave in the middle of the night."

"I'm not ready yet."

"Why? Do you want to be free to find someone else? Someone better than me?"

"You're the best. Who else can dance like you? Or understand me like you do?"

"Then why not? Don't you want me to be part of your life, Mica? At least think about it. You don't have to decide tonight."

"I will," she said and she kissed him on the neck over and over and then she pretended to bite him while laughing.

The question of living together came up several times in the following months, but Mica kept repeating, "I'm not ready yet."

For a time, that was enough to satisfy André, and he didn't push, until one night over dinner, when he announced he had been offered a fellowship in cardiology at Yale-New Haven Hospital.

"I plan to accept the offer. I start on July first. It's something I've always wanted."

"Of course. I'm happy for you." She put down her knife and fork and looked at her lap to keep him from seeing that she was about to cry.

"I'll be working longer hours including nights and weekends. I won't have time to go to New York—that is, if you're here."

She tried to appear calm, but instead of continuing the conversation, she asked him, "What do you think of these vegetables? I think I cooked them too long."

He shook his head. "We have to discuss this. I know your life is your dancing. But come with me to New Haven."

"What will I do in New Haven? I can't leave Juilliard. I've been tapped by the Martha Graham Company. Your dream is Yale, but my dream is to join the Graham group after graduation."

"You can commute to New York by train. It wouldn't be so difficult; you only take classes at Juilliard three times a week. Maybe you can find someone in New Haven to dance with on the other days."

"I have a career also," she protested. "Can't you get a fellowship in New York?"

"I've always wanted Yale, and I don't want to lose it."

"You're being selfish. You want me to give up my life? The one I sacrificed so much for?"

She got up and walked over to the window. She loved André, and she didn't want to be away from him. She couldn't bear to leave New York, and she also couldn't bear to lose him. She feared, that he could find someone else—perhaps one of the beautiful women who approached their table in the restaurants. Jealousy overcame her.

Mica looked at her watch. "It's late. I have a master class tomorrow. I should get a full night's sleep. I have to go."

"Wait! You may think I'm selfish, but let me make a confession," he said quietly, coming over to stand next to her. "I always wanted to go to an Ivy League college, but I couldn't get in. I didn't go to a private high school. My parents couldn't afford it. I went to Forest Hills High School. A good one, but not the best. From there, I went to Queens College. Good, but not Ivy League. Now, I can finally be a fellow at Yale. Dancing is your dream, but this is a dream for me also."

He took her hand. "I want to be a great doctor, Mica, not just a good one and not a rich one. At Yale, I'll be learning from the best."

"I understand." She put her face in her hands and cried.

SHE AND ANDRÉ CONTINUED TO SEE EACH OTHER AS IF NOTHING HAD changed. André accepted the offer at Yale, and he traveled back and forth to New Haven several times to arrange a place to live and to finalize the details of his work at the hospital. In his absence, Mica tried to make a decision. She didn't know what to do, but she couldn't help thinking that after all she'd been through, she couldn't give up Juilliard and the chance to dance with Martha Graham's group. The dilemma was difficult. She asked Annabel for advice.

"How much do you love André?" her best friend asked. "Can you live without him? Do you want to live with him before you're married or wait? What about Juilliard?"

After an hour on the phone with Annabel, Mica called her aunt Diane for her opinion and to talk through the situation. Her uncle, listening in, was adamant against the idea of her moving to New Haven. "You're too young to live with a man. Even though you're no longer eighteen, not even twenty-one, I'm responsible. What will I tell your father? That I let you shack up with a guy I've only met a few times? No! Absolutely not!"

Diane agreed that Mica was too young to even think about

living with André. Yet Diane told her she had to admit that he was a wonderful guy.

Mica talked herself through what it would mean to live in New Haven—commuting, attending her classes, and sleeping in New Haven. Yet, Mica could not decide what to do. She procrastinated giving André her decision, still saying, "I'm not sure," and "I need more time to decide."

July 1st came and André went to New Haven alone.

───────

MICA WAS DEVASTATED WITHOUT ANDRÉ. SHE LOVED HIM WITH ALL her soul and being without him made her love him more. She missed his jokes, laughing with him, telling him everything she was doing, everything she thought. Without him, she realized how empty she felt inside, how much she needed him—for his strength, for his happiness. She missed his optimism, his telling her that everything is meant for a reason, and that reason is what's right. She admired the joy inside him, his *joie de vivre*, that was so contagious.

To try to forget him, she danced more and practiced harder to drive away her demons. She spent hours with Annabel, stretching, dancing, rehearsing, and in between, crying. Annabel advised her to go to New Haven. "You can commute a couple of days a week. It's not far. You're strong enough to continue your dancing schedule even traveling back and forth. You'll be happier!"

In anguish over the separation and frantic because she couldn't decide what to do, she lost her appetite, lost weight, and couldn't sleep. She was miserable. She had found the man she loved—and lost him.

After three weeks, Mica finally made up her mind. She wanted to be with André. She loved him too much to be without him. Would he forgive her? Still love her? She wanted to call him, but she decided to send him a letter instead. She wrote that, yes, she missed him very much. Yes, she wanted to be with him. Her life had no meaning without him. She mailed the letter express.

Will you dance with me?
Suddenly there was thunder from the sky. Rain.
Come here.
And I followed for the first time.
You kissed my wet lips and stroked the leaves from my breast. I fell into the straw and you drank the rain from my thighs and dried my skin with your kisses.
I forgot where I was, what I was doing, where I was going, only wanting you more and more.

CHAPTER 33
THREE MONTHS LATER

IT HAD BEEN two years of working with lawyers, two years of wire transfers and negotiations, and two and a half years since she escaped Romania. Still, the fate of Anton and Corina Mihailescu remained uncertain. Mica dreamed of them often. Sometimes they were in danger; sometimes they were next to her in New York. But one thing was the same: in both her dreams and in reality, Mica was anxious. She ravenously read the news about Romania and Ceausescu's regime. She tried to put together what she was reading in the newspapers and hearing on TV with the information she'd received from her lawyers. It was a puzzle, and she was determined to solve it.

Mica and André got engaged soon after they arrived in New Haven. They wanted a simple party on the beach, which Diane and Simion helped Mica arrange in nearby Branford. Many of Mica's friends from high school and Juilliard joined the engagement celebration. André's friends came out from the city in a bus they had decorated with a huge wrap-around photo of Mica and André bicycling in Central Park.

Sadly, though, Mica's parents were not there. During the celebration, Mica lit a candle and prayed, "I wish my parents can soon meet André and know how happy we are. I hope they will be with us for our wedding."

For the first dance, the couple chose their favorite song from the Beatles and Mica sang along, *"Michelle, ma belle..."* André swung her several times, and when she stopped laughing, she whispered in his ear, "This is the song that helped me run toward freedom when I escaped Romania."

They timed the ceremony to coincide with the setting sun and when Mica and André kissed to seal their engagement, the red and orange above them colored a rainbow more vibrant than diamonds. Their friends lit fireworks to announce the couple's new life together.

ANDRÉ WAS BUSY IN THE CARDIOLOGY CLINIC AT YALE-NEW HAVEN Hospital. He was becoming more confident about observing, diagnosing, and talking to patients. He especially believed that if a doctor listened carefully to a patient while taking the history, it would help him make the right diagnosis. He took his Hippocratic oath seriously, as he did his love for Mica, never ceasing to admire her courage and determination.

Mica had her own busy schedule, commuting to Juilliard on Mondays, Wednesdays and Fridays, volunteering at New York Hospital Monday evenings, dining Wednesday evenings with Diane and Simion, and meeting their lawyers on Friday evenings. But there were four other days in the week when she was not in New York, and she wanted to dance more.

One evening, as she was walking on Chapel Street toward the hospital to meet André for dinner, she passed Yale's School of Drama and its theater. Billboards were posted that announced a coming event: "Shakespeare's *A Midsummer Night's Dream:* A

Modern Interpretation with Music and Dance." She smiled, remembering her beloved bard.

Curious, she entered the theater and asked if there was someone in charge of the dance program. A petite middle-aged woman, dressed in a black leotard and ballet slippers, her black hair pulled back in a chignon bun, greeted her. After several minutes of chatting, Mica learned that Nina Obolensky was Russian-born and had danced with the Bolshoi Ballet. Miss Obolensky exuded an unmistakable air of old-world aristocracy. Mica stared at her, recalling photos of her that she had seen in George Szabo's dance magazines.

Mica told her how much she loves dancing, but most of all, choreography, as she has been working with the Martha Graham group and Juilliard students.

"Did you ever do a choreography on your own?" the Russian ballerina asked.

"Yes." Mica told her how she arranged to dance in Budapest at an Easter celebration. "Dancing on stage in the American Embassy while playing the flute amidst lit candles had been a turning point in my life."

Then Mica asked Miss Obolensky, "Could I become your student? I could learn so much from you."

The Russian prima donna answered, "We will practice together and we will see."

Every other day, Mica and Nina Obolensky met in the theater basement to explore how they could merge ballet with modern dance to create a more colorful and bold interpretation of dance. The goal they shared was to use music to better feel the movement of dance—a fusion of music with dance to create an elevated expression of art.

One day, Mica had the idea that to feel more intensely while she danced, she would dance with her eyes closed. In this way, she'd be able to concentrate on what she was feeling inside her and not be distracted with what was outside. "Dancing is feeling my soul," she said.

Obolensky cleared the stage, then set up a video camera to capture the practice. Mica put a white bandage over her eyes and Miss Obolensky cued the music—Tchaikovsky's *Romeo and Juliet*.

Mica got into position, listened to the music for several minutes, allowing the opening clarinet and bassoon melody of the lovers to take her back to when she was Juliet, loving Romeo, and wanting him to love only her or she would die. She danced while taking her cues from the music as it turned violent and she remembered how she had looked for her parents in the audience and they were not there. And then again, the melody of love transported her as tenderness fought violence.

As she danced, she cried, and her soul filled with love and the music took her outside herself to a height where she was no longer a body, but a soul uniting with music and dance. When Tchaikovsky's violins finished in a minor key announcing the tragic end, Mica fell down to the hard stage, a bird who had flown too high.

Obolensky stopped filming and ran to Mica. She picked her up in her arms and hugged her. "It was beautiful!"

Each day they met, Mica began her practice session, blindfolded. Her mentor wanted Mica never to forget that she had attained a fusion of music and dance with her soul. She didn't want it to be an isolated experience. "Repetition is important," she told Mica, "but repetition when it's repeated over and over again is not repetition. The same action makes you feel something completely different by the end. We both want you to feel emotions—that is dance, that is music—and they enhance each other. Repetition makes art as perfect as possible."

For Mica, her dancing with Miss Obolensky's guidance was a time of great creativity and excitement.

Meanwhile at Juilliard, she continued practicing with the

Martha Graham group. Annabel became an intern in the troupe's corps de ballet and Mica became an intern with the choreography team. With this new opportunity, Mica was able to fuse her dance talents and love for music with her eye for stage design, as she had done in Budapest. Drama, music and dance came together instinctively in her vision. And choreography gave her free rein to create a new interpretation of modern dance.

Life was full of promise and pleasure. Yet, there was still persistent anxiety in Mica's soul. Her lawyers had not yet succeeded in getting her parents free. Then, fate intervened once again when the Martha Graham students, including Mica and Annabel, were asked to perform *Sleeping Beauty* as part of a fundraiser for UNICEF, the UN's children's organization. Sam Mayer, Mica's mentor at the pediatric-oncology clinic, was a board member for UNICEF and attended the New York fundraiser. After the performance, he went backstage with several colleagues and introduced them to Mica.

"There's no one who is more dedicated in my volunteer unit at New York Hospital than Mica," Sam told Dr. Brad Andrews, the director of UNICEF. "She knows every child's name and brings books and toys for each one. She has even taught the children to dance while she plays her Romanian flute."

"Are you Romanian?" Andrews asked her.

"Yes. I was born in Transylvania."

"Have you heard about what's happening there?"

Mica shook her head no.

"It seems that Ceausescu has forbidden birth control and abortion; so unwed mothers abandon their newborns to orphanages. To make the babies stronger, Ceausescu has this crazy idea that they should receive blood transfusions. The orphanages use and reuse unsterilized needles to save money, and thousands of babies have been infected and are dying."

"I can't believe it," Mica said, covering her mouth in horror. "Is there anything we can do to help?"

"UNICEF is working with several orphanages to send medical aid for the infected children, but the process is slow."

"I'm working on this, too," Sam told Mica. "But we've already encountered obstacles. The biggest one is that we have a language barrier."

"I speak Romanian and Hungarian," Mica told him. "I'd be happy to translate for you. That was part of my job when I was at the American Embassy in Budapest."

"It would be more effective if someone from our group could actually *get into* Romania, *go there*, and hand-deliver the medicines," Andrews said, looking hard at Mica. "We want to make sure the right people get them."

Mica understood. "I've been trying for years to get my parents *out of* the country. If you find a way *to get in*, let me know. I volunteer. If your project works, I'd love to set up a fund for Romanian families to adopt the children and get them out of orphanages." Instinctively, Mica thought if she could get *into* the country, she could *leave* the country with her parents.

"Shows you have heart. But expensive," Andrews commented.

"I hope to have the chance to plant the seeds and start such a project," she said.

"We can work together on this," Sam told Mica, and she was happy to have his support to begin.

The same week that Mica proposed to help the Romanian orphans, her team of lawyers made contact with Romania's newly appointed chief minister of health, Eugèn Florescu, who assured them that Mica's parents were alive and healthy, but still under house arrest.

At the next lawyers' meeting, Mica and Simion were briefed about a plan Florescu had put forward. Bernard set up three telephones at the conference table in his office and dialed Florescu's number. Mica took one phone, Simion another, and Bernard the third. After the lawyer greeted the minister, Florescu explained his offer.

"As the new chief of health, I'm alarmed at the increase of HIV-infected children. I don't want to wait any longer to treat them. Children are dying and the press got wind of it. It would be beneficial if you, Mica, could immediately establish a foundation to supply medicines and antibiotics for the orphans, and bring the medicines, yourself. I can facilitate distribution in Transylvania first. I can get you a visa to enter the country for humanitarian purposes—linked to supplying medicines and medical care that we do not have in Romania."

Mica was thrilled at the idea, yet calmly replied, "I'm willing to be the courier, and I can discuss with UNICEF what medicines are needed."

"Good. Once in Transylvania," he said, "you can go to your parents' house and bring them home with you to New York."

Those were the words that Mica was dreaming of for three years. "How much will this cost?" she asked, trying to stay calm.

"Fifty thousand dollars. Wire money into my Swiss account for the project," Mr. Florescu instructed. "Some will go toward the Foundation, some for my colleagues and their paper work, and some for my consultation services."

Mica took a deep breath. Could she trust this new minister? "How about $25,000 now and $25,000 when my parents and I arrive in New York?"

"That's fair."

"How can we plan the transaction?"

"Come to Spera. I can arrange to meet you at your parents' house on a mutually agreed day and time," he explained. "I'll have visas and travel documents signed and stamped, authorizing that they can leave with their daughter for medical treatment in the West. At the same time, you will bring by hand in a suitcase, the medical supplies. When I receive the first wire transfer of $25,000, I have the power to grease the wheels."

Bernard slipped a note to Mica, saying: *Ask him HOW he'll grease the wheels.*

"I'll give you the following papers for your parents: One. from the mayor of Spera, an affidavit of approval that your parents do not owe any town taxes. And another stamped letter that confirms they have no judgment or debt against them. Another from the medical director of the region: two certificates with medical diagnoses, naming diseases that cannot be treated in Romania, but can in America. He'll make up the diagnoses."

He stopped talking as if he were thinking. "From your first $25,000, I'll pay the mayor and medical director." He hesitated again. "But your parents need authorization for visas. The minister of the interior is the only who can provide that. What would you like to do for him?"

Mica looked at Mr. Bernard. He wrote on a paper: *Give the minister of interior your parents' house.*

She eyed Uncle Simion. He nodded his head yes. She looked down feeling guilty and prayed her parents wouldn't object.

She continued her negotiations. "My parents have a rustic home in the woods, designed and built by my father, who is an engineer, and his students."

Florescu understood. "Fine. The minister is looking for a country retreat."

Bernard wrote another note for Mica. *"Your parents need visas to enter the U.S. as political refugees. Our law firm can do that, for an extra fee."*

"Is there anything else I should do?" Mica returned her attention to the phone.

"This is my private telephone number. I will arrange for everything to be ready when we meet at your parents' home. Call me when you arrive in Romania."

"One more thing," she added. "If I need protection in Romania, can I also call you?"

"Of course. It's in my interest that you return safely to New York. My $25,000."

In order to travel to Romania, Mica had to register with the U.S. Department of State. The only way to get to her parents was to be part of an official humanitarian aid group. She arranged with Andrews to join the UNICEF delegation as a translator. If anyone asked, she was visiting several orphanages in Transylvania and bringing medical supplies. The plan for her parents would remain secret.

Mica tried not to think that she could be detained at the airport, or stopped while traveling to Transylvania. She was trusting Mr. Florescu and yet, she knew nothing about him. Perhaps he had enemies. Could he keep everything secret? He had to arrange the plan with several other ministers. Could she trust them? She had to take the chance, the risks. She had to suppress her fears and think only about the outcome—to save her parents.

CHAPTER 34

Mica moved slowly through the customs line at Bucharest's Otopeni International Airport. She followed the Romanian signs reading, *"Pasaport."*

"Buna dimineata. Good morning."* The customs official eyed her fur hat, her soft leather gloves, her warm coat.

Nonchalantly, she handed him her American passport, visa, and the return half of her plane ticket.

"Translator, hmm," he mumbled. "Pasaport American. Hmm. Hmm."

Mica held her breath. She wanted no long conversation in Romanian, no complications.

"Nascuta in Spera," he said. "Born in Spera. How did you leave?"

He studied every page of her passport, even the blank ones. Then he read her visa again—UNICEF. He looked at her plane ticket—New York, Geneva, Bucharest, New York. Why Geneva?"

She quickly explained. "I'm part of a humanitarian aid group. Part of the UN and Red Cross. We met in Geneva. I'm going to several orphanages. Here is a letter from UNICEF stating that, as a translator, I will arrange distribution of medical supplies for children."

The official sneered. "Why would you want to help after living *comfortably* in America?" he asked sarcastically.

She answered calmly that she felt sorry for the children of her country. She looked him in the eyes, but also counted the number of broken capillaries on his cheeks and hypothesized how many liters of wine did he drink every day. She smelled the stale wine oozing from his pores.

"Where are you going now?" he asked.

"Transylvania. Spera first and then Cluj to several orphanages."

"It's dangerous there for a woman alone." His eyes surveyed her body from head to toe.

Mica stuck to her story. "I've been asked to prepare the paperwork for the medical supplies." Now Mica knew she needed to move along and to deflect attention from her.

She played her trump card. "I have a Christmas present for you." She took out a carton of Kent cigarettes.

He smiled at her with the shrewd eyes of a peasant and quickly hid the baksheesh under his counter. "What else does Santa's little elf have?"

His slyness repulsed her. The constant demand for bribes, payoffs, kickbacks, but she smiled. "One more thing and then *I must go*," she stated firmly—and handed him a bottle of Johnnie Walker Red. She had brought two bottles with her, and she knew from the start that the first bottle of scotch would go to him. She stared at him fiercely and then indicated with a nod, the two policemen, carrying rifles, surveying the slow line.

He hid the bottle under the counter next to the cigarettes. Then he returned her passport, visa, and plane ticket. "Happy Birthday," he said in English and waved her on. She knew he meant to say "Merry Christmas."

Mica picked up her two suitcases and put her pocketbook on

her shoulder. In spite of the freezing cold, her lips were parched—
she had jumped a big hurdle. As she walked toward the exit, she
noticed there was one electric bulb for the entire room, and the
40-watt bulb flickered and then died. It reminded her of the
theater in Spera where she had played Juliet three years ago.
Nothing had changed, if anything, it all looked worse from her
Americanized eyes.

The airport was relatively empty except for several policemen.
Each one had a knife strapped to his ankle. Mica stared at them,
smooth-skinned boys dressed up as soldiers. The cold wind of
winter blew through broken windowpanes, and Mica was
reminded how desolate the airport always was. No one could
travel. No one could leave.

She walked over to the empty Tarom Airlines counter. "Is there
a plane to Spera?" she asked the young woman behind the desk.

"No."

"A train?"

"Depends… but no, not dependable."

There had been no way for Mica to plan ahead of time to get to
Spera, and the woman at the counter didn't seem to know
anything about Spera or even care. Mica was angry. Frustrated,
she started thinking how could she get to Transylvania, *now?*

"See if there's a taxi outside. Sometimes there is, sometimes
not… depends." The woman turned her attention to another
customer.

Mica stepped outside into the freezing morning. A thin
youngish man, wearing his Sunday best, got out of a Romanian
car. *"Buna dimineata."* He bowed to Mica and removed his woolen
cap. "My name is Dinu. Are you looking for a car?" He bowed
again.

"Da," she answered and looked around to see if she had a
choice. But his small Dacia was the only car there. Not one taxi in
the entire airport.

"Where are you going?" he asked, not raising his eyes from the ground—a sign of giving respect.

"Spera first, and then we'll see. How much will it cost?"

"Seventy-five American dollars to Spera, plus the gas. Then we'll see."

"That's okay."

She looked around to check if anyone was watching them and wondered if she could trust him. Her old suspicions had come back the moment she set foot in Romania, and she couldn't help but think that he might be working for the secret police. She needed to telephone Florescu to reconfirm their meeting at her parents' house the next day at 5:00 p.m. But there was no phone in sight, and if the driver was a member of the Securitate, she couldn't very well ask him to take her to a phone and then explain why. That would ruin the entire plan.

"How are the roads?" she asked, trying to sound nonchalant and looking around surreptitiously. Everything looked gray- the terminal building, the sky, the snow.

"Not bad. I can do it, even if we have a lot of ice. Let's go to the city center and try Calea Victoriei. There's one gas station open near Cismigiu Gardens. If we find gas, we'll continue north." He hesitated, looking to the sky. "The weather looks bad. It could take all day."

She didn't care that it would take more time. She wanted to study the situation and make sure the driver was trustworthy. Getting into the car she told him, "As we drive toward Bucharest, I'd like to pass through some villages and see what has happened in the past few years. Besides," she smiled, "I have a Christmas present for you." And she gave him the second bottle of Johnnie Walker Red. She knew he expected a gift. And she knew she would need him for an extra day or two.

They drove looking for gas. Suddenly, a checkpoint appeared and the police waved at the driver to stop the car. Dinu quickly opened his door and got out of the car as a way to divert attention away from Mica. "I work at the airport as a taxi driver. Here are my papers."

"Take the detour toward Snagov," the policeman ordered as he returned the papers. Dinu got back into the car, stepped on the gas pedal and drove away without further discussion.

"What was that all about?" Mica asked.

"We don't ask why in this country." Then he added more calmly, "A slight detour. You'll be able to see some villages."

Mica looked out the window and concentrated on the scenes before her, which were slightly familiar. People walked on dirt roads without sidewalks. Mothers had no strollers, and carried their babies in their arms. In between the trees lining the road, she saw strips of farmland. In a field, a little boy dressed in red was walking next to a shepherd dog. Hundreds of white dots painted the grass. As they traveled on, the dots became sheep and Mica saw the shepherd boy wave his wand to the herd.

A group of peasants raised their heads as the black car appeared. They were arranging piles of goat cheese on a stand, and Mica breathed in the fragrance. She imagined her mother in their old kitchen next to the fireplace baking cakes filled with the same cheese. But suddenly, the sweet smell turned bitter and the image of her mother disappeared as a motorcade of police cars and motorcycles pulled up behind them. She wondered if the secret police were following them.

"I'm going to take another road," Dinu announced. She didn't know if that had been his plan all along or if he wanted to evade the police, but she didn't ask.

As the car stopped at the rotary, Mica noticed a group of wild dogs barking and scavenging a pile of garbage. It had been bad when she left three years ago, but since Ceausescu, life in Romania had gotten even worse. With each kilometer she traveled toward

Bucharest, her soft, protected world in America moved further away.

"We're getting closer to the center of town," Dinu told her.

She didn't know Bucharest at all. Her family had never traveled there when she was a child. Then suddenly, the car stopped short. A group of small children swarmed in front of their car. They wore hats that were larger than their faces. They had eyes that were darker than any winter night. They looked like bats ready to attack.

"Here, lady, look!" They opened her car door, flashed cards in front of her nose, pulled her coat, tried to grab her pocketbook.

Dinu, locked the car doors, got out and picked up a stick.

"What do they want?" Mica asked through her open window.

"Money. They're orphans. They're showing you a card stamped by the police that gives them the right to beg." Dinu shook his stick and chased them away.

"Why do they need a card?"

"Because homeless children come to the capital to beg. And the residents of Bucharest went to the police to complain. The magistrate solved the problem by declaring that only kids from Bucharest can ask for money."

Mica opened her car door and stepped out. Dinu followed her, carrying his stick. She waved the children toward her, threw a handful of coins into the empty space, and watched the coins and children drop to the ground. A male figure jumped out from the group. Mica didn't know if he was a boy or a man. He was as broad as he was tall and every line of his square face spoke of cruelty. He had no age. He could have been a youth turned old from evil or an old man made young by his power to harm. He grabbed Mica's money from the ground and snarled at her with hatred.

She stared at his open mouth and pointed teeth. He jumped toward her hand, ready to bite, but Dinu knocked the urchin down and pulled Mica away.

"That's enough," Dinu said, swinging his stick. "Don't give away money. Let's get back in the car."

Upon entering Bucharest, Mica noticed a group of children sitting on the sidewalk, passing a small tube from one to the other. "What are they doing?" she asked Dinu.

"Sniffing glue. Their drug."

"But they look like they're ten years old."

"Maybe younger. Ceausescu's children, we call them. The enlightened leader has banned contraceptives. Girls get pregnant and not knowing what to do with the infants, abandon them. The seven-year-olds take care of the babies while the ten-year-olds rob the people and sniff glue. Their food."

Mica thought of the children in the pediatric-oncology clinic where she volunteered. They loved her stories about Romania and Gypsies. Last week she had brought them scarves and dressed them up as Gypsy children. She had played her flute like the Pied Piper. And now, looking at these children in front of her, she wished she could help them also.

But her thoughts returned to her mission. "Is there a telephone nearby?" She had to call Florescu.

"I don't even think we'll find gas."

"We have to find a telephone." She took several deep breaths. She didn't want to make a scene with Dinu, not now. She'd find a telephone somewhere. She had until they reached Spera.

Dinu pulled into the gas station. A boy ran out and shouted, "What do ya want?"

Lowering his window, Dinu answered, "Gas. Fill it up. I have American dollars."

"You're Hungarian! We have nothing for you. Get out of here!"

Dinu argued, but in vain. Then, he cranked his window closed. Ashamed, he turned to Mica and said, "No gas left."

"What do you mean? He's giving another customer some gas."

Dinu said, "I'm from Transylvania. He heard my Hungarian accent when I spoke Romanian."

The two countries had fought for years over who owned Transylvania. The result? The Hungarians and Romanians living there didn't like each other.

What rotten luck, she thought. "Can I rent a car and drive myself?"

"Rent a car?" He laughed. "There are no car agencies here."

"Can I pay someone else to drive me to Transylvania?"

"Very few people have a license to drive someone. There are checkpoints, and police are stationed at both ends of every town."

"The driver can say I'm his sister."

"In that fancy coat with those beautiful soft leather gloves? It's obvious you're not from here. They'll ask to see your passport, see you were born in Romania, and start asking you how you escaped. It's better if you stay with me. I picked you up at the airport, and I'll vouch that you're a tourist."

Mica knew he was right. She couldn't allow the police to question her.

"Let's see if you can take a train," Dinu suggested. "I know the stationmaster. Maybe he won't ask for your passport and let you on the train for Spera."

"Let me? Isn't the train public?"

"Public, yes. But every Romanian has to show ID when they buy a ticket."

Dinu drove fifteen minutes until he reached a small stone hut located next to the train tracks. An old man, dressed in a ragged coat and dragging his right foot, walked slowly toward them.

"Ce mai faci? How are you?" Dinu greeted him as he got out of the car. "This young lady," Dinu pointed.

Mica folded a hundred-dollar bill into her hand and walked toward the stationmaster.

"Buna dimineata," she greeted him, shaking his hand American-

style and giving him the folded bill, Romanian-style. "I would like to go to Spera."

"One way?"

"One way." She hesitated. "And then back to Bucharest with two other passengers."

"That's suspicious. The conductor on the train will ask for your passport. He'll have to report you to the police."

"If it's a question of more money…"

"No. I'll lose my job. My pension."

"*No?* Then give me back my $100!"

"What hundred dollars? You haven't even bought a ticket yet. As far as I'm concerned, you haven't given me anything."

Dinu whispered to Mica that they should leave and led her to the car. But even as she backed away, she was still arguing with the stationmaster to give her a ticket or refund her money.

"I have to get to Spera! *I must. I must!*" Mica was beside herself with fury. To have come so far and be turned back! She had sworn to herself she wouldn't return to New York without her parents. She had to meet the minister at their house in one day. Twenty-four hours! It was all arranged— the clock was ticking.

"I don't want to see you arrested. Then you'll never be able to return to America."

Mica stared at Dinu. There was nothing more he could do. Then she had an idea.

"Dinu, follow me." She took another hundred-dollar bill and folded it in her hand.

She approached the stationmaster, took a deep breath, and smiled at him. "Do you have a car?"

"*Da.* An old one."

"Do you live nearby?"

"Two kilometers away."

"Would you like another $100?" She moved closer. "Can we *buy* the gas that's in your car?"

He didn't answer for several seconds. Then he laughed. "That's not a bad idea. I did that once for my neighbor. I have a hand pump and rubber hose. We can drain my gas into your car."

"Yes!" she shouted before he could finish his words. "And one more thing. Do you have a telephone at the train station?"

CHAPTER 35

MICA AND DINU continued north toward Transylvania. The aroma of burning leaves filled the moving car. Mica relaxed somewhat and looked out the window.

With every kilometer, it was as if she were going back in time. The deeper they traveled into the countryside, the more carriages she saw pulled by horses. When Dinu slowed down to pass one, she waved to the people. The excitement of remembering overtook her, and for a moment, she wished she was no longer the outsider observing. She wanted so much to be part of the nature she was traveling through. She swayed in the back seat of the car and wished the small vehicle would not keep her at bay from the past.

The car climbed the serpentine road, and Mica felt her ears clog as they approached the Carpathian Mountains. With each village they passed, the pieces of her childhood broke through the restraints of memory and emerged from the shadow of time. Her present merged with the past and she was transported into her old world and enjoying the thrill of going home.

It was the soft mist of early evening that Mica remembered

most of all. The fragile vapor had a way of magically spreading its drops from the mountains to the meadows that she loved so much. In the winter, the dew turned to fine particles of ice and all the fields were covered in a blanket of white sparkling frost as if to put the day to rest.

She was going home, and the thought filled her with an excitement she thought she had lost forever. As she looked through the window, time confused its borders, months turned into seconds. Outside nothing had changed; inside, though, she was trying to find her old self.

Upon nearing the center of Spera, Mica saw the steeple of the town church and next to it the theater where she had played Juliet. "Just one stop, Dinu. I want to remember where my story began."

She got out of the car and put her nose to the window. The tattered red velvet curtain was still there. She looked at the stage and hoped to see Mr. Marinescu wave his beret and shout, "Juliet, act with all your heart."

She returned to the car, thinking, "Wherefore art thou Romeo?" *Whatever happened to Romeo?*

"Okay, Dinu," she said in a breaking voice, "Please, let's go on. I'm already three years late."

She was finally nearing her parents' house. Florescu had told Mica on the phone that he would visit her parents and get them prepared; tell them that Mica was in Transylvania, traveling to their home.

Mica opened the window to breathe better. Her hands were trembling and she couldn't stop the thumping in her chest. The excitement of returning home now turned to fear, fear that her parents would be angry with her for taking three years to save them.

"Forgive me," she kept repeating. And she prayed, "I hope you are both in good health."

Dinu continued on and then stopped short. The weather had

suddenly turned colder and he had encountered heavy snow, blocking his car from moving. Dinu took a shovel from his trunk and dug a path the width of the car.

After they passed a group of dark buildings, Mica recognized the headquarters of Spera's secret police. She put her pinky in her mouth and with the tip of her tongue, caressed her finger. Then she saw a girl, about seventeen, biking up a hill, struggling in the snow. She was wearing black leggings, pedaling hard, legs pumping up and down. Dancer's legs. Strong. She stared at the girl. Did she have short black hair? Was she wearing boots? A Shakespearean coat? Dinu swerved his car to avoid hitting her. The girl disappeared.

"Dinu," Mica said. "Take this hill slowly." She had always had to stand up on her bike to pedal the last minute until she saw her mother at the front door waving and waiting for her. Up she would stretch, down she would pedal, and she'd rush to see if Mama was cooking dinner. Her mother would greet her at the door and kiss her. "*Draga*, you're late."

Yes, I'm late. Mica rubbed the tears from her cheeks. *I tried, Mama, believe me. Tata, don't judge me. Please still love me.* She opened the window to see better and to clear her mind. She reviewed the documents she needed to get from Mr. Florescu.

Then she saw her house perched on top of the hill, just as it had always been, surrounded by blue spruce trees.

"Dinu, we're here!" She tried to stay calm. It was hard for her to breathe. Her heart pounded faster. She took her purse, pulled out her make-up case, examined her hazel eyes, and wiped them dry. "Dinu, could I ask you to stay in the car?"

"I was just going to tell you that I have an aunt who lives in the next town. I thought to spend the night there and come back for you in the morning to take you to the orphanages. Then we can come back here for your meeting at 5:00."

Slowly she got out of the car. She felt the same tinge of nausea she felt before she danced on stage—stage fright. She'd miss her rhythm and lose her balance. She looked down so as not to trip. There were three steps at the front door. One, two...

Before she could knock, the door opened wide. She stared at the two people in front of her. At first, she didn't recognize them. Her father's red mustache was now gray. His full head of hair wasn't so bushy, wasn't so reddish-orange; it was more a brownish-gray. His broad shoulders looked narrower, and his six-foot frame less powerful. Her mother looked smaller, shorter, thinner. Her back was bent with the weight of suffering and waiting for three years.

Mica felt her body tremble, her legs weaken. Her knees lost strength, and she thought the wooden step would disappear from under her feet. She felt herself falling but was saved in mid-air by her father's arms.

"Mica! Mica!" they yelled, and she was brought back to her senses.

"Mama, Tata." She kissed them over and over, not wanting to stop.

"I can't believe it."

"My little girl, my love."

"My dream has come true!" She took each one in her arms and kissed their wet cheeks.

"I've wanted this moment so much," she sobbed. "Every day I thought of it." She placed the palms of her hands on her mother's face and stared into her beautiful blue eyes. Then she placed her cheek next to her father's mustache and rubbed his bristles hard.

"Mama, Tata, I'm sorry it took me so long. I tried. I tried so much. Forgive me."

"We know. We understand. There is nothing to forgive!"

Her father put his arms around her and took her deep into his chest. Her legs became wobbly again. She felt faint. Her father helped her walk from the front door to the living room. He placed her in his large green armchair and rubbed her cold hands. She smelled his espresso sweet as he kissed her cheek. Slowly, strength came back to her. She looked around the living room, so dear with remembering- the furniture, so scratched with memories.

"I can't believe I'm here." She put her face in her hands and cried.

Mica sat at the kitchen table watching her father put several logs into the fireplace while her mother prepared her favorite dinner of grilled meat and goat-cheese cakes. Every two minutes, her parents stopped what they were doing to kiss or hug her, to make sure she was truly there.

"Tell us from the beginning—what did you do when you realized we'd been arrested?"

"I remembered the colored diamonds hidden in the basement."

"Good." Her father nodded his head. "The last time we saw each other, I tried to give you the most important lesson of your life, and I couldn't tell you why."

"Every day for three years I suffered, thinking I left you both without saying I love you."

Anton wiped a tear from his cheek. Corina did the same and then asked, "How did you bike to the Hungarian border in the middle of the night? Was it snowing?"

Mica narrated every detail of her journey, beginning with Marinescu, then the miners, the fascist witch, the secret police, the electrified fence, how cold it was, the frost, ice…

"We received your postcards from Budapest, so we knew you got there. At the beginning, for six months, the postman slipped the mail under our back door. After that, the ministers watched us very carefully. The postman was afraid to deliver mail, and we thought you must be negotiating with someone from the government."

"Did you find what I left for you?"

They looked at her blankly. "What did you leave us?"

Mica was about to explain, but then she hesitated. Their lack of an answer indicated they had not gone back to the bunker, and she thought it best to explain when they were safe in New York. Instead, she talked about her stay in Budapest at the American Embassy.

"I got the visa for America because of Mr. Bridge, but it was complicated." Tomorrow she'd explain why.

She told them about Magda Bartha, Ben, and Tibi, how they took care of her so she wouldn't be alone. And of course, Simion and Diane, how good they've been to her. How they've treated her like a daughter with so much heart and love.

Anton said, "I can't wait to see my brother. It's been more than twenty years."

"He says he wants you to work with him in his business. He's back to building houses. He has capital now and needs an engineer."

"I would like that."

"I wonder where we should live once we're in New York," Corina said, looking pensive.

"Near me," Mica quickly replied. "I'll find you an apartment in my building."

"I don't want to invade your privacy," her mother answered.

"You've become so independent," Anton added. "We don't want to take that achievement away from you."

Mica put her arm around her father, kissed him on the cheek, and rubbed her face against his bristly mustache. "Uncle Simion told me he's negotiating to buy four acres of waterfront property in Hewlett Harbor. It's beautiful there. He has the right to sub-divide the land."

"I'd like to be his neighbor," Anton said.

"Mama, Aunt Diane wants to rent a store in Hewlett village for a needlepoint studio. She always wanted to do that and can't work alone. She said you can help her arrange classes and get special designs from museums of master paintings. You'll see what she does. Reproductions from Chagall and Van Gogh. It's so awesome. So cool!"

Her mother laughed at Mica's use of American slang. "I would love that. Your father is eager to work again. We both want to work." She hugged Mica.

Her father smiled. "Mica, you've become a beautiful woman inside as well as outside."

She was so excited, and continued talking. "Let me tell you about the American Embassy in Budapest and my work there—Dr. Ingel, the two refugees and what they said about Ceausescu, Gaddafi, Arafat, and terrorism." And she explained.

"*Da, da,*" her father mumbled. "It's all true. One day the world will know. Terrorism! A reign of terror. There will be no turning back."

"My poor Mica," her mother cried. "You've gone through so much. You've suffered a lot."

"Not 'poor Mica.' I survived. I think how hard it was for you, being arrested, interrogated, put under house arrest for three years. I feared you had been tortured." Mica bit her lip to hold back her tears.

"No, we were protected because so many Romanian ministers were dealing with your lawyers. We understood the strategy and it kept us hopeful. They wanted to make sure we stayed safe and that you continued to pay."

"Your gift of diamonds paid," Mica said laughing. "That reminds me, important business. Can you be packed and ready in twenty-four hours? Mr. Florescu will meet us here tomorrow at five o'clock with the necessary documents. We'll leave immediately for New York."

"Is it all legal?"

"Everything has been arranged," she assured them. Yet, until they were all safe in New York, she couldn't relax. "The regional director is making up a medical diagnosis for you both. I don't know what he's writing, but you're both okay?"

She moved closer and touched their cheeks. They had changed physically and also psychologically. She could see that. Her father stuttered very slightly, and Mica wondered if it was because he had a stroke. His eyes had lost their spark. She promised herself she'd take care of him and make sure his eyes would shine again. Her mother also had paid dearly for the years of suffering. She kept forgetting where she'd hid their documents, placed her eyeglasses—and what was Simion's wife's name, again? Their sufferings had worn them down. And she hoped not permanently.

Anton's voice interrupted her thoughts and sounded stronger than when he had greeted her at the door. "We're fine, Mica. Especially now. You're not to worry any more about us."

"And you, Mica?" her mother asked. "You look thin."

Mica rubbed her right arm and smiled. "I'm fine." She would tell them about her scare and scars when they were safely on the plane.

She put her arms around her mother and cuddled next to her as if she were a child. "It took me too long to save you. I can't forgive myself."

"We never gave up hope."

"I suffered every day, feeling how much pain I was putting you through, that you worried so much about me. After all this time, I realize that the diamonds are important only because they helped to reunite us as a family."

Her father hugged her and her mother took her hand, kissing each finger. Then she smiled as she touched a pearl ring on Mica's finger. "What's this?"

"I'm engaged. To André, the man I love. Let me show you his picture." She took from her neck a silver locket in the shape of a heart that André had given her. "Tata, will you walk me down the aisle at our wedding? I didn't want to get married without you."

Mica laughed, happy to share with them all the wonderful things about her life in America.

"Let me tell you the whole story from the very beginning. It all started three years ago on February second. I was seventeen, rehearsing as Juliet…"

EPILOGUE
TWENTY-FOUR YEARS LATER

February 2, 1989

MICA WALKED over to the line of taxis and looked in each window hoping to see Dinu, but in her heart, she knew he wouldn't be there. Instead, she chose a car that was larger than most of the Romanian Dacias. She knocked on the window of a Renault. She needed a car with a sizable trunk for her two large suitcases that were filled to the brim with medicines.

"Buna dimineata." The driver rolled down his window. "My name is Adi. Are you looking for a car?"

"Da."

"Where are you going?"

"Spera first, and then Cluj."

"That's a long day's journey."

"I know. How much will it cost?"

"Well… not sure." He eyed her oversized suitcases, her soft leather gloves, her overcoat, cashmere scarf. "Well… $150 per day, plus the gas."

Wow, Mica thought. Romania has become Westernized quickly.

"That's okay." She didn't want to bargain. He put her suitcases in the trunk. She sat in the back seat and placed her backpack next to her feet.

As they rode away from the airport, Mica opened the window to see better. She was excited, thinking she was going home to the world she had thought she had lost forever. Time confused its borders, years turned into seconds. Outside nothing had changed; inside, though, Mica was trying to find her seventeen-year-old self.

The fragrance of the burning leaves brought her back to the night of her escape and she could feel again the rolling of the train carrying her away from Transylvania. She had thought she'd never return again. She had feared she had lost her parents forever. And yet, she had not. *Determination*, her father had said, *that's what helps people overcome hardships.*

Mica remembered how twenty-one years ago, her parents had arrived in America and had seen New York for the first time. From the airport, they made a detour to Brooklyn Heights, Mica's favorite vantage point, and together, they walked on the promenade, stopping in front of the Statue of Liberty, to pay homage and offer their gratitude.

Mica had thought also that she'd never see her friends again, Anca, Marina, and Cristina. But she sees them often. Anca had escaped Romania, about the same time as Mica did, in a daring feat, equally as frightening as Mica's, hidden in a defective tractor as it was transported on a hydrofoil up the Danube to Vienna for repairs. Anca became a pediatrician at New York Hospital, where André helped her when an opening became available as clinical director of the teaching department in pediatrics.

She helped Marina and Cristina, too. They were what Ceausescu had labeled German-Romanians, ethnics who had a German heritage and spoke German at home. There were thousands of them living in Transylvania. Ceausescu realized he could make money by selling them, like he did with the Jews. Germany had been destroyed after the war and needed people to build up the country. Mica arranged with her lawyers to pay for Marina's and Cristina's freedom and their passage to West Germany. Cristina continued on to France to study fashion and Marina to America to become an entrepreneur.

Mica leased an apartment for Marina in Manhattan where they transformed her kitchen into a lab. Marina set out to analyze chemical makeup of facial creams from Transylvania. She added a dab of collagen to retin-A, mixed bee pollen to vitamin E, pulverized shark cartilage with honey, and created a rejuvenating, wrinkle-less facial cream. Everyone swore it worked. Women looked younger, felt happier, loved longer. Marina got rich. Her strategy was to teach women that their appearance was an asset. *Use your beauty for power* was her motto. The words were written in gold letters in her expensive salon's waiting room.

Cristina decided to live in Paris and work as an intern for Yves Saint Laurent. Now, she was one of France's top fashion designers. Every few months, the Four Musketeers spent a weekend in Paris at Cristina's home.

Mica recalled all the fun they'd had as the Four Musketeers, walking in a line, holding hands and singing, *"We are the poets of our lives."* They had proved they were the creators of their fate.

Mica felt the car jump into second gear, and she moved in her seat to find a more comfortable spot. She reasoned to herself that it was a good time for her to return to Transylvania. It was twenty-four years to the day that she had escaped. She remembered how freezing cold it was that night, but she had her Shakespearean coat. In addition, the timing was perfect, for now she could legally return. The Ceausescus had been executed six weeks prior, on Christmas day, a gift for each Romanian. Communism was finished.

Mica also had a couple of weeks to relax from work. As

director of choreography for the Martha Graham troupe, she had finished the season's performances on New Year's Eve. During January, she usually worked with a few students to create new dance scenes, and during February, there was always a slight lull.

Her parents were still living in Long Island and active in their work with Simion and Diane. Her sons, Craig and Nicky, twins, were back at Princeton after a month of winter break. And André was busy with patients at New York Hospital. Mica smiled, thinking of her husband. He had chosen the specialty that fit him well—cardiology—because he felt so strongly with his heart.

The car climbed the serpentine road, and Mica felt her ears clog as they approached the Carpathian Mountains. The car was her protective shield, allowing her to travel through the kaleidoscope of her past that had been painted with chips of colored facets. As she looked out the window, she realized that no painter could have brushed green so passionately on white and blue. And no musician could have created the sounds that were softer than the timbre of the silent fields.

She was going home again and she wondered, if her eyes were seeing all this beauty in a different way, now that she was older. *Am I a better person for having lived in two different worlds? Have I learned from them both?*

Adi stopped at the rotary. "We're nearing Spera," he said, turning to her in the backseat.

"Can we stop? I'd like to stretch my legs." She took her backpack.

"Sure, I'll get a cup of coffee. How about if we meet here in an hour?"

Coffee. At the thought, her heart started to throb. She reasoned that it would be better to calm herself first, prepare herself psychologically. "I'll take a stroll," she told him. "Then I'll get some coffee."

She walked over to the town clinic, and remembered another

clinic, the one at the American Embassy in Budapest, her refuge for six months. She couldn't wait to see Magda, Ben and Tibi. They would be coming to New York in a month to spend several weeks with her. She smiled, imagining how happy they will be to meet André, Mama, Tata, the twins, Simion and Diane. Mica had planned a big welcoming party for them.

Since the end of communism, they had spoken weekly on the telephone. None of them had married, living together very much as before. But Magda had retired and bought a cottage on Lake Balaton where she spent the summers. Ben had been writing a book about Tavernier and the legends of the Grand Blue diamond. And Tibi? He said he'd been inspired by Mica's story and was trying to uncover the truth about what happened to the Romanov diamonds. Some had been recovered over the years and were exhibited in the Kremlin Diamond Museum in Moscow. But Tibi realized that two bluish-white diamonds were missing. Had they been lost or stolen? He was searching for the diamonds and the truth.

Mica returned to the theater to take the dirt path to the bunker. She told herself that she was ready. She had worked up the courage, and needed her cup of coffee.

She looked up to the tip of the highest mountain and calculated where the underground bunker had been. She walked over to the area and saw broken logs and brush that now hid the path she had taken so often with her bike.

She kept her eye on the mountain and continued walking northwest. *It's a good thing I came prepared*, she said to herself— rubber-soled hiking boots so I don't slip on the ice. She looked for the chimney of the abandoned glass factory and hoped it would still be standing, trying to reassure herself that it was made of brick and was three meters tall.

Her stomach started to rumble; her lips were parched. She feared someone would see her walking all alone in the woods.

Then she saw the chimney. "Oh my God," she whispered. "It's still there." She saw the steel bike rack. *Amazing; it's also there.*

"I'll count twenty paces." She remembered the spot: one, two, three. "Stop. Look down." She opened up her backpack for her tools. "Good thing you brought a hand rake and flashlight. Look for the iron covering. It's there.

"Dig, Mica, dig faster, deeper," she continued, talking to herself. "Use your hand rake, get all the leaves and branches off the iron lid. Clean it. Lift it. Ooooh, it's heavy. The hinges are stuck. Bang the caked dirt off the lid with the hand rake. Yes! Descend the staircase. Use the flashlight. Oh, what a smell! Be careful, Mica, the ladder is icy and slippery. Keep your gloves on. It's colder down there. Okay, you're finished with the steps. Tata's office is to the left, remember? Through the corridor. Keep the light on straight ahead. The door should be on the left. There it is. Wow, the door is closed."

Her heart jumped with hope that if the door were closed, perhaps that meant that no one had entered the office all these years.

She continued talking so that she wouldn't be afraid. "Pull hard. Keep the light directed to the right. That's where the desk was. Yes! The desk is still there. Oh, what a mess. Cobwebs, a nest, mice running off the desk." She took off her gloves to wipe the desk clean.

"The counter. The espresso coffee pot. Oh, my God, the cup– it's still there! Pick up the cup. Put the flashlight on the desk and angle it to the cup. The false bottom. Open it."

She felt the weight of the ashes inside the false bottom—hard. They were all stuck together in a solid block. But her fingers touched two pieces that protruded out of the ashes. They felt like stones. Diamonds. "Put the chunk of ashes with the diamonds in your coat pocket. Deep inside. Cover them with your gloves. Leave the cup for good luck."

Mica tried to walk out the office, but her knees were shaking. She held on to her father's desk for support. She started to talk to herself again to keep her nerves intact.

"Walk out quietly. Don't rush. Close the door just as it was before. Take the corridor to the right. Up the stairs. Up, up. Slowly. Close the iron lid. There's light. You're outside now. Walk calmly as if you're taking a stroll. Look around. No one is near. Keep your pace. Like dancing. Steady and in rhythm. Don't rush. Relax. Stay in control. There's the car."

She closed her eyes and took several deep breaths.

"Hello," she addressed Adi, smiling.

He asked her if she had enjoyed her walk. Did she get some coffee?

She smiled and answered, "Yes, strong and tasty, and I had time to stroll in the woods that I loved as a child."

"Pretty spot," he commented. "Where would you like to go now?"

"To the first orphanage," she answered. "It's five kilometers from Cluj."

"That'll take some time. We've traveled already the whole day. I'm not tired, but are you?"

"No, I feel rejuvenated."

As the car rumbled through the mountain roads, she put her hand in her pocket and fingered the chunk of hard ashes surrounding the two pink diamond that she had left for her father so many years ago. She fingered their rough edges. Maybe twenty carats each. And pink, a rare color. Mr. Reinhardt could have his jewelers cut out the flaws and polish out the impurities for another sale. *It'll assure my parents a good life for their remaining years.*

She opened the window to let in the pure mountain air. It appeared as if the pine trees were reaching to the sky. The beauty of her Transylvania. She sighed and wondered if the colored diamonds had brought her bad luck or good luck. Would she redo her life, if she could? Her life of bad and good? No, she wouldn't change anything, despite the hardships and challenges.

Yet, she knew that one thing had remained the same—the diamonds had once been owned by Auschwitz prisoners. As Tibi had told her, "Sell them as quickly as you can, and use the money to do good."

She had listened to Tibi. Three months after arriving in New York, she took action to undertake an auction of three diamonds. The money from this first auction had been used to pay bribes and get her parents safely to America. A second auction came five years later, after Willy Reinhardt cut and polished the remaining thirteen diamonds for another sale. All the proceeds went into the NGO she had created with UNICEF, to set up an adoption agency for orphans. Her parents and André agreed that the thirteen diamonds should be used solely to help others.

Mica established the adoption agency in Transylvania next door to an orphanage, so as to simplify the adoption process logistically. Her NGO's mission was to take care of children younger than three years old. For the past twenty years, she had supervised the adoption agency and orphanage from New York with help from friends in Transylvania. One thing was agreed upon: no child was to get a blood transfusion of the kind Ceausescu had decreed. No needles used for inoculations could be reused. All the children at her orphanage were HIV-free, and more than two hundred fifty children had found families.

"We're here. Faster than I expected. No snow."

A good omen, she thought. "Can you park at the shed?" she asked him. "Then help me with these large suitcases?"

"Of course."

"Someone's coming. According to their clothes, they must be the doctor and nurse."

The man and woman walked over to Mica, took her hand, and kissed it Romanian-style, to thank her for her goodness.

"It's very little," she said. "I just want to help."

"Glad you arrived today. Good timing," the doctor told her. "A young woman, seventeen years old, just beginning medical school, wants to leave her baby here. She confessed she had an affair with a senior doctor who was married and refused to leave his family. The girl is an orphan, has no family to help her. She wants to study."

"Is she still here?" Mica asked.

"Yes, with her two-week-old baby. He has a high fever. Did you bring antibiotics?"

"I have a big supply in the suitcases. Over there."

"I'll start immediately," the doctor said. "Did you bring syringes?"

"In the plastic bags." Mica pointed and then asked him, "Can I go with you to see her? Perhaps I can help."

The young woman was holding her baby, feeding him at her breast. He was chubby and didn't look sick except for the red flush covering his little face. He had fine blond hair like golden silk. His eyes were closed, sucking peacefully. Mica smiled, admiring his beauty. He resembled an infant from a Renaissance painting, being held by his blonde, full-faced, beautiful mother. She looked so loving, yet so sad.

Mica watched the doctor take the baby's little arm and give a quick prick of the needle and cover it with a Band-Aid. Then he returned the baby to his mother's breast. Mica was mesmerized as the mother rocked her infant, kissed him, took the small hand into hers, caressed his fingers, and sang to him. Her voice sounded like a harp playing to an angel.

Mica went to the infirmary's storage room and gave the contents of her suitcases to the nurse in charge.

"Did you get the delivery of thirty cribs?" Mica asked her. "Also twenty beds, clean sheets, boxes of formula, toys—all the supplies on your list?"

"Yes, three truck-loads. Now, all of the fifty children have their own beds."

Mica was pleased. "Can I stay here tonight?" she asked. "I'm tired. It was a long day and tomorrow the driver can take me to the next orphanage."

"Of course. We have a separate guest cottage, as you know. We'll put one of the new beds there for you."

Mica went outside to find the driver to ask if he was willing to stay the night and then continue tomorrow. He agreed

Mica took a stroll through the garden. She saw the young woman sitting alone on a bench and decided to join her. She was reading a large book. It reminded Mica of André, studying.

"May I sit down?" Mica asked.

"Please," she answered, shyly, and closed her book.

"My name is Mica. What's your baby's name?"

"Luca, after my father."

"And your name?"

"Andrea."

Mica thought of Andrea del Sarto, the Florentine Renaissance painter. How he would have loved to have painted Andrea as a Madonna holding her baby. "Your son will be better soon," Mica said, to reassure her.

"Thank you." The girl looked up and smiled. Her eyes were deep blue, bright and warm.

"The doctor told me you're a student in medicine. My husband is a doctor."

"I dream of being a doctor." She looked down and said quietly, "I'm poor. I'm an orphan." She hesitated and rubbed her moist eyes. She bit her lip and then in a burst, said, "They tell me you have an adoption agency here next to the orphanage. Can you find a good family for my baby?" She started to cry, a soft whimpering. Her body trembled.

Mica took her into her arms, held her. "I will try to find the most loving family for him."

Mica thought: *What a tragedy. She'll never be happy knowing she had given away her beautiful baby.*

The doctor walked over to them. "Ladies, would you like to see a miracle of modern medicine? Come with me."

He led them to a small infirmary where one of the new cribs was set up. Inside was a bundle wrapped in a new white blanket. Mica approached the crib, looked inside, and saw the most beautiful baby, sleeping contentedly. The feverish redness on his face was gone. His skin was now clear in color with a pinkish glow. Mica watched him, mesmerized. An angel. Sleeping peacefully.

Andrea went over to her baby. He had his small fist in his mouth, sucking it as if to tell his mother he was hungry. She picked him up and his eyes opened and she sat down, holding Luca tightly to her breast, kissing his brow, stroking his soft skin, his silky hair. She opened her blouse and put him close to her heart, rocking him softly, singing to him while he suckled. After several minutes, he fell asleep again. Andrea held him, rocking him, singing to him, closing her eyes. After several minutes, she carefully placed him in his crib.

She turned to Mica and asked, "Do you have a few minutes more to talk with me?"

"Of course."

They returned to the garden and sat down on the bench, which was surrounded by blue spruce trees. Mica looked up to admire the white mountains. Flakes of snow started to fall. It was this soft mist of snow that she had missed so much. She remembered that the grass around her parent's house would be covered in a blanket of pink and white frost, and she could smell the mountain air, so pure, crisp and good.

"Is it too cold for you?" Andrea asked. "We can go inside."

"No, it's lovely here. Why go elsewhere?"

"You live in New York?" Andrea wanted to know, but she didn't wait for an answer. "You have children? Do you work?" The questions came in an unexpected rush.

Mica looked at her, a little surprised.

"Would you like to have a baby?" Andrea asked her.

Mica was stunned. She couldn't absorb the question. Mica just stared at her. Then she answered, "I-I-I never thought of it. I have two sons, all grown up, just beginning college. I'm forty-one years old."

"That's not old."

"Not as young as you or when I had my sons."

"But you're full of energy, and you look so young. I can tell. I'll be a doctor." She picked up the heavy book next to her as proof. Mica smiled. Andrea reminded her of her seventeen-year-old-self. Determined.

"What are you thinking?" Mica asked Andrea, still not absorbing the essence of the girl's words.

"Take my baby to America. He'll have a better future there. Educate him. Love him. Make him your son."

Mica took a deep breath. Not sure what to say or do, she took her gloves off, and when she stuffed them into her pocket, her fingers touched the two diamonds enmeshed in ashes. She thought about how all twenty diamonds had colored her life. How fortunate she had been, after all, to have had such a rare gift. She wondered, had God led her fingers now to the jewels? Was he giving her a message? Offering her the chance to save a life? Was Andrea the seventeen-year-old-guide that Mica had been searching for in the airport?

She asked herself: *How should I answer her? Should I say I'll think about it? That I want to go home and speak to my husband? To my sons?*

Mica remembered how her father had told her years ago, when he was showing her how to make her escape, "Whatever may happen, you must be strong. Think with your mind and act with all your heart. When in doubt, go with your instincts."

She stood up, looked at the indomitable mountain peak being covered by fine snow. Purification. Redemption.

She sat down, took Andrea's hand, and said, "I am very honored by your request. You're giving me what is the dearest to you, and I am humbled by such a gift. I will take this beautiful treasure under one condition: I will arrange that you see him every couple of months, on Christmas, Easter, his birthday, your birthday, every holiday, whenever you want. Often. Either in New York or here, in Transylvania. We will share him. We will give him what we have the best inside us. Two mothers will give him double love. He will have two mothers to love."

Both women stood up. They kissed each other's cheeks. Andrea's were wet and so were Mica's. Yet they were both happy. They were at peace. They would share this beautiful baby, this gift from God.

THE END

Prologue

I have often tried to understand love.

Is there a logic, a pattern, a process? Does it begin as a chemical reaction? Does the heart tell reason that there is no place for logic? Or does the mind direct all feelings? How does it happen that love can transport us to a state of being that we have never known before? And why do we journey so far, so blindly, so willingly, for the person we love?

I have wondered if we love only once. Or can we love different people with different loves at different times? Is it possible that love can transform itself into something sinister and unrecognizable and still be love? And if we should choose to reject love completely, what is life without loving?

My story is one of love, colored with tender moments of pleasure and heights of ecstasy. But it is also shadowed gray when love was crushed by shame—when lies turned passion to pain.

On an autumn night in Transylvania, October 1970, the golden days of yellow leaves had turned into smoky evenings tinged with the smell of wood-burning fireplaces. Communism was at its peak under Nicolae Ceausescu. No one could do what they wanted unless the government approved. I was outspoken, independent, and uncooperative. I was being watched.

Alec, my best friend from childhood, had come to our two-room cottage late at night to give me and Petre, my husband of three years, some confidential information. I remember the storm that night, with its lightning and thunder, and even hail. But luck was in our favor; the police preferred to stay indoors, drinking with their buddies rather than patrolling the town or watching people like us.

Alec had been my father's student at the Technical University of Civil Engineering and his helper on Sundays in our basement, where they both sent secret messages to people in other countries. He had graduated to become the chief engineer at the Ministry of Agriculture. Petre was a doctor, specializing in endocrinology. He was in charge of the clinic in our small town, Dova.

Alec came to tell us some news: one of the Austrian tractors the government was using to work the farms was defective. The parts weren't available in Romania and the tractor would have to be sent to Vienna for repairs. Alec knew that I was pregnant. He had been working on a plan to get me out of Romania, to hide me in the tractor as it traveled from Transylvania to Budapest, and then by hydrofoil up the Danube to trustworthy contacts in Vienna.

"I won't go," I told Alec and Petre.

Petre insisted. "Anca, this is your only chance. You can't have a baby in this country."

"I will not leave without you."

"I'll follow," he promised.

Alec persisted. "I can make another defective tractor for Petre in two months by detaching some wires needed to start the engine," he told me. "Your husband can leave then. But you must take this one first."

Petre paced our small living room. I had never seen him so agitated. He was almost shouting at me. "The secret police have started an investigation on you. I know this from a patient. Someone I trust."

"How will I be transported to Budapest?" I asked them. "The borders are locked as tight as an iron gate."

"The tractor will be hauled in a truck from our town to Budapest," Alec answered. "I'll create space for you under the tractor's seat where you'll be hidden."

"What about food and water?"

"It'll be next to where you'll lay comfortably on a mattress."

"Comfortably?" I said, raising my voice. "Do you realize what will happen to me if the secret police come searching with their dogs?"

Alec shook his head. "As director of the agricultural project, I have the right to escort the tractor from here to Budapest and onto the hydrofoil, which I will do. Once on the hydrofoil, you'll be on the Danube and safe."

Petre took my hand. "Alec will protect you. He has the contacts from the Danube to the hotel in Vienna, and then…"

"No! It's too risky."

"You must take this opportunity," Petre insisted. "The chief of the region is in charge of your case. He has proof you've given antibiotics to Gypsies and non-communists. The police will very likely torture you. You could lose the baby."

I was crying, and pleading my case to both men, but as I felt the baby kick inside me, I knew they were right. "Petre, you promise to take the next available tractor?"

"Yes," he assured me. "I'll be at your side when you give birth. You have my word."

Was I wrong to have agreed? I can't help but wonder now: what was Petre's true motive for getting me out of the country? Did he know then that his promise to follow me in just two months was simply a subterfuge? Over the years, I have tried to analyze the truth as well as the lies. I've wanted to forgive Petre, to feel less for him, to live my life guided by reason—and accept my fate. I have struggled with this. Then one morning, a newspaper and a telephone call tore my orderly world apart.